FRIEDA'S SONG

KATHLEEN SCARTH

HUMBLECREEK
INSPIRATION FOR LIFE

Scripture taken from the HOLY BIBLE, NEW INTERNATIONAL VERSION®. NIV®. Copyright © 1973, 1978, 1984 by the International Bible Society. Used by permission of Zondervan. All rights reserved.

Cover illustration by Victoria Lisi and Julius.

Published by Humble Creek, P.O. Box 719, Uhrichsville, Ohio 44683

Printed in the United States of America.
5 4 3 2 1

KATHLEEN SCARTH

Kathleen writes about what she loves: music and the Lord. Kathy can sing and play a variety of instruments. She also loves history and chose old Germany, a location not often seen in historical novels, for the setting of her books. Kathy lives in Oregon with her husband and two youngest children and works in sales.

For my daughter, Margaret,
who has delighted me and kept me on my toes for fourteen years.

Chapter 1

"I will not have him," Frieda asserted, smoldering within as she strove to keep her voice down. She sat stiff on the edge of her chair in the castle solar as she glared at her father, her fingers white where they gripped her bunched surcoat. Her mother's tears nearly broke down her resolve, but she hardened her heart lest her father pounce on her weakness.

Lord Friedrich scrubbed his face with his hand. He had grown a small chin beard recently and it looked ridiculous. "Your choices are very limited."

"My sister," she spat, "was permitted to choose her husband."

"She was. And you were to be allowed to choose yours as well. But you have driven off or refused every eligible man in the Schwarzwald. Now this offer comes to us from Bavaria, and we will accept it."

Frieda squeezed her eyes shut. She knew that firm tone her father took when his mind was made up. She could think of no excuse that her parents would accept this time.

"*Liebchen*," her mother said softly, "you met all of the brothers at your sister's wedding. You do remember which one he is, do you not?"

"I think so," she agreed. "Ludwig, the oldest, has a skinny wife. Albert is the youngest, and he had a besotted look and a blond girl on his arm. Gottfried is the giant with the silly red beard. Gregor is the buffoon my sister favored until her music teacher was suddenly found worthy of her hand." She shrugged and affected her innocent look. "Klaus must be the one left over."

Lady Ida leaned forward, her pretty face framed by braids coiled around her ears and marred by the wrinkles in her forehead as she strove to understand her youngest daughter. "When we were there, you said that Klaus was the handsomest man you had ever seen. That was before you knew he was one of Lord Otto's sons and one of the wealthiest men in the valley."

"And powerful, Mutti—don't forget to mention that he is powerful," she said, completely without enthusiasm.

Her father spoke in ringing tones better suited to addressing the great hall than in their family's quarters. "And in marrying him you will form an alliance not just between his family and ours, but between the Schwarzwald and Bavaria. It is a chance we must not pass up."

"Then *you* go and marry him, Papa, for I will not!"

She heard her mother's sharp intake of breath while she watched the color rise in her father's face. His next words were clipped. "Go to your chamber now, Frieda. If you decide to speak civilly with me, you may join the family for supper."

She rose and looked at him for a moment while extending her hand to her mother, who pressed it briefly. Frieda stalked out of the solar and into the hallway. She kicked at the floor rushes and turned to see whether her father watched to see what direction she took. He was addressing the young page by the door while watching her departure. The page pelted down the stairs as Frieda reached her chamber.

There she removed her veil and circlet, a small respite from the heat, tossed them on the bed, then unlatched the glass window and tossed it aside, heedless of its cost. She steadied her breathing, striving to ease the ache in her chest while she stood and looked out over the castle wall to her beloved Black Forest, the Schwarzwald from which this region took its name. With a fist she jabbed at the tears that dared to slide down her cheeks. If only she could get out into the forest where it was cool, she would feel better. She would be able to think in her favorite places beneath the trees. She had always done her best thinking and planning there.

Frieda peered out her door until she was satisfied that neither her father nor his spies were watching. She closed her bedchamber door quietly behind her, crept slowly to the stairs, then dashed down them as fast as she could. She took the circuitous route to the stables she had devised when she was just a girl. On no part of the route was she visible to anyone watching from the solar windows.

Upon reaching the stable she found the youngest groom seated on a bench outside, oiling a harness. With wariness he watched her approach while Frieda donned her most charming smile. He rose in her presence. "Will you please bring me my horse, sir?" she asked, all reasonable congeniality.

"I am sorry that I cannot do that, my lady. Lord Friedrich sent word that I must not," he said, twisting the harness in his hands as he spoke. Her father would think of her most likely means of escape.

"I would not ask you to do anything contrary to my father's orders. What were the exact words used?"

"I was told that I must not saddle your horse for you. That is all that I was told."

"You were told not to saddle my horse. . . . I don't object to riding my mother's horse."

The groom studied the twisted harness he held. "Yes, my lady. And what horse will your escort require?"

Her father's rules followed her everywhere she went. "This is a civilized land. What need do I have of an escort?"

"You know my lord requires you to have an escort. Have pity on me, my lady." Frieda did pity him, for he looked completely ill at ease. It was bad enough that she was miserable. She would not make others so.

"I do require an escort. *You* ride with me today." The man raised his head and eyebrows, then hastened away, returning shortly with two saddled horses. Frieda mounted and led the way out of the castle and kept up a good pace down the road, through the meadows, and into the cool forest.

There she slowed and rode along a familiar track she loved. Riding with the young groom was nearly as good as being alone, for he would not speak unless spoken to. She calmed herself by looking at the huge trees around her and the squirrels and rabbits that either watched or scampered away before them, and breathing deeply of the conifer and soil scents. This was the only place she could truly find peace. Her stomach tightened as she thought of leaving her cherished home.

Frieda could tell when her father's mind was made up about something, and his mind was definitely made up about her marrying this Klaus. Belatedly she wished that she had accepted the suit of one of the men who had asked for her hand before, someone who lived in her homeland. She thought about each of them and sighed. Even faced with marrying and moving far away, each of her former prospects seemed dreary. And it didn't matter, for it was too late now.

Her marriage might be bearable if she had her parents nearby and her forest to retreat into. Bavaria had nothing like this, she reflected as she looked up into the dark canopy overhead, glinting with bits of sunlight as stars in a clear night sky. And Bavaria did not have her parents, the parents she wanted so badly to please.

She knew they loved Margarethe best—the truth of that she had seen at the wedding, where her mother treated her sister with great affection and laughed at every one of her jests. Frieda's own perfect embroidery and the designs that everyone else exclaimed over did not earn her mother's esteem. Her horsemanship did not gain her father's admiration. She tried so hard and got so little notice for it that she sometimes wanted to scream.

Yet still she wanted to please them. Perhaps marrying this Klaus would do it. Though she did not feel ready for it, she was grown now and it was time for her to leave home and make another one with a husband. Maybe this was her last chance to please her parents. She would go willingly to do as they wished, and maybe. . .

Maybe what would happen was that she would exchange parents she could not please for a husband she could not please. She had no idea what Klaus was like, except that he was incredibly handsome, that he owned two estates with castles—perhaps one was far away from Margarethe, she mused—and that she had never seen him smile.

If Klaus proved as difficult to please as her mother and father. . . Frieda fought against the lump in her throat as she watched a deer bound off ahead of her on the trail. She could not start all over again, spending her life striving for a goal that could not be reached. Her parents cared something for her; even if it was not as much as she would have liked, it was something.

She would do as her father demanded. She would make a show of willing compliance, pleasure, even. Then she would make a life of her own in this Klaus's home. She would enjoy her time there as much as she could, buying pretty things and embroidering as much as she liked. She would play her favorite amusements on a new set of servants. She would ride as much and as often as she liked with or without escort, and perhaps Klaus would tire of her and bring her back home. If not, at least she would be doing things she truly enjoyed.

"My lady, look," the groom called out, interrupting her pondering. "There is the cuckoo who has been calling out to us." He was pointing at a large bird perched on a branch. Its white breast looked strangely clean in the midst of her dark thoughts. Odd that she had not heard the bird's call.

☙

Frieda went down to the great hall to supper that evening with her soft brown hair freshly braided and a carefully contrite expression. "I am sorry that I was so rude to you, Papa," she said to him as she made her way to her place beside her mother at the head table on the dais. The servants were already bringing in the heavily laden trays of meats.

She hugged her mother, who eyed her with suspicion. "You smell like a horse, my girl," she observed.

"That is not very nice, Mutti. It is hot, after all."

"Hmm," was her mother's only reply. Lady Ida was seated between Frieda and her father, which suited Frieda fine.

After the last course of cheese and small cakes was cleared away, Frieda leaned forward and addressed her father. "I have decided to do what you have asked me to do, Papa. I will marry Klaus."

"Good for you, Frieda. After supper I will draft a reply for the messenger to take back and you may write a letter to Klaus as well."

"Yes, Papa. And I want to leave for Bavaria as soon as possible so that I won't become frightened again." She glanced at her mother to see whether her remark triggered the proper sympathetic response. It did. Her parents were nicely reliable. Now they would be completely tractable for her until her wedding day. She would be able to talk them into buying her huge amounts of cloth to take with her to her new home.

What they did not realize was that she had agreed only to marry this Bavarian. She never said that she would make him happy.

Klaus approached the heavy oaken door of Willem and Margarethe's solar, which stood open to admit every possible breeze on this warm evening. He tapped lightly on the door.

"Klaus! How good to see you," said Willem, rising to shake his hand and clap him on the shoulder.

Margarethe also rose and kissed his cheek. "Too warm for hugging," she said, smiling an apology.

"It is, in truth." He sat with them and they talked about small things as his news boiled around inside of him. Finally, they sat looking at him with expectation. "It is about your sister, Frieda," he began.

Margarethe interrupted. "Oh, yes. Gregor was thinking of asking for her hand."

Klaus cleared his throat and stared at his clasped hands as he shook his head. "No. I spoke with my brother at length about this, and he does not think he can make a match with her." How his brother had reached this conclusion was a matter for which Klaus felt some guilt. "I, however, was most impressed with her seriousness and—"

"Oh, Klaus," said Margarethe, "Frieda was not so much serious as she was angry. My mother said she was upset about something almost the whole time she was here, and that she is often angry. You are such a gentle soul that I fear she would make you miserable."

Klaus thought that Margarethe would not think him gentle had she ever seen him on the battlefield. "Well, for good or ill, the deed is done. I have made an offer for her hand and my messenger returned with an answer. In three weeks Frieda will be here for our wedding."

Klaus made note of the stunned look on Margarethe's face as Willem again jumped to his feet, shouting and lifting him in a rough embrace. "Don't listen to her. If Frieda needs some gentling, you're the man to do it. You'll be so happy. These girls from the Schwarzwald—there is nothing like them."

Klaus patted his back as he withdrew from the hug. "I hope you're right. And if she proves challenging, so much the better. I have been needing a challenge ever since the war ended."

He looked to a frowning Margarethe, his future sister-in-law, as she stood. "God bless you, Klaus. I hope you'll be very happy."

"Thank you, Margarethe. I know you did not grow up together since you lived here with your aunt and uncle, but perhaps you know something about Frieda, some small thing she likes that I could get or do to please her?"

Margarethe sat down, and the men did, too. "Flowers," she said slowly. "She loves flowers." She paused and Klaus nodded, making a note in his heart. "And she's fashionable."

"She might like for you to be fashionable as well," Willem suggested with a grin. "These," he said, stroking his small chin beard, "are the latest thing."

"Those are very silly. You look like a goat."

Margarethe giggled behind her hand while Willem laughed. "Klaus made a joke, *Liebchen*. I think it was his first."

"It was no joke. The resemblance is quite striking."

Willem rubbed his beard while Margarethe grinned. "Well, you have a different sort of face and it might look good on you," Willem said. "If you do not shave your chin until she arrives, you could have something substantial started there."

"I may do that. If it looks bad, it is easy enough to remedy."

"When will the wedding be?" Margarethe asked.

"Frieda wrote me a letter saying that she does not want to wait, so we will be married almost as soon as she arrives."

"This will be my mother's second trip here this summer and my father's third since he went home to escort Frieda between our betrothal announcement and the wedding."

"I hope they don't mind all the traveling," said Klaus.

"Oh, no. They have only us two daughters, so no more trips will be needed for weddings. I'm glad they're coming. Maybe I'll get to spend some time with my parents and get to know my sister as well."

☙

This was Frieda's last night in a tent, thanks be to God. She enjoyed riding every day, but the sleeping was tedious. It was not just the hardness of the ground beneath her pallet but the lack of privacy. She shared a tent with her maid and good friend, Jeanne. Jeanne had been with her since her father's trip to Lorraine two years earlier. She enjoyed her company but was not used to sleeping with anyone.

And soon she would be sleeping with Klaus. It was a completely strange idea, and she came near to panic every time she thought about it.

Frieda squirmed on her pallet, seeking a comfortable position, then settled on her side staring at the bit of firelight she could see through the tent material and listening to the insects singing their monotonous song.

She remembered what Klaus looked like. His hair was straight and a plain brown like hers, his eyes dark. He did not go in for these foolish chin beards that were in style but was clean-shaven. He had a noble look and did not waste time laughing and jesting as so many people did. He was taller than she was and nicely muscled. He would be nice to hug, she thought, and smiled in the dark.

Her life would be easier if Margarethe was not already the ruling beauty of Bavaria. Of course people would compare the two of them, and Margarethe shone like a jewel—a singer, a songwriter, a blond beauty married to a war hero and diplomat. If she could avoid Margarethe as much as possible, eventually she would be able to establish her own reputation as she had at home. She was the finest embroideress and designer in the Schwarzwald, and the best chess player as well. It was not widely known that she was the best chess player, though, for she lost a few games to army commanders and the like for strategic reasons of her own. She loved the shocked look men wore when a woman beat them.

And now everything was changing. If she had to be married, it did not hurt that her husband was handsome and rich. It made her look good to have such a man make an offer for her hand. If she could please him and keep a good reputation, it would go far toward making her life a happy one. She knew it was impossible, of course, since she was so flawed. She had never been able to please her parents, who were naturally inclined to love her because they were related. How could a stranger ever love her?

⟨⟩

"Father, give me wisdom as I start this marriage," Klaus prayed as he knelt in the darkness in his bedchamber the night before he would ride out to meet his bride. "Help me not to listen to the bad things people have told me about Frieda. You guided me to choose her as my wife, and I know You would not give me anything that would hinder me in my life with You. Help me not to offend her in any way, and let me know how to treat her at all times. Father, she is so beautiful—help me not to overlook any of her other good qualities.

"Please bless Frieda this night. Give her peace. She will be living far from her homeland and family except for Margarethe and Willem. Comfort her and give me patience to put up with frequent visits with them. You know how impatient I can be with their constant music and jesting. I see no point in such frivolity but will endure it for Frieda's sake. Thank You, my God, for giving me a godly woman to be my wife."

⟨⟩

It was near midday and warm as Frieda rode at her mother's side. "Someone approaches," her father called back.

"It may be Klaus," her mother said. Frieda stood in the stirrups but could see little with the men at arms in the way and her father's pennant flying back toward them in the hot east wind.

"Mutti, do I look all right?" Her throat felt dry, her chest tight.

"You look fine, Frieda," her mother assured her with a smile. Frieda urged her horse forward to draw even with her father. Her mother followed. Still she could not see and did not know if it was Klaus and his men who approached.

Then one rider broke away and galloped his horse toward them. She saw that it was indeed Klaus. He dismounted and greeted her father first, then her mother; then as he came up to her, she had a hard time looking him in the eye since his silly chin beard distracted her. Oh well. She could deal with it later.

"Greetings, Lady Frieda. I am glad to see you," he said as he searched her eyes.

She endeavored to show pleasure at seeing him, which was not overly difficult since he was so handsome, with the exception of the despised beard. "Greetings, my lord," she replied. She was not sure what else this occasion called for. Neither of her parents had dismounted, but she wanted to.

She must have somehow conveyed this, for Klaus smiled—he smiled!—and stretched both hands up for her. Frieda slid off her horse, allowing him to ease her landing. He did not take his hands from her waist, so it seemed natural to hug him. She recalled speculating that he would be nice to hug; she was right.

Klaus had his men fall in with Lord Friedrich's and he rode at Frieda's side, pointing out landmarks as they went and talking of the journey with her father.

After a time, Klaus asked Frieda to ride a little apart with him. She followed, wondering which of the many things they had to discuss he wanted to talk about. "We have not yet talked about the wedding, my lady. How soon do you want it to take place?"

"As soon as may be, my lord."

"My mother requested three days' notice. Will three days be enough to get ready?"

"Oh, yes." Klaus was proving to be most agreeable.

"My parents' castle is the one best situated for most of the guests, but we can marry at our own home if you prefer."

Frieda was startled at the words "our own home." Was he referring to his castle as partly hers?

"Your parents' home will be fine. I would like to go. . .home the day after the wedding, though, if that is acceptable to you."

Klaus shifted in the saddle. "Will you not want time to bid your parents farewell?"

"They will stay in Bavaria for some time and can visit us later. Since we do not know each other, I think I would feel more comfortable without relatives around at first."

Klaus nodded agreement. "That is a good idea, my lady." He appeared lost in thought.

Frieda watched him until he looked back at her. "What will you wear to the wedding?"

"I was not sure what would look well with your clothing, so I had several new garments made in various colors."

Frieda was impressed in spite of herself. "That is excellent, my lord. If you will allow me to see your clothes, I will help you choose."

"That was my hope. I wonder what color you will wear?"

"I will wear green and gold, and you will not see my gown until the wedding so that you will be surprised."

"It is well. How many of these people will be staying on as a part of our household?"

"Just one: my maid, Jeanne."

"I will see to hiring everyone else you need. Do not hesitate to ask me for anything. Anything at all."

Frieda nodded. Perhaps she would have some nice things to amuse herself with during her exile in this man's home.

Chapter 2

All were greeted warmly upon their arrival at Beroburg, Klaus's family home, a gray castle with square towers in the old style. Lady Edeltraud, Klaus's mother, was especially tender toward Frieda, kissing her cheek and keeping her close as she might a daughter.

Frieda was glad to see a bath prepared for her when she reached her assigned chamber, and a large crockery jar full of flowers. Jeanne, always considerate, quickly removed the daisies and tossed them out the window. Frieda wasted no time climbing into the bath and had Jeanne wash her hair for her. "They have given you the best room, I think, my lady."

Frieda looked around. It was about the same size as the room she'd had at Adlerschloss when she had come for Margarethe's wedding, but then this was an older castle, and the rooms, except for the great hall, were smaller. The furniture had turned wood legs and there were imported carpets on the floor instead of the ubiquitous rushes. "I think you're right."

She did not feel tired after her bath, so she went to the solar where Lady Edeltraud had said she would be if Frieda wanted to visit. Klaus was there as well, and both of them smiled as she entered, so Frieda smiled back. "We were just discussing the wedding plans, my lady," said Klaus.

She noticed that Klaus looked different. "Oh. You shaved off your beard."

"Yes. You did not like it."

"How did you know that?"

"You have a face that is easy to read."

Frieda was not encouraged by that remark. She would have to be careful.

After supper she accepted Klaus's invitation to walk with him out through the castle grounds and to the top of a tower. They could see in all directions from there with the golden sunset spreading its glow over the fertile rise and fall of the countryside, the dark shapes that were woods following the wandering paths of streams.

Klaus pointed out a castle a few miles away, its turrets ruddy in the sunset. She could not see it well, but it looked large. "There is Apfelburg, your new home."

She gazed for some moments, unsure of what to say. "It is near enough to visit often."

"Nothing would make Mother happier."

"You also hold another castle?"

"Hohenstein. It is some distance to the east. We cannot see it from here."

She watched mounted men leaving the castle and going in all directions from the castle. "My lord? Where are all those people traveling at this late hour?"

"Messengers," he said in a voice tinged with satisfaction. "They are carrying the wedding invitations that Mother has had the scribes working on all afternoon."

Her hand flew to her mouth. "Oh. I hope I have not caused any trouble by asking for the wedding to be so soon. Will the messengers be safe, traveling at night?"

"None of them have far to go. They will lodge with the families they visit."

She looked out over the land as darkness fell, noting the differences between this and her beloved Schwarzwald, and seeing something lovely all the same. "It is a beautiful country, Klaus."

Standing close beside her, he spoke softly. "And you have made it even more beautiful by your presence."

She quickly turned and looked at him. To her amazement, he looked perfectly serious.

⟨☙⟩

Klaus sat across the old oak table from Frieda in the solar on this, the evening before their wedding day. They had talked much in the last few days, but now he needed to tell her of something he had decided. He hoped that she would understand and agree to it. Her face was expectant and just a bit wary, as he had come to expect of her.

"My lady, you know that I have been on the battlefield for the past twelve years." She nodded slowly. "I have commanded troops for most of that time. I am lord of several estates and command there as well. I am weary of command and will not be commanding you."

Frieda looked down at the table before her. After a moment, she looked back at him. "Then am I to be your ally?"

"Yes. My second closest ally."

Her brow creased and she tipped her head. "Who is first?"

Klaus swallowed. "God is first." She often seemed not to recognize his references to the Almighty, and he wondered at it. He had yet to see her at Mass, but she had been here but a few days and was likely still tired from her journey and could not rise at dawn.

"Of course," she murmured.

Klaus struggled to remember what he was going to say. He clasped his hands before him on the table and cleared his throat. "Allies sometimes disagree about things, and sometimes even fight." He risked a glance at Frieda and found her eyebrows raised, her eyes large. "We are both strong people and we may disagree about things from time to time. But to help us remember that we are allies, we need to have a time or place agreed upon where we do not fight or argue about anything."

"As the Lord's Day in time of war?"

"Just so. Would you agree to this?"

"Yes, Klaus. I think it is a very good idea, though I cannot imagine ever fighting with you."

She looked innocent, but something was not completely right. Every once in a while Frieda seemed false to him. He would have to think about it and pray. Likely he was nervous about the marriage and saw things that were not there.

"I am glad we are in agreement about this. I think that the best place of peace for us would be our bedchamber. That way we may remember every day that we are on the same side and can get a good night's rest as well."

Frieda rose and looked out the window for some time before replying, her face turned away from him. When she finally turned back to him, she had the look of someone who had made a decision. "I agree, Klaus."

"I am glad." He rose and strode toward her, stopping a step from her. "It is getting late, and tomorrow will be very busy, but the moon is out. Will you go up to the tower with me?"

"Is there not a sentry at this hour?"

"Yes, but I know how to get rid of him." Frieda's smile served as her reply and she walked at his side through the grounds to the tower. There was little light on the stairs and Klaus guided her with his hand lightly on her back. He dismissed the sentry, asking him to return to his post in an hour.

Frieda stood looking out over the land, then up at the stars while Klaus looked mainly at her. She was so lovely. He hoped he could make her happy.

Frieda shivered a little with a breeze and Klaus moved close and put his arm around her shoulders, watching all the while to make sure she would not mind. She leaned close and put her arm around his waist—more than he had hoped for. They stood thus, each thinking their own thoughts. Klaus prayed that Frieda's were happy.

◌◌

Jeanne helped Frieda dress for the wedding, and her mother came to her chamber and fussed over her, as did her sister, Margarethe. "Mutti says you did all the embroidery on this yourself."

"I did. I think it turned out well," she said while admiring the gold embroidery on her surcoat. It was of a deeper shade of green than her tunic and embroidered all over in a pattern with gold thread.

"It is beautiful. I wish I could make something so splendid. Alas, I lack the imagination and the patience."

"That's not true, sister. You have made some nice things yourself." Frieda charitably stifled her smile. Margarethe's embroidery was poor at best. But then, everyone's was, in comparison to her own.

Their mother sighed. "It is hard to believe that both of my little girls are married. But you knew it would happen, Frieda. You began to work on this over a year ago."

"I knew I would marry, but I didn't know whom. I am glad I waited so long, for Klaus is a fine man." She brushed at a tiny wrinkle she noticed on her sleeve to keep the others from seeing her smirk. Klaus was a fine man if you counted generosity and gullibility as assets.

"I hope you will be very happy, *Liebchen*."

"Thank you, Mutti."

"Frieda, are you sure you don't want all us women to put you to bed tonight?" Margarethe asked. Frieda met Jeanne's eyes, for the two had had a lively discussion on this point earlier that morning. Jeanne had been most informative, having three married sisters. Margarethe persisted. "It is a fun custom. We would get you into your gown and tuck you in and put flowers everywhere, then all of the men would bring Klaus in. Our friends did it for Willem and me. The jokes were not too bad."

"No, thank you, Margarethe. Klaus and I do not know each other well and I would be too embarrassed. I talked with Klaus about it and he feels the same way."

"Well, Klaus is not much for jokes, and that's the truth."

Frieda held her tongue.

Lady Mechthild, the aunt who had reared Margarethe, came in with her daughter, Jolan, and paid their respects to the bride. When Lady Edeltraud, Klaus's mother, came in, Frieda knew it was nearly time for the wedding. Frieda lifted a hand to check the position of her gold circlet, her only head ornament. She wore her hair loose as brides did. It was a shame it covered so much of her embroidery in the back, but it could not be helped.

Frieda tried to pay attention during the wedding, but everything seemed like a dream to her. Klaus was handsome in his green clothes, a stylish super-tunic worn over snug breeches. He could not seem to take his eyes from her. There was a feast, then music and dancing. Frieda had never danced so much in her life.

There was a brief respite from dancing during supper, and then it all started up again. Klaus was dancing with her to a couples' dance and looking into her eyes. "Are you getting tired, *Liebchen*?"

"Yes, my lord, I am."

He smiled gently. "Let us see if we can sneak out of here then." At the end of the dance, he maneuvered her to the back of the hall, and they had taken three steps up the stairs when Willem, Frieda's brother-in-law, who was leading the music, began playing a lullaby.

Everyone turned and looked at them as they froze for a moment on the stairs. Frieda's cheeks burned and Klaus's were bright as well, though he looked pleased. "We have been caught. We might as well wave, I suppose." They waved and people laughed as they waved back.

At the top of the stairs, Frieda said, "I think that was almost as embarrassing as letting them put us to bed."

"At least we did not have to listen to the jesting." They reached the door of the chamber they would use that night, and Klaus opened the door and let Frieda enter first.

There were flowers everywhere, even strewn on the bed and floor. Their fragrance was delightful, like a field on a warm summer day. Happily, there were no daisies to be seen. Candles burned on small tables on either side of the bed, whose velvet curtains were pulled back and tied as befitting a warm evening. "This is lovely. Who did it?"

"My valet and your maid, most likely."

She belatedly remembered Jeanne. "Oh. I will need Jeanne's help."

"Since we did not want anyone putting us to bed, she will not come. I will assist you this night."

Suddenly Frieda realized that she truly was married and that Klaus was here to stay. Her mouth grew dry and she tried to swallow. After Klaus helped her out of her surcoat, he carried it to the light and examined the stitchery. "This work is striking. Too bad you did not bring your embroideress with you."

"I designed the pattern and did all the work myself. Do you really like it?"

"Oh, yes. So I have married an artist." He hung the garment and asked her to turn around. "So the back of your tunic is laced. I wondered how it was made to fit so nicely."

He loosed the lacing and gathered the tunic as Frieda held her breath and made sure her smock was not gathered along with it as he lifted it off over her head. She wore a light summer smock without sleeves. While Klaus hung the tunic, she removed her circlet and other jewelry and laid it on a table. She felt very strange.

He turned and faced her as she stood in nothing but her smock. "Now I will braid your hair. One braid or two?"

"One is enough. It is a big job to do even one."

"I love your hair," he remarked as he turned her around and began the daunting task. "It sparkles in the candlelight with all different colors." Klaus continued talking to her as he worked until Frieda understood that he was just as nervous as she was. She took courage from that.

Frieda and Klaus had allowed their servants to bring them breakfast, and Jeanne made Frieda's hair presentable, two braids coiled about the ears in the conventional way. After they left, Frieda noticed that Klaus had grown formal once more and very proper. She would go to work right away on his excess of dignity. Under her care, soon he would have none. She stifled her own feeling of awkwardness, rose and crossed to him, and sat on his lap. His ears turned red, but otherwise he adapted well. They talked for a long time as they had before their wedding.

"We will be teased today, my lady, especially if we stay up here much longer."

"Had we gone down to the hall to breakfast we would have been teased as well. This way we had some time away from all those people."

"We will go home right after dinner and no one will visit for two weeks."

"I am looking forward to that, my lord. I will go down with you now, if you like."

"Very well," he said. They got up and walked together to the chamber door, where he turned to her, a wistful expression on his handsome face. "One more kiss first?"

She slid her arms around his neck. He was falling for it very nicely. "As many as you like, my lord," she whispered. He was warm and sweet to kiss. If only he truly loved her. . .but that was impossible. If her own parents couldn't love her, no one could.

They descended the stairs, and some of the people in the hall grinned as they walked by. Frieda saw her parents sitting at a table playing some wind instruments with Lady Mechthild and the ever-present Margarethe. Klaus took her hand as they walked over to the group at the table.

"Greetings, newlyweds," said Lord Friedrich. "Dinner was exquisite. We tried to save you some, but—"

"Oh, stop," said Lady Ida. "Good morning, Frieda. Good morning, Son." She extended her hand, and he took and kissed it while Frieda bent and kissed her mother's cheek. There were greetings all around.

"What are you playing?" Klaus asked.

Margarethe grinned. "Oh, just some old songs we all know. Would you like to join us?" Frieda wondered about the grin until Klaus answered.

"Oh, you know I am not too much for music. I do not mind hearing it, but making it is not my favorite thing to do. Would you like to play with these good people, my lady?"

"Not I. I am in agreement with you about music, my lord."

Margarethe and Lady Mechthild chuckled at Frieda's reply. "They truly are a good match, are they not? Likely my little sister is deadly at chess as well."

Lord Friedrich said, "She truly is. That is how she drove away—" he stopped abruptly, then continued—"many a great chess player." Lady Ida sat stiff in her chair. Frieda relished the memory of one particular suitor she could not get rid of any other way. She would not play less than her best to please any man, unless she had her own reason to do so.

"That is wonderful," Klaus said, looking Frieda in the eye. "I enjoy chess as well. We can enjoy many a friendly game in the days to come."

"I hope we can keep the games friendly, my lord."

"If we cannot, there is always backgammon."

"Or I can teach you to embroider." She kept her face straight as she made this outrageous suggestion.

"In exchange for jousting lessons, perhaps?" He looked perfectly serious, but Frieda caught a little twitch by his left eye.

Margarethe and the others burst into laughter. Klaus put his arm around Frieda's shoulders and steered her away. His parents had come into the hall, and they went to greet them.

Immediately after dinner they bade everyone good-bye and set out with the waiting servants and men at arms for Apfelburg. Frieda and Klaus rode in the front where she could enjoy seeing the countryside for the first time.

"Everything is so lovely, Klaus."

"It is lovelier still in early summer when everything is still green."

"I love all the seasons. I'm glad there is variety in the year instead of everything being always the same."

"Yes. God is most considerate of us." Frieda looked at him with curiosity. He mentioned God frequently, and it seemed strange to her that anyone not a priest or monk should do so. God was someone far away, large and powerful. Someone she would rather not take much notice of her.

As they descended the last small valley before the castle, Frieda saw a large orchard spread before her. "Apples, Klaus?"

"Yes. In about a month the entire household will turn out to pick apples for cider. I sell both apples and cider to many households."

"I have never seen anything like this. I imagine it is beautiful in springtime." Most people got their apples from wild trees, but these were obviously planted on purpose, like a crop of smaller plants would be. A wonderful idea.

"It is. And the fragrance blows on the wind up to the castle."

"Can we see the orchard from the castle?"

"A part of it. We are nearly home," he said. He spoke the word "home" with warmth.

Frieda and Klaus rode straight up to the donjon and dismounted while the servants who came with them and the ones who came out at their arrival hurried to take the horses and unload things. Frieda made sure it was Jeanne who directed the unloading of her things.

A dignified man with gray threaded through his beard came up to them at the door and bowed. "My lady, this is Hagen, my steward. Hagen, my bride, Lady Frieda."

"I am glad to make your acquaintance, my lady. I am at your disposal for whatever you would like to learn about this household."

"Thank you, Hagen. Your management has been highly spoken of. I am looking forward to the apple harvest."

"It looks to be a good year for apples," he said.

Klaus took her hand. "Come, my lady. I will show you the house."

They went into the great hall first, where all was fresh, new rushes on the floor, the trestle tables set up for supper. There were jars of flowers on every table. "You must like flowers as much as I do."

"I like flowers," he replied. Frieda sneezed.

He took her upstairs and showed her the chapel, the solar, and the bedchambers. Frieda walked with him throughout the donjon, and then the rest of the castle, including the kitchens and stables. All was neatness and efficiency. Frieda felt totally unneeded even while she took note of people who would be vulnerable to her mischievous games.

☙

Klaus noted Frieda's quietness during their tour of the castle. He hoped that she was not displeased at how it was run, or that it was not too small for her liking. Perhaps she was just tired. Yesterday they were wed and today she came to her new home. Likely it was all quite tiring.

"Will you rest before supper, my lady?"

"I would like to change. You might do the same." He looked down at his dusty garments and agreed. He showed Frieda the wardrobe next to their chamber. She chose fresh garments of brown and a bright tan color.

She enlisted his help with the lacing on the back of her tunic, a task he didn't mind. They changed quietly and washed their hands. He did not ask her if she liked her new home.

Frieda was quiet at supper as well, though she seemed happier, except for sneezing a few times. He feared she was becoming ill. Perhaps he had tired her too much. The servants all treated her with respect, and the higher-ranking people were openly friendly toward her.

At one point, she leaned over to him and pointed out that her maid, Jeanne, was seated with Hagen, the steward. "They seem to have much to talk about."

"Hagen spent several years in Lorraine when he was learning how to run a household. Likely they speak of Lorraine."

"You have good people here, Klaus. Everything is run well. I congratulate you."

Klaus nearly sagged with relief. "Oh, thank you, my lady. Do you see anything that needs improvement?"

She waved him away as she covered her mouth and sneezed again.

"You need rest, my lady. I will have my physician see to you. She has many potions that are—"

"No, Klaus. Forgive me. There is one thing that needs improvement here." He sat still as he waited and she wiped her nose. "It is the flowers. They are pretty, but daisies make me sneeze." Klaus called a servant over and had the flowers removed from their table immediately. "Other than that, I like all that you have done here."

He covered her hand with his on the table and squeezed it, wondering how long she might have waited to tell him of her difficulty with the flowers. She was far too considerate of his feelings.

After the last course was cleared away, a few musicians began to play and servants brought out games. Klaus was eager to see how well Frieda played chess, but she politely declined. "I want to hear all about your lands, Klaus."

Touched that she cared about that which was so close to his own heart, he kissed her hand. "*Our* lands, *Liebchen*. We hold all together now." The moment would have been most satisfactory, were it not for the little glint in his bride's eye.

Chapter 3

Frieda's old mare, Fraulein, stamped and switched her tail, reflecting Frieda's own eagerness for the tour of all the estate. Truly, though, Frieda was nearly as eager to see what Klaus would make of her little joke. It was a harmless one, since his horse was a well-behaved animal and Klaus was a fine horseman. She recalled with amusement Jeanne's reaction when she asked if there was any fish soup left over from the night before. She grimaced and said, "I hope not, madame." She'd rolled her eyes when Frieda sent her to fetch some and carry it to the stable.

Klaus met Frieda at the stable and mounted. "The orchard first, my lady? To check on the apples?"

"Yes, my lord. That will be fine." They rode to the orchard along the old cart track, curving around the hill that hid most of it from view. The morning breeze was already warm and carried a light scent of apples.

Frieda was glad to see other kinds of fruit trees besides apples planted there. "Pears. I'll be back in a moment," she said. Klaus followed her and caught the pear she tossed him.

"I have heard that these are not good to eat raw."

"I eat them raw whenever I get a chance. They've never harmed me." She inspected the fruit, then took a big bite.

Klaus smiled. "I have often done the same thing. Don't tell my mother."

"Have you ever had pear cider?"

"I don't think so. Do you know how to make it?"

"I know basically how to do it. It looks like there are many pears this year. Cider would be a good use of them. I can speak with the brewer and the vintner to see how to proceed."

"If it pleases you, my lady, then I am content." Frieda thought he looked content, eating another pear as he sat on his horse. His horse stamped his right forefoot several times, and Frieda looked away.

They continued the tour, and Frieda was impressed with the size of the estate and the way it was being managed. They started to ride past a pasture with hogs grazing. "I'd like to see the hogs better."

Klaus led the way, then Frieda detoured to the manure pile. Klaus followed and said nothing about their odd destination. "You have a good number of young pigs."

"Thank you." He reined in his fussing horse, which was stamping that right forefoot again. "Is this the same variety of hogs your family has?"

"I think so. Hogs are hogs." She watched Klaus's horse with interest. His right forefoot was covered with flies.

"Excuse me, my lady. My horse is misbehaving." He dismounted and looked at the offending hoof. "What have you gotten into?" He slid his hand down his cannon and fetlock, then sniffed at his hand and shook his head. He mounted again and pointed. "We will ride to the creek over there. I will find out who did this, and that groom will answer for this little joke."

"What joke?"

"Something smelly has been put on his foot to attract flies. What if my horse had shied and you were hurt?"

The thought of some innocent groom being punished for her silliness dismayed her. "Oh, but he's a good horse, and I know he wouldn't have shied."

"Nevertheless. I will ride him through the creek a few times to wash whatever it is off, then we can continue our tour."

Frieda watched Klaus ride his obedient stallion through the creek. She never admitted to any of her jokes, but she never let any innocent person take the blame, either. She made it look as if someone who deserved trouble got blamed, if anyone. Unfortunately, in her new home she hadn't yet discovered who deserved what. She bit her lip. What a foolish thing she had done.

When Klaus rode up to her, she said, "You're so busy with the estate. I'm in the stable a great deal. I'll find out whose joke this was and let him know you didn't care for it."

She wore her best innocent expression, and Klaus said nothing for a bit but looked at her with speculation. He nodded. "I will let you deal with it. Thank you, my lady."

They rode up a high hill and watched people harvesting grain. "And that field beyond this one, Klaus, is it yours as well?"

"It is ours, Frieda; yours and mine."

"Ours. It's wonderful." She turned to see him regarding her. "I don't know if I can ever get used to calling this fine place ours. I have done nothing to deserve such an honor."

"You have married me and made me happy. That is no small feat," he said, chest expanded, shoulders held back. He looked proud—proud of her? Incomprehensible. It must be that he was proud of his lands.

"I'd like to see Hohenstein. Are you working its lands as well?"

"Yes. The steward there has full charge, not seeing me often. We can visit there soon, if you like. He will be pleased that you are taking an interest in the place when we are so newly wed."

"Do you ever stay there?"

"When I do go, I usually spend the night. It is easier than making two trips in one day. We will likely spend the night when we go."

"What about staying longer? Do you ever do that?"

"I haven't done that for years. During spring and summer I was often at war, and the other seasons. . ." As he sat looking out over the land, Frieda watched his countenance change to that of a much younger man, a boy, even. "One winter when I was small, Father and Mother gathered all of us children, fosterlings as well, and took us to Hohenstein just as it was beginning to snow. It is higher than here and gets much snow, and there is a great hill. We played there for days, sliding on sleds we made and waging battles with snowballs. I have not thought about that for a long time."

She couldn't imagine Klaus acting like a playful child. It would be another blow to his treasured dignity, and she wanted to see it. "Perhaps we can go there at first snow this winter and take your family and all of the children of the household. I think it would be great fun."

"Wonderful, Frieda. A good way to celebrate the first winter without war preparations. I don't think we'll run into any opposition to this idea." He smiled at her. "My life was so dull without you. We have been married scarcely three days, and already you have introduced a new cider to the castle and given us a new winter holiday."

She laughed. "Neither one of those things has come to pass yet. I hope that I can continue to please you so easily." Lightly she spoke the words that expressed a deep longing she did not want to admit having—not even to herself.

☙

At dawn on the Lord's Day, Klaus leaned on one elbow gazing at his young wife before gently waking her. "It's time for Mass, *Liebchen*. We don't want to be late."

She stretched and looked up at him. She smiled sweetly, then pushed him over, kissed his cheek, and tossed off the covers. They dressed quickly and went to Mass together for the first time.

Klaus glanced at Frieda occasionally during the service and found her looking bored. Most people did not pay attention during Mass, for it was much the same every time, but prayed their own prayers in their hearts while the priest said Mass. Frieda looked to be waiting for it to be over.

Klaus prayed for her, that God would make Himself known to her. Then he felt bad for assuming she did not have a close relationship with Him. He did not really know her very well yet, after all. Perhaps one day soon they would be able to talk about Him together.

☙

Frieda watched with delight as her parents, Lady Ida and Lord Friedrich, asked questions and exclaimed over Klaus's holdings on their tour. She knew they were genuinely impressed.

Later, they sat together in the solar. "And the pear cider was truly Frieda's idea?" her mother asked.

Klaus squeezed Frieda's hand as he answered. "It was. She has contributed several good ideas. I do not know how I ran the place without her." He looked at her with undisguised affection.

"She has always been one for original thinking," Lord Friedrich observed. "Our Frieda is not content with things as they have always been."

"I discovered that for myself when playing chess with her."

Frieda smiled as she recalled his astonishment at losing a game, something that had happened to him only rarely since he was thirteen. "Mutti, have you ever seen such fine sheep?"

"They are fine, *Liebchen*. They are a different kind than we have at home. I would like to see some of their wool."

"There is much of their wool about the place, but it is all made up into cloth or yarn," Frieda said.

"I don't know much about sheep," said Klaus, his hands now politely folded together in his lap. Frieda caught his eye and smiled. "When we come to visit, I would like to learn the merits of your sheep."

"That might be a good time to transport some animals for the breeding experiments Frieda suggested," Lord Friedrich said. "We will be traveling too quickly this time to include sheep in our party."

Frieda barely kept from giggling as she suggested, "You and Mutti could each carry a ewe lamb on your lap as you ride. That wouldn't slow you down at all."

"A very good idea," her mother said, eyes dancing. "Then when you and Klaus visit, we will be sure to send home some little pigs with you by the same method." Frieda laughed with her mother.

"Lady Ida, will you stay for my brother's wedding in three weeks?"

"No, we need to return home. Friedrich likes to oversee the harvest, and there is other business. I am pleased that your family invited us, though."

"Most thoughtful of them," Lord Friedrich agreed. "A big year for weddings, what with the war ending. First Margarethe and Willem, then you and our Frieda, now Albert and Hilda. I have heard many things about them. How did they meet?"

Klaus looked at the floor as he answered. Frieda knew from the quiet way he spoke that he was carefully considering every word. "This spring, Ewald's troops attacked Albert's village. He rode in afterwards to see what damage was done and to persuade the survivors to take refuge in the castle. He heard screams coming from the mill and rescued the miller and his daughter from two of Ewald's soldiers who had stayed behind to do mischief." Klaus paused and seemed to gather his thoughts. "The miller was unarmed and the girl was injured. It was soldiers who had harmed her, and so she was distrustful of any soldier save Albert, so he did not entrust her to any of his men but carried her to Beroburg himself to be cared for by your niece, Jolan, and Margarethe.

"Albert felt responsible for the girl and visited her whenever we were not on the battlefield and came to love her."

"So she *is* a miller's daughter. That is the part of the story I did not credit," Lord Friedrich admitted.

"Her mother was high-born," Klaus said.

"Yours is the only conventional marriage of the summer then," said Lady Ida. "Willem came along and won Margarethe's hand away from your brother on the day they were to announce their betrothal."

"That is true. But he and Gregor had agreed upon it, and Willem loved Margarethe for a long time," Klaus said. "It was only because he had no land that he was ineligible to marry her. Once he distinguished himself in the war by his encouragement of the troops and his diplomacy and was rewarded with land, my brother stood no chance."

"It is good that he stepped down gracefully," Lord Friedrich said. "He was most persuasive in Willem's favor, as a matter of fact."

"Still, Margarethe was prepared to go ahead with wedding Gregor that he might not be dishonored. I was proud of her," said Lady Ida.

Klaus nodded agreement. "She is a woman of honor. But it is better to marry where one's heart is, I think."

Frieda remained silent during all of this conversation, her heart torn anew as she heard the pride in her mother's voice when she spoke of Margarethe. She had seldom heard that pride when either of her parents spoke of her.

Klaus took her hand and held it as if it was a delicate and priceless thing, then spoke with a quiet intensity. "In spite of my brother's loss, my family still has the alliance they desired with your family through Frieda and me. And I have in my house a greater treasure than I ever imagined."

Frieda looked up at him and saw both respect and affection in his eyes. Her breath caught as she drank in a great draught of his approval, fleeting though she knew it would be, and gazed at him until she remembered that her parents were there. She glanced at them and found them smiling at one another.

⚭

Frieda watched Klaus as he checked the girths on their mounts, his expression serious as usual as they prepared to set out for his brother's wedding. "It is not so long a ride to my parents' house, *Liebchen*." He searched her face for a moment. "You look as if you are dreading it."

"Oh, no, Klaus. It will be a fine ride, I am sure."

"Would you like to tell me what you are thinking about then?"

She did not like to lie to Klaus, but she did not want to tell him how she dreaded being near Margarethe and her fame. "Oh, I was wondering when I would ever get to see my parents again." She concentrated on recalling her mother's farewell and was able to summon a small tear.

"I will take you home for a visit next summer, you know. It is but ten to twenty days on the road, and since Ewald's surrender, there is little danger on the roads."

"You could protect me even if there *were* enemies on the road, I am sure," she said, her head lowered demurely. His eyes narrowed. She had best be careful.

"I have mentioned this visit home before. Does it not help to know you will be able to see your parents then?"

"Oh, yes, my husband. And I want to show you all the forest tracks I liked to ride on and everything about the Schwarzwald."

Klaus tugged on Frieda's saddle, checking where he had checked before. "I heard something about the market fairs in the Schwarzwald."

"Those are always good to visit."

"There is a fair not far from Beroburg. Would you like to go after the wedding?"

Frieda turned around, pretending to assess the small party they were traveling with, then smiled broadly at her husband. "I don't think we have enough pack horses."

He answered seriously. "We can always buy or borrow more." He turned then and met her eye. "Wait. Will you buy more cloth? You brought enough with you to clothe the entire household."

Frieda chuckled. "I have something in mind other than clothing. I would like to employ an embroideress or two."

"Whatever you desire, my lady."

She laughed as he helped her mount her horse and smiled as they rode. They arrived at Beroburg just at dinnertime and took places at a trestle table since the lord's table was full and the servants were already bringing in the food. They wore traveling clothes, simple garments that did not reveal their rank and were not recognized at the table. Klaus sat next to Frieda, and across from them sat two old women whom Frieda did not remember ever seeing before.

Frieda was hungry and content to sit and listen to conversation around her rather than participate. The women at the table with them discussed the nobility at the lord's table. Some of their identification work was faulty, but some was quite good.

Frieda glanced at Klaus. He appeared to be paying no attention to what was said, simply serving the woman across from him as was his duty while

Frieda served the woman across from her as well. It was an unfamiliar duty to her since she had rarely been partnered with someone who outranked her, as this woman assumed she did since she was older.

Her dining partner was speaking authoritatively. ". . .and next to her is Willem."

"Oh, I have heard of him," the other woman said. "He's the man who won a castle and a princess for a song. Which one is he?"

"The man who looks like a goat, there."

Frieda could hear no more, for she burst out laughing and turned her face into Klaus's shoulder, trying to hide her laughter as a coughing fit. When she recovered she drew back and met his eye. He winked.

"Are you all right, dear?" the old woman asked her.

"Thank you, old mother, I am well."

Satisfied that her dining partner was not going to die in her presence, she turned to the other woman. "Anyway, Lady Margarethe is not a princess, but she might as well be one. She composes music and sings like an angel and plays every instrument there is."

"Well, I am disappointed that she is not a princess. It makes a better story if she is. Is she not the one who nursed our Hilda after she was hurt?"

Now Frieda understood that these two must come from Albert's village.

"That is true, and before Willem won her hand, she was betrothed to Lord Gregor and called down an angel to rescue him from death on the battlefield."

"I heard that she has a sister who last month married the handsomest of the five sons of Lord Otto."

"I have never seen him, but I don't see how he could be any more handsome than our Lord Albert."

"Nevertheless, everyone says he is the handsomest of the five brothers, so it must be true."

"Well, be that as it may, his name is Klaus, and he was the fiercest of the army captains."

"The war is over now. I hope that he'll be kind to his people and not remain the fierce warrior he was."

"I hope so, too. But it is said that he never laughs. Likely it is because of the war."

"I feel sorry for the girl he married. What if he should hurt her?"

Frieda was outraged at this ridiculous remark. She drew a deep breath to speak and felt her husband—her fierce, warlike husband—gently squeeze her knee. He frowned slightly. He was right. It was better to keep silent.

"Do not waste your time feeling sorry for her. She has a nasty temper and can quite likely take care of herself."

"I had not heard that. I do know that she cannot sing or play any instrument at all, and that she has neither her sister's looks nor her charm. It is a pity."

Frieda looked down at her dinner until she realized that the hand Klaus rested on her knee was trembling. She looked and saw that his face was nearly red. He looked about to speak, and Frieda turned his face to her and kissed him on the lips, silencing him the quickest way she knew.

When she had his startled attention, she narrowed her eyes. He moved to look around her at the old women, so Frieda kissed him again. He blinked and nodded.

Frieda settled down to her dinner once more, then noticed the women's silence. She looked at her dinner partner, then at the woman beside her. Their wary looks caused her to laugh, and she couldn't stop but kept on laughing until they also laughed, looking somewhat bewildered, and Klaus put his arm around her.

The servants cleared that course and brought out the next before the old women resumed their conversation, discussing other people, mercifully. During the last course of sweet cakes and raisins, Willem waved at them from the head table. Frieda ignored him, as did Klaus. Willem then left the lord's table and strode down to them while Frieda waited stiffly. "Klaus, I didn't know you had arrived," he said as he grasped his shoulder and shook his hand.

"Greetings, Willem. We arrived just as dinner was being served."

"And how is my charming sister-in-law?" he said as he bent to kiss Frieda.

"I am well, though life with this fierce man is sometimes trying."

"Oh, no. Your mother said he beat you. I am so sorry," he said with a grin.

"Well, I beat him four times before he managed it, so I am content." She glanced over at the old women. Her dining partner's eyes were huge, her face pale. Frieda was pleased.

Willem followed her look and reached over and patted the old woman's hand. "Do not fear, old mother. We speak of chess. These people are as dangerous as month-old puppies."

Willem turned at hearing his name called. "Likely they want a song. Let's get together this afternoon."

"We shall do that," Klaus agreed. As Willem retreated, Klaus faced the old women, leaning close, his face as unyielding as his words were soft. "Now you see how dangerous gossip can be. Many of the things you said in our hearing were not true. My wife is not bad-tempered, and when it pleases her to sing, she does a very good job of it. She is an artist and a good and beautiful woman. I hope that you will watch your tongues from this day forward."

"Yes, my lord," said the quieter of the two.

"Yes, my lord, I will," said the other, a pale reflection of her former garrulous self. "Begging your pardon, my lord, my lady."

◌ß

At supper that evening, Frieda and Klaus sat at the head table where they belonged. Toward the end of the meal, Frieda kept an eye on the table where the household officials sat; the steward sat there tonight since all of the lord's family filled the head table, also the chief brewer, the chief vintner, the kitchen manager, and others. When people began to get up, she especially watched the chief baker. During her previous visit, she and Jeanne had come to know him as a deserving person. He rose from his place, and people around him started laughing at the large number of feathers stuck to his backside. Frieda nudged Klaus and nodded toward the disturbance.

He smiled and shook his head. "What would make them stick like that?"

"Oh, any number of things. Honey comes to mind. Bakers use a lot of honey, do they not?"

"Honey, of course. Hmm."

She glanced at him and noticed that his smile was directed at her.

◌ß

Late that night Frieda lay beside Klaus, recalling things that had been spoken that day.

"*Liebchen*, I hope you did not listen to those gossiping women today. People who have nothing to say sometimes make something up."

Frieda sighed. "I know there was some truth in what they said, for their words about Margarethe were nearly right, and they said some truth about you as well."

Klaus said nothing for a while, then, "In war one does what needs to be done. I don't think I was any more fierce than the other captains, whatever that means."

"I know nothing of that. But I do know that you are the handsomest of the five von Beroburg brothers, just as they said."

"I thank you, Frieda." A friendly silence lay between them until he spoke again. "About us brothers, you can see that no two of us are alike?"

"Yes, I can see that," she agreed as she wondered what he might be trying to say.

"God made us different from one another, and so He did with you and your sister. She. . .makes more noise than you do, and she has been here longer as well, so people know more of her."

"So you are saying that they don't know anything about me, and so they make something up?"

"That is what I think."

Frieda snuggled close to him and kissed him. "Thank you, Klaus. I will remember that."

They bade one another good night, and Frieda tried to dwell on Klaus's words. But instead she kept remembering, ". . .nasty temper and can quite likely take care of herself. . .cannot sing or play any instrument. . .she has neither her sister's looks nor her charm. It is a pity. . .it is a pity."

Chapter 4

Frieda stood talking with Klaus and her aunt Mechthild when Margarethe came to her and invited her to visit Hilda as she prepared for her wedding. "Are you certain I would be welcome? I know her but slightly."

"I know you'll be welcome, for she asked for you. Your reputation, you know," Margarethe said, looking smug. Their aunt chuckled.

Frieda walked along with Margarethe, completely unenlightened about why Hilda might have asked for her, to Hilda's chamber where they joined a giggling group of young women. "Thanks be to God that Frieda is here. Now we can get this thing settled," their cousin Jolan said.

Frieda went to the happy but anxious bride. "Greetings, Lady Hilda. God bless you on this day. What thing am I to help settle?" She was puzzled, for all seemed normal to her, and she was no expert on anything that she knew of.

"Greetings, Lady Frieda. It's about this veil. I don't know whether to wear it or not." The veil she held was of an old-fashioned style but daintily embroidered with thread that matched the fabric.

"It's very pretty, perfectly acceptable for a bride. Where did you get it?"

"My mother made it and wore it when she married my father. She. . . died a year ago and I wanted to honor her, but. . ."

"Do you not like it?" Frieda asked gently, still not seeing why Hilda had asked for her.

"I do, but it truly doesn't look right with my gown. These ladies," she gestured around the room at the grinning friends, "pointed out that you did not wear a veil at your wedding and that it is likely out of style for brides to wear veils. And it doesn't go with this, in truth, but it was my mother's and it would please my father if I wore it, but. . ."

The veil truly didn't go with her other clothes. She wore a plain, light blue tunic with a nicely worked surcoat of purple over it, the embroidery worked in gold. The veil was a pale yellow, which did not blend with the tunic at all.

Frieda took only a few moments to decide what to say. "First of all, do not feel obligated to do something to please your father. You are between lords today. Up until today you had to please your father, and as of tonight you will have to please your husband." Here she was interrupted by friendly laughter from the other women, which caused Hilda to blush. "So this is your only day to do as you please. If your veil looked well with your other clothing, would you wear it?"

"Without a doubt."

"Very well. Let me see your wardrobe." Hilda led her, with the other ladies following and whispering, to the coffers in the corner. She had not many garments with her, but one of them was a tunic of a slightly stronger yellow than the veil. Frieda took it and carried it, along with the veil, to a window. The colors looked well together.

"Lady Hilda, do you need to wear that tunic? Could you wear this one instead?"

Hilda frowned. "I like purple with blue. . ."

"So does Margarethe," Jolan pointed out. "She wears it all the time."

"She wore purple and blue to her wedding as well," Frieda remembered aloud. "Your coloring is different than hers, and I think this yellow would bring out the lovely green of your eyes, and then the veil would look right with the whole. The purple surcoat will look striking with the yellow. See?" Frieda held the tunic next to Hilda's surcoat and looked to see her begin to smile.

"But would I not be out of style to wear a veil?" she asked as if it was her last doubt.

"Who cares? A wedding like this of a great lord and a well-loved lady sets styles; it does not follow them," Frieda asserted, completely confident in her manner and voice.

"Then I shall do it. Someone help me, please," Hilda said. Jolan and Margarethe rushed to assist her, Margarethe beaming a big smile Frieda's way. As she watched, Frieda felt shaky. Who was she to advise a bride?

The ladies stood back and gazed at Hilda when she was once more dressed. "Oh, yes. This is just what you needed," Margarethe said. "I did not want to worry you, but you looked pale before. Now you look radiant."

"Beautiful," Jolan agreed. "Now aren't you glad you called for Frieda?"

"Yes, I am. This is the perfect solution, Lady Frieda. Thank you so much," she said as she held her hands out to her.

Frieda stepped up, thinking to clasp both hands, but Hilda drew her close and hugged her instead. "Why did you think I might be able to help?"

"Because you always look perfect, and your sister suggested that you might be generous with your fashion knowledge. I'm glad she was right."

Startled by Margarethe's unexpected kindness in drawing her in, she nodded and moved toward the door. "Please stay with us, Frieda," Hilda said, and Frieda hesitated. It would be nice to have women friends, but she knew none of these well.

"My husband will be wondering what has become of me. I wish the best for you this day, Hilda." She slipped out and glided down the stairs and into the rapidly filling hall, where she found Klaus seated near the front of the hall. He rose to greet her.

"How is Hilda this morning?" he asked as he seated her.

"She is well. She wanted to consult me on a fashion matter," she said, her voice sounding a little proud even to her own ears as she settled her skirts.

"A wise choice on her part. You are always well dressed. But is she only now deciding what to wear?"

"She is dressed. Is Albert worried?"

"He is nervous, but mostly he is happy, as I was on our wedding day."

Frieda noted that he looked as serious as ever. She recalled their wedding day and did not remember feeling nervous at all. "Why do people get nervous on their wedding day, I wonder."

"I cannot speak for everyone, but I was nervous about promising to spend my life with someone I didn't know very well."

"Oh," Frieda breathed, realizing that her lack of nervousness showed how lightly she had taken her vows. From the day she told her father she would accept Klaus's proposal, she had not considered the permanence of marriage, only the possibilities for making it less tedious. She felt Klaus's strong hand taking hers and holding it.

"If we were marrying today, I would not be nearly so nervous and even happier than I was then," he said softly.

She looked at him in wonder. She carefully chose what she could truthfully say, for he deserved only the truth. "I think that if we were to marry today, I would not be nervous at all, for you are an even better man than I thought you were."

He squeezed her hand. "I am glad. I want you to be happy."

People were stirring now as the ladies who had been with Hilda came in and took their seats. Klaus and Frieda continued to hold hands as the wedding began. Hilda did indeed look beautiful, and Frieda sat close enough to see the appreciation in Albert's eyes. The wedding itself was in the great hall, followed by the blessing in the chapel. The chapel would not hold all the people, so some remained in the hall while it was set up for the feast. Dancing followed the feast. All of this was familiar to Frieda from her own wedding in this castle a few weeks before.

She enjoyed dancing and danced with everyone who asked her. During a ring dance, which did not require partners, she got away from the dance floor and found Klaus at a side table and dropped to a seat beside him. "Thirsty, *Liebchen?*" he asked as he pushed their cup toward her.

"Yes, thank you, Klaus." She drank. "I want to dance some more after I rest a little. I am hoping that you will dance with me more so that all the men will remember that I am married."

Klaus shifted in his chair. "Is someone bothering you? I can let him know that you do not like it."

"Oh, no. Everyone is very nice. I'm just a little uncomfortable. My family at home is not much for kissing, and your family seems to be different."

"There is always a lot of kissing at weddings. Who has kissed you?" He looked as if he was simply making a polite inquiry, but the glitter in his eyes spoke ill for anyone who was out of line.

"Well, Uncle Einhard and Willem. . ."

"Both are members of *your* family," he pointed out.

"That's true. And your father and your brothers—"

"Which brothers?" The steel in his voice was unmistakable.

"Albert, of course. The new husband is kissing everyone, and Gottfried and Ludwig."

"Not Gregor?" Klaus asked.

She shook her head, and Klaus's hands on the table relaxed and his brow smoothed. "No. And Hilda's father, but that doesn't count, for I kissed him."

"I saw you do that. I am almost jealous."

Frieda feigned surprise. "Why? Did he not kiss you?"

Klaus shook his head, and Frieda thought she saw a twinkle in his eye. "I think you are done with all the men who are likely to kiss you."

"Not all, I hope," she said, her eyebrows raised.

"Not all," he agreed and leaned forward and kissed her tenderly on the lips.

"Well, I'm glad you two are getting along," Willem said as he came up to them with a laughing Margarethe.

"Everyone is getting along today, it seems," Klaus answered as he pulled a chair back.

Willem held the chair as Margarethe sat down. "Will you be staying the night or rushing back to apple harvest?" she asked, smiling up at Willem, then looked at Frieda as Willem took his seat.

"We will stay the night. We want to go to the market fair tomorrow."

"Oh. . ." She turned glowing eyes on Willem. "Can we go as well? You know I need fabric for clothes, and I want to see everything. . . ."

"Certainly we may go, *Liebchen*. I know you need clothes. I am tired of seeing you in such rags," he said, flicking her delicately dyed and richly embroidered sleeve as she laughed merrily.

Frieda strove to look pleased at the prospect of her sister coming along. The men began discussing something else, as men so often do when women speak of shopping, and Frieda leaned close to Margarethe and whispered in a conspiratorial tone, "I am planning to purchase material to make a surprise for Klaus. Don't tell him what it is for."

"I love surprises, and I would never spoil yours." Margarethe looked hurt, and Frieda was ashamed. "Shall we get rid of these men so we can talk about it?"

"I will need to lose Klaus for a time tomorrow while I buy my linen. Today, though, I need to talk with someone knowledgeable about," she whispered in her sister's ear, "the war."

Margarethe grinned and pressed her hand. "That's easy enough to do. Trust me?"

"Of course," she said, though dubious.

Margarethe nodded and winked. Then she sighed and drummed the table until both of the men looked at her. "Is it not time to go back to dancing? It is such luxury to be a guest instead of a musician that I loathe to waste any of the music." She raised her eyebrows. "Klaus?"

He glanced at Frieda before he rose and held out his hand to Margarethe. "I will dance with you, little sister. Come." He held her chair as she got up. Frieda kept her eye on Margarethe, wondering what she had in mind. Margarethe nodded toward Willem and winked. Of course. Who was more knowledgeable about the war than the man who had had a key role in bringing about its end?

Margarethe watched her husband take her sister off to the dance and did not hear all of what Willem was saying to her. ". . .any help, we will be glad to come with some of our men." Frieda turned to Willem, and her look must have been quite blank. "I have just offered myself and my wife and our men to help with the apple harvest."

"Thank you. I will let Klaus know right way." She looked back at Klaus dancing with Margarethe.

"I got the impression that Margarethe was removing Klaus for a purpose?"

Frieda forced herself to focus her attention upon what she wanted to learn about the war from Willem, asking about the final days and what parts the different allies played, and what their banners and shields looked like. "And what banner did you use?"

"I used none. I considered myself a man of Gregor's battalion since it was he who heard my request and allowed me to join the troops. I was also connected to your Uncle Einhard, though, having only recently left his employ, and I shared a tent with one of his knights. A very new knight, with a very new tent, for which I was grateful since the rain was terrible."

"I have slept in a tent on a rainy night and was grateful that it was a good one. Do you have a shield design now?"

"Yes. Margarethe and I have put one together to be our own. I would be entitled to use my family's, of course, but since my lands do not derive from them, we decided to have our own. Your family's arms are cluttered, having been quartered several times, and so we used the colors of your mother's and uncle's family. They have a gold bear on a black ground with a red border."

"And the bear clutches a sword."

"Yes. We use a gold lute on a black ground with a red border. We thought of using the sword behind, but the lute is unusual enough."

"Do you feel Uncle Einhard was the one who was largely responsible for getting you involved in the war?"

"Definitely. I would not have come to the war at all had he not released me to go to work for your father-in-law."

"All of Lord Otto's family uses that bear. What about the enemy, the main enemy, Ewald? What was on his banners and shields?"

"A red dragon."

"Oh, Willem, that is just perfect. Don't tell Klaus about this conversation, please? I will use the information to make a surprise for him."

Willem's face crinkled in amusement. "A wall hanging for the hall. An excellent idea, my lady."

Frieda was dismayed. "You don't think he'll guess this easily, do you?"

"Not unless you ask him the questions you just asked me. And Klaus is always gallant. Even if he did guess, he would say nothing."

"Good. He'll know I'm doing something, though, because I will be hiring two embroideresses."

Willem whistled. "You really are embarking on a big project. Say," he said, covering her hand with his larger one, "should we not dance? We have been sitting here through several songs. It is bound to look suspect."

Frieda looked out over the dancers until she spotted Klaus. He held Margarethe and was smiling, apparently at something she was saying. "What is it, little sister?" Willem asked gently.

"I know Margarethe loves only you, but Klaus once made an offer for her hand, and I wonder—" She broke it off when she realized that she was complaining about her husband to a man of her family. It was wrong.

Willem still held her hand as he answered softly. "Klaus made that offer long ago, and now his attention is focused in another direction. He loves you, you know."

"I hope you're right." She saw compassion on Willem's face. "I should not have spoken so. Pray forgive me."

"It is done. Now will you dance?"

"Certainly." They made their way to the dancing and joined the others in the midst of a song. Willem kissed her hand at the end of it and asked for another dance just as she saw Klaus and Margarethe weaving their way through the crowd toward them.

"Frieda, will you dance with me?" Klaus asked.

"Well, Willem already asked me, and—"

"Go ahead, Frieda. I know you'd rather dance with your husband, and even though it's not fair, I don't mind."

Frieda saw Klaus's face tighten as he looked at someone behind her, then she heard a man's voice saying, "What is not fair is that I have not had a chance to dance with Frieda today. I hope you don't mind, Klaus?"

Frieda turned and saw that it was Gregor, Klaus's brother who had been betrothed to Margarethe. She glanced back at Klaus. He looked perfectly friendly now except for a little twitch of his jaw muscle. "Go ahead, Gregor, if my wife is willing to dance with you." There was a slight emphasis on the words "my wife."

Frieda wondered what this was all about and looked to Margarethe, but her perfectly composed face gave no clue. Willem was grinning, so it could not have been anything serious.

"Frieda?" Gregor inquired as the music began. She nodded and blew a kiss to Klaus as she danced away with Gregor.

They danced without speaking for a time, Gregor holding her gaze and smiling. "I am bold to say so," he began, Frieda bracing herself in case he was preparing to say something mean, "but my brother has not smiled so much in his entire life as he has since you have been here. He was right. You are very good for him."

Frieda considered this before answering. "So. He thought I would be good for him?"

"What he said, I believe, was that you two would be well suited to one another."

"When did he say this?"

"When he was talking me out of making an offer for your hand."

Frieda missed a step. "Were you seriously considering it?"

"I was." Frieda shook her head in amazement.

They danced without speaking for a few minutes until Gregor cleared his throat. "There is something I have to know, if you are willing to answer, and I will never tell a soul." Frieda looked at him with misgiving, and he laughed and drew her closer. "I want to know; if Klaus and I had both made offers for your hand, who would you have chosen?"

"My father would have chosen Klaus. He is the older of the two of you, and the richer."

Gregor narrowed his eyes. "I happen to know that your father allows his daughters to choose their husbands. And I want to know. . ."

Frieda couldn't resist teasing her brother-in-law a little. "Come here," she said, tugging on his shoulders to draw him closer. She tiptoed and whispered in his ear, "I would have chosen. . .Klaus."

Gregor relaxed his hold on her to the loosest possible dance position. "Not only are you two well suited; you deserve one another."

Frieda laughed until Gregor did, too. "I know you and Klaus were once close. Don't stay away because of any small dispute between you. I want you to be a frequent visitor at our home. Can you do that?"

"Are you trying to get me to help with your wretched apple harvest?"

"Yes," she agreed, grinning.

He sighed dramatically. "I shall never marry. These sisters-in-law God has given me are enough of a trial." He removed any sting from the words by resuming a normal, friendly dance position.

At the end of the song, Gregor bent and kissed her cheek. Frieda scanned the dance floor for Klaus. He was heading her way, and her smile widened as she caught sight of him. He seemed tense but then relaxed as he joined them.

"Your *wife*," said Gregor, "is a fine dancer. She also has diplomatic skills not unlike your own. So if you want my help with the apple harvest, you shall have it."

Frieda held her breath at the sight of Klaus's cautious smile. "Day after tomorrow then. And don't dress up. I think I will use you in a tree."

"It won't be the first time," Gregor said, grinning, relief evident on his homely face. "And of course next month I will be needing help in my vineyards. . . ."

Klaus caught Frieda's eye. "This is how we brothers stay close. By working one another to death."

"Willem also offered to help. I said I would let you know."

"Excellent," said Gregor. "Another source of cheap labor."

Klaus grinned and took his brother by both arms, and Gregor did the same to him. Frieda looked on wistfully. If only she and Margarethe could solve their problems so easily. It would be wonderful to have a sister to love and be friends with.

Chapter 5

The booths and colorful pennants blowing in the hot breeze, the mingled odors of animals and roasting meats reminded Frieda of the market fairs near her home. This one was smaller but familiar and welcoming.

Klaus supplied her with a generous amount of gold coins and winked at her. "Likely our tastes run to different merchandise, sweet lady, so I will leave you to shop with your sister." He turned then to Margarethe. "Did your husband give you enough coins before he went off to look at the horses?"

"If I say that he did not, will you give me some more?"

"I will, and I will extract payment from that rascal at first opportunity."

"In that case, I have plenty, thank you, my handsome brother." Klaus bowed to the ladies, kissed Frieda's cheek, and strode off in the direction of the horses.

Frieda grinned at Margarethe. "He *is* handsome, isn't he?"

"Everyone knows that. What shall we look at first? Linen, maybe?"

"Yes, while Klaus is nowhere near. I hope there is some nice dyed wool thread as well. I have some at home, but I don't want Klaus to come upon me dying it."

"That's a good idea." Together they walked to all three stalls that carried quality linen goods where Frieda chose a length of linen and had it trimmed to the size she wanted. Then they found wool thread. Klaus's man, who followed at a discreet distance, took the packages from her when she beckoned him over.

Frieda watched him carry the packages to a horse. "I wish I could go right to work on my project, but I have to wait until after the apple harvest."

Margarethe steered her back toward the stalls they hadn't seen yet. "I thought you were looking forward to that."

"I am, but a new project like this is so exciting. I hope Klaus will be pleased with it." She reached beneath her veil to check on her hair.

"Me, too. You said something about hiring an embroideress?"

"I think I will check around with the people we already have—see if any of them do nice work and would like to help."

Margarethe took Frieda's arm, and they walked off through the stalls. They stopped at one that displayed glassware. Margarethe lifted a cup and examined it as they continued their conversation. Frieda likewise turned her attention to the nice things at hand.

Frieda, noticing that the young woman tending the booth fidgeted, nudged Margarethe into silence from her chatter. The girl curtsied when she realized both ladies were looking at her. "I beg your pardon, my ladies, but I heard the name 'Margarethe' used and have just realized who I have here in my father's shop. To honor you and your friend, I would like to give each of you a goblet."

Margarethe graciously thanked the girl while Frieda stared. "I will think of you when I drink from this."

"I, too," Frieda murmured. She examined the goblet for a moment. "I have been wanting some goblets, and yours are very fine." She proceeded to bargain for a set of green glass goblets for the head table and arranged to pick them up when she had a man to carry them for her.

"Thank you, miss, for honoring us," Margarethe said as they left the stall.

Frieda regarded her sister until Margarethe stole a sideways glance at her in return and grinned. Frieda couldn't help grinning back, then Margarethe giggled. "Do you always attract admirers in public like that?"

"This one was bolder than most, I think." Frieda shook her head. Her sister really *was* the ruling beauty of Bavaria.

Margarethe bought cloth for clothing for herself and Willem, consulting Frieda on each purchase. They surveyed the goods in every stall, then headed for the horse market where their husbands were sure to be found.

They found them side by side, leaning on a fence discussing horses. Klaus straightened when he saw Frieda and greeted her with a shy smile and a kiss. Willem greeted Margarethe with a hug and whispered something in her ear, then they watched Frieda, to her puzzlement.

Klaus took both of her hands and all of her attention as she stood facing him, the warm wind causing her veil to flutter. "*Liebchen*, I know you love your old horse, but would you be unhappy if I gave you another horse?" His face was earnest as he studied her and went on. "Perhaps a yearling filly who cannot be ridden for another year. . ."

Frieda felt her face breaking into a smile that matched her husband's. "I have been thinking about another horse. How did you know?"

Klaus shook his head. "I didn't know, but I saw this filly and thought she would suit you."

"Show her to me then, Klaus, unless someone else has bought her while we stand idly chatting."

The others laughed as Klaus led her by the hand toward the younger horses. Frieda glanced back to see Margarethe and Willem following. Her sister looked just as happy as the men did, though she couldn't have seen the filly they spoke of.

Klaus stopped among some young horses, and Frieda found she could not take her eyes from one beautiful filly. She was perfectly proportioned and graceful in appearance and had a look of intelligence and liveliness about her. She tossed her head up and down as they approached. She was pure white, the most desired and rarest color.

Frieda moved closer, and the young horse watched her closely as she began speaking to her in a soft, friendly way. "Greetings, little lady. I would like to get acquainted with you." She murmured other things as she walked up to her.

The horse showed no fear and allowed Frieda to stroke her as she continued talking softly. After a while the filly nuzzled her. Frieda was completely charmed and whispered, "Are you mine?"

Gradually she sensed Klaus behind her. What if this was not the horse he had chosen? Surely this fine animal would be far too expensive. He might not like it that she had gone directly to this horse and ignored all the others, even the one he had chosen for her.

Klaus spoke near her ear. "Frieda, did I choose wisely?"

She turned and flung her arms around his neck. "Is she truly mine?"

"She is, for I already bought her."

Willem chuckled. "He promised all next year's crops, but he bought her." Margarethe smiled as she hit him.

☜☞

Late that night Frieda lay awake after Klaus fell asleep and thought about her wonderful new filly. She had been given nice gifts before, but never anything like this. She recalled the horse's response to her and her sister's and brother-in-law's reactions. Margarethe had looked so happy, tears in her eyes.

But mostly she remembered Klaus. His eager look as he asked her if she would mind if he got her a horse. His voice behind her as she stroked the filly. His delight as she threw her arms around his neck.

She hugged him often, but he had seemed especially touched by this hug. He had held her tight and his voice was husky when next he spoke. Frieda wondered about that. The only explanation was that he had wanted to please her and was glad that he had.

When she was a little girl, her mother had sometimes given her presents to appease her when something had gone wrong between them. Her father had done this a few times as well.

But she and Klaus had not quarreled. They had yet, in fact, to invoke the rule about not arguing in the bedchamber; they had never argued anywhere.

And he was not asking for anything and trying to gain her favor with the gift. She was sure of that. Klaus was a diplomat, true; but he was always direct with her.

By his open and eager look when he asked if she would like a horse, and by his happy response to her hug, she was fairly certain why he had given her such an extravagant thing. And it was extravagant, she knew, for white horses were rare and highly prized.

Frieda sighed, quietly so as not to disturb Klaus, and smiled in the darkness. It looked as if her husband might love her. She had pondered his actions late at night and watched him for clues. He was consistent in his care and affection for her, and the gift of the filly added weight to the evidence.

Still, he said nothing, so she didn't know for sure. Klaus was a great one for the truth, so she knew that when he did say he loved her—if he ever did—she could be certain that it was true.

It had long been her dream to be married to a man who loved her. Even if he were despised by every other person on the earth, she would find a way to love him in return.

And Klaus was nearly perfect, as far as she could tell. He did act a little prideful at times, when he was right about something and wanted everyone to know it. A small thing—it even made her smile. But his treatment of others was always fair. His men at arms had all served under him during the war and respected him greatly.

Yes, Klaus was a beautiful man. Surely he deserved a better wife than her. She knew herself to be thoroughly wicked. She had only agreed to marry him in the first place because her father told her she had to. Even as they stood in the tower the night before their wedding with their arms around one another, Frieda had intended to make him as miserable as she was.

It was only after the wedding that she began to consider treating him well. He was so considerate, so loving. And, oh, those kisses were enough to change any girl's opinion.

She was unworthy of such a man, yet here he was. She looked over at him where he lay sleeping at her side, the moonlight just enough that she could make out his profile. She carefully turned on her side to see him more easily.

Why was he so good and she so wicked? She had always been so and she could not blame her parents, for they had done what they could to help her change. Even when she was little, she had been bad. She lost her closest companion, Margarethe, when she was but six years old. Heartsick and desperately lonely, she wandered about the castle seeking someone to play with, but everyone was too busy for her, including her old nurse and her parents. She had never noticed how busy everyone was until her sister was gone.

Gradually she learned to entertain herself, and her loneliness grew less. Her parents did not act the same as before toward her, and she didn't understand it. Now that she was an adult, she knew that they missed Margarethe as much as she did, but didn't want to say anything to her about it.

When she was young, she only knew that she could no longer please her parents—and how badly that hurt. She strove to please them and never stopped all of her years at home.

While still trying to please her parents, Frieda also found things to do to please herself. Sneaking around, eavesdropping, and bribing people did not bother her conscience especially, but she burned with shame at the memory of having stolen. Another thing began to bother her now.

It was about her sister, Margarethe. She had loved her as only a child could. Then when she left and her parents became impossible to please, and especially when her father compared her to Margarethe, Frieda began to resent her, even to hate her.

It did not help that she didn't get to see her sister for nine long years. Margarethe grew to be a monster in her eyes. Now she knew that her parents hadn't allowed her to come for fear of the danger on the roads, for even the children of Lord Otto's allies were not safe. But at the time, she only knew that her sister would not come for a visit and that she was not allowed to go to visit her.

Now that she was getting to know Margarethe once more, she liked her. They could become friends she felt sure, in spite of Margarethe's preoccupation with music.

Yet Margarethe's popularity remained a problem. Frieda would have liked to be adored as her sister was. It seemed to be the same thing she endured growing up; her parents loved Margarethe, not her. And now it seemed that all of Bavaria loved Margarethe.

It wasn't fair. Why could someone not favor her for once?

Suddenly her eyes stung as she smiled through tears. Klaus favored her. It wasn't fair that someone as good as he should care for a wicked person like her, but it seemed that he did.

All those years of trying to please her parents, and now she hardly tried to please Klaus at all, and he was pleased with her. Frieda gazed at her sleeping husband through the tears pooling in her eyes, then sliding across her face. She wiped her face with her hand and sighed. Surely he deserved better.

But for how long could she please him? Sooner or later he would find out what she was really like, and then he wouldn't care for her anymore. Tears came again.

Klaus was a genuinely good person. He had to have gotten that way somehow. She would find out his secret and adopt it as her own. Frieda considered possibilities as to the secret and dismissed them one by one.

Then she recalled the way he mentioned God all the time as others might mention a friend they spoke with regularly. That was the only thing it could be. Klaus must actually have some kind of friendship with the Almighty God.

Frieda knew God existed, but He seemed far away. She would rather He didn't take notice of her, since much of what she did was wicked.

That was going to change. From now on, she would do only good things. She would confess to their priest the sins she had thus far accumulated in her life and go on from there. Her habits of jealousy and deceit were so strong, though, that she doubted she could overcome them on her own. She would need help.

Klaus stirred in his sleep, and she suddenly wanted to ask him to pray for her. God would hear him and give her the strength she needed. She had to ask him now, before she lost her courage.

"Klaus? Are you still awake?" she whispered. She didn't know if she was hoping that he was awake or that he wasn't.

"I think so," he answered. "Is something wrong, *Liebchen*?"

His handsome face looked worried in the moonlight, and she couldn't bear to add to his worries. "Oh, it's nothing. I just wanted you to hold me, if you're not asleep or too busy."

His voice rumbled as he answered, "Heaven forbid that I should ever be too busy to hold my Frieda." He moved nearer and took her in his arms. "If ever I am asleep when you want holding, wake me up. I don't mind."

She nodded against his neck. "As I just did?"

"Exactly. And I hope that I may do the same with you?"

Frieda choked. How good he was. "Of course, my sweetheart," she whispered. She tipped her head back and kissed his chin.

As he held her and drifted back to sleep, she knew she couldn't find the courage to ask him to pray for her. She would have to draw on her own strength.

Chapter 6

Apple harvest began the next morning. Willem and Margarethe had spent the night so that they and their men would be handy. Gregor came early in the morning with about twenty of his people, and Albert sent some men as well. Since he and Hilda were so recently married, no one expected them to come.

Klaus went down to the great hall before Frieda since he wanted to make sure all was ready. Jeanne helped Frieda dress in something she felt was old enough to work in. Klaus greeted her in the hall with a smile as he looked her up and down.

"Ready to catch apples, I see."

"Catch?"

"When the person picking tosses apples down to you. You need not work if you don't want to, but—"

"Of course I want to work, but. . ." Frieda frowned as she searched his face. She had hoped to climb a tree and do some picking. Apparently this was not to be. Klaus looked puzzled. Frieda decided to tell him what she wanted. Maybe there was a chance. . . "Don't tell my papa, but I can climb a tree quite well."

"Can you, now?" His lips smiled as he squeezed her hands, but his eyes did not. He looked as if he would say more, but Margarethe interrupted.

"Frieda, are you ready to work?" Frieda liked her sister's old clothes, both tunic and surcoat too short.

"I'm ready."

People walked to the orchard together, and horses gamely carried more than one rider while carts were filled with laughing workers. Frieda watched these people—her people—amazed at how happy they were to begin apple harvest.

On arriving at the orchard, Frieda and Margarethe handed out baskets and smiles to every pair of apple pickers as they followed the cart that carried the baskets. People could have gotten their own baskets, but this showed them that the lords and ladies were working as well, something Klaus wanted everyone to know.

"This orchard is huge," said Margarethe as she looked around at the trees stretching far in every direction. "No wonder they call this place Apfelburg."

"And Klaus planted more trees every year he has held it. If my pear cider turns out well, I will have more pear trees planted. Perhaps plums and apricots as well. I know apricots don't grow well where the winters are hard, but this is a fairly sheltered valley, and I think it might be worthwhile to start a few trees."

Margarethe's smile was proud. "You have the makings of a great lady, my little sister. I feel certain you'll bring Klaus even more prosperity than he has now."

Frieda grinned as she handed a chambermaid a basket. "I hope so, sister."

Margarethe was paired with Willem for picking, and Frieda's partner was Warren, Klaus's valet. He climbed the tree awkwardly as she smirked at his slow ascent. Frieda easily caught every apple he sent her way and found herself irritated with his gentle tosses.

As he moved around in the tree, she followed below with the basket. Eventually it became too heavy to lift easily and she dragged it.

"*Liebchen*, don't do that," Klaus said behind her. She straightened and turned to him. "This basket has enough apples in it; let me dump them. I don't want you to get hurt."

"Oh, Klaus, I can fit a few more in," she protested.

"Ah, but I don't want to get hurt, either," he admitted as he lifted the basket.

She matched his quiet tone. "Then stop carrying full baskets and help us pick."

He smiled as he carried the basket to the waiting cart. He returned to her and stood looking up at Warren, who held apples in his tunic. "I'll take those apples now, Warren. Then come down and take a short rest."

Warren threw the apples down rapidly, one after the other. During his slow descent, Frieda made her appeal. "Klaus, I want to pick apples."

"I cannot allow it, *Liebchen*." His answer was soft yet firm.

"But it has been years since I climbed a tree, and I want to do it. I wouldn't hurt the tree, and I can get higher than Warren since I'm lighter, and I know that it's not improper, for I see other women in the trees, and. . ." She stopped at his warning look, her temper slowly heating. He was acting just like her father, his arbitrary rules governing her life. Surely she had exchanged one taskmaster for another, and it was not to be tolerated.

Warren hopped down to the ground from the lowest branch. Frieda decided that she would do as she pleased, no matter what her husband said or did to stop her. If there was to be a battle of wills, they had best get on with it before too much longer and see how the land lay. She tucked her skirts into her belt while Klaus watched. Warren watched them both, alarm growing on his face. Frieda faced Klaus, hands on hips.

Klaus glanced at Warren, then back to Frieda. "Show me your climbing skills then, my lady. But promise something?"

"What is it?"

"That you will come down if I ask you to."

The fear she read in his eyes gave her pause and convinced her to agree. Was it fear that made him tell her not to climb? "Of course, my lord."

She walked to the tree and surveyed it. She found Klaus at her side. If it was fear that had made him so stubborn. . . "Be careful, sweet lady," he whispered. She searched his eyes, gave him a quick kiss, and swung up into the tree.

Almost instantly, Frieda was in the area Warren had been picking. "Has she had a squirrel for a teacher?" Warren marveled.

"She can do just about anything, I think. A remarkable woman."

That wonderful, free feeling she remembered so well from years ago overwhelmed Frieda with a playful mood. "Is someone going to catch these apples, or am I to let them fall?" Frieda called. She heard men laughing and looked to see that she had an audience of several of Klaus's men at arms.

Warren held out his hands to catch apples and Frieda tossed them down, one by one. She could not hear what Klaus said to his men, for he faced away from her, but she heard their chuckling. Frieda picked an apple and threw it at Klaus, hitting him in the back of the head.

Klaus put his hand on his head and turned, looking comically astonished. She waved and blew a kiss while his men laughed. Klaus bowed then went back to his job of picking up apple baskets.

At dinnertime, she climbed down from the tree. She was looking rough, she knew, dirt and tree litter all over her. Heedless of her appearance, she left Warren while he brushed at his clothes. She walked to the middle of the orchard where all the harvesters were to be served a simple dinner. Frieda did not see Klaus or anyone else she knew, so she approached a group of women who were seated on the ground. "I don't see anyone I know, so may I sit with you?"

"Of course, miss," one answered while the others looked her over. Two of them wore friendly smiles as she lowered herself to a seat in the dry grass. "We are all from Lord Gregor's household. And you?"

"Apfelburg is my home."

"The town or the castle?"

"Castle."

"What do you there?" the first woman asked.

Frieda frowned inwardly. She should have anticipated the questions. "I will begin a large work of embroidery as soon as the apples are in." It was the truth, but she hoped these people would find something else to talk about.

They looked at one another then back at Frieda with approval. The first one said, "I so admire people who can do beautiful needlework. I am only an assistant to the baker."

A little woman with bright-red hands crowed, "And it's not only baking she 'assists' him with, either, I'll wager."

The others laughed, and Frieda saw that the first woman blushed but denied nothing.

One who had not spoken before asked Frieda, "And how are things in Apfelburg? Can a girl find anyone to 'assist' there?"

Frieda felt her cheeks burning while the others grinned and waited for her response. "Well, I do manage to keep busy." She blushed even more at their sudden laughter.

Servants brought the meal, and one stumbled when he saw Frieda. She winked at him. After they were served and had begun eating, one of them remarked, "Lord Klaus has put his heart into his harvest, as always."

"And his back as well," another observed. "And we have Lady Margarethe and her Willem with us as well."

Frieda thought it would have been more proper of them to refer to him as "Lord Willem," but she said nothing.

"They are so happy together," the young woman next to her remarked, her face a reflection of a dream. "I hope that I can marry a wonderful man like that someday."

"Keep on dreaming, Anna," said the red-handed woman. "Chambermaids don't get many chances to marry wonderful men."

"Leave her alone," another said. "She has been praying every day, and the good Lord may hear her."

Frieda thought she would have a better chance at success if she petitioned Gregor for a husband, but she held her tongue.

"I think it is important to be a wonderful woman if you want to have a wonderful man," said an older woman. "After all, Lady Margarethe did not dream and pray, but she studied her music and became quite accomplished."

The young girl called Anna cleared her throat. "Actually, she *did* pray. And so did Lord Willem; for years, in fact. I heard it from Lady Jolan's maid when she was visiting with her lady not too long ago."

The older woman patted her hand. "Then perhaps you are on the right road after all. But the lady also worked hard. Do not forget that." Frieda cynically wondered if she was the girl's overseer.

"Lady Margarethe had considerable gifts to work with as well. I hear that when she was a small girl she could pick up any instrument and play it," someone put in.

"And she sings so beautifully. It's a pity she's not a soprano, though."

"What is a pity is that she did not marry our Lord Gregor. Then we could hear her songs more often." The red-handed woman's remark was met with a stiff silence. Frieda concentrated on her food.

The girl was the next to speak up. "Speaking of gifts, I wonder if Lady Margarethe's sister can sing? The Lady Frieda, who married Lord Klaus."

Frieda continued eating but felt eyes upon her and smiled weakly. Of course they would look to her for information since she had said she belonged to Klaus's household. She should have just told them straight out who she was. She looked around at the expectant faces. "Lady Frieda can sing, and she is a soprano, but she is not skilled at it since she has put her efforts into other pursuits."

"Oh, so you know her," the girl breathed. "I am so curious about her. What can you tell us?"

"Yes, what?" the first woman asked. "I have heard that she has a bad temper."

Frieda felt the stirring of that temper now.

"That is foolish. People always say that about people with green eyes, and it's just not so," Red Hands said with some heat.

"And what color are your eyes, *Liebchen*?" the baker's assistant asked as everyone laughed and Red Hands blushed.

"I heard that Lord Klaus is completely enchanted with her and will not let her out of his sight."

"I heard that he bought her a unicorn."

Frieda laughed. "It is only a white yearling filly." She spotted Klaus approaching. How could she ever keep him from giving her away?

She jumped to her feet and gave him a deep curtsey, beating him to the first greeting and surprising him greatly, judging by his face and posture. "Greetings, my lord. I did not find any of your other people here, so these good women of your lord brother's household allowed me to sit with them."

Klaus's eyes held an amused twinkle. Frieda sighed with relief that he had caught on. He bowed to the women seated on the ground. "May I also join you good women?"

Agreement was swift and accompanied by much patting of headdresses and wiping of mouths. The girl who wanted a husband, Anna, was sitting on Frieda's other side. "So," Klaus began, "what have you good women been talking about today?"

Red Hands spoke up boldly. "We have been talking about men, my lord." The others tittered.

"And what have you concluded?" Klaus's inquiry was entirely polite, as if they had been discussing the weather.

"That we like them," the baker's assistant said. The laughter was general at that, and Klaus smiled.

Frieda noticed the girl next to her had been leaning forward to get a view of Klaus. Now she leaned toward Frieda and whispered, "He is as handsome as ever." Frieda grinned and nodded, then turned to Klaus.

"We were also wondering about your bride, my lord. It is likely that I know her better than any of these others, but perhaps you will tell us all about her?"

Klaus raised an eyebrow at her, then looked thoughtful as the others held their breaths. Likely they thought Frieda audacious indeed, but she looked forward to his answer as much as anyone else did.

"Lady Frieda is not what I expected her to be from our first meeting. I had thought her a serious person, but she is full of mischief. Harmless mischief," he hastened to add. "Of course, she is every bit as beautiful as I remembered. Her smile lights up the entire hall. She is a dangerous chess opponent and a fine embroideress. She has excellent ideas for the running of a household, and she is a good worker. Today she picked apples along with everyone else."

"Where is she, my lord?" one asked timidly. "I would like to see her beauty."

Frieda peered anxiously at Klaus, who spared her a swift glance. "Oh, she is nearby. Likely she has leaves in her hair." Frieda had to discipline herself sternly to keep from passing her hand over her hair.

Red Hands shifted position, and the baker's assistant shot her a warning glance. She spoke her thought with defiance in her tone. "I heard that she has green eyes." She waited for Klaus's nod. "And some say that green eyes denote a bad temper. I do not think that is so. What think you, my lord?"

Klaus looked as if he were seriously considering the question, and Frieda was apprehensive when he would not meet her eye. "Well, I cannot say anything about green-eyed people in general, but up until today my lady has shown no signs of ill temper in my presence. Up until today," he repeated, his voice and face sad.

Frieda felt he was preparing for some sport at her expense, but that was impossible. This was, after all, Klaus.

The girl leaned forward and asked, "What happened today, my lord?"

Klaus sighed with what seemed to be regret. "She hit me in the head with an apple. I feel certain that a lump is forming there."

"Oh," someone sighed. The looks Frieda saw around the circle were of sympathy, shock, and amusement.

"I. . .she could not have hit you that hard. Let me see it, my lord. I have some training in healing," Frieda said.

"Very well." He sat still as Frieda examined his head all over. "She has great healing skills," he informed the watching group as she searched for a lump. "She can make a lump on the head go away with just a kiss." He looked so serious that only the oldest woman grinned.

Frieda wondered what he was doing. She concluded her examination of his head. "There is no lump, my lord."

"Alas," he said, looking her in the eye. "May I have the kiss anyway?"

Frieda heard gasps, and the girl next to her whispered, "Oh, glory."

Frieda shrugged. "I suppose." She struggled against the laughter that bubbled up inside her as he slowly leaned toward her and put his hand—the hand farthest from the audience—on her face and drew her to him and kissed her lips. It was no peck, either, but a kiss that took awhile. Frieda would have found it easy to forget their audience, were it not for the gasps and indignant whispers.

The oldest woman's comment was the one she heard most clearly, coming at the end of the kiss. "Obviously, she is Lady Frieda."

Frieda's guilt made her reluctant to turn back to her companions. "Are you?" Red Hands demanded.

She swallowed. "I am Lady Frieda, and I am pleased to make your acquaintance." She spoke the truth, for the meal had been mostly pleasant and quite informative.

"Please forgive me, good women, for my mischief. It was my idea. My lady wife is innocent."

His remark was met by a hostile glare from Red Hands and by grins from the baker's assistant and the older woman, and a happy sigh from Anna, the girl with a dream. Frieda smiled at each of them in turn and failed to notice Gregor's approach.

"Well, here you are. Klaus, I found your wife. She's been gossiping with the women of my household, I see." He kissed Frieda on the cheek as he made himself a place on the ground beside her. The girl happily scooted over.

"Was I missing?" Frieda asked.

"Well, you knew where you were, but none of the rest of us did," Gregor replied.

"My lady enjoys eating with people she does not know. She does this often." Klaus took her hand and squeezed it as he spoke. Frieda found it reassuring when she was not sure of the response of some of the women here.

"Soon you won't be able to do that anymore, my lady—" Gregor's look was half serious—"for you will know everyone in the country."

Frieda laughed. "Or at least they will know me and will avoid me when they see me coming." The woman with red hands held her hands in her lap and looked down at them. "I am glad these women let me sit with them today, for now I am assured that you have good people at home. These are fine folk."

Gregor frowned. "They *let* you sit with them? Did you not tell them who you are?"

"No. I wanted to be just one of a group of women. Is there something wrong with that?"

Klaus said, "We were deceitful. Gregor, I will tell you my mischief later today. Did you good women enjoy it?"

"Oh, yes," they chorused, heads nodding.

"*Liebchen*, we should get back to work," he said as he rose, then extended his hand to her. Gregor also got to his feet.

"I want to talk with you and hear about this mischief. I can't picture you making mischief of any kind, big brother."

Frieda turned and bade the women good-bye. She hesitated for a moment, then bent to speak to the girl, Anna. "If you like, I'll keep my eyes open for a suitable husband for you." She watched the girl's expression change from disbelief to delight.

"Oh, yes, please, my lady."

"Do you like men with blue eyes?"

"I like all colors, my lady." She blushed as the others laughed. Frieda grinned as she turned to join the men. When they had walked out of the women's hearing, Gregor demanded to hear about the deceit. Frieda enjoyed Klaus's very accurate account. When he got to the kiss, Gregor asked for a demonstration, which she laughingly agreed to.

"You have really changed, Klaus. Used to be you would hardly ever even smile, and now you're making mischief? What has happened to you?"

"It is this lady, I think," said Klaus, looking at her sideways. He smiled back at her smile.

"Oh, Gregor? The young chambermaid, Anna?"

"Yes?"

"She wants to marry. I said that I would cast about for a husband for her. I did not think to ask you whether she would be free to marry," she said, then bit her lip.

Gregor snorted. "My family and I owe her a good turn. Her mother was a widow in my parents' employ when she was born."

"Oh, that's sad."

Klaus said, "I didn't recognize the girl, though I knew you had taken her in. But making a chambermaid of her?" Klaus looked disapproving. Cleaning was hard work.

"It was only for her good and the safety of the household. She is likely the poorest seamstress I have ever seen. She tried working in the kitchen but kept getting burned."

"Her work will improve once she is married," said Frieda in a knowing way. "She's clumsy now because she is dreaming of the wonderful man she will marry."

"Romantic notions like that are what caused her mother's downfall. You see, she had been a widow for two years when Anna was born."

"Oh, dear," Frieda said.

"Yes. Father felt partly to blame, for he had a houseguest that winter whom Anna's mother named as the father of her babe, and he did not deny it." Gregor looked thoughtful. "If you can find her someone suitable, I will give my blessing."

Klaus grasped Frieda's sleeve and said near her ear, "Do you think. . ." then whispered the rest.

She nodded. "He is whom I was thinking of. But she is only a chambermaid."

"True," said Klaus with a grin, "but a chambermaid of noble blood."

Chapter 7

Frieda massaged Klaus's nicely muscled back as he lay facedown on the bed. She found several tender spots and knotted muscles and worked at them relentlessly. Klaus was mostly silent under the vigorous kneading. She shook her head as she worked on one especially vicious knot.

"Why do you insist on carrying full baskets all three days of harvest? Surely someone else could share that chore." She doubted he would listen to her. She had uncovered two of his faults—pride and stubbornness.

Klaus allowed himself a small groan. "I don't want my people to think I am lazy."

"Oh, I see. You would rather they think you mad. That makes sense."

"Why should carrying baskets of apples hurt me? They weigh less than my armor, and I can wear it all day while riding a horse and swinging a sword and it doesn't hurt this much."

A picture of Klaus riding his warhorse in full armor and carrying a basket of apples sprung into Frieda's mind, and she smiled as she worked. "The weight of the armor is carried all over you, while the apples are carried in front."

"I see," he said, though Frieda suspected that he didn't.

She worked the last bit of resistance out of the last tight place, then went back to the long, soothing strokes she had started the massage with. Klaus's sigh of relief could be felt as well as heard. "I'm nearly done with your back now, sweetheart. Are you sure you don't want to roll over and let me massage your neck and arms as well?"

"You are good to me, Frieda. My back is enough for tonight. I don't want to tire you."

She snorted, an unladylike sound Klaus seemed to enjoy hearing. "Too bad you didn't think of that before having me spend three days in a tree."

"But you like trees. I imagine your legs are sore. Do you want me to—"

"No, Jeanne gave me a massage. I'm fine." He was so considerate to think of her when he had to be in pain, judging by the knots and spasms she found.

She finished the massage and wiped the excess oil from his skin and her hands and arms with a towel. "Something I could use, though," she said as he rolled over to face her, "is a few kisses."

"I could probably manage to give you a few." His eyes twinkled as they met hers. She sat beside him on the bed and leaned over to kiss his cheek. He took her hand and held it.

"Good. I have a busy day planned tomorrow, and a few kisses will help a great deal."

"I have a lot to do as well. I have been too long in the orchard and done nothing in the castle. I will be meeting with Hagen in the morning and seeing how many apples we got in and—" He paused to yawn as Frieda watched, amazed at how relaxed he had become with her in such a short time. "Excuse me, *Liebchen*. What are you doing tomorrow?"

"I am starting an embroidery project."

"I wish you would tell me what it is. I have heard only rumors," he said, brow furrowed.

"That is as it should be, my husband, when the thing is a surprise for you."

"Ah," he said, a shrewd expression on his face. "So perhaps you *do* like me, after all."

"Perhaps," she agreed, one eyebrow raised. "I also want to spend time with Lady. I visit her morning and evening, but it's not enough."

"Oh, you want her to grow still more attached to you? Already she thinks you are the only person worth anything."

Frieda thought about her beautiful filly. "She is partial to me, I think."

Klaus snorted. "Why should she not be? You are always grooming her and giving her treats and telling her she's wonderful. . . ." He looked thoughtful, then startled as he met her eye. "That is exactly how you treat me."

Frieda stood, took off her robe, and draped it over a chair. "That's silly. You are no horse, Klaus." She went back to the bed and lay down beside him.

"Nevertheless, when you call my name, I shall come to you."

Frieda smiled as she put out the candles.

Later, after Klaus fell asleep beside her, Frieda wondered if she *did* treat Klaus as she did her horse. Maybe she did, except her compliments to him were not so lavish. He did know how to talk, after all, and would likely be either insulted or amused at the sort of silly things she said to Lady.

She had real affection for her filly; it was not a calculated attempt to gain her favor as Klaus had implied. What about Klaus? Was she trying to gain his affection? That could not be, for she already had it, in abundance. She remembered her manipulative attempts to win favor from people in the past. She hoped she wasn't doing that with Klaus.

She thought about these things as she stroked his back. She could do this now without waking him, he was so used to her, so trusting. And why did she want to stroke his back when he wasn't awake to appreciate it? Of course, it was because she felt affection for him. Maybe she even loved him.

Maybe she loved him. She thought that he might love her, but he had said nothing. Of course it would not last, for everyone disliked her once they got to know her. Still, she would like to enjoy it while she could. She had to wait for him to speak of love first; she would not force his hand. But now he was asleep. . . .

She whispered in the darkness, ever so softly, "I love you." Klaus did not stir. She could not see him well at all in the dark, their faces close together. "I love you," she whispered again, then drifted into sleep.

☙

Frieda forced herself to wake before dawn to attend Mass with Klaus. This was the first time she had managed to go when it was not the Lord's Day. Klaus seemed pleased. Frieda had noticed that he went to Mass every day and thought that perhaps that had something to do with his ability to be so good. She was determined to do whatever was necessary to improve herself.

While they knelt side by side in the chapel, Frieda prayed, *Help me, God, to be good. I ask You this not for my sake, but for Your friend, Klaus.*

Walking hand in hand to the great hall to break fast, they discussed their plans for the day. "I would like to go see Lady with you," Klaus said, "if you don't mind. You may fetch me from Hagen's office chamber when you are ready to go."

"I wouldn't be interrupting?"

"Oh, no. I will need a break by the time you are ready to go to the stable."

"I'd like to have you with me."

"Good."

After the morning meal, Frieda gathered Jeanne and Ida, one of the kitchen servants, to her. Jeanne was a good embroideress and had volunteered to help as she had on so many of Frieda's other projects. Ida was glad of the extra pay she would get for assisting. It gave Frieda satisfaction to have someone in her employ with the same name as her mother.

Together they went to Frieda's sewing room. It had both east and south facing windows, so there was plenty of light. Frieda brought out the sketches she had made of her plan for the wall hanging. The other women were intrigued.

"Such large shapes, my lady. How will we fill them in?" Ida asked.

"Mostly with Bayeux stitch, or a variation upon it that I have devised. And we will use outline stitch to define the edges."

"I am not familiar with Bayeux stitch," Ida admitted, gripping the table edge.

"You will be soon enough, if you work with Lady Frieda," said Jeanne. "She likes it well, as you will soon learn. It is quick and easy, economical of thread, and gives a very nice finish."

"Is it a pattern stitch? Or laid work?"

"Laid work," Frieda answered. "We will need to stretch the cloth on a frame as we work it."

"These soldiers look vague, madame," said Jeanne.

"Yes. We'll work the features of the ones in front clearly, then suggest the others, else we will be working on this until Eastertide. If you two will get the thread and prepare the linen in the frame, I will draw this to scale."

The others got out the materials while Frieda drew the main figures in the size she wanted for the actual work. She drew the large dragon facing left, which made it a sinister figure, and all of the others facing right. Actually, they appeared to be facing left, but the insignia must appear in the direction of the symbols as it would appear to one having the figures on a shield, and wearing the shield.

Then each of them set to work outlining the shapes in large basting stitches that would be removed later. The linen piece was so large that each woman could work without hindering the others.

They were still involved in this when they heard a knock at the door. Frieda got up to answer. "Yes?" she called through the door.

"Are you ready to visit Lady?" Klaus called out to her. Frieda glanced back at Jeanne and Ida, both sitting wide-eyed at the sound of the lord's voice, the one person who must not see what they were making.

"Yes, Klaus. I will meet you on the stairs in a moment." She returned to her helpers and spoke softly. "You may work as long as you like, but put it away when you are done. Jeanne, I would like you to show Ida the Bayeux stitch, if she has time before going to her other duties."

"Yes, madame. Have a good visit with your Lady," said Jeanne.

Frieda picked up her cloak before slipping from the room as she heard Ida say, "Her lady?"

Klaus awaited her at the head of the stairs. He held out his arms to her, and Frieda stepped into them. "It is so nice to see you again," he murmured as he held her fast.

"It's nice to see you again, too." She smiled at her silliness while feeling the same way herself.

"And what a morning it has been." He took her hand, and they descended the stairs and left the donjon. Klaus draped Frieda's cloak around her shoulders. As they crossed the bailey, he quietly confided, "Hagen is a fine manager when I am not around. But when I am here, he thinks he needs to consult me on every tiny matter. It was most tedious."

"Poor Klaus."

"Oh, and I remembered your words to Anna and spoke with the man we were thinking of for her. He has been talking about marrying for some time—"

"He hints to us about it every day. And what did Warren say?" Frieda was impatient with Warren's treating her like a delicate flower, but Anna might well enjoy it.

"He seemed hopeful, though cautious on account of her being a mere chambermaid. He would like to meet her."

"Wonderful. You're doing a good job for one not given to matchmaking."

"We need to get her into the house somehow so Warren can see her without her knowing that he might be interested."

"Klaus, that's not fair. Is she to be looked over as if she were a horse for purchase?"

"It doesn't seem fair, but I wouldn't want to get her hopes up before introducing him as someone who would make a good husband for her, then have him not like her for some reason."

"And what if she doesn't like him?" Frieda tossed back. She had to slow her steps to match her husband's and noticed her breathing had quickened, as well as her pace.

"That is a possibility, too, and I had thought of it."

Frieda doubted his words. "Humph."

"Perhaps you could bring her into the house as trying out for some job and see if any man catches her eye. I think she would say something if she saw someone she liked."

"That she would, but I think it would make her clumsy to be thinking about which man might. . . Warren is impatient with clumsiness, is he not?"

"He is. We'll think of something, *Liebchen*, if it's meant to be."

As they drew near the stable, Frieda pondered on a way to get Anna into the house. She had an egg of an idea and would let it incubate awhile.

Lady was at the far end of a run behind the stable. When Frieda and Klaus walked up, she lifted her head and cocked her ears. "Lady," Frieda called, and the filly trotted up and put her head over the fence. She nibbled at her veil in greeting and stood still while Frieda stroked her muzzle, then she nuzzled her, looking for a treat.

"I forgot to bring you something, my pretty girl. I hope you will forgive me."

Klaus spoke softly beside her. "I brought her something."

Frieda glanced at the apple in his hand while holding the horse's head. "Good choice. But cut it up so you get credit for bringing more treats."

He stepped back and turned around and sliced the apple, then turned back to Frieda, extending a hand full of apple pieces. "Here you are."

"She needs to know you, too, so that when we're riding together she won't shy away from you and your horse."

Klaus walked a few steps along the fence and called Lady. She ignored him. Frieda stepped away from her and he called again, and Lady looked at him. He held out a piece of apple, and she moved over to him and delicately took the bit of apple from the flat of his hand with her lips.

Frieda followed and spoke to Lady in the usual warm tone of voice she used when talking to her: "There's a pretty little traitor, yes, she is." Lady regarded her for a moment, then went to searching Klaus. He grinned as the search continued. An apple slice was balanced on his shoulder.

Frieda beckoned to the waiting groom. He brought her grooming tools, including a large apron. She began to put it on when Klaus said, "*Liebchen*, you should take off your cloak. I would not like for something to happen to it."

It was one of her favorites, with crimson silk embroidery on slate gray wool that she and her mother had worked together. "You're right." She draped the apron across the fence, removed the cloak, and looked for a place to put it. Klaus held out a hand and took it from her.

Frieda donned the apron and picked up a brush. She made sure Lady had eaten all her apple slices, then went in through the gate and called her horse. Lady came to her, and Frieda began to groom her, talking all the while. Occasionally she glanced at her husband, who was watching with no signs of boredom.

Lady fidgeted, and partway through grooming, Frieda stood back and said, "Do you want to run? Go then. Get it over with and run." Lady stared at her. Frieda said, "Go," and swatted her on the rump. Lady galloped off, and Frieda joined Klaus by the fence.

"It is amazing that she can get going so well in this little run," he said. "I fear she may misjudge and hit the fence, though. You'd better come out."

Lady was making the turn at the far end, and Frieda saw the wisdom in Klaus's words and hurried to the gate. Frieda passed through the gate just as the filly tore past Klaus.

She turned at the near end of the run and galloped for the other end, turned, and headed back. She looked a little too close, and Klaus and Frieda both stepped back as she came by. Lady came very close to the fence, perhaps lured by their presence, and Frieda's cloak, which Klaus had draped over the fence, fell into the run. Lady's rear hoof caught it as she sped by.

Klaus put a hand on top of the fence post and hopped over, retrieved the cloak, and looked at it with sorrow. Lady stopped and looked back at him. He looked at her, then returned to Frieda through the gate. "This would have been safer on you, after all, *Liebchen*. It is my fault. I should not have put it on the fence."

Frieda, looking at the damage, saw that it was not a large piece of material, but it was in a place that could not be gracefully repaired. She would never wear it again. Her eyes stung.

"Can it be fixed?" Klaus asked. She kept her eyes down as she shook her head. "I am sorry. Did you do the embroidery yourself?"

She didn't answer, and Klaus tipped her chin up. His brows lifted in dismay as he looked into her face. "Oh, Frieda." He hugged her close while she felt foolish. It was only a garment. Nothing worth crying over.

"I'm being silly. Forgive me."

"Did you do the embroidery yourself?"

"My mother and I did it together. Why?" She pulled back in his arms so that she could see his face; the compassion she heard in his voice was reflected there.

"That is likely why you feel like crying." She wondered what he meant. "Forgive me?"

"Of course, Klaus. It was Lady who stepped on it, after all. And I have no business coming to the stable dressed like a great lady."

"Ah, but you *are* a great lady."

She sniffed. "Nevertheless. Now would you like to help me finish grooming that beast?"

Frieda watched as he groomed the horse and noticed that he moved stiffly as he bent, so she did not let him do very much of the work. "Would you like to go for a ride after dinner?" he asked.

She considered as she brushed. The wall hanging could wait. She searched the sky and found no excuse in the weather. Without excuse, she resorted to the truth. "I would worry about your back, sweetheart. Last night you had spasms, and today you seem a little stiff."

"I am fine, Frieda. Nothing better than riding to loosen muscles."

"Very well. I would like to go for a ride. After three days in an apple tree, I want to see some of the countryside."

"I know just the place for that."

Frieda surrendered her torn cloak to Jeanne and clasped her arm and shook her head when she would have exclaimed over it. Jeanne found her another cloak while Klaus changed his supertunic. Warren was nowhere near, so both women helped him with his sleeve buttons.

During dinner, Frieda watched a self-important brewer's assistant get more hugs than ever before in his life. He looked baffled, and Frieda grinned. Klaus tapped her hand. "What is that on his back?"

"Whose back?" she asked, her innocent look in place.

"That brewer's lad, there. He has a bit of parchment or some such on his back."

"I wonder what it could be," she said.

Hagen, on the other side of her, said, "I saw it, my lord. It says, 'I need a hug.' Ingenious, really. Everyone is offering sympathy, and he has no idea why."

Frieda dared a peek at Klaus. He was regarding her with a bit of amusement. She quickly looked away.

After dinner they set out, Frieda riding Fraulein and feeling guilty about how much she was looking forward to riding Lady. The day was warm except for the cool breeze, and only the changing colors of the trees indicated the season. The castle was on the highest hill in the area, of course, but its walls and buildings prevented a good view of the land from there. Klaus led the way up another high hill and stopped when they reached a clearing at the top.

"From here, my lady, all you can see is yours to command." With difficulty she turned away from looking at his handsome profile, all satisfaction and pride written there, to be awed by the view of rolling hills, forest, and farmland. Frieda turned her horse to look in every direction. All was beauty and prosperity.

She looked at her husband. He himself was more than she had bargained for. He caught her looking and rode over to her. "Yes, my lady, even I am included in that."

She frowned. "You are included in what?"

"I told you that all you can see is yours to command, and here you see me. . . ."

Frieda laughed. Oh, that it were so. He drew alongside, took her hand, and kissed it.

Chapter 8

If anything happened during the day to stir up Frieda's feelings, she could be certain that Klaus would bring it up at night when they were alone, whether she wanted to talk about it or not.

Tonight Klaus sat in a great, carved oak chair by the table, wearing his robe and watching as Jeanne braided her hair. Frieda knew they would be talking by his contemplative look. When Jeanne had taken her leave, Frieda sat in her chair, waiting. He took her hand across the corner of the table.

"Are you and your mother close?"

Frieda did not know what she'd been expecting, but it was not this. "Why?"

"It's just that when she and your father were here, I got the impression that you were not entirely comfortable with her, nor with your father."

"Yet I cried when a garment we worked on together was spoiled, so you wonder about it."

"Yes." He stroked her hand with his thumb.

"I was surprised that I felt like crying. Mutti and I really are not close. She was sometimes an ally against my father, but not much more than that." Frieda looked at the linked hands as the silence lengthened.

"Were you two allies when you embroidered together?"

"Perhaps. And we worked well together, and as long as we talked only of the work, I didn't get into trouble." Oddly, she felt the sting of tears again. She looked down. Klaus would think she cried all the time.

"Trouble?" He sounded hurt, and she looked up at him quickly, revealing her tears. "Come here." He moved his chair back from the table and held out his arms.

Frieda went to him and sat on his lap. "Tell me, *Liebchen*. Tell me about getting into trouble."

She sighed, and because she needed to talk, and because she felt safe with him, she told him of a few of the wicked things she had done as a child. When she finished, the silence lengthened, and she began to fear that he, too, would not approve of her. He rumbled, "It sounds as if you were not caught very often."

"I was very good at what I did."

"And so you cannot imagine why you were not good at the one thing you most wanted to do."

"How did you know? I could not please my parents no matter what I did."

"Were they not pleased with you just because you were their own little Frieda?"

"No. Sometimes I think that is what displeased them the most." She sobbed and clung to Klaus as he hugged her close. When she quieted, he dried her face and kissed her cheek. "I'll get up now. Surely you are tired of me sitting on your lap."

She got up, and Klaus did, too, and captured her hand and pulled her close. He placed his hands on her waist and held her gaze with his own. "The days when you must please your parents are over. Now you have only me to please." She felt anxious in spite of his smile. "And I, my sweetheart, am *very* pleased with you."

He kissed her forehead, then looked into her eyes again. She was sorry he would see the anxiety there, but she had to tell him her fear. "I know I please you now, but I am afraid that when you find out how awful I really am. . ."

"It does not matter to me, for I am awful myself, so I know how it can be. Would you stop. . .caring for me if I did something horrible?"

"Never. You are my Klaus, after all, and you are far from awful. You are the best person I know. I have been wanting to ask you your secret." She swallowed. There. It was out now, and she hoped he would tell her the truth without thinking less of her.

He folded her into his arms. "My secret is God, Frieda. I simply ask Him for His help each day, and I ask Him more often than that if I need to."

"I thought that was it. I asked Him to help me, too. But I need to ask every day?"

"It is not because He forgets and needs to be asked again. But because we forget." She nodded against his shoulder. "I would like to keep talking, if you are not too sleepy, but can we do it in bed, where it's warmer?"

"Of course." She helped him out of his robe, which was not necessary, but a friendly thing to do, and he did the same for her. She put out the candles while he loosed the curtains on the bed for the first time this fall. The night was cool enough that they would give welcome warmth.

They climbed into bed and lay close together. "My sweet lady. You missed out on a mother's love when you were little, and I know it would not be the same, but I know someone who would love to be a mother to you now."

"Lady Edeltraud?"

"Yes. She cares a great deal for you."

"I am fond of her. But we do not know each other well. Why does she care for me?"

"She just does. She was impressed that you wanted to marry as soon as you arrived here."

"Strange. I thought that I was making her a lot of work."

"True." His face was next to hers, and she could feel his smile. "But she enjoys being busy. And she assumed that your reason for haste was your concern for purity. That you were worried that you would not be able to resist my charm once you spent time with me, hence the hurry."

Frieda found that amusing. "She didn't realize what a gentleman you are."

"Oh, she knew. She was thinking that was *your* reason, and she was impressed. Your real reason was more that you wanted to get it over with before you changed your mind."

Frieda gasped and dared to look over at Klaus. "Don't look so startled. You were fairly obvious," he said.

"Oh, Klaus. I'm so sorry now. I didn't know—"

"Hush, *Liebchen*. I knew, or at least hoped, that you would be glad you married me. Are you?"

"Oh, yes. You're the man I always dreamed of marrying, though I didn't know it when I agreed to marry you."

"Why did you agree to marry me? I have always wondered."

Frieda closed her eyes and turned away, but not in time, for Klaus was gently drawing her back to face him. "Sweetheart, did they make you?" She squeezed her eyes tightly shut. She never wanted Klaus to know this. Never. Tears leaked out beneath her eyelids. Would there be no end to crying this day?

Klaus was kissing her face, and she gradually relaxed and returned his kisses. When she opened her eyes, she found pain on his face. "I'm sorry. It's not that I objected to you, just that I didn't know you and that I didn't want to move to Bavaria."

"I see. I had thought that you wanted to be with me. I'm sad that you did not."

"Oh, darling. I want to be with you now. Does that not count?" She was desperate for him to see that she cared and for him to keep on caring for her.

"Of course it does. I am so glad that you have grown to care for me." She kissed him, and he returned it soundly. "Now how did we come to talk about all of this? I wanted to speak to you about my mother."

"I like her. She is serious and formal, like you; at least that is the way you *used* to seem. But she is warm, too."

"Yes. And she wanted to have daughters as well as sons."

"Yet all she had was you five boys. Did you wish for sisters?"

"I would have liked sisters, but I did have a sister for a short time."

"I didn't know. Tell me about her."

"Ludwig was but one year old when I was born, then when I was two,

Eleanor was born. Something was wrong with her from the beginning. Her head seemed to be too large and she could not make her eyes work as one. She ate poorly, though Mutti nursed her herself in addition to the wet nurse.

"Eleanor was named for the great ladies of the ruling family, but she never got to be a lady herself. She died at eight months. She was never even able to hold her head up."

Frieda squeezed his hand and waited for him to go on. "Mother blamed herself. She thought there must be something wrong with her that she could give birth to such an unfortunate child. No one could change her mind. She was afraid to have any more children and kept Father away.

"Finally, she listened to your uncle's old priest, Father Bernard. He pointed out to her, as others had, that she had two healthy children. Then he told her that to live is to risk, and that the greatest things, the things most worth having, often call for the greatest risks of all.

"She took it to heart and went on with life. When she found out she was with child once more, she was anxious the whole time. The household was quiet, and there was much prayer going on.

"When she gave birth to Gregor, she looked at him carefully to make sure he was healthy. The midwife laid him on his stomach while she tended to my mother, and Mother was certain that Gregor lifted his head and looked around.

"That is when she knew that he did not have the same illness that Eleanor had. That is also how he got his name, for Gregor means 'vigilant.'"

Frieda knew there was more, for her husband looked far away. "Gregor brought joy to the entire household. He was a happy baby, and he was funny. You have seen how he looks; his nose and chin are too big and his eyebrows go nearly to the ceiling when he is surprised. Everyone loved him.

"But I carried the scars from the time of doubt and rarely laughed or smiled the rest of my life. Many have teased me about it, but I cannot help it; it is how I am. Ludwig is serious, too, though not as much. Mother thinks it is because I feel so deeply the pain of others."

Frieda now understood the differences among the brothers. It was as if they were from two different families, Ludwig and Klaus were serious, while Gregor, Gottfried, and Albert were always making people laugh, Gregor most of all.

And poor Lady Edeltraud. What a heavy burden she had carried. Little Eleanor was to be pitied, never having had the chance to grow up and enjoy life.

Frieda grew conscious of Klaus's gaze and turned to him. "Thank you for telling me. But I see you smile all the time. And I will try to be a daughter to your mother, for she needs one and I need a mother." She laid her hand on his face and he kissed it. "If you will agree—" she searched his face before going on— "I would like to name our first daughter Eleanor."

Klaus closed his eyes tightly while he held her. Frieda thought she saw a tear in one.

⊙৪

Neither of them managed to wake in time to go to Mass in the morning, but they broke fast together in the great hall. Afterwards, Klaus went off to do some business with Hagen. Frieda took a few minutes to do some sewing in their chamber, a bit of stitching Klaus might find amusing some morning, then hid his slightly altered breeches away among his other clothing. Then she was free to work on the wall hanging.

Jeanne and Ida had made some progress on it after she left the day before, and she was pleased to see a scrap worked in Bayeux stitch. Jeanne must have demonstrated it to Ida.

Frieda set to work. When Ida came in, she showed her what to do, then did the same for Jeanne when she came in soon after. They worked and talked until there was a knock on the door. Jeanne went to answer, then came to Frieda looking troubled. "It is the lord for you."

Klaus was to have been occupied for some time. She slipped out and met him in the passageway. He looked more distressed than she had ever seen him. She grasped his arm. "What is it, Klaus?"

He pulled her into an unused chamber nearby. "I will be making a quick trip to Hohenstein. I just received a message from the sheriff there."

Now she began to share his distress. "What has happened?"

"A man stole some cattle, and the farmer's son caught him at it, and the thief killed the boy. There were witnesses, so the trial will be short."

"Oh, Klaus, it is too bad."

"These things happen, Frieda." He gathered her into his arms. "I have had to sentence a man to death twice before, and it is so hard. No matter what they have done, they are still people."

"Should I come with you?"

"No, *Liebchen*. It will not be a pleasant trip." She stepped back from him as he released her.

"Of course not. And that is why I am offering to come. To share the burden with you." She willed him to understand, to see that she would gladly share this with him.

"Thank you, darling, but no. I would have the people there associate you with happy times. Is that acceptable?"

"I understand. Will you bring to me the names of the dead boy's parents? I want to write to them. And is there anything I can do for you?"

"Hagen will likely come to you with a few small requests. Decide whatever you like on those things. I will bring you the parents' names."

He hesitated. "There is another thing. . . ."

"Whatever you need."

"Pray for me?"

Frieda was surprised, but she agreed. "And pray for the thief. The sheriff says he has refused to see the priest."

"Oh, Klaus, I will pray. Is this a private matter? Or may I ask Jeanne to pray, too?"

"I would appreciate that. Our priest will be praying, too." His longing to forget the matter was evident on his face. "Thank you for caring so much, Frieda."

He opened his arms to her yet again, and she hugged him, wanting to lend him her strength for this day. While he still held her, he murmured, "I must go. I will see you tomorrow."

She had not thought he would be gone overnight, but it made sense, for it was a long trip to make twice in one day. "Tomorrow then, my husband." She raised her face for his kiss, which was hard and fierce in his distress. He smiled a little as he stroked her face; then he was gone.

Frieda felt an emptiness inside as she rejoined her companions in the sewing room. "What is happening, madame?" Jeanne asked as Frieda seated herself.

"Lord Klaus has gone to Hohenstein to conduct a trial. He asks that we pray for him and also for the murderer."

"A murderer!" Ida was indignant. "Why waste prayers on a murderer?"

Jeanne explained, though the answer was obvious: "We will pray that he repents so that he does not go straight to hell."

"Hell is where he should go, and directly." Frieda was surprised at Ida's harsh attitude. She herself might once have felt that way. It seemed familiar to her—and repugnant.

Jeanne said, "If he does not repent today, he will likely go there directly, for the castle has no jail."

"No jail?" Frieda asked. Every castle had a jail of some sort. And how did Jeanne know?

"Yes. Hagen told me that Lord Klaus will not permit the ancient jail there to be used, for it is nothing but a pit. A man can neither lie down full length in it nor stand up straight."

"I see," Frieda said. She was heartsick for her husband. Not only would he have to condemn a man today, but also it seemed he would have to witness the execution. "Will either of you consent to pray with me?"

Jeanne nodded, and then they both looked at Ida, who stared at her work. After a time, she sighed. "I will pray with you for the lord. But I cannot honestly pray for the murderer. I will ask to be excused from that part, if it pleases my lady."

"Of course, Ida. It is always best to be honest before God." Frieda was surprised to hear herself say that and wondered what it might mean.

∽◎∾

Frieda accomplished much on the wall hanging, for she worked on it most of the day, working alone after dinner and nearly until supper.

Hagen came to her once with a dispute between two bakers. He asked for her decision only, but she wanted more information and walked with him to the bakery. The two were so awed that the lady herself would take an interest in their problem that they ended the dispute on the spot.

Hagen was most gratified. "If there is anything I can do for you, my lady, I will do it."

"There is something, Hagen. And since my lord will not be here tonight, it may be an opportune time." Hagen looked a bit apprehensive, and Frieda wondered whether it was Jeanne or Klaus who had made him fear her. "Klaus tells me that before I came you were the only worthy chess opponent in the castle. I would like to match wits with you."

He bowed. "Yes, my lady. I would like that as well."

The brewery was near the bakery, and Frieda stopped there to check on the pear cider. The brewer cleared his throat several times before reporting. "Perhaps it is because the days are still warm, my lady. That may be it." He wiped his hands on his apron for the fourth time. "But some of the cider, some of it has turned to vinegar."

"Show me."

She spent the rest of her visit on the brewery tasting and listening to increasingly complex explanations. Much of the pear cider was now vinegar, but some of it was good. "Good man, this is not a thing you could have helped. Work with the chief cook on finding a use for the vinegar. And please give me two small jars so that I may show my lord both the vinegar and the cider."

Frieda called on Lady before supper, then after supper had a chess match with Hagen. Frieda was thinking about Klaus and was afraid her concentration would be poor, but they had a large audience, and that always served to sharpen her wits. She had to work to do it, but she won.

"Excellent playing, my lady. And do you sometimes beat Lord Klaus?"

"Sometimes. I think it is most interesting if the same person does not win all the time."

People laughed, and Hagen blushed. "Lord Klaus beat me every match for three winters."

"He's very good. And very patient." That met with more laughter.

Frieda excused herself, and Jeanne helped her get ready for bed. She got into bed, drew the curtains, and put out the candles. She remembered too late that she had forgotten to latch the door. But she was already warm and did not bother with it. It was strange to be in bed without Klaus, and it took her a long time to fall asleep.

Frieda was awakened by some noise in the night and peeked out from behind the curtains and saw Klaus taking off his clothes. She tossed the covers off. "Stay abed, *Liebchen*. It's not warm tonight." She put the covers back on and watched as he finished stripping and washed his hands and face.

"I did not expect you tonight," she said. He got into bed and lay facing her across the width of it.

"I wanted to be with you, to know there is still some good in the world."

She scooted next to him and gave him the hug she knew he desperately needed. "I'm glad you came home, darling. Let me know when you are ready to tell me what happened."

"That day may never come," he murmured as he clung to her.

Chapter 9

"Frieda, wake up. It is almost time for Mass." Klaus spoke softly, leaning over her. She stretched, her eyes still closed, and tried to remember what was different about this day.

Suddenly it all tumbled back into her memory: Klaus's intense look when he told her of the murder, him coming home cold and quiet in the night, his gasping for breath as he dreamed. She woke him, and he would not tell her what it had been about but urged her to wake him right away if he gasped that way again.

"It is the Lord's Day, *Liebchen*, and we need to get up." She opened her eyes. Klaus looked tired but awake and determined.

"Are you not tired, sweetheart? You came home late last night. We could sleep for a while."

"I would like to do that, but many of our people know what happened yesterday. I need to show them that I am still able to rule today."

She pushed the cover aside and swung her legs out of bed. "I had not thought of that. I will be at your side. Maybe we can sneak up here and take a nap later."

Klaus went to the door to admit Jeanne and Warren, then came back to her as they began their work. "Have you forgotten we are going to visit Gregor today?"

"Oh, do you still want to go?" She thought he would like to stay close to home for a few days. She washed and dried her face, then untied the ribbon at the end of her long night plait.

Jeanne laid Frieda's clothes for the day on the bed. "Turn around for a moment, Warren," she said. When he complied, she removed Frieda's gown and dropped her smock over her head. "It is safe now, Warren."

"Very well," he said and went back to gathering Klaus's clothes. "Why is it, Jeanne, that you may see the lord unclothed but I may never see the lady so?"

"Because, Warren, I am a lady and do not really look. I believe that you, sir, are another matter."

She prepared Frieda's tunic to go over her head as she spoke, looking as haughty as possible. Her French accent added to the effect; something she knew and used to full advantage.

"It is true that I am no lady, yet if I had a lovely wife to look upon every

72

day, Lady Frieda would be in no danger from my gaze." He allowed himself one dramatic sigh as he handed Klaus his hose.

It was the latest variation in his campaign, a campaign Frieda and Klaus had been enjoying. It was a nice diversion on this sad morning. "Have you talked to Jeanne, Frieda?" Klaus asked.

"No. Shall I do it now?"

"I think it a good idea, considering our destination."

Frieda told Jeanne their idea for bringing Anna into the household on a temporary basis. Jeanne was happy to agree. "And it will be a good thing, madame, for many ladies have more than one maid, and you truly run me ragged at times." Frieda laughed, not believing it at all.

"My lord? Am I to get some help as well?" Warren politely inquired. Klaus's foot was not passing through his breeches as it should. Warren tried again, then pulled them off and examined them.

Klaus exchanged looks with Frieda, who could barely contain her merriment. "That remains to be seen, Warren," he said in his most pompous manner. "You seem to be having more trouble than usual this morning. I suppose getting help will be your next great cause once you have your pretty wife?"

Frieda covered her mouth with her hand. Jeanne looked over at Warren and laughed when he couldn't get his hand through one of the legs of Klaus's breeches. He looked baffled. Jeanne intervened. "Just get another pair. I'll repair these later."

While he went to get another pair, Frieda felt Klaus's gaze upon her. Those particular breeches had to show up this morning. She dared a peek at her husband and found him smiling with a certain speculative look.

After Mass and breaking fast, Frieda and Klaus set out for Gregor's castle with a few men at arms. They were greeted warmly there and given a tour of the vineyard with its ripening grapes. "You had best be good to your back, sweetheart, for it will be needed again soon," she told Klaus.

"Amen," said Gregor.

Once inside the castle, they settled comfortably and Gregor had cider brought. He leaned forward and asked, "Now, Klaus. Tell me what is bothering you."

Klaus stared at the floor for some time before beginning. Frieda was glad he was talking about it. He told all. From the letter from the sheriff to leaving the castle after moonrise. Gregor listened as well, stopping him occasionally for clarification of a point. When Klaus finished, he sat in silence, and Frieda took his hand.

Gregor was thoughtful as he said, "I think you handled it very well, brother. You were more merciful than the criminal deserved by persuading him to see the priest and by having the sheriff use a horse for the hanging. Your people will remember your mercy."

Frieda frowned and Gregor answered her unspoken question. "Death comes most quickly when the thing the man stands on is quickly removed from under him. That way the neck is broken; otherwise it is like being strangled, slow and horrible."

Frieda closed her eyes as Gregor continued what he had been saying to Klaus. "Besides your mercy, they will remember that justice was served, and swiftly. Not many executions are carried out on the day of sentencing."

"I must build a decent jail. I can see that now. What if this had happened when I was away from home? The sheriff could not have held the man in his office chamber for several days or even weeks. And what if the murderer had not been willing to see the priest even after I talked to him? I would be loath to send a man to his death unshriven when a few days to think about eternity might change his mind." Klaus ran a hand through his hair, a hand that shook a little.

"Yes, you do need a jail there," Gregor agreed. "But all worked out well this time. God was with you."

"I know He was. Frieda was praying, as was I. I cannot say that I felt His presence yesterday, though, especially when. . ." They waited, but he did not continue.

A page came to the door and announced visitors. "I can be lonely for weeks, and today I am inundated with company." Gregor's delight was apparent as he rose to greet the newcomers.

Frieda and Klaus also rose as Margarethe and Willem came in. Greetings and hugs were exchanged all around. "And how is the lord of the apples?" Willem asked as he greeted Klaus.

"I will be fine, I think," he said. He said nothing else, and Willem turned to Frieda.

"Klaus had to conduct a trial yesterday at Hohenstein. A boy was killed during a robbery."

"Oh, I am so sorry. That must have been difficult." Margarethe looked on with sympathy. "Will you tell us about it? Or would you rather not?"

"It may do me good to tell it again, if you want to hear."

"Please, Klaus," Willem said as he and Margarethe and Klaus found seats.

Gregor motioned Frieda to follow him. They walked to a window at the far end of the room where they looked out. "He will be fine, you know. He has been through things just as bad before."

"He loves his people so much that everything that affects them affects him. I can only listen and offer what comfort I have within me."

"It is enough, my sister. I'm glad that he has you."

"Thank you." She looked out over the countryside, over Gregor's lands. She especially liked the looks of a dark wood not far from the castle.

"How is your little white filly?"

"She is doing very well. She is more lively than necessary at times. . . ." He chuckled. She decided to go ahead and ask what she had been thinking of without consulting Klaus.

"Gregor, might we spend the night? Klaus will probably want to ride home, but he is tired, and his back is sore. I want him to rest and will try to persuade him."

"I can help you in this direction, if need be. I also have a healer who gives an excellent massage. . . ."

"I have skills in that area myself, and I like to use them, so no thank you."

"I hope you don't mind my saying so, but you look tired yourself. All of my household is at your disposal."

He was so kind. Why had she ever thought him a buffoon? "Actually, I would like to borrow Anna for a week or two, possibly to become permanent."

"Oh, yes. So the man you were thinking of for her is interested?"

"He is. I'd like to see them wed."

"Do I know him?"

"I think so. He is Warren, Klaus's valet."

"Blue eyes? Startling?"

She nodded. "Women seem to find him attractive."

"Anna likes good-looking men."

"She seems to be rather taken with Klaus, I've noticed."

"Ah, but Klaus is oblivious to every woman but you."

Frieda felt her cheeks warm. "I hope so." She looked away from her brother-in-law and out over the countryside once more. The dark wood caught her eye again. "That little dark wood there, does it have trails to ride on?"

"It does. And it is not as small as it looks from here. I could take you there after dinner if you wish."

"I don't want Klaus riding so soon after this morning's ride. But I like the look of that wood. It reminds me of the Schwarzwald. Are those fir and spruce trees?"

"Yes. It's nice and open beneath them. I hunt there."

"What game do you find?"

Gregor told her all of the different kinds of animals he had seen there. "But I take only deer and rabbits, for that is what I like to eat."

"It reminds me so strongly of home."

She didn't hear Klaus come up behind her. "Then we shall have to ride there this afternoon, with Gregor's leave," he said, his voice a soft rumble, his hand light on her shoulder.

Frieda turned to him and searched his face for the effects of the retelling of yesterday's events. "Truly, Klaus, I wonder if it would be hard on your back to ride since you rode so much yesterday. . . ."

"It is fine, *Liebchen*. Don't worry about me. I am wise enough to stop doing something that is hurting me." Gregor cleared his throat, and Frieda saw him grinning and shaking his head. He covered his grin by scratching his nose when Klaus turned around and looked at him.

"Frieda, dear one, don't let this man fool you. He does what he wants to do, whether it hurts him or not," said Gregor. Margarethe and Willem joined them at the window.

Klaus spoke softly near Frieda's ear. "I would like to go riding in the wood today if you want to go. My back will be fine."

Frieda nodded agreement. If he said his back was well enough to ride, she would take his word for it. His dignity was worth more than his back. "I would like to ride there. It looks like a lovely place."

"It truly is. We can get to it easily from our home as well. Just to ride or walk in," he hastened to add, "for it is Gregor's land, and I would never poach."

"That's good to know, esteemed brother, since much of your orchard adjoins my land."

"Feel free to poach fruit any time you like, Brother; just don't go in with a large crew."

Frieda smiled with Klaus while Gregor, Margarethe, and Willem laughed. They looked out the window once more. "I don't see how to get to the wood from our home. I don't remember seeing anything like this from there."

"That hill hides it from view. I'll show you the first time I get a chance."

A page summoned them for dinner, and they walked to the great hall together. On the way, Willem said, "You and Frieda be the guests of honor today since you were here first."

"How generous of you, Willem, seeing Klaus outranks you," Gregor said.

"The war is over and we have no rank among us." Klaus was ever the diplomat. "Seat us however you like, Gregor. It does not matter."

"Now *that* is what I like to hear. Very well then, the ladies are the guests of honor. I will have one on either side of me and you two may sit where you will." Gregor looked pleased with himself, and Willem laughed.

It was a good dinner, with plenty of talking and laughter. Frieda was amused at Gregor's largely effective efforts to entertain both her and Margarethe. Klaus and Willem talked quietly during dinner, smiling occasionally at their wives.

As they all ate the cheese and nuts that made up the last course, Gregor asked Margarethe, "Will you ride with us in the forest? Frieda says it looks much like the Schwarzwald."

"I would like to, but I think Willem intends to return home."

Willem spoke up. "We'll ride in with you for a way to see it, then ride for home. Frieda can tell us whether it resembles her old home."

"I don't remember the Schwarzwald at all." Margarethe sounded regretful.

"Coming, Klaus?"

"I am, of course. And I am ready to go." Frieda smiled as her sister caught her eye. Klaus did not care for waiting around once something had been decided. Frieda popped one more morsel of cheese into her mouth.

Gregor sent a page out to the stable to have the grooms ready their horses, and then they walked out together. It was another fine day, cooler than last week had been, with a few high clouds—the benign kind.

Klaus's men at arms stayed behind, but Willem's few came along as they rode out together. The forest was easy to get to from a road. And once inside it lost all appearance of smallness. It was notably cooler under the trees. "This would be wonderful to ride in during the summer," Margarethe said.

"Yes, it would. This is much like the forest near our old home. Margarethe, do you remember anything like this?"

Margarethe drew her horse nearer to Frieda's Fraulein. "It does seem familiar. And. . .happy, somehow."

"Maybe you are remembering our games of hide-and-seek."

Margarethe laughed, a delighted, girlish sound. "Yes! That's it! We used to play that for hours. Willem, I *do* recall something of my childhood."

"Good, *Liebchen*. Hide-and-seek?"

"Someone hides, someone looks. It is a simple game. We could play it now, but we'd have to dismount. These trees are big, but not big enough to hide a horse."

Frieda looked over at Klaus and was surprised by the happy smile on his face. Then she looked at her clothes, the extra-fine clothing she had chosen to wear this day. "Let's play it some time when we are dressed less well."

"Yes, please," Klaus agreed. "My laundry men are unhappy enough with me when I spill things. I don't want to send them clothes with pitch on them." Frieda tried to picture Klaus spilling something and could not.

"We'll play that some time," said Gregor. "Which way on this track, ladies? Left or right?"

After a pleasant hour, Willem and Margarethe turned around. "We will go home now. It was a good visit, and I am glad we ran into you, Klaus and Frieda. Thank you, Gregor," Willem said.

"It's always good to see you. Keep on appearing like this. I rather like it."

"You appear at our house next Lord's Day. You, too, Klaus, Frieda. Albert and Hilda are coming, so we should have a good visit." Klaus raised his eyebrows at Frieda, and she nodded.

After they left, Gregor showed them the main track through the forest, including the branch that went to Apfelburg. "It's not an especially good shortcut but can be used when there is some reason to avoid the main road. Early in the war when it was still this far north, we used this route to move troops a few times."

"I had almost forgotten about that. This place brings back memories for me as well as for Margarethe."

"I think every beautiful place does that for people, husband. Jeanne saw the ocean when she was little, then saw it again when she was older and was overwhelmed with the memories of her childhood trip."

Klaus said, "I have never seen the ocean. Would you like to see it, *Liebchen?*"

"I would, but it's so far away. I would like to see the Alps up closer, though."

"Let's go then sometime. I am through with dedicating my life to war. Now I plan to enjoy life with my lady and go places."

Gregor grinned. "That sounds like a good idea, Klaus. I'm thinking of going to Lorraine next summer and buying some horses for breeding. I've never been to a place where all they speak is French."

"Don't let Jeanne hear of your plans, or she will want to go along. She's been wanting to visit her family for a long time." Frieda felt badly that she had moved Jeanne farther from her family.

"Now Jeanne is something more than a maid, is she not?" Gregor asked.

"She's my good friend, and a lady. Her father met mine when he stopped in Lorraine on his way back from a trip to France. The family had fallen upon some hard times, and no husband was found for Jeanne. She is the fourth daughter."

"Fourth! No wonder," said Gregor.

"Since she could not marry anyway, her father asked her if she would like to travel to the Schwarzwald and become my maid. She is a perfect lady's maid and companion for me, and a fine embroideress, as well. She's helping me with the project I am working on."

"I want to see this famous embroidery project when it is finished. I may want to commission you ladies to make one for me, as well. I will warn you that I am orderly and difficult to please."

Klaus snorted. "That's apparent by the deer antlers hanging in your solar with swords and such hanging from them."

Chapter 10

K laus sat at the table stretching his back while Gregor's servants brought games out. Frieda noticed and knew that he must be hurting. "Darling, let me give you a massage now. You know how much it helps."

"It does, *Liebchen*, but I want you to have some entertainment tonight. I will be fine. Maybe later on I will allow you to massage just my back."

Gregor had apparently overheard and came and squatted between their chairs. "Klaus, if you'll take advantage of my healer's skills, you'll feel much better. I have wanted to try to best your lady wife at chess, so we would be profitably entertained in the hall. I know you're hurting, and I know you don't want to take Frieda from the hall just now. Don't be stubborn."

"How good is this healer of yours? I don't want to end up hurting worse than I do."

Gregor chuckled. "He never hurts me. But I can post a page outside the door. If he hears you scream, he will come get Frieda and me."

Klaus winced. "Oh, that makes me feel completely safe, brother. Very well. I will do it." Gregor stood and beckoned to a man across the hall. Klaus continued. "And I want you, brother, to keep your guard up while playing chess with my wife. She is a treacherous opponent."

"I hope it helps, sweetheart," Frieda said as Gregor led him away. Gregor was soon back with a chessboard under his arm and swinging a little bag of men. He grinned as he drew near the dais. "I have been looking forward to this for a long time. I have heard from several sources that you are a formidable chess player."

"Well, it's nice to be famous for something, I suppose." They set up the board and began. Frieda did well, and Gregor proved to be more a challenge than she expected. Toward the end of the game, they had an audience. Frieda thought it was due more to Gregor's impassioned groans than to any fame on her part.

"Checkmate," she announced at last.

Gregor studied the board for every possible way out before conceding and groaning loudly in mock despair. Then he grinned and shook hands with Frieda. "What a good game. I hear you have beaten Klaus?"

"The first four times I played him, and several times since."

"I don't feel too bad then. He is the family—and army—chess champion."

"He's discerned my strategy now, and we are more evenly matched. He is always a challenge to play."

"He sharpened his wits with Hagen. Have you played him?"

"We played for the first time last night. The whole household gathered to watch."

"Well, shall I show you to your chamber and your husband? Or were you wanting to talk for a while?"

"I would like to see how Klaus is doing. And is Anna about? I would like to have her help me."

Gregor looked somber. "I don't know how much help she'll be, but I'll summon her."

Gregor peeked in as Frieda opened the chamber door. Frieda went in and looked at Klaus, who was sound asleep. She went back out to Gregor. "It looks as if he got what he needed. He's as playful as a dead rabbit."

"So you will have no one to talk to. Shall I lend you a book?"

Her curiosity stirred. "Yes, I would like that. I can read softly enough not to disturb Klaus, I think."

He strode to his own chamber while she waited, wondering what kind of book he might have in mind. He was back in a moment and handed her a small book. "Thank you, Gregor. I'll take good care of it."

"I will greatly appreciate it if you don't let anyone other than yourself and Klaus see it."

"All right," she agreed, her curiosity piqued.

Anna arrived then, and Frieda slipped the book inside her surcoat to Gregor's amused smile. "Greetings, my lady," Anna said as she curtsied.

"Greetings, Anna. I would like your help in getting ready for bed tonight and in getting dressed in the morning, if it does not conflict with your other duties?"

"Oh, yes, my lady."

"And in the morning I will talk with you about coming for a visit at our home. But tonight we must be quiet, for Lord Klaus is already asleep."

"Of course, my lady. I understand." Her eyes were bright with happiness.

"Well, Frieda, good night," Gregor said. He stood with his arms at his sides, leaving the kind of good night up to her.

She stepped up to him and gave him a hug and a kiss on the cheek. "Good night, Gregor. Thank you for everything."

He returned the hug and the kiss and said, "God bless you."

Anna silently followed Frieda into the room and picked Klaus's clothes up off the floor and laid them neatly across a chair. She was making a good start. While she did that, Frieda slipped the little book out of her garment and put it on a chair that was pushed under the table.

Frieda removed the pins that kept her braids coiled. Anna approached and silently offered to remove her clothes. Frieda consented and found that Anna knew exactly what she was doing. She would have to ask her about this tomorrow.

When Frieda was wearing nothing but her smock, she dismissed Anna and latched the door behind her. She sat at the table and began to read the little book. Parts of it were hard to understand, but it was beautiful. She recognized some parts of it as scripture from having heard it read at Mass, but this book was in German and far more comprehensible than Latin, a subject she had not grasped well at all.

She stopped partway through the book and sat and thought. Klaus stirred and rose up on one elbow. "Frieda, *Liebchen*? Are you coming to bed?"

She rose and went to him, carrying the precious book. "How are you feeling, darling?"

"I feel fine. I imagine you are cold. It is not a warm night, and you are wearing no robe. Have you been reading?"

"Yes. Gregor lent me this book. I have never read anything like it," she said, its words still tumbling through her mind. She sat on the edge of the bed, and Klaus raised a hand to her cheek.

"You have been crying," he said, wonder in his voice. "What is this book?"

"It's about righteousness and sin, about death and life. It's about wanting to do good and doing sin instead, about sin coming through Adam, but life through Jesus Christ. Gregor asked that no one but you and I see it. Don't lose my place," she warned as she handed it to him.

Klaus kept a finger in her place and looked at the beginning of the book. "This is Gregor's handwriting. I had no idea he was doing anything like this."

"We're not supposed to have the scriptures in German, are we? I mean, isn't Latin the proper language?" Klaus looked at her searchingly. "But why can we not have the scriptures in our language when it's so much easier to understand? I have had this read to me, though just in bits, since I was a little girl. Now I read it one time in my own tongue and I feel as if I have walked from a donjon into a great, bright meadow." Frieda could not help the tears that began rolling down her face once more.

Klaus sat up and got out of bed. Frieda stood and watched as he began getting dressed. "What are you doing?" she asked.

"I want to read with you, and I do not want to be cold."

Frieda sat and read for Klaus the passages she wanted to be sure about. He explained and she nodded. "So then, this is saying that I am wicked because it is my nature."

"As it is mine, and all men's."

"And sinning is dying, but I want to live—and Christ is the answer to that?"

"He is."

"Klaus, you told me that you ask God every day to help you be good."

"I do that, but I know that it's only because I belong to Christ that I can be good at all. I still am what I am."

"I want to be good. I want to be a part of all this." She patted the open book.

Joy shone from Klaus's face. "You have decided then?"

"Yes. I want to belong to God. Whatever He wants, that's what I want, too."

Klaus rose and crossed to her chair, bent, and hugged her with a fierce abandon that made her cry once more.

☙

Klaus stayed in bed and watched as Anna helped Frieda dress. She did a good job and only rarely stole a glance at him. Frieda looked over at him and smiled several times. "Anna, I can tell that you've done this work before. Why are you not a lady's maid?"

"At Lord Gregor's house? It is impossible."

Klaus grinned. Gregor would have little use for such.

"Well, your lord has given me leave to have you come stay at our house for a week or two. I would like you to act as one of my maids for a time, to see how I like your work. Is that agreeable?"

Anna bit her lip prettily and curtsied with Frieda's braid in her hand. "I would like to do that, my lady. And I thank you."

Klaus wanted to get up but didn't want to appear as he was in front of Anna. "Will you ladies please turn away for a moment?"

They both looked right at him then giggled as they turned away. "Is he always so modest, my lady?" Anna asked.

"By no means, I am happy to say," Frieda replied as their giggling resumed. He had always thought Frieda dignified, but now he suspected that she was influenced considerably by Jeanne.

Frieda was conversing with the steward's wife during breakfast, and Klaus remarked to Gregor, "Frieda is rather taken with a little book she borrowed from you."

A smile spread over his brother's homely face. "I hoped she might like it. Did she read it all?"

"Only twice. I was reading it, too. Have you done anything else along that line?" He thought Gregor might appreciate his oblique approach to the question. There was no telling who might listen.

"Oh, yes. It has become a little hobby of mine."

"That is wonderful. I wonder if I might keep that book a few days so that I might make a copy for my lady?"

"I would consider it an honor."

They stopped talking when Frieda turned to Gregor. "This cider tastes familiar. Where did you get it?"

Gregor's laugh was her only answer.

⁂

About two hours before dinner, Klaus and Frieda arrived home. Frieda wanted to change her clothes since she was wearing those she had worn the day before. Jeanne greeted them in the hallway near their chamber. "Welcome home, my lord, my lady. I did not know you were going to be gone all night."

Frieda squeezed her hand. "We decided late in the day. Jeanne, I want you to meet Anna. She will be working with you to keep me presentable."

"Welcome, Anna. I hope you will like it here," Jeanne said warmly. Anna looked less nervous instantly.

Klaus went into the bedchamber first, then Frieda and the maids followed. "I want to wear something looser today. My back is still a little tired. Ho, Warren, there you are," he said as he spotted Warren looking through a coffer of clothing.

Warren stood and bowed to him, then to Frieda. He froze in place and Frieda looked behind her to see what he was looking at. Anna was frozen as well and turning a becoming shade of pink. Klaus spoke. "Anna, I would like you to meet Warren, my valet. He is the one who keeps me presentable."

Warren roused himself enough to bow again but said nothing for a few moments, then, finally, "I am pleased to meet you, miss."

"Anna will be assisting Jeanne," Frieda said. "Jeanne, I'd like to change into something green, if there is anything suitable available. I will be embroidering and visiting Lady. Nothing too fine."

"Yes, madame. Anna, come see where Lady Frieda's clothes are kept." Anna followed Jeanne, and Frieda sat on a bench and removed her shoes as she watched Klaus and Warren. Warren seemed a little clumsy, and Klaus looked amused. She caught his eye, and he blew her a kiss.

Somehow, Frieda and Klaus both got into clean clothes. He wore the old supertunic style today instead of one of the tight jackets that were coming into style. He came to her as he got ready to leave their chamber. With his hands on her shoulders, he said, "I will see you at dinner. Will you embroider for a while first? Or go see Lady?"

"Embroider. I will go see Lady right after dinner. I hope she remembers me," she said ruefully.

"She will. I will go with you, if that is all right?"

"Oh, yes. I will see you soon." She stood on tiptoe and kissed him before he left. "Ready, Jeanne?"

"Yes, madame. Shall Anna come with us to the sewing room today?"

Frieda looked thoughtfully at the girl. "I think," she said slowly, "that

I don't want to overwhelm her with duties at first. Anna, you may come to the sewing room if you wish, but perhaps you would rather have a tour of the castle?"

"Oh, yes, my lady. I would like a tour of the castle," she eagerly agreed, "but I don't want to take anyone away from her duties," she said more quietly, a little unsure.

Frieda began to answer, but Warren was suddenly beside them. "Please, my lady, I have no pressing duties. I would be honored to escort Anna about the place. I know it well."

"You do, Warren. Is that acceptable, Anna?"

The girl's eyes gave a more emphatic answer than her soft, "Yes, my lady."

Frieda and Jeanne joined Ida in the sewing room and got right to work. Frieda allowed Jeanne to tell her about Anna. ". . .and she will be assisting me as our lady's maid, though she was working of late as a chambermaid in Lord Gregor's household." Ida's lips tightened, and her stitches were made with white fingertips on the needle until she left for her duties in the kitchen.

⌘

Just before supper, Frieda sent for the jars of cider she had set aside and had them brought to her at table. When Klaus joined her, she had a cup of the vinegar waiting for him. "Here, husband. Try some of our pear cider."

He sat straight and proud beside her as he took up the cup and tipped in a good mouthful. His eyes grew wide as he cast about looking for something to do with it. He swallowed and shuddered. Frieda schooled her face to seriousness. He wiped his lips and shook his head.

"What do you think?"

"Not at all what I was expecting."

"Better then?"

"Ah, no."

Frieda stuck out her lip.

"I'm sorry. I'm sure this is not what you intended it to taste like. I hope. Is it?"

She poured out the rest of the cup and poured cider from the other jar. "Perhaps this batch is better."

Klaus sniffed before tasting. "Yes. This is good. I think that other batch is almost vinegar."

"Do you think so? I wonder what it might be used for?"

"Hmm. . .well, we have other kinds of vinegar already. But maybe a new kind of sauerkraut if we get a good cabbage crop. . ."

"Or maybe for cleaning the stables," she suggested. Klaus's eyebrows rose.

After supper, there was music and dancing. Klaus was up to some dancing, but not for the entire evening, so Frieda encouraged him to have a game of chess with Hagen. Jeanne watched this avidly while Frieda watched everyone else, continually coming back to Anna. Warren was going out of his way to make her feel welcome. Indeed, he couldn't seem to keep his eyes from her. Good.

Frieda was watching people form into a huge circle when Jeanne spoke by her ear. "Come, madame. The chief musician is calling for everyone to join in."

Frieda agreed as she glanced at her husband. He was deeply involved in his strategy and did not look up when she kissed his cheek. She let Jeanne lead her by the hand. A cheer went up when she joined the circle, then the musicians began to play.

It was a standard ring dance, larger than most since everyone got in one large circle instead of separating into two groups: nobles and commoners. There was a lot of laughing during the dancing. It was too bad Klaus didn't join them. She saw him make a move then rub his hands together—a bad sign for Hagen.

At the end of the dance, the musicians began a couples' dance, and Frieda moved off to the side to watch. Anna danced with Warren, of course, and looked enchanted. Frieda smiled and looked around at the other spectators. Ida, her embroidering companion, sat nearby. Frieda's breath caught as she saw the hateful glare Ida fixed on Anna.

Chapter 11

Frieda had Anna join them in the sewing room the next day. Anna seemed ill at ease and spoke very little. Frieda showed her the project and listened to her praise for it. Then she had Jeanne show her how to execute the stitches they were using and had her do a few stitches. She was keeping an eye on this, and when Jeanne met her gaze over Anna's head, Frieda was relieved at her nod. She had yet to see any evidence of the clumsiness Gregor said she had in abundance.

Frieda noticed that Ida was quiet and a little stiff. She did not know her well enough to ask what was bothering her, so she just kept including her in the conversation.

"Anna, I think you know all about Jeanne and me by now," she said. "You do not know Ida yet. Perhaps you would like to get acquainted with her?"

Anna hesitated, then plunged in, keeping her eyes on her stitching. "I know that you're a fine embroideress, Ida. Did you learn it from your mother?"

"Yes," she said sullenly, "as every girl does."

"Well, it's obvious that you paid attention to her. What is your work in the castle?"

"I am a kitchen servant," she spat. Her hostility was enough to make Jeanne gasp. Frieda kept watching her for a few minutes, then she decided to dismiss her.

"Ida, we will be needing more purple thread soon. Come with me to the storage area and we'll see if there is some more." Ida tied off her work, apparently seeing how it would go, then walked with her to the shelves on the far wall. There she spoke quietly to her. "Ida, something is bothering you today."

"Yes, my lady."

Frieda waited, but Ida said no more.

"I know that we do not know each other well yet, but is there something that I can do to help?"

Ida dropped her gaze to the floor and shrugged.

"What would make you feel better today, working with the rest of us and talking pleasantly or having the rest of the forenoon off?"

"I would like to be alone."

"That is fine then. I hope that whatever it is works out well for you. I will see you tomorrow."

"Yes, my lady," she said and stalked out. She closed the door quietly behind her, so it seemed that her hostility was controllable.

Frieda joined Jeanne and Anna at the table, their eyes following her. "Do either of you know what is the matter with her?"

Jeanne shook her head, then looked at Anna. "Madame, she seems not to like Anna."

"We have all gotten along so well until just now, so maybe that's true."

"I know it's true," Anna blurted out. "Last night, my lady, in the hall she looked at me as if she hated me. And we had not even been introduced. I had never seen her before. I was afraid." She looked frightened still.

"What were you doing when she was looking at you that way?" Frieda asked.

"I was dancing with Warren."

"Oh," Frieda breathed. Then Frieda had not imagined it. "Maybe she is fond of Warren."

"Most of the girls in the household are fond of Warren, but Ida is not one of them. She pays him no mind," Jeanne said.

"This is very strange. I hope she gets over whatever is bothering her soon. I want to get this wall hanging done." They all three went to work in peace, and the conversation picked up after a while.

After their work session, Frieda met Klaus for dinner. "I cannot visit Lady with you today, *Liebchen*, because I am meeting with Father's steward about adding a jail to Hohenstein. He is good at designing such."

"Oh, I am glad you are taking care of that. Will you ride there today, though?"

"No, he is coming here, and we will work from a drawing of the castle."

"Good. I want you to stay off your horse for a few days." She smiled mischief at him. "Though perhaps I should say that I want you to ride, and then you will insist that you do not want to."

"Now you are beginning to figure me out."

"I want to ride today. Whom shall I call on as escort?"

"Anyone you like. Any of the men at arms are reliable. Perhaps if you ask the captain of the guard, he will make a suggestion."

"All right. Will you be needing Warren for anything this afternoon?"

Klaus looked pained. "Oh, Frieda. Have you gone and fallen in love with him as all the other women in the castle?"

Frieda was shocked until she noticed the crinkles at the corners of his eyes. "That is silly. I thought that he would like to ride with Anna and me. Jeanne never did see any point in riding for pleasure, and I do not know how Anna feels about it, but if Warren is along. . ."

"So you think they are getting along well?"

"Definitely."

"Good. Do whatever you like with Warren. I do not need him."

Frieda looked out over the hall and spotted Anna and Warren sitting together, laughing. She pointed this out to Klaus, and he looked pleased.

That afternoon Anna and Warren were delighted to ride out with her. They sought out the entrance to Gregor's wood and a number of other places. Warren entertained them with stories of different things that had happened at some of the places they saw. He had lived in the village and the castle all his life.

They stopped on a hill to look out over the land and rest the horses. "Here now, Warren. Trade me horses for a while."

"You would be welcome to ride this fellow anytime, my lady, even though he is my favorite. But I cannot ride a lady's horse. Pray excuse me."

"My lady, why do you want to ride that horse? He's not very pretty," Anna said. He was a medium-sized gelding, a nice brown color, well built. His face was nearly all white, though, and it was not attractive.

"I know. But he picks up his feet well and is most tractable." She patted her horse's neck. "I have a nice enough horse. It's a shame Warren will never get a chance to try her out." Anna laughed and Warren sighed.

The next morning Ida came in and took her place quietly. "My lady, Jeanne, Anna, I ask you to forgive me for my rudeness yesterday. I was feeling poorly."

"Of course we forgive you, Ida," Frieda said for all. She did not believe her excuse, but as long as she was pleasant and they could get some work done, she was content. Ida was more pleasant, and though she could not be said to be friendly toward Anna, she seemed to have accepted her.

They talked about various things as they worked, and eventually Jeanne asked Anna, "Anna, what think you of Warren?"

Anna blushed. "I like him well enough. He has lovely manners, and I enjoy talking with him."

"Do you think you could be friends?" Jeanne gently pressed.

"Oh, yes, I think so," Anna agreed. Frieda caught Jeanne's eye and shook her head a little. It would be better not to embarrass the girl too much. And she still wondered whether Ida might be fond of Warren.

❦

Frieda lay remembering the entrance to Gregor's wood from their side of it. It seemed to have many tracks in it, both winding and straight. That day with Anna and Warren and the men at arms, she had found a pretty little stream. She wondered where it came out. She fell asleep thinking she watched a rabbit hop along the bank of the stream.

A few days later, Klaus came to supper distressed about something. Frieda waited for him to tell her about it, and after the first course was served, he squeezed her hand and spoke so as not to be overheard. "I hope it's just a mistake. Sometimes a horse can go astray somehow, get into the wrong pasture. . ."

Frieda swallowed. "A horse is missing?"

He nodded. "We have plenty of horses, you know. It is just one. Still, they are valuable, and I would not like to think that someone is stealing them from us."

"What horse is it? Any one that I know?"

"Baldy."

"Baldy? A soldier's horse?"

"No, he is one of the household horses, a brown with a white face. . . ."

"Warren's favorite. I hope we find him. He is a nice horse."

"He is a nice horse."

Frieda frowned. "Is that why you're unhappy? Because he is such a nice horse?"

Klaus sighed and looked her in the eye as he tightened his grip on her hand. "Perhaps I am just borrowing trouble. But if Baldy was stolen, it had to be one of our own people who took him. No one else could do it."

☙

"Well, my good women, we are nearly finished with this wall hanging." Frieda was so happy that she announced the obvious on this fine autumn morning. "I would like each of you to think how you would like to sign your names on it."

Jeanne protested. "But, madame, this is your design, and you had more of the work of it than anyone. We are only stitchers, after all."

Anna and Ida murmured similar things but looked pleased nonetheless. "I want each of your names on here somewhere. If you want to put only your initials or first name, that will be fine. Now we can put them all in a group here in the corner, or spread them out, or. . ."

Frieda trailed off and left the others to their thoughts. She was working Klaus's crescent design in the upper left-hand corner, which was a place of honor. It did not look exactly like a moon, since the opening was aimed upward. It was on Klaus's banners and shields, along with the family's bear. She stole a peek at the others' faces to make sure they didn't know what she was doing.

Anna led the way in signing the work by stitching her first name only in the very bottom of the lower right corner. Frieda looked at it there. "You may put your last name there as well, if you use one."

Anna's dimple showed. "We share a last name since I was born in Lord Otto's house."

To people who did not know, then, she would appear to be a close relative rather than a servant. "Then perhaps you would like to sign the last name of your father, the noble who sired you."

"Really, my lady?" she said, looking more mischievous than ever. "Then I would have to rip the stitches out and start further back, for my last name would be. . ." She came to Frieda and whispered in her ear.

She gasped. "Oh, my word. We cannot put that. I had no idea." She stared at Anna in consternation. "Your first name alone will be plenty, Anna, thank you." She was shaken. Likely many people were related to that family, but still.

"Are you finished there, Anna? For I would like to get to that corner now," Jeanne said. Anna yielded her spot. Jeanne embroidered her name with a flourish, first name only, though she was entitled to use the name of her noble family. "I, too, am using my first name only so we match better."

Ida came around and took Jeanne's place next. She studied the space with Anna's simple script and Jeanne's flowing, French-style letters. She chose to print her name in perfectly upright capitals with large serifs.

"Beautiful. Perhaps we will work on something next where we can each use our own style. Your signatures are all so lovely; I don't know how mine will look." She contemplated while she viewed the signatures upside down from her place in the upper left-hand corner.

"Make yours large, my lady," Jeanne suggested.

"If I sign all of my name, it will be large. But I will leave off 'von Quelle Donau' and sign just my married name. That is, after all, who I am." She finished the crescent shape she was working on and came around to the signature corner and signed her name.

The others gathered around and admired their work. "Well," Frieda said, "we are done. Since we finished the edges as soon as the laid work was complete, we have no finishing to do. All there is left to do is to hang it."

They all four shared a big hug, then looked at their work again. "I hope your lord likes it," Jeanne said, "though how could he not?"

"Anyone would like this," Ida said. "It is really something beautiful." Frieda noted that she looked sad.

"I thank you all for letting me join in on this. It has been an honor to work with you," Anna said.

"Let us start something else soon," Frieda said.

"Will you show it to Lord Klaus today?" Jeanne asked.

"Yes, after dinner. I want to show it to him alone first, then we will let others see it. I am sure each of you will want to show it to your friends, but Klaus gets to see it first since I made it for him." She moved to gather the embroidery materials that lay about, and the others rushed to do the cleaning up for her.

It was near to dinnertime, and Ida had to get to the kitchen. Frieda opened the purse at her belt and spoke quietly to her. "I thank you again for helping me with this. I feel it is worth more than I originally told you I would pay. You don't mind, do you?" Ida looked blank. "Is it acceptable if I pay you more than I said I would?"

Ida grinned then and dipped her head. "If you must, my lady." Frieda placed six French gold pieces in her hand. Ida gaped, whispered her thanks, and slipped out the door.

∽∾

After dinner, Frieda led Klaus by the hand to the sewing room. "I cannot believe that I am finally to be admitted to this private female place," he said.

Frieda laughed. At the door she turned and warned him, "It is still lying on a table, so it will look different when hung in the hall. And I have never done anything quite like this before, so be kind." She waited for his nod, then opened the door.

Klaus walked in and Frieda anxiously followed. His first reaction was a delighted, "Oh!" Then he stood looking in silence at it for a long time, his eyes taking in everything. After a bit he looked concerned.

"What are you wondering about, Klaus?"

"The bear. Who does it symbolize?"

"Your family, of course. Since you all use the bear, I made just one."

"That is good," he said, his eyes still on the work. "I have never seen anything like this. It is wonderful. The symbolism is so obvious, and it is so well executed. The color choices add to it." He looked at her with a smile and offered a hug, but she saw something in his eyes. Something was troubling him, but he didn't want to say what.

Frieda accepted the hug and, when she was sure she wouldn't laugh, asked while still snuggled against her husband's broad chest, "What is wrong with it, sweetheart? I do not know a great deal about designing an insignia. Did I make some blunder?"

He released her and held her by the shoulders, looking her in the eye. His eyes now held a glint of amusement. "Are the stitches hard to remove? If you want to remove just, oh, one small thing?"

"It depends. It's usually not too much trouble. What shall I take out?"

"The crescent symbol in the upper corner; why did you put it there?"

"Well, I thought it was something important. I have seen it on all your banners and shields."

He smiled and hugged her again. "Many wives think their husbands are wonderful. You are the same, for you have attributed the entire victory to me." She wanted to lean back and get a look at his face, but he held her fast. His belly shook a little, but she knew he never laughed, so it had to be something else.

"What are you talking about, Klaus?" she demanded. He still would not let her go, so she stopped struggling and waited, trying not to laugh or grin.

"The crescent is the symbol of the second son. By placing it in the upper corner there, you give me credit for winning the war single-handedly."

"Oh, no. I will take that off right away." He would not let go of her, so she gave a small struggle and fixed her innocent look firmly on her face. She struggled again. He was holding on to her a little too long to suit her. The sport would be more enjoyable if she could see his reaction.

"Now, *Liebchen*, I do not mind if you want to think I am so wonderful, but if we hang it in the hall as it is, my brothers and father may well take offense. . . ."

"Or laugh at me, as you are," she accused. She pushed against him. "Let me go so I can fix it."

"Oh, I feel I have to hold on to you until you understand that I think this wall hanging you have made is wonderful." She nodded against him. "And that you are wonderful as well."

He released her far enough that she could look up at him, her face carefully innocent. She watched a smile spread across his face. She lifted her chin, and he happily took her up on her offer and kissed her tenderly. One of his hands stole up to the back of her head and sneaked a pin from her hair. She noticed but was busy enjoying the kiss. He took another pin and she laughed, twisting away.

"Frieda, I wonder if you did this on purpose? You aren't acting embarrassed in the slightest, and I think you would be if this had been an accident."

"Why, whatever do you mean? Why would I do such a thing?"

He stepped to the embroidered crescent and touched it. "These stitches seem a bit looser than the others."

He looked so suspicious, one eyebrow raised, that she couldn't help laughing. She admitted nothing, but Klaus's smile showed her that he knew. She walked to the storage area to get her scissors, and Klaus went to the door and latched it. She raised her eyebrows as she came back to the table. "Why, Klaus? Do you not want anyone to catch you working on embroidery?"

"You are very perceptive, *Liebchen*," he said. He sat down beside her and picked out stitches as she instructed him.

Chapter 12

That afternoon, Klaus had the wall hanging hung in the great hall, and people kept coming in and admiring it. Frieda's practiced eye could see the picked out place in the corner, but it was hardly noticeable even to her. She and Klaus stayed nearby and listened to the things people said. Hagen especially admired the work and gazed at it for a long time.

Frieda did not see Klaus send a messenger, but he must have, for soon enough Gregor was in the hall. "This is a workday, but everyone is standing around admiring some—my word, it's a painting," he said as he approached it. "No, it's not. But the colors. . ."

"Good day, Gregor," Klaus greeted him with a slap on the back.

Gregor turned to him, grinning. "Greetings, Klaus, Frieda. I do not usually greet the artwork first. Sorry."

Frieda laughed and kissed his cheek. "What do you think of it?"

He looked again and stood looking for some time. "It's wonderful. I want one for my hall." He turned to her and said seriously, "I will pay whatever you ask, and it will be well worth it."

Frieda looked over at her husband, who was looking proud. "Well, it was a lot of work. And since I have everything I need. . ."

"Oh, Frieda. I can tell when I'm being set up. What do you want?" He looked amused and only a little apprehensive.

Frieda beckoned to him and whispered in his ear, "Books."

He chuckled and nodded agreement. "Of course. We will discuss specifics later." He kissed her hand, and then he and Klaus exchanged smiles.

While Gregor stood looking at the wall hanging, Klaus came to her and asked near her ear, "What did you ask him for?"

Frieda thought that he had guessed, since he smiled at his brother after their words. "I asked for books."

Klaus shook his head sadly. "You should let me do the negotiations for you. Gregor would happily give you books anyway, for he loves to share those. I would ask for something he would not normally give. . . ."

She raised an eyebrow. "Such as?"

"Such as hunting rights in that forest of his."

Frieda laughed, then as Klaus tried to look dignified, she laughed louder. Gregor turned to watch them. Frieda leaned toward her husband.

"Gregor wonders what we are talking about. I shall go and tell him what you said."

"No, for if he knows what I want, he will have me pay dearly." Frieda pretended to start toward Gregor, and Klaus grabbed her arm. She pretended that it hurt and pouted. "Oh, *Liebchen*. Let me kiss it better," he said mockingly. He lifted her hand and kissed it.

"That is not," she said with all her dignity, "where it hurts. Later I will show you where it hurts so that you can kiss it better, better."

"Very well," he said with twinkling eyes in an otherwise serious face. She kept looking at him, watching his face as he began to grin, then she heard something that sounded suspiciously like a chuckle.

"I do not know what I shall do with you," she whispered.

"I can make some suggestions," he whispered back. Frieda was amazed. Somehow Klaus had been transformed into a big, playful bear, and she really didn't know what to do with him.

She took his hand. "Let us see if Gregor wants to see Lady."

Klaus called to Gregor, "Are you interested only in embroidery now? Or would you like to see Frieda's filly?"

"Oh, I would like to see her. Are you going now?"

"As soon as you are ready," Klaus said.

They walked together to the stable, Gregor congratulating Frieda on the wall hanging. "I especially like the way you all signed your names, each in a different way."

"I wish I could write my name as prettily as Jeanne does."

Klaus put his arm about her waist. "I love the way you wrote your name," he said and kissed her temple. She wondered at the gladness in his eyes.

The next day Frieda wanted to speak with Gregor but had lost track of him soon after breakfast. She found her husband in the great hall talking with some men at arms and went up to them. Klaus was speaking and continued in spite of her arrival and gathered her into his arm. He was certainly growing casual with her. He never would have done this even a week before, but would have stopped his conversation with his men and bowed to her and treated her entirely properly. She thought this new way was better. . .maybe.

He turned to her, eyebrows raised. "I wonder if you have seen Gregor?"

"He asked to borrow a book and went off somewhere. I know he has not gone home, for he did not say good-bye."

"Thank you, my lord," she said. To her surprise, he bent to kiss her, right there, where his men stood waiting and watching. She accepted his kiss and the wink that followed, then went looking for her brother-in-law again.

If he was reading a book, he might be in the solar. She found him there seated beside the table, his feet on a chair. "Good morning, Gregor. I was just wondering what kind of wall hanging you would like to have."

He had evidently been thinking about this already, for he answered immediately. "I would like a smaller version of the one you made here, simplified. Just a bear killing a dragon. I need no background, unless you want to put in a few fir trees. Would that work?"

She nodded as she thought. "Yes. That would look good, I think, and will be different from ours, too."

❦

"I am getting smarter about these family visits, Klaus," Frieda said after Mass as they got ready to set off for Waldbergen. "This time I am bringing us some extra clothes."

"A good idea, *Liebchen*. We need to have everyone come to our house next. That would be wonderful."

Klaus and Frieda rode with a few men at arms, meeting Gregor on the road. He fell in with them, and they visited pleasantly all the way to Waldbergen.

On their arrival, Margarethe and Willem greeted them warmly. Margarethe drew Frieda aside and asked how the project was going. "All finished. It turned out well, too."

"Oh, you got it done so quickly. But when I have a good idea for a song, I write it down fast. I suppose things like that can run in families."

Frieda gritted her teeth. What did Margarethe know about family? Frieda felt arms go around her from behind and heard Klaus's low rumble saying, "What things run in families, ladies? Besides whispering in corners while husbands languish neglected?"

Frieda turned in his arms and looked mockingly into his handsome face. "Poor languishing creature."

He winked, kissed her, and took some pins out of her hair while she tried to catch his hand. He let go of her, exhibited the pins, and lifted them out of her reach. He walked away smiling.

Margarethe was wide-eyed. "Was that Klaus?" she demanded. "What has happened to him?"

"He's been like that of late. It's amusing but unsettling. I was used to him being formal and proper, but now. . .he tickled me yesterday."

Margarethe's mouth dropped open. "Has he had a blow to the head?"

Frieda shook her head slowly. "Only from the apple I tossed at him from the tree that day."

"Oh. You have been doing things to him, and now he is doing things back. That could seem logical and proper to him. Maybe." Margarethe's frown was doubtful.

"You know, he's been teasing like that since Friday when I gave him the wall hanging."

"Oh, I want to see it. We'll have to come over right away. I love your work on clothing and can't wait to see what you do with a wall."

Her response pleased Frieda. She noticed Klaus doing something at the table, and Willem watching carefully. He was unrolling something wrapped in heavy cloth. "What is he doing? Come, Margarethe, let's go see."

As they approached, Klaus looked apologetically at Frieda. "I hope you don't mind that I brought this along. I couldn't wait to show Willem and Albert what you made."

So he was truly proud of it then. He was proud of her. It was wonderful to know. "Oh, Frieda, it's so beautiful," Margarethe breathed.

"Good craftsmanship," Willem commented. "I cannot say I am surprised about the content, though." Frieda suddenly remembered the day of Hilda and Albert's wedding when Willem had answered her questions about the war and everyone's shields. Also that day he had assured her of Klaus's love for her. That had been but three weeks ago, and now she felt assured of his love by his actions and did not need her brother-in-law's words.

"I wish that I could embroider as beautifully as you do." Frieda looked up at the wistful tone in Margarethe's voice. "It is just another thing I missed out on, along with everything else."

Frieda's stomach tightened. She spoke softly yet with steel in her tone. "How can you say you missed out on so much? You got an education."

"I did, but I did not have my family."

"Aunt and Uncle and Jolan are family."

"That's not the same, and you know it, sister of mine."

"And you were always Papa and Mutti's favorite."

"I was not!"

"You most certainly were." Frieda shook Klaus's hand from her elbow. She heard no conversation in the room. "They always loved you more, no matter what I did."

"Oh. I see. And that's why they sent me off to live here and kept you close to them."

Frieda frowned. They could have sent her off, too. Why had they not? But facts were facts, and she knew for certain that her parents always compared the two of them and she came up lacking. "They wanted me nearby to compare me to you and tell me how little I was worth."

Margarethe moved a little away from the men, then said, "That's absurd."

"They never said those exact words, but it was made clear to me nevertheless."

"I don't believe it. Mutti taught you to embroider, and she never took the time to teach me anything."

"Well, you were not there to be taught."

"I could have been. They didn't ask me if I wanted to leave home, you know. I was told that I had to go."

"And when you left, I had no one. You never came home to visit, not even once."

"And you never came to see me. I begged Mutti and Papa to bring you, and they said that you didn't want to travel."

"That's not true! I wanted to see you. They wouldn't bring me. They said the roads were too dangerous."

"But not too dangerous for me. Just too dangerous for their favorite."

Frieda caught her breath and bit her lip to keep from saying anything. She sensed Klaus at her side and this time allowed his hand to stay on her arm. Willem stepped up behind Margarethe. Margarethe bowed her head. Frieda stood locked in place. Could there be some truth to her sister's words? When Margarethe raised her head, Frieda was surprised to see her shaky smile. "Here I am, fighting with the sister I always longed for."

"Me? You always wanted to be with me?"

Margarethe nodded. Frieda saw that she was holding her breath as well. She quickly wet her lips. "I have heard that sisters always fight."

Margarethe stepped forward, and Frieda closed the gap between them. They embraced, then laughed as they held hands.

"Maybe now we'll have some peace, eh, Willem?" Klaus suggested.

"I pray you're right. . .brother!" Willem laughed and Klaus chuckled. Margarethe's mouth dropped open, and Frieda laughed at her, then saw Hilda and Albert coming into the room.

"Ho, the newlyweds," Willem called out. They smiled and joined them at the table, greeted everyone, then viewed the wall hanging.

"Oh, Frieda, this is wonderful," said Hilda. "Do you think you will make something like this again someday? I would dearly love to help."

"I wish we lived closer together so that we could do things like this. You are the farthest away of all my sisters," Frieda said as she gripped Hilda's hands, turning her head to smile at Margarethe, who winked in return.

"One day we will have a good long visit. You and I. These men will come around if we manage it right," Hilda said.

Frieda laughed. "I think you're right."

⚬⚬

In the morning Klaus, Frieda, and Gregor traveled toward home. They had decided earlier to stop on the way and visit Lord Otto and Lady Edeltraud. Frieda had been wanting to see Lady Edeltraud, and Gregor and Klaus had things to discuss with their father.

Frieda could smell rain. She studied the clouds to see how long it would be before the rain began. It looked as if it would be early afternoon when it started. The birds seemed to be enjoying the different winds, swooping about high in the sky.

"Still watching birds, my lady?" Klaus asked as he looked over at her from his horse.

"I like them," she said. "They seem to be having fun today."

"They do. And I had fun last night. Did you?"

"I did. I should be scandalized that we danced on the Lord's Day, but I liked it."

"I enjoy dancing any day. It might be politic not to mention it to Father, though. He is firm about that. But we were at Willem's house, and what could we do?"

Frieda chuckled. "What could we do, indeed? And I enjoyed all the singing. I have never heard that arguing duet Gregor sang with Margarethe. It was so funny, and I didn't even know Gregor could sing."

Gregor drew his horse up even with hers. "Ho, I hear my name being bandied about. What are you talking about?"

"Your singing. Frieda actually likes it."

"I like your singing, Klaus. I wish you were more generous with it."

"If it will not frighten the horses excessively, I will sing with you now. Go ahead and start something—unless you are just talking."

"Ha!" said Gregor and launched into an old love song. Klaus joined him, making a harmony beneath his melody. Frieda hardly breathed as she listened.

When they had finished, she exclaimed, "Wonderful! What a talented family I have married into." Too late, she detected a bit of mischief in her husband's eyes.

"Now I think it only fair that Frieda sing for us," he announced.

"Completely fair," Gregor agreed.

Frieda sighed and tried to think of something to sing that Margarethe had not already made famous. She remembered a song she had sung with Jeanne when they first met and she had been intrigued by the idea of singing in French. She started it out, daring a peek at Klaus, who looked utterly enchanted.

At the end of the song, the men were loud in their praises. "And if I knew more French, I would know what that song was about," Klaus said.

"I shall not enlighten you, my lord, for that is likely one of the silliest songs ever sung."

"I am glad to hear it, for it made no sense to me. I was afraid that my French was worse than I thought," Gregor said. Frieda laughed at that, for he was the army's translator when one was called for.

The rest of the trip to Beroburg was spent in discussing and trying out different songs in three-part harmony.

They had a good visit with Lord Otto and Lady Edeltraud. When Klaus showed them the wall hanging, Frieda enjoyed their praises but puzzled over Lady Edeltraud's proud look. Klaus talked with his parents about the jail he was adding to Hohenstein.

After dinner, Klaus was looking out the window at the sky. Frieda joined him, and he circled her waist with his arm. "What do you think, *Liebchen*? Do we leave now or spend the night?"

"I think we should ride for home. What does Gregor want to do?"

Then Frieda saw Lord Otto approaching and said, in his hearing, "You brothers are all most charming. I think you got it from your father."

Klaus grinned at Frieda, and Lord Otto winked at her. "Looking at the weather, Klaus? You are most welcome to stay."

"Thank you, Father, but I think we will go home. We will go as soon as we say our good-byes."

He walked with them over to Lady Edeltraud. She was warm toward Frieda as they said good-bye. "Anytime, you are welcome here anytime, with or without this Klaus," she told her as they held hands.

"Thank you, *Mutti*," Frieda said, and Lady Edeltraud dropped her hands and gently hugged her.

Gregor rode out with them, as Klaus had predicted, and they set a swift pace to beat the rain. At the junction where Gregor would turn off for home, he said he would stay with them. "I brought no men with me and would not want to be riding alone in bad weather, you see."

"Whatever you say, Brother."

The rains had just begun with large drops when they arrived at Apfelburg, so they rode right up to the donjon and let the grooms take the horses to the stable.

Jeanne met them at the door and kissed Frieda's cheek. As they all mounted the stairs, Klaus said, "It may be lazy of me, but I want a hot bath before supper. How about you, *Liebchen*?"

"It sounds good."

Jeanne said, "I will tell Warren. What would you like to wear, my lady?"

"Oh, Jeanne, rest. Let Anna do some work."

Jeanne grinned as she remembered something. "I never told you this, my lady, but one day after you bathed in the morning, I went back into your bedchamber and Warren was using your bathwater himself."

"What did he say?"

"He said he saw no reason to waste water that was still warm. I offered to wash his back for him, and he was quite alarmed."

Frieda laughed, and Klaus said, "I imagine."

Warren and Anna appeared as they reached the top of the stairs. Joy shone on their faces. "We heard you come into the bailey. How may I serve you, my lord, my lady?"

All of them stood outside Klaus and Frieda's chamber now. "I am wanting a hot bath, as is my lady."

"I am content for now," said Gregor, starting to walk off.

"Wait, my lord," Anna called.

Gregor turned and looked at her, his smile growing. Frieda noticed that Anna was fidgeting and blushing. "Yes, Anna?"

"Anna and I have something to tell you. I have assured her that all the proper permissions have been given." Warren's customary eloquence faltered, and he stuttered, "Anna has agreed to marry me."

Everyone congratulated them at once, and Klaus said, "Well, good. Now he will stop pestering me every day to find him a pretty wife."

⌒⌒

The next morning Frieda laid out two more wall hangings and got Jeanne, Anna, and Ida to agree to help her with them. They came in for two hours before dinner and began them, then returned after dinner. "It's nice to be able to work with all of you again," Anna ventured.

"I enjoy working with each of you as well. Do let me know if you have any ideas we may put into the work."

"Madame, have you thought of anything we could do where we each use our own style?" Jeanne asked.

"Not yet. I did enjoy the different styles of lettering we used, though. Ida? Have you thought of anything?"

"No, my lady. I like the idea, though."

"We will keep thinking. These will be enough work for now."

Chapter 13

Anna greeted Frieda shyly as she came to her in her bedchamber, nodding to Jeanne. Klaus had already left for Mass, and Warren was gone as well. "Good morning to you, too, Anna. How are you this morning?"

"I am happy, my lady. Today after dinner, if you do not need me for anything, Warren wants me to go with him to meet his family." She smiled as she got the comb she would use on Frieda's hair.

"Oh, that will be fine. Let me know how you like them," she said. "You haven't met them yet?"

"Only his mother. She is kind and has a good sense of humor. She is dramatic, like Warren. She has eyes as blue as his, and her hair has two white streaks. I wonder if Warren will get those?"

Frieda smiled as she watched her work. "My father has two white streaks in his beard when he grows it out. I wonder if I will get those," she said, stroking her chin. Anna and Jeanne laughed merrily, and Frieda joined them.

After breaking fast Frieda walked to the stable to see her filly. Lady was always happy to see her, but today Frieda carried some carrots with her—a thing that always assured her a warm welcome.

She entered the stable and stood still as she allowed her eyes to adjust to the lower light. "Lady, I'm here," she called as she started toward her stall. She did not hear her usual nicker of greeting, nor did she see Lady's head pop over the stall. "Lady?" She walked up to the stall without seeing or hearing anything of her; it was a little odd. It was very early in the day for her to be out in the enclosure.

Frieda walked out the back door of the stable and looked for Lady in the fenced area. There were no horses there at all. Frieda felt a jab of fear. There had to be an explanation. Slapping the tops of the carrots against her surcoat, she set out looking for the answer.

She nearly ran into a stable boy just inside the door. "I beg your pardon, my lady."

Frieda squinted at him until he became easier to see. "Have you seen Lady? She is not in her stall this morning."

"I. . .no, I haven't seen her, my lady. She is not outside, is she? It's early."

"She is not; I looked. Can it be that someone moved her to clean her stall?"

"I do not think so, my lady. I am the one who cleans her stall, and I always do it with her in there. She is very gentle and nice to be around."

Frieda's eyes stung. "Yes, she is, thank you. Where is the avener?"

"Tack room, I think."

Frieda nodded and strode off. She had to find Lady. Something was not right here.

The avener looked alarmed when he heard what Frieda had to say and walked with her to each stall looking for Lady. "A lot of horses are missing today, it seems. These stalls are usually in use, are they not?"

"They are. The weather will turn soon, and Hans wanted to take the warhorses out to the pasture north of the village for some exercise and grass before the mud confines them.

"Hans," she repeated.

"The groom who cares for the warhorses. Blond fellow, missing a front tooth."

"Oh, yes. A competent groom."

"All of our grooms are competent, my lady."

"Of course they are, Axel," she agreed idly. They had reached the last stall without finding Lady. She turned to the avener. "I will want to talk to each of the grooms to see if any might know where Lady has gone."

The man looked near to tears. "Yes, my lady."

Frieda turned to go back to the donjon to find Klaus, then turned back as she remembered something. "Was Baldy ever found?"

Axel hesitated. "No, my lady."

She nodded, turned, and strode out of the stable, then ran to the donjon.

She found Klaus in Hagen's office. He rose as she entered and clasped her in his arms as she broke into tears. "*Liebchen*, what is it? Tell me." She shook her head, and he gently took her by the arms and held her a little away from him. "Frieda. Frieda, look at me." She met his eye and took a deep breath. "Now tell me."

"Lady is gone. She is not in the stable and not in the enclosure. Axel does not know where she could be, either. We looked in every stall."

Klaus gathered her close again and held her tight. "We will find her, *Liebchen*. She is the only perfect white filly in the region. She cannot disappear. Trust me in this?"

She tipped her head back to look at him. "Yes, Klaus. I hope no one hurts her, though."

He frowned for a second, then regained his calm and serious look. "No one would hurt her. She is too sweet. Come, let us get the search started."

Frieda went with him to the stable and listened as he stopped to talk with some of the men at arms on the way. They ran to the stable ahead of them and rode out right away. While Frieda consoled herself by petting her old horse, Klaus talked with the avener and every groom who was nearby. Then he had his horse saddled and rode to the gate to talk with the men there.

He came straight back to Frieda where she waited by the door. "Ride with me, Frieda. Let us talk."

She mounted and rode with him out through the gate and toward the village. "I think I may have found out how someone got her out."

"What do you think?"

"Hans rode out at dawn with a group of the warhorses. They are large, and Lady could have been in the midst of them."

"So you think Hans, our own man, took her away?"

"He may have. I do not know why, though. Perhaps he thought she could use some fresh grass, too. He should have gotten permission if he wanted to do that."

Frieda noted a closed look on her husband's face. He was not telling her something. "What do you think, Klaus? Do you think he wanted her to have fresh grass?"

"No, not really. The guards are acting a little odd; too eager to share information and too nervous."

"Someone bribed them to keep quiet about Lady."

He looked at her with compassion. "If that is the case, we are dealing with a professional thief. Hans would not have money on his own with which to bribe guards."

"How will we find Lady? I don't care who took her; I only want to have her back."

"That is what I want, as well. Finding out who did it might help. The sheriff will question the guards and Hans; he is quite good at finding out things."

"The guards may be innocent. He's not too rough, is he?"

"He is a fair man. I also have men going to every stable in the area looking for Lady. I would not be surprised if we have her back by dinnertime."

"I hope you're right, Husband. I hope so."

At dinner Frieda sat next to Klaus in her usual place at the head table and pretended to be hungry. Several times during the meal, he took her hand, and once he raised it to his lips. She could see his care for her. "We will find her, *Liebchen*."

"I know."

She wanted to be held, and after dinner Klaus went with her to the solar and sat her on his lap and reassured her without words. Thus they sat when there was a tap at the door. Frieda answered it and was surprised to see Ida standing there, twisting her hands.

"Come in, Ida. What is it?"

Ida stepped in and glanced around the room and bobbed her head to Klaus. "I know who took your little Lady."

"Who?"

"Well, I was watching this morning at dawn when a groom was taking some of the warhorses out. There was a man following them leading a small horse with a large blanket on it. I saw that it had a white head."

Klaus spoke from behind Frieda, softly. "You said that you knew who it was, good woman."

"Yes, my lord," she said, bobbing her head again. "I know who it was. It was Warren Schmidt."

Frieda gasped. Warren would never do such a thing. He knew how much she loved Lady, and he was an honest man, no thief. She wanted to say all of this, but Klaus was thanking Ida for telling them and showing her to the door. "Go to the sheriff and tell him what you just told us. It would be most helpful."

Once she was gone, he latched the door and took both of her hands. "How well do you know this Ida?"

Frieda shook her head. "She has worked with me quite a bit but says little. I truly do not know her well."

"Has she always told you the truth, as far as you know?"

Frieda had to think for a few moments. "No, I don't think she has. She was very rude to Anna once, and I dismissed her for the day. The next day she came back and apologized, but she gave a false reason for her rudeness."

"Was she lying today when she said she saw Warren leading Lady?"

"I can't say for sure, but I have a feeling that she was."

"I have that feeling, as well, but because I know Warren."

"Warren could not have been leading Lady out at dawn anyway, for he was here helping you."

Klaus winced. "He was not. I gave him the morning off so that he could go see his parents and help his mother get the house ready for Anna's visit."

"I slept late and didn't know that. I wonder when he rode out and if the guards will remember that he rode alone, not leading a horse."

"The guards will help us find out who did this thing, and Ida will help us, too—whether or not she means to."

Frieda wrapped her arms around Klaus, and he held her close. "Soon, *Liebchen*. We will have her back soon."

"Let's go look for her," she said. He stroked her cheek with a gentle finger, then offered his arm.

An hour before supper, Frieda dismounted back at the stable with Klaus when Ida walked up to her. "Greetings, my lady. Has your filly come home yet?"

Frieda thought it a strange turn of phrase, for everyone else asked whether the filly had been found yet. "Not yet. We were out looking for her."

Ida looked toward the gate, then back at her lady. "I hope you get her back soon."

"I hope so, too."

Klaus came beside Frieda and took her hand. "Ida? Is it not your suppertime? Surely the servants get to eat a little before beginning to serve."

"Yes, but I was worried about my lady and came to see how she fares."

"How good of you," said Klaus.

"Yes, Ida. I do appreciate your concern for me." Ida looked ill at ease and kept glancing toward the gate. Frieda met Klaus's eye and saw that he thought something was odd, too.

Frieda looked toward the gate herself—she could not resist since Ida kept looking that way. Suddenly the men there started stirring and shouting. She was too far away to hear what was said. Then she heard Klaus speaking and listened.

"Yes, Ida, I think you deserve a little supper after this long day. Do go back to the kitchen now."

Ida looked frantic, torn between obeying the lord and seeing what was going on at the gate. Frieda had no time to puzzle over this as a soldier rode up to them. "The filly has been found."

Frieda laughed and ran toward Hans, the groom, as he trotted up leading Lady behind him. She looked fine, none the worse for her day away from home, and was groomed well beneath a layer of road dust. Frieda hugged her and patted her all over. "Where did you find her?" Klaus was asking.

"An old stable on a farm north of the village that was abandoned at the beginning of the war." Frieda turned her head and saw that Hans had dismounted and was standing before Klaus, fidgeting with the reins and scratching his leg with his other foot. Frieda looked back to the stable and saw Ida standing, watching.

Frieda's joy at supper was diminished by the tension she sensed in her husband. As far as she was concerned, the incident was over. Klaus felt differently, she knew, and she was afraid for whomever had taken Lady.

Another thing that distressed her was the poor way the other servants were treating Ida. They pushed her when her hands were full and laughed at her. One even tripped her. If they were this open with their cruelty in the hall, how bad might it be in the kitchens when everyone settled down to sleep for the night?

As Ida was taking the last course's dishes from their table, Frieda smiled at her. Ida's smile was tight. "Until all this is settled, I want to give you a chamber of your own to keep you from the ridicule the others are giving you."

Ida's eyes widened, and she held perfectly still. "Thank you, my lady."

She looked ashamed. Odd.

Frieda talked with Ida again that evening, then checked on Lady before bed, and when she got to their bedchamber, Klaus was not yet there. She thought she would find him in the hall. She stopped in the solar, but he wasn't there. There was something on the table, though, that she did not remember seeing, and she went to look at it. There were no candles lit in the room, and it was too dark to see what it was.

"There you are, Frieda. I see you have found the gift I made you," Klaus said. He sounded tired, his voice flat.

"Klaus, greetings. What is it?" She did not feel especially curious, but since he said it was a gift. . .

"Gregor let me keep the little book he lent you, and I have made you your own copy," he replied.

"Oh, thank you. You don't know how much I need its words tonight."

He sat at the table with her, his hand over hers. "Why, *Liebchen*?"

"I have been thinking about Ida. I think she could benefit from this message."

Klaus said quietly, "I think you are right. Frieda, we need to talk."

"Yes, we do. Shall we just go to bed?"

He hesitated. "Let us light the candles in here and sit together." He picked up flint and tinder and lit the candles on the table while Frieda closed the door.

"One day I will have a door made between the solar and the bedchamber," he said. Frieda had heard this before. "Sit down, *Liebchen*." He held her chair for her, then seated himself. Perhaps it was the candlelight, but Frieda thought he looked older than usual tonight.

"I talked with the sheriff after supper. He thinks there is a strong case against Warren."

Frieda gasped. "Oh, no! On Ida's word?"

"Hans also said he saw Warren following him out with Lady."

"Did the guards see him, too?"

"One of them says he did, but that he was not leading a horse."

"I believe that he is the one speaking the truth."

"I believe that, too. But the testimony of two witnesses is of more weight than that of one."

"But Lady is back now, unharmed, and I am content. Why do we need to pursue it at all?"

"A thief will steal again if he is not stopped. And we must not allow this lest others be encouraged to steal, thinking that they will get away with it." He looked at her with weary eyes and took her hands. "There is something else."

She nodded.

"Warren came to me tonight and told me that he had found Baldy."

"Good. Where was he?"

"In his family's stable behind the smithy."

Frieda could scarcely breathe. "Someone is trying to make it look as if Warren is the thief."

"That seems obvious to me. But the sheriff arrested him and put him in the jail."

Frieda sobbed, then cried quietly as Klaus stroked her arms and face. Eventually she dried her tears and asked, "When will there be a hearing? And how on earth can you conduct it when you know everyone involved?"

"I cannot. I am certain Warren is not guilty, and I could not be impartial about it. In a case like this, a lord calls in a neighboring lord, usually one with more standing than himself, to conduct a hearing. The sheriff says we can have a preliminary hearing tomorrow. My father will be here to conduct it."

Relief washed over Frieda. Klaus would not have to suffer through conducting a hearing or trial so soon after that painful one at Hohenstein. "I'm glad, Klaus. Your father will be fair. But tomorrow? It's so soon."

Klaus's brow furrowed as he slowly nodded. "I know. But the sheriff wants to do it soon and says he has reasons. Has Ida told you any more than what she did at first?"

"No. And I assured her that if she wanted to talk, I would listen. She said that she had talked enough to the sheriff to last her a lifetime." She had been in tears when she said that, too."

"And has she asked you any questions? Has she expressed any concern for Anna? They worked together for you, and Ida should realize that Anna must be suffering when her sweetheart has been accused of a crime."

"She has said nothing to me about Anna."

"Does that not seem strange to you?"

"Not really, for she does not like Anna. I do not know why, but from the day she met her in the sewing room, Ida has been barely civil to her."

"Have you told the sheriff what you just told me?"

"Yes. He asked me things one by one, and I did not put it together until just now. Ida is accusing Warren to be mean to Anna, isn't she?"

"That is what it sounds like to me."

"How horrible. What is the punishment for a thief?"

"Hanging."

A coldness went through her. "Warren may be hanged?"

"If he is found guilty, yes." Klaus leaned forward, and his gaze grew intent. "If Ida withdraws her testimony, he could go free, and there would not need to be any hearing."

"I do not think she would do that, for she would look foolish. That seems to be the one thing she hates most of all, as far as I have seen of her."

"You have some influence over her. Will you talk to her, try to get her to tell the truth? A false accusation is a crime, too, and she can make it right by telling the truth tonight."

"Tonight! I cannot go to her tonight. She was exhausted when I left her. Jeanne and Anna are not speaking to her; the other household and kitchen servants are treating her poorly. She has no one but me. No one. I must stick by her no matter how absurd her story is."

Frieda saw Klaus's eyes darken just before he dropped his head into his hands. "She is playing you for a fool."

"I am sorry. If she is, then so be it. At least I am being a loyal friend to someone who needs one."

"What about the friend Warren needs right now? And Anna? What if she has found the love she has always dreamed of only to lose him to the hangman?"

Frieda began to cry, burying her face in her hands, feeling that her own love was slipping away from her. She had to do what was right, though, and defending one who had no one else was right. After a while she looked up and saw Klaus standing beside her. "Let us go to bed now, Frieda. We will not talk about this anymore. Tomorrow will take care of itself."

She rose while he extinguished the candles. They reminded her, and she asked, "Klaus, why did you want to talk in here instead of going to bed earlier?"

His face was hard to read in the darkness as he hesitated. "Remember before we wed we agreed that we would never argue or fight in the bed-chamber? But that it would be a place of peace for us?"

"So you knew we might disagree."

"I knew. Now we must remember that we are allies."

"Yes, please," she said. They were moving toward the doorway, and Frieda touched his sleeve, wanting to hold his hand, but he did not respond.

The bedchamber was empty and dark. Of course, the valet was in jail and one maid was weeping for him. Jeanne was comforting Anna. Frieda offered to help Klaus with his sleeve buttons, but he shook his head. She removed her surcoat, but her tunic was laced in back, and she struggled with it until Klaus helped her. "Thank you, Husband. And now let me help you with those sleeve buttons."

He extended his arms to her, one at a time. At last they were ready, and Frieda climbed into bed and released the ties on the bed curtains while Klaus latched the door and put out the candles.

When he got into bed, he lay on his side facing away from her. Frieda waited, but he did not say good night or move toward her. She laid her hand on his shoulder and got no response.

Chapter 14

After a lonely night, Frieda woke as tired as she was when she went to bed. It was not yet dawn, and Klaus was already gone. Frieda dressed quickly in the early morning chill, determined now to talk to Ida and make her see that she was doing wrong. Even if she convinced her to do something she did not want to do now, she would be glad one day that she had done the right thing.

She went up to the chamber she had given Ida and found two men guarding the door, wearing swords. "Good morning," she greeted them and made to open the door.

"My lady, we have orders to admit no one," one of them said. He looked distinctly uncomfortable.

"It is good to know that Ida is being protected. Obviously, your orders would not pertain to me, however. Let me pass."

"No, my lady. We cannot. You may speak to the sheriff about it if you wish."

So the orders came from the sheriff. That was good to know. Good to know that Klaus was not preventing her from seeing Ida. "I will do that. Good day, sirs."

She knew she would be late for Mass if she went now, so she went back to the solar and took up the little book Klaus had copied for her. Its cover was made of leather, awkwardly made. It was all the more dear for being in his handwriting.

She opened it near the middle and began to read. She read the part again that spoke of wanting to do good but doing evil instead. And Klaus maintained that it was a universal problem. So Ida must—in some part of her soul—want to do good. Today Frieda would find that part of her and urge it to the forefront.

Frieda read for a while longer, and the book's words became more encouraging. She could not understand it all, but she liked it. And she wished that she had gotten up a little earlier and gone to Mass so she could have prayed.

But it did not matter. God was here as well. She got down on her knees and prayed for wisdom and strength. She prayed for all the people involved in the hearing, especially Ida and Warren, and Lord Otto who would be the judge. And she prayed that her husband would love her. This was the first time since reading the little book that she felt she needed to pray that prayer.

Klaus was at the table when she arrived for breakfast and sat beside him. "Good morning," she ventured.

"I pray that it will be a good morning," was his reply, in a tone that chilled her.

"I also pray that."

"Your prayers might have been more effective had you bothered to attend Mass."

Frieda looked at his handsome face, handsome as a statue carved of cold marble. "I woke late and prayed in the solar. I think God can hear me from there."

"Likely you were praying for Ida. I hear you already tried to visit your good friend this morning."

The servants were bringing the meal now, and Frieda sat in silence, not wanting them to overhear. Klaus had never treated her this way before. She wanted things to be different, so much different. She wanted him as he was before, the playful Klaus he had been lately, or even the polite, considerate Klaus he was before that.

When their food was set before them, Klaus said, "I need to talk to the sheriff. Please excuse me." And he was gone.

Frieda ate a little bit, each bite a task, and drank a goblet of cider. The goblet was one of the ones she had bought at the market fair with Margarethe. The wall hanging they'd shopped for that day was on the wall nearby. She felt like pulling it down and picking Ida's signature out of it.

After breaking fast, the great hall was cleared for the hearing. The trestle tables were taken down and some of the benches aligned near the front. Guards were posted at all the doors to keep the curious out. There was no way to keep the most determined away, for every passage in the donjon led to the great hall, but the hearing would be kept as close to private as possible. The only other room large enough to hold all the people who belonged there was the chapel, and Klaus deemed it an unseemly use of a chapel. Frieda agreed.

Lord Otto arrived and was seated at the head table, in Frieda's chair. She kissed his cheek. "Greetings, Papa. I wish you were visiting only and not here for this unpleasantness."

He smiled and returned the kiss. "I, too, Frieda. You know all the people involved. Please tell me your impression. Did Warren do this thing?"

"He did not, Papa. Hans and Ida are playing some game, and I will try to get Ida to tell the truth. I have befriended her, and she may listen to me."

"Klaus also believes in Warren's innocence. Does anyone believe the groom or the girl?"

"No, my lord. And that is why I have befriended her," she said. Lord Otto's look of sad understanding pierced her.

Klaus came up to them on the dais looking grim. "Father, thank you for coming. Has Frieda told you anything?"

"Yes. She is trying to prejudice the judge into setting your valet free."

She looked quickly at Klaus, who gazed at her with some of his old tenderness. "She is a soft-hearted creature."

"And that is why you love her. I will do my best to honor her wishes, but if the weight of evidence is against him, there is little I will be able to do." His warning turned her breakfast to lead within her as the thought of Warren's death grew more terribly real.

Frieda's eyes teared up, and she reached a hand toward Klaus. He clasped it firmly, then brought it to his lips and kissed it. She blinked to clear her vision and found him looking at his feet.

They stood and talked with Lord Otto for a few minutes, avoiding any mention of the hearing soon to begin. Frieda anxiously watched all the people come in. She whispered to her father-in-law, "That is Ida."

"Go and sit beside her, Frieda. I will be calling on you soon."

"Yes, Papa."

Frieda touched Klaus's hand before walking to sit with Ida. "Good morning, Ida. I tried to visit you this morning and your guards would not admit me."

She looked tired and worried. "Thank you for trying, my lady."

"The hearing will begin soon, for here comes Warren." He also looked tired; it seemed that everyone looked tired this morning. There was pain in his eyes as he spotted her and Ida, and then he was looking away again. The sheriff's men had him sitting off to one side, alone except for themselves.

Frieda spotted Anna sitting with Jeanne. She tried to catch Jeanne's eye, but she glanced at her, then lifted her chin and looked away. So she had lost even Jeanne.

Lord Otto called Hans first and had him tell his story. He questioned him closely on several points. "You led a group of twenty warhorses to pasture all by yourself."

"I beg your pardon, my lord; there were eighteen warhorses. They are very obedient from their war training and no problem for an experienced horseman to lead."

"And you saw Warren Schmidt following the horses you led."

"Yes, my lord."

"And he led Lady."

"Yes, my lord. She was covered with a large blanket, but there is no horse like Lady. I would recognize her anywhere."

"Why did you not stop him and ask him what he was doing?"

"Why, because of the horses, my lord. I could not leave them."

"I see. You could not trust those very obedient horses for a few minutes to question a thief. Thank you for your interesting testimony."

Frieda met Klaus's eye for a moment but could not discern his thoughts.

Lord Otto called Axel, the avener, next. "Has Hans often taken the warhorses out to pasture?"

"He has."

"Has he always taken them alone, with no one to help?"

"He has never done that before."

"Did you ask him to take them out yesterday?"

"No, it was his idea. He takes care of the warhorses."

"And so he would normally be the one to decide when to take them out?"

"No, I generally suggest when it should be done."

Ida continually brushed and plucked at one small circle on her surcoat. Frieda took her hand and squeezed it. Ida turned her face away. Lord Otto called Ida next, and she told the same thing that she had before. "And where exactly were you when you saw Warren?"

"I was standing in the kitchen doorway."

Lord Otto looked across the room at a man standing in the back. "Rudolf, are you still in charge of the kitchen here?"

"Yes, my lord."

"Can you see the castle gate from the kitchen doorway?"

"No, my lord."

"Was this woman, Ida, on duty at sunrise yesterday morning?"

"She was. She is a good worker, my lord."

"Did she leave at any time yesterday morning?"

"I am not sure, my lord."

"Very well. Thank you." He turned back to Ida once more. "I will not embarrass you by asking you again where you were when you saw Warren leading Lady out of the castle. I understand that sometimes it is easy to forget something that happened the day before. But I am sure you remember what color blanket Lady wore."

"It was green, my lord."

"Thank you, Ida."

He called the sheriff next and asked him first what color Hans had said the blanket was. "Tan, my lord."

"Very well. You questioned the gate guards also, did you not?"

"I did."

"Did they see anything unusual?"

"It is hard to say. Each of them changed his story a bit while we visited." Frieda swallowed as she wondered what manner of visit it had been.

"Did you discover anything from either of them by any other means?"

"I did ask them to empty their purses. Each of them had an unusual coin, identical to one another. It seemed odd to me."

"May I see those coins?"

"Certainly." He stepped up to Lord Otto and handed him two coins. He studied them, then looked directly at Frieda.

Ida, seated at her side, began to tremble. Frieda said softly, "There is still time to do right. Do you truly want to see Warren hanged for something he did not do?"

She bowed her head, shook it, then turned toward Hans, who was seated across the room. Frieda watched as he got up and walked over to them.

"Lady Frieda, will you please come here and look at these coins with me?" said Lord Otto. Frieda rose and glanced at Ida, who was engaged in earnest conversation with Hans. Frieda aimed a quick prayer heavenward as she went to her father-in-law.

"Have you ever seen coins like this before, my lady?"

"Yes, Papa." Her face warmed as the sheriff chuckled. "My lord, these are gold pieces from France. Why do you say they are unusual?"

"Because they are unusual here. I suppose you saw quite a few of them at your former home in the Schwarzwald."

"Yes, my lord. They are used in trade there. I have quite a few of them in my—" Stricken, she stopped. She had paid Ida with coins like these.

"Don't worry, my lady. I know you didn't bribe the guards to help someone steal your own horse."

Lord Otto then looked at someone behind Frieda. "Hans, do you wish to add to your testimony?"

"Yes, my lord."

"Come here then." Frieda began to move aside, but Lord Otto motioned her to stay. "What would you like to say?"

"Please, my lord, I cannot let this happen. I lied about Warren following the warhorses and leading Lady. I also paid the guards to keep quiet about. . ."

"About what, Hans?"

"About me having Lady in amongst the warhorses. I am the one who took her, no one else."

"What did you tell the guards?"

"That I was playing some mischief on Lord Klaus, and they were not to mention that they saw Lady with me."

Lord Otto looked at Ida, who stood behind Hans, gripping her hands so tightly together that her knuckles were white. "Well, Ida? Have you also remembered something else?"

"Yes, my lord. I did not see Warren taking Lady out of the castle. And

I am the one who gave Hans the money for the guards. The whole thing was my idea. I am to blame."

"Why did you do this thing? Lady Frieda loves that filly, and you caused her much pain."

"I did not mean to hurt Lady Frieda. I wanted to do something mean to Anna." She hung her head, whether out of remorse or embarrassment Frieda couldn't guess.

"Why did you want to do something mean to Anna? I have never before met a person who did not like her."

"I am a kitchen servant. When Lady Frieda asked me to help her with an embroidery project, I was glad to do it for the extra money, but also for the chance to be near the lady. I have always wanted to be a lady's maid, and I thought I might have a chance if she liked me. But instead, she brought Anna into the household, who was nothing but a chambermaid, and let her be her maid."

Lord Otto turned to Hans. "And you, sir, agreed to help her, even to the point of doing the crime and risking your life. Why?"

Hans shrugged. "I love her."

Frieda saw that Ida was holding her breath.

"That is no excuse. What about this other horse, Baldy? Did you take him, too?"

"Yes, but that was not done to make Warren look guilty. I like Baldy and was hoping to make a home of my own and thought he would not be missed. When I found out that he was, I decided to make it look as if Warren had taken him."

"You stole Baldy."

"Yes, my lord."

"What do you call what you did with Lady?"

"I borrowed her. I treated her well while I had her, but I did not even have her a whole day. It was still wrong, I know, my lord."

"Indeed, it was. Borrowing without asking is called stealing, sir." Lord Otto leaned back and drummed his fingers on the table. He looked around the room from under lowered brows, then sat forward again. "I have made my decision. Warren Schmidt?"

Warren rose and walked up to the dais. "Yes, my lord?"

"Have you heard all that has been said?"

"Most of it, my lord."

"You are found not guilty. Any fines levied here today shall be given to you to compensate you for your anguish and your time in jail."

"Thank you, my lord."

"I would like your opinion as to what to do with these two thieves."

Warren was dismayed. "I, I do not know, my lord, what to do with

Hans. He came forward with the truth before I could be hanged, and I am glad of that." He glanced around the hall, his eyes resting in the direction Frieda knew Anna sat. "As for Ida, I would suggest you send her somewhere far away from my Anna, for her own safety."

"Thank you, Warren. The guards took bribes, but as soon as the sheriff asked for the truth, they gave it. They were both alarmed; they believed it was merely harmless mischief as they had been told. The guards forfeited their bribe money, and each will lose one month's pay."

The guards looked at each other, then bowed to Lord Otto.

"Hans and Ida are together guilty of a serious crime. I have never hanged a woman before—"

"Papa, no!" Frieda cried out, then clapped her hand over her mouth. Lord Otto gave her his attention. Klaus, seated beside him, also looked, leaning forward. She was not sure, but she thought she saw a glint of amusement in her father-in-law's eyes. She plunged in. "They have done wrong, but they did not really steal Lady, not really, for she was returned unharmed, and it was their intention to do that all along. I did not suffer overmuch, for she was not gone even one night. I am willing to forgive them, and I think Warren is, too." She slid her gaze over to Warren and found him nodding. "Warren is being compensated for his anxiety, and I am willing to accept something like that, too; only please do not hang either of these people. Lady is valuable and lovable, but she is only a horse, and these people are people. Please, Papa—I mean, my lord."

Lord Otto nodded. "For your sake I will not hang either one of them. I will, however, remove them from this household. Klaus and I will decide where their skills can best be used. Each forfeits three months' wages as well. Will that be acceptable?"

Frieda smiled and Hans and Ida both agreed quietly and gripped one another's hands. Warren smiled, and Frieda realized that the forfeit wages might make him and Anna a nice cottage.

Frieda went to Warren, as did many other people, who all stood aside for the lady. "Oh, Warren, I'm so glad."

"Then you did believe in me? The guards were taunting me, saying that you had gone over to Ida."

Frieda saw the hurt in his eyes. "Ida had no one to be with her; I was only there acting as a friend. When the opportunity came, I urged her to do what was right. That is all."

He nodded. His other well-wishers were crowding in, but all deferred to the lady, of course. "God bless you, my lady," he choked out as he bowed. She extended her arms for a hug, but he stepped back and looked alarmed.

So much for his belief in her.

Frieda sought Anna. She had thought she would be the first to come to Warren. She spotted her off to the side a little, hanging back, Jeanne at her side. Frieda tried to catch their eyes, but neither of them would look at her. So she had lost both of these women she had counted as friends, even Jeanne, who had been her friend for over two years and had come to this country with her. Bavaria grew more horrible by the minute.

Frieda withdrew and sought out Klaus. He was on the dais talking with his father. She wondered where they would send Ida and Hans.

Frieda watched Klaus and wished that he loved her. His love would make any loss of friends, anything at all bearable. There had been times that she thought he loved her, but now she knew better. He treated her well when she pleased him, and she did not know what would please him. She could not know what to expect of him, so it would be better to be with people who, while not often kind, were at least consistent.

She watched Klaus for a few minutes, wanting to always remember the face of the man who nearly loved her, then she went to find the captain of the guard.

Chapter 15

Frieda found the captain of the guard at the rear of the great hall. She drew him aside where no one would overhear. "I will be riding out in one hour. I want you and however many men you deem necessary to meet me just inside the entrance to Lord Gregor's wood."

"Yes, my lady. How far the journey?"

"Bring provisions for twenty days."

His normally imperturbable face grew alarmed. "Twenty days, my lady?"

"The journey probably will not take that long, but it is good to be prepared this time of year. You will be reprovisioned at the other end for your return trip."

He swallowed as he stared. "The provisions are to be for how many people?"

"For you and me and your men."

"Then the lord will not be going?" he blurted.

"No, Captain, he will not. Are you not able to protect me?"

"Of course I am," he said, drawing himself up and looking wounded. "But I will need to talk to the lord. . . ."

That was the last thing she needed. "What are your orders concerning me?"

"I am to obey you without question, as I do the lord."

"Good. Then obey me in this and do not speak to the lord or anyone else about it."

"Yes, my lady," he said and bowed. The glimpse of his face she saw before he left the hall showed her that he was not the least bit happy.

Frieda left the hall and ascended the stairs to her bedchamber. She changed into a warmer tunic and an older surcoat, put on an extra pair of hose, and packed a few garments. She took a couple of pairs of Klaus's old pants in case it was cold when they skirted the mountains and she needed the extra warmth. She knelt on the floor looking at them, remembering the apple trees she had climbed during harvest and how proudly Klaus had watched.

She shook her head. This was not profitable. She stood with her bag and looked around the room. She wondered where the little book was that Klaus had given her. She had been reading it in the solar. She put on her favorite cloak, then with one last look around the room, she closed the door.

In the solar, she unlocked the coffer Klaus kept the money in. She knew she would need some but had no idea how much. There were so many variables. She might need to stay in inns a few times, and she might need to have a horse shod or buy extra provisions. She decided it was better to have too much money than not enough and chose a good number of gold coins. She counted them carefully and recorded the amount in the ledger. She puzzled over what to write as the purpose of the withdrawal, then wrote that it was personal expenses. She put the heavy coins into her belt purse.

Frieda picked up the little book Klaus had made her and tucked it into her bag. She fastened it shut and headed for the door. There she hesitated. She did not want to be seen with the bag, but she did not usually use the back stairs, so being seen there carrying it might be worse than using her usual route.

She took a deep breath and began walking down the hallway. A page hurtled past. "Boy," she called. He reversed course and came to a halt in front of her.

He bowed and said, "Yes, my lady."

"Please carry this bag to the stable for me."

"Yes, my lady. With whom do I leave it in the stable?"

"Just leave it by my horse's stall." He bowed again and tore off down the passage with the bag. Frieda was able to leave the donjon without speaking to anyone else and sighed in relief as she walked through the bailey. She looked at the sky and noted that it was nearly time to set out.

She reached the stable and went to her horse, who was pleased to see her, and her bag was not there. Given the page's tendency to speed, he surely had gotten here and left by now. She casually glanced around, not wanting to attract a groom's attention.

Frieda heard a nicker and looked across to see Lady looking at her. How could she have forgotten Lady? She went to her and found her bag there. Of course, that would be the horse a young boy would think of as hers. She stroked the horse's smooth coat. "Greetings, my sweet Lady. I hope that you will forgive me."

She picked up her bag and went to Fraulein's stall. There she began to saddle her, and a groom rushed up. "Forgive me, my lady. So many people want to ride today, and we are short a man."

"It is well, good man. Will you tie this bag on there, too, for me?"

"Yes, my lady." He finished the work and led the horse out. Frieda mounted just outside the stable and rode out through the bailey. She saluted the guards at the outer wall as she passed and took a familiar trail off the main road. When she knew she could not be seen from the castle, she cut over to the track that led to the wood.

Frieda felt the cooler air and smelled the fragrance of the huge trees as she rode into their shadow. There Captain Gernst awaited her. She quickly counted eight men and wondered if that would be enough. The captain greeted her as she drew even with him. "Good day, my lady. I felt it prudent to arrive here one by one so that our departure would not be noted. We are all here now except four who have gone on ahead to Tanneburg to purchase additional provisions. I apologize for not getting permission from you to do that, but we could not get enough traveling food at home on short notice."

"You did well, Captain. I thank you. Shall we ride?"

"Yes, my lady." He urged his mount forward and signaled his men to follow. "You left much to my discretion, my lady, and I took the liberty of bringing a tent and winter weight bedroll for you. I did not know if you had such."

Frieda had been thinking of the traveling and not much of the sleeping. The nights would be long and cold. On the trip here, she had been with Jeanne. On this one, she would sleep alone. The men would be nearby, but it was still frightening. "I thank you for doing so much for me on such short notice, Captain. Does anyone at the castle know where we are going?"

The captain grinned, a rare unguarded moment for him. "No, my lady. I could hardly reveal what I myself do not know."

"We will be taking the road west. I am going to visit my people in the Schwarzwald. I know that the road can be joined from this one near Beroburg, but is there not also a junction farther south?"

"Yes, my lady. We could make it that far easily today. It looks as if we will be having a heavy rain late this afternoon, so we will need to choose our campsite carefully."

"That is another matter I will leave to you, Captain."

For some time, they rode without speaking. If she had not played so many tricks on Klaus, perhaps he would have trusted her more, would have judged her kindness to Ida less harshly. Removing herself from him was taking her wickedness away as well, surely a good thing for all concerned. She knew, though, that she was leaving for her own reasons, not to spare Klaus her wickedness. She couldn't bear to be near the man she loved knowing that he neither loved nor trusted her.

Sad to be leaving, she focused on the beauty of the forest they passed through so as not to remember. She saw a pair of fat squirrels chasing through the trees. "I love the forest. I always have."

"I have been told that the Schwarzwald looks much like this forest. Is that true, my lady?"

"It is. It is vast, though, containing mountains and streams and countless tracks. But you will see for yourself soon." Gernst looked pleased.

Soon they reached the edge of the forest on Gregor's end. There they waited for the men who had gone to his castle for food. "Captain, I have room on my horse to carry things if we need it."

"It is well, my lady. You carry little, I noticed."

"I have enough. Oh. I have something you should probably help me carry."

She took her purse off her belt and tossed it to him. He caught it and gaped at the weight before peering inside. "Oh, my lady. It would not be wise to carry this much money. May I divide the care of it among several men?"

"If you think it best." She watched him give coins to each of the men to carry. Each of them somberly put them away in their own purses.

When the men who had been to Tanneburg joined them, they set off to join the road south.

∽

Klaus was seated at his place at the head table at dinnertime. Servants had begun to bring the food, and still Frieda had not taken her place. It was odd. She was rarely late and never without him knowing the reason.

After the hearing, he had wanted to share with her his idea of what to do with Ida and Hans, but he could not find her. She was neither in the sewing room, nor their chamber, nor with Anna or Jeanne.

Anna, Jeanne, and Warren were upset when he asked if they had seen Frieda. "I was looking for her as well, my lord," Jeanne said. "Warren has just told us the truth about what my lady was doing with Ida, how she befriended her and then encouraged her to tell the truth. I have wronged her badly."

"As have I," Anna moaned. "I thought that she believed Warren guilty. I did not speak to her after the hearing, and I have been avoiding her."

"I avoided her also, my lord," Jeanne said. "When you find her, please summon me, my lord. I want to make things right."

"I am afraid I hurt her feelings as well, my lord," said Warren. "After the hearing I talked with her for a bit and was glad to learn that she believed in my innocence. I bowed to her, and she put out her hands as if to hug me, but I stepped back. My care was for her reputation, for she should not be seen to hug a servant, especially one who has been accused of a crime, but I fear she took my actions as scorn."

Klaus also had apologies to make to her, but it was not fitting for him to share that with them. "I will let you know when I find my lady."

He remembered all this now and wondered if Frieda had sought comfort elsewhere. Heaven knows he had not been a likely source of that commodity of late.

Lord Otto was staying for dinner and spoke to him now across Frieda's empty place. "I wonder why Frieda is so late."

"I do not know. I have not seen her since the end of the hearing. Likely she is busy with something. She has been taking an interest in the running of the estate. When I was gone for the trial at Hohenstein, she helped Hagen settle a dispute between two bakers. Have I told you about that?"

Lord Otto listened with amusement to the story, and they went on to talk about other amusing things that had gone on in both their homes recently.

After dinner, Lord Otto took his leave, and Klaus went back to wondering where Frieda might be. He went up to check their chambers and the sewing room once more in case she had been away for a moment when he had been there before.

He thought she might be with Lady. He surveyed the sky on the way to the stable, a habit acquired in his years of commanding troops. It would rain late in the afternoon. A groom greeted him at the stable. They were shorthanded now, he recalled, with Hans where he was. Frieda was not there, nor was there any sign that she had been there. Lady had not been groomed yet. "Shall I groom you, Lady? Will you allow that today?" he asked as he stroked her. It would not take long, and perhaps Frieda would come and enjoy seeing him doing this.

Klaus called for the equipment he would need and went into the stall. Lady was playful and nudged him when he bent over. He laughed and talked to her while he worked. A groom came and offered to finish for him, and he agreed. His heart was in finding Frieda.

Klaus went to Fraulein's stall and found her gone. Now he had an idea where Frieda might be. Besides her embroidery and Lady, Frieda loved to ride, especially in the forest. That is where she must be.

"Saddle my horse," he called to a stable boy. He sent a boy to the donjon for his cloak. When his horse was ready, he rode to the main gate. "Greetings," he called to the guards. "Have you seen my lady today?"

"Yes, my lord. She rode through some time ago."

"Which direction did she take?"

"The main road, my lord, then she took the first track heading south."

A different direction than he would have thought, but she could have gone that way and then cut off for the forest road. She loved that forest. But why would she try to disguise the way she went? Unease stirred within him.

"How long ago did she ride through, would you say?"

"Three hours or so."

"Thank you," he said and started to ride on. He pulled up and asked, "Who did she have as escort?"

"She rode out alone, my lord."

"Alone?"

The guard glanced at his partner, who stood at attention and did not meet his gaze. "Yes, my lord. Unless she was escorted by one of the guards and was meeting him down the road. . . . Quite a few men rode out this morning, one at a time."

"Thank you," he called and urged his horse forward. He strained to remember Gernst telling him about any exercise he had planned for today or for any other reason for men to be riding out. He recalled nothing of the sort. If he did not run across Frieda in the forest, he would ask him about it.

Klaus rode straight to the edge of the forest, sure that was where Frieda had gone. The track was churned by hooves where it lost its grassy cover under the great trees. Not churned by the passing of horses, but by horses standing and waiting, moving about—as if their masters were gathering for an excursion, such as a hunt. If his men were hunting in Gregor's forest without permission, there would be trouble.

Klaus rode in, following the trail of the riders before him. Several times he stopped and listened, quieting his horse with a hand. He heard no human sounds at any time and rode on.

Klaus worried more the farther he rode into the forest. Since Frieda had come this way, she might have met up with these men and rode with them. What if they were going farther than she knew and none of them would stop and take her home?

That was impossible. Any of his men would take care of his lady or forfeit his life.

What if this was not the trail of his men but of some robbers? Lady Frieda would make a fine prize for ransom. It was too horrible. "Help me, God, to think right about this. Help me to find Frieda."

Klaus rode to a place where there was more of the churned earth. So they, whoever they were, met more people here. The trail went on toward the main road from there, so there was little point in following it. The road could give few clues.

Instead, Klaus followed the trail of the men who had met the ones he had followed. Klaus worried more the farther he went into the forest. The road led straight to Tanneburg. Klaus would check with Gregor and see if he knew anything.

On arriving, Klaus handed his horse to a servant. He entered the donjon and found Gregor in the steward's office. "So, Klaus," Gregor greeted him with a grin, "are you hungry, too?"

"Hungry?"

"Yes. We had some of your men here this morning buying dried meat and fruit, bread, you name it."

Klaus felt he had been hit with a battering ram. "What is it, Klaus?" Gregor was instantly at his side, his arm steadying him. Truly, Klaus felt he needed the support or he would not have kept to his feet.

Gregor produced a chair and dismissed the steward. Klaus sat heavily and told Gregor what had been going on and what he had seen in the wood. "She has left me, Gregor. She must be going home to her parents."

Gregor sat and stared. "Why are you sitting here? You have to bring her home."

"How? My men are at home, nearly an hour away in the wrong direction. And if I take the road as I think she went, I could be wrong and miss her."

Gregor shook his head. "I'll help you out, Brother, since you are too shocked to plan strategy. Here's what we will do. . . ."

☙

"My lady, we have come some way today and should seek a campsite," said the captain.

They sat where the road leading to the west road branched off from the one they were on. Frieda could smell the approaching rain and thought with distaste of sleeping in the damp. "Would it be safer to be a few miles from any junction?"

"Yes, my lady. But that would be a considerable distance since there are two junctions: this one and the one with the west road four miles from here. If it is safety you are concerned with, we should seek to stay in a neighboring castle."

Frieda looked across the countryside. Not more than two miles away, she saw a castle on a large hill. She did not know who lived there, but it looked a likely place to spend the night. "Captain, do friends live there?"

"Yes, my lady."

"Then let us go there for tonight."

"A good choice, my lady. We can be there before the rain starts, I think."

He gave the order to move out. As they rode through the village on the way to the castle, they saw a church being built and several houses as well. Some buildings stood empty, charred wood for walls.

Frieda pulled up even with Captain Gernst. "Captain, what happened here?"

"This village was attacked in the spring, my lady."

It seemed to her that they should have traveled far enough today that they would be far from Klaus's family's lands, so she had not asked whose land this was. Albert's village had been attacked that spring. She had never been to visit Albert and Hilda, but perhaps she would be doing that today.

"Is this Lord Albert's village?"

"Yes, my lady."

"Very well. As soon as we get to a more private place, I would like to stop that you may instruct the men."

Outside the village, approaching the castle gates, the captain called a halt and listened to her instructions, then passed them along to the men.

At the castle, Hilda was delighted to see Frieda, and Albert was friendly enough. Frieda did not say why she was there, but Hilda did not seem to care, so glad she was to see her. "We live so far from everyone else that we do not have enough family visits. It is yet awhile before supper. Would you like to see my new clothes?"

"Oh, yes, Hilda. I do like clothes."

"Albert, darling, you can spare us, can't you?"

"Certainly, *Liebchen*. If you forget about supper, I will come and get you."

Frieda thought that unlikely since she had had no dinner.

☙

Albert wondered why Frieda had come to visit without Klaus, and why she had such a hefty, well-armed, and well-packed escort. She had not given a reason for the visit, but Albert had other ways to learn what was going on.

He went to talk with Gernst, who was known to him from the army when he had been one of Klaus's lieutenants. He returned to the solar still ignorant and sat at the table pondering what to do.

Finally, he called for a messenger and bade him to get ready to ride. He took up a quill and wrote to Klaus to let him know that his wife had arrived safely.

Chapter 16

Frieda was given a comfortable room with a fire burning. She read her book until she felt tired enough to sleep, then crawled into bed. She wondered what Klaus was thinking about tonight, wondered if he missed her. She drifted into a troubled sleep like an autumn leaf falling into a stream.

Frieda struggled to rouse herself when she heard a knocking. Once she realized what the sound was, she listened longer to make sure it was at her door. Surely it was not morning already. She had asked to be awakened just before dawn, not at midnight.

She threw off the covers and went to the door, unlatched it, and opened it. She gasped when she saw Klaus standing before her, his cloak hanging heavy with the rain that soaked it. She could not speak, did not know what she would say if she could. He stood looking at her, worry marring his handsome face. "May I come in, Frieda?" he asked softly.

She nodded and stepped back to admit him, then closed the door behind him. She shivered in the nighttime chill and took up the tunic she had taken off earlier and pulled it on over her head. Klaus took off his sword and laid it on the table, then stirred up the fire and added wood to it.

Frieda went closer and watched him. "Let me take your cloak, Klaus." He nodded, stood and took it off, and handed it to her. She stood with it, looking at him, wanting so badly to hold him, to have him hold her. She looked away and hung the wet cloak over a chair.

Klaus gestured for her to be seated, and he chose the chair next to her across the corner of the table. She watched him as she waited for him to speak. "Tell me, *Liebchen*. Tell me how I can make it right."

She shook her head. How could she tell him when she did not understand it herself? She kept her hands close to herself lest she reach out for him as she longed to do.

He held her gaze as he spoke. "I treated you badly before the hearing. I was cold to you, and I am sorry."

She nodded and looked away. "You were mean to me, and I didn't know what to do because you have never done that before. You told me once that you would always be pleased with me because I. . ." She had to stop, take a deep breath, and swallow. "You said I was your Frieda. But I found out it was not true."

"No, Frieda. I did not agree with how you were acting with Ida, but I did not stop caring for you." His voice and his look were both intense, loaded with caring.

"That is exactly how it seemed to me. I was the only one who cared about Ida, and I chose to care because she was alone and needed someone. My reward was to be abandoned by all of my people, and the one loss that hurt the most was you, for I thought you would always care for me."

"I do, Frieda. I do care for you."

"I thought about what you said last night and decided that you were right. I tried to get in to see Ida to convince her to tell the truth, but the guards would not let me in. Then you made a remark at breakfast about me going to see my good friend and—"

"I am so sorry, *Liebchen*. Please forgive me. Even though we disagreed, I never should have treated you so."

"Why did you do it, Klaus?"

"I was afraid that Warren would hang for something he did not do. I care for him not only as a friend, but as one of my people. If one in my care died because of a false accusation, I would have failed. I am responsible for my people, and I love them."

Yet he did not love her, Frieda, who loved him. It was horribly unfair. He glanced at the fire as a piece of wood fell. "Can you not forgive me, Frieda?"

She hesitated, then said, "I forgive you, Klaus."

He smiled and reached for her hands, but she kept them close and drew back. "But what then? Will you not come home?" he asked.

"No. I don't belong there. I'm going home to my family."

Pain washed across Klaus's features. "When will you be back?" he whispered.

"I am not coming back."

"But think about what you told me about your parents, about how you could never please them. You can please me, just by being yourself."

She nodded. "Oh, yes—unless I back the wrong side in a dispute among your people. My parents I *know* I cannot please. There is some security in that."

Klaus hung his head, and Frieda walked to the fire, not wanting him to see her tears. When her grief was under control, she went back to him. He still sat there but had turned toward the fire. Had he been watching her there? She wondered if he knew that she loved him, that she would gladly go home with him if only he loved her.

There was no way that she could ask him, for he would say what she wanted to hear to get her to go home, and she would never know the truth.

Yet he looked so broken. She had to ease his pain somehow, even if it was with a lie. She quickly prayed in her heart that God would forgive her. "Klaus, it is not you, mostly. I do not care for Bavaria. The people do not care for me and compare me unfavorably to my sister. I miss my parents and friends in the Schwarzwald. It may be that I was too young to marry, in spite of my years. I do not know."

"You may need some time to grow up; I can understand that. I want to help you. If you do not object, I will still visit the Schwarzwald come summer. I can bring Lady to you."

Tears filled her eyes again. "Would you really do that for me? After I have left you?"

"I would do almost anything for you, *Liebchen*."

Touched, she extended her hand to him. He held it, then kissed her fingers one by one. She smiled and stepped back, renewing the distance between them. "Klaus, it is late, and I want to leave immediately after breaking fast. I need to go to bed, and you had best go to bed, too."

He sighed deeply as he got up from the table. To her dismay, he pulled his supertunic over his head.

"What are you doing? Did Albert not give you a room?"

"Why would he do that? We are married, after all."

She watched as he pulled off his boots and pulled his shirt out of his pants and got into bed that way. She followed wearing her smock and tunic.

All the rest of the night she did not speak to him, and he did not speak to her, but she felt that he did not sleep as he lay silent and perfectly still beside her. She did not sleep for hours. Of that she was certain.

Frieda woke just before dawn with Klaus leaning over her on one elbow. She started to smile, then remembered, and was able to stop.

"*Liebchen*, I know you wanted to leave right after breakfast, but are you willing to wait an additional hour so that I might write some letters and power of attorney for the stewards?"

She frowned. What was he talking about? She tried to lick her lips, but her mouth was dusty with sleep. Klaus reached up to the headboard where there was a shelf and got her a cup of cider. She drank gratefully. "Mmm. It tastes like some of ours."

He smiled. "It is." He waited as she drank some more and handed the cup back to him. "Will you wait for me?"

"Why? What are you doing?"

"I want to come with you, if you will have me."

She stared at him. "I have a good escort already."

"No, *Liebchen*. I am not offering to escort you. I want to be with you, always. If you do not care for Bavaria, then I shall leave, too." In spite of his casual tone, his expression was earnest, longing. He raised a hand, hesitated, and then brushed a loose strand of hair from her face.

Frieda closed her eyes. It was tempting. She enjoyed his company so much, but. . .

"Wait. How can you leave your lands, your towns, your people?"

He shrugged. "That is why I need to write to the stewards and give them power of attorney to act in my stead. Gregor will agree to look in on things from time to time, I am sure."

"But you love this land. I cannot ask you to leave."

"You are not asking me to leave; I want to be with you. We belong together. Please, sweet lady, let me come with you." He found her hand beneath the covers and brought it to his lips, keeping his gaze on her face as he kissed it. "It's true that I love the land and my people, but I love you more."

Her eyes filled with tears as she took her hand from his grasp and slipped it around his neck. "Oh, Klaus," she whispered. He gathered her into his arms and held her tight. She cried quietly in his embrace, wanting to stay in his arms forever.

Klaus loosened his hold and looked at her. His eyes looked moist as he asked, "I take it that you mean to say yes?"

She smiled and softly said, "No." His face fell, and she hastened to smile encouragement while stroking his face and laughing through her tears. "You cannot go with me, because I am not going."

"You are not?"

"No. My home is with the man I love." She looked steadily at him as comprehension came to him.

"Then you love me, too?"

She nodded.

"I wish I had told you that I love you. But I was afraid that maybe you didn't love me and would feel pressured to say that you did if I told you." She laughed and sniffed. "I felt the same way. We are stupid."

He pulled her close. "We were stupid. We have both just gotten smarter."

He laughed, and Frieda held her breath at the sound of it, a wonderful sound she had never heard before. She tried to push herself back to get a look at him, but he would not let her go. "Be still. I want to hug you," he growled. Then he started kissing her, and all thought of pulling back dissolved away.

When dawn was long past, Klaus said, "We need to get up. Gernst is likely puzzled, if not scandalized."

"He will be disappointed we are going home."

"Why?"

"He was looking forward to seeing the Schwarzwald. And I feel bad about having him gather all those provisions and tents and things just to pack it all back home. He was most helpful to me. You will have to give him a nice bonus."

Klaus snorted. "*You* give him a nice bonus. I took some money before I rode out last night and saw your ledger entry. Were you planning on buying a castle when you got to the Schwarzwald?"

She laughed. "I don't know how much things cost, so I took enough to be sure I had things covered, like staying in inns, replacing horseshoes. . ."

"Replacing all the horses, more like." He tossed the covers off both of them, and they dressed, helping one another here and there. While Klaus rebraided Frieda's hair, he said, "I have been thinking that it *is* a waste of good packing to go right home. It is late enough in the year that there is much snow in the Alps. Did you not want to see them some time?"

"Oh, yes! That's a wonderful idea, darling." She turned around slowly, so as not to disturb his braiding, and kissed him.

"I think we have everything we need, except some clothes for me. I can borrow some things from Albert, but his breeches would be too small. This pair may get pretty sorry."

"I have a couple of pairs of your old breeches with me. I did not know if I might need the extra warmth, or if I might need to climb a tree."

Klaus laughed, and this time she was able to get a look at his face. He looked so happy and free. Freedom. That was what had been missing in him. And now. . .now he seemed complete.

She put her arms around him, and he hugged her back while keeping a grip on her braid. "We should go to the hall soon," he rumbled. She loved that nice bass rumble.

"Very well. We can go as soon as the last braid is done. I will finish it if you have other things to do."

"No, I like playing with your hair." He gave the braid a tug.

"I will have some woman pin it up for me, though. You are not very good at that."

"Hmm. I am good at unpinning it, though."

Albert and Hilda greeted them in the hall, and Captain Gernst looked up, relieved, as they passed.

"You have missed breakfast, sleepies, but I know someone is in the kitchen," said Hilda. She sent a page for food. They sat together at the head table.

"We have not been much company this trip, and that is the truth," Klaus apologized.

"Next time, you can stay longer. And we have been wanting to see you. Hilda has not been to your home yet," Albert said.

"Oh, Hilda. I hope you will come soon. If you are not careful, though, you will get talked into joining the grape harvest at Gregor's."

Albert and Klaus went to get Klaus some clothes after breakfast, and Frieda excused herself to talk with Gernst.

"Captain, there has been a change of plans."

"Yes, my lady," he said as he bowed.

"We will not be traveling to the Schwarzwald after all." He nodded and looked vaguely disappointed. "But we will take a trip south to see the Alps. I am sure Lord Klaus will talk with you about it. I just wanted to thank you for all the work you did for me on short notice."

He bowed again. "My pleasure, my lady."

She stood for a minute, then decided to go ahead and tell him something she had been thinking of. "Captain, Klaus and I will be traveling to the Schwarzwald this coming summer. If you are interested in coming along, I can use my influence on your behalf."

His eyes lit up, but he shook his head. "I have duties. . . ."

"Of course. But surely you have a good man who could see to things while you are away. Let me know if you are interested."

She turned to go, and he said, "My lady." She turned back and looked at his grin. "Thank you."

They rode for three days at a good pace to reach a place where they could see the Alps well. The weather was with them after the first day, and the riding was pleasant, but the nights were cold. Frieda was glad Klaus was there to help her keep warm.

When they arrived at the place Klaus had in mind, they sat on their horses looking, just looking at the snow-draped majesty. "We can go closer if you want to, *Liebchen*, but this is the best view you can get."

Frieda had not imagined anything so big and beautiful could exist. "I am content. They are beautiful. I have never seen anything like this."

They spent the night near that spot and looked at the mountains again in the morning. Frieda was delighted to see that they were even more stunning in the morning light. Klaus came to her and put his arm around her. "God makes the most wonderful things, doesn't He?"

"He does," Frieda agreed, but she was looking at Klaus, not the mountains. "We head for home today. Anna and Jeanne and Warren must be most anxious by now."

"I know someone else who is likely to be anxious by now."

Frieda did not know whom he might mean. "Whom?"

"Ida and her sweetheart. They are in jail. I thought I would be gone but two days or so. . . ."

Frieda laughed, and Klaus joined her. The captain looked at them, then politely looked away.

"What will you do with them, darling?"

"The avener at Hohenstein has been begging for an experienced groom, so I thought I would send him there. Ida had agreed to marry Hans, so she will go there, too."

"They deserve each other, I suppose," she said.

"That is what Father and I thought."

☙

Four days later they arrived home. Frieda had enjoyed the trip, but coming home was even better somehow. People greeted them in the hall, but Frieda did not see Jeanne, Warren, or Anna, the people she most wanted to see. She looked at Klaus to see if he was wondering, but he looked satisfied.

Hand in hand, they ascended the stairs, and Klaus allowed her to enter their bedchamber first. Jeanne greeted her with a glad smile and a hug. Frieda hugged her in return, moved to tears. "Oh, madame, how sorry I am for being so cold. Can you forgive me?"

"I have already, my friend."

They stepped back from one another and smiled until Anna came forward. She, too, offered a hug, more hesitantly. Frieda took her in her arms and hugged her tight. Anna cried as she asked for forgiveness. "Of course, Anna."

Warren was right beside them now. Anna squeezed Frieda's hands and let go. Warren stepped into the gap his betrothed left and asked, "Me, too?"

Frieda laughed, and he wrapped his arms around her and gently squeezed. He held on for a minute, and she laughed again as she made to step back and Warren still held on. Anna giggled, and Klaus said, "That will *do*, Warren." He sounded testy, but as Frieda got free, she saw his eyes twinkle.

Klaus took her in his arms and rumbled, "What would you need to make you feel truly at home, *Liebchen*?"

"Hmm, without a doubt, a hot bath and clean clothes. I have everything else I ever wanted. Everything."

FOR A SONG

KATHLEEN SCARTH

HUMBLECREEK
INSPIRATION FOR LIFE

ISBN 1-59310-741-2

Cover illustration by Lorraine Bush.

Published by Humble Creek, P.O. Box 719, Uhrichsville, Ohio 44683

Printed in the United States of America.
5 4 3 2 1

KATHLEEN SCARTH

Kathleen writes about what she loves: music and the Lord. Kathy can sing and play a variety of instruments. She also loves history and chose old Germany, a location not often seen in historical novels, for the setting of her books. Kathy lives in Oregon with her husband and two youngest children and works in sales.

For Franci, my daughter and friend,
who is always asking for more chapters

Chapter 1

Adlerschloss
Southwestern Bavaria
AD 1327

A n untimely March snow melted in the thin morning sunshine as Margarethe hugged herself for warmth at the open castle window. Though she wore a blue wool tunic over her woolen smock and a purple velvet surcoat over that, it was still much too cold to be comfortable. But Father Bernard had not yet arrived for her lessons, and she refused to sit by the fire like some old village woman at her spinning wheel.

This third-story window in the room where she had studied since she was seven offered a view of both bailey and countryside. She knew every outbuilding, the stables, the gardens, the great round towers atop crenelated walls. Uncle Einhard was quite proud of his castle, built in the modern style in this, the fourteenth century since the coming of Christ.

She could see beyond the walls to rolling hills and forests, fertile farmlands stirring to life beneath the light mantle of white. And far beyond that, the great, dark forest, shrouded in fog and mist. Somewhere out there—over the horizon and many furlongs distant—there was fighting and bloodshed. But here in her own corner of Bavaria, the seasons came and went on schedule, undisturbed by man's foolish disputes over boundaries and borders.

Margarethe left off her musings, for she had spotted something more interesting nearer at hand. A kitchen maid, plump as a Christmas pudding, stood against the stone wall by the brewery door. She glanced up, her mouth dropping open as she met Margarethe's eye, then took her hand from the folds of her russet cloak to reveal a large snowball. Margarethe grinned and put a finger to her lips, signaling her complicity. The maid resumed her vigil in anticipation of the ambush.

At that moment Margarethe heard Father Bernard's ponderous approach through the rushes in the hallway and tucked a stray wisp of hair back under her cap. She turned and beckoned him over to the window. He joined her just in time to see the kitchen maid hurl her snowball at the brewer.

It struck the fellow on the shoulder, and he started after the maid but slipped in the mud, flailing his arms and legs to avoid a fall. The maid's laughter rang out, rising to drift through the open shutters and mingle with

Margarethe's and Father Bernard's. Hearing them, the ruddy-faced brewer looked up and gave a jaunty little wave, upon which Father Bernard saluted him and turned to Margarethe, who closed the shutters and drew the draperies against the chill.

"A good morning to you, my lady. Pray forgive my tardiness. I was detained by your uncle." He bowed and smiled.

Margarethe's breath caught in her throat at the sadness clouding his dear old face. Father Bernard took her arm and led her over to the study table near the fire. "Did my uncle say something that would lead you to believe he is thinking of. . .ending my time as your student soon?"

Father Bernard was exceedingly gentle as he seated her. "He is considering several matrimonial prospects for you now that you have seen sixteen summers."

Margarethe sighed and settled into her chair at the spot where she had studied for nearly nine years. "Then I am glad it is too muddy to send messengers to the Schwarzwald. Uncle Einhard can't arrange for me to marry anyone without my parents' approval."

"Your family loves you far too much not to choose wisely for you." He regarded her kindly, tapping a finger on the sturdy oak table, then continued. "Your Uncle Otto will be here for supper tonight."

"He is no uncle of mine!" Margarethe scowled, then quickly sobered. "I am torn, Father. Should I pray that the mud lingers so that messengers can't get through? Or should I pray that the mud dries up so that Lord Otto and his sons will stop bothering about me and go back to their silly war?"

There was a note of reproval in the priest's voice. "Any of Lord Otto's sons would make a fine match for you, Margarethe. All hold lands nearby."

"And holding land is vital to a match, I know." She could not restrain her bitterness and was relieved when her old tutor opened a book to begin their studies.

After the Latin lesson, they reviewed the medicinal properties of several herbs, which reminded Margarethe once more of the passage of time. She had seen a few daffodils this morning blooming bravely in the snow by the herb garden.

Father Bernard took his leave early. "Willem has asked for extra time with you today," he said, while Margarethe carefully schooled her face to a look of disinterest. "I believe he has in mind the composition of a new song to entertain your uncle's dinner guests."

"Very well, Father." At the mention of the music instructor's name, Margarethe had felt her pulse quicken. "I am looking forward to our history lesson tomorrow."

As soon as he left, she pulled a strand of hair from her cap, curling it around one finger, then shook out her surcoat over her tunic. Pinching

her cheeks for color, she hurried to fetch her lute and was tuning it when Willem appeared, his steps silent except for the whisper of the rushes.

She smiled up at him, and he held her gaze as he bowed over her hand. He was wearing a new green tunic in a shade that brought out the jade of his eyes. "Good morning, my lady. I see that you are already hard at work."

"Certainly, good sir," she replied, allowing herself a slightly flirtatious tone. "I am weary with studying and, were my relative not coming tonight, would enjoy playing only a few simple tunes today."

Willem shook his head. "Alas, it is not to be. Lord Einhard advised me that a special song was in order for this evening." He slanted her a knowing look. "I thought we might debut our latest composition."

She sighed, dropping the banter for the moment. "I suppose. I do wish you'd let me play some easier part for the instrumental passage, though. My fingers aren't wise to it yet." She looked down at her lute in dismay.

Willem came and sat beside her with his burlap sack of wind instruments. "It is you who composed the words and the melody. And since that passage is my only contribution to the piece, I do hope you will permit it to remain." He dropped his gaze to her hands on the lute. "Those fingers may be soft, my lady, but they are nimble and skillful beyond your admission."

She felt a blush stain her cheeks and hastened to tune the last string.

Willem strummed his own instrument, and they played some chords to warm their fingers before applying themselves to the new song. It was a love song, to be performed as a duet, and it would have been most pleasant were it not for that tricky part.

They ran through the tune several times. Then, tiring of the tedious exercise, Margarethe smiled mischievously. "I think I need your help with this, Willem. Can you show me once more how to get my two hands to work together?"

He cocked an eyebrow and glanced out the doorway. "I would have thought by now, you'd be able to do this quite easily." His look was one of amusement before he tiptoed to the thick timber door and pulled it closed.

Coming around behind her chair, Willem bent over, putting his hands over hers and guiding her through the intricate passage so that she could get a feel for the places where the fingering changes intersected with the plucking pattern. Margarethe, savoring his closeness, missed a few notes.

"You're not paying attention, my lady," Willem chided, his breath warm on her ear.

"Oh, I am paying attention—but not to the music."

His familiar chuckle rumbled deep in his chest. "Play it through once more."

She played it again—better than before. "I think you must be part

magician—you instruct me so artfully."

"It is *you* who have enchanted me—with your skill and beauty," he whispered, then rose to fetch his chair nearer. "Let us try the Schwarzwald tune, but without the lyrics. "I would speak with you without being overheard."

Margarethe nodded and strummed the simple song about the Black Forest, where she had spent her early years. "What would you speak with me about?"

"Lord Einhard has asked that the new music celebrate. . .your betrothal."

She stumbled over a chord. "My betrothal? But when? And to whom?"

"He mentioned May Day, I believe." Willem turned to regard her in surprise. "And you have no notion who it is to be?"

"No. I only know who I want it to be." She fought the lump in her throat, then concentrated on her playing.

They played without further conversation for a full chorus before Willem broke the somber silence. "I have no prospect of acquiring land. My brother is not in poor health, nor is he given to war. I cannot ask him to divide the land with me, for there is not enough for both of us. And I am a second son, as you know, and there is no remedy for that."

"Second sons often end up as priests or monks." In this case, Margarethe mused, it was not a happy thought.

"I am grateful that I did not, else I could never have been even this close to you, sweet Greta."

Margarethe frowned as she played the sprightly number. "I care nothing for land or palaces. I want only to be with the man I love," she said, leaning close so Willem could catch her words above the music.

"But we knew this day would come. I am praying for strength when the time comes, but I fear I cannot bear to see you wed to another. By May, I might have become a traveling minstrel or even a foot soldier—anything to be away from here on your betrothal day."

Margarethe nodded, and a tear slid down her face as Willem signaled the end of the song. He wiped the tear with his finger and anointed his own cheek with it, smiling sadly. "Do you remember the first time we spoke openly of our love?"

"Yes," she breathed. "We would not have spoken of it then. . .except I was so young and impetuous."

"I had wounded you," he admitted with a shrug, "though completely unintentionally. It will be two years come summer—that day when we rode out to our creek."

Margarethe remained silent, remembering.

"You did not mean it, but I, too, was hurt that day," he said. "In my heart

I knew I loved you, though I had not confessed it. We sat side by side on the grass by the creek while you tossed daisies onto the surface of the water. Then you asked me, 'I want to know why you do not love me anymore.'"

"I am sorry, Willem. I never meant to hurt you."

"I know. Nevertheless, the truth of your words stung like the tip of a lance. I had indeed been pushing you away. I could not permit you to continue your childish displays of affection for me. But I should have explained. I should not have turned my face from your kisses or held you away from me without a word. Still, I hoped you would understand."

"I understood only that the man I loved no longer loved me."

His laugh was brittle. "Ha! Nothing could have been further from the truth. I loved you from the day we met—sweet mischief and all. But as you blossomed from a child into a woman, I knew that I must put all such thoughts of love away. Even then, I knew there would be no hope for us ever to marry."

Margarethe stormed to her feet and paced in front of the blazing fire in the grate. "It is all so unfair! That I should be forced to wed someone I *don't* love and be denied the one person in all the world I *do* love!"

When her fury subsided, Willem risked a comment. "I never told you, but I was tempted by your logic."

Hope renewed, she returned to her place beside him. "Were you?"

His eyes roamed her face as he reached for her hands. "I'm afraid so. . . until the next day, when we made up our rules."

"I never did agree to the no kissing rule," she maintained.

"How well I know, little one. But it was necessary. You will be glad one day that you never kissed me."

"But I *have* kissed you."

"Not since you were no taller than a yearling fawn. And not since we both guessed the other's true feelings."

"Only because you will not let me!" She pursed her lips in a pout. "Tell me again why we may not kiss anymore."

Willem's usual explanation was accompanied by a playful grin. "Because once your lips have touched mine, you would be completely spoiled for anyone else's kisses forever."

"Oh, now I remember." She gave him a coy smile. "Sometimes I feel I should like to take a chance, though. Then at least I would have something pleasant to remember you by."

"Ah, *Liebchen,* we are not prophets that we can foretell the future. Perhaps there is still a chance for us." Margarethe searched his eyes, but they held no spark of promise. "Come, let's stand and stretch. We should practice the vocals before the hour's end."

She heaved another sigh and rose. "Could we stand near the window

then? I want to see if our kitchen maid is still throwing snowballs."

Willem led the way to the window and opened the shutters, then tipped his head to one side as he studied the landscape. "Snowballs? You have not looked out lately. There is no snow."

Margarethe followed his gaze. Out in the fields, where the snow had melted into the soft bosom of the earth, there was the hint of greening.

Chapter 2

S upper was a lavish affair. Following an oxtail soup flavored with leeks and garlic, the servants processed from the kitchens, bearing great platters of roasted pheasant nested in a bed of rice, wild boar with apples, and a rack of lamb. There were cheeses and breads and even exotic preserved foods from Spain.

Much to Margarethe's discomfort, Lord Otto and his four sons were seated at her table, along with Lord Einhard and Lady Mechthild. So there was to be no escape from boring conversation this night. It was all she could do to avoid casting glances in Willem's direction. As was the custom, he, along with the other hirelings of the household, was seated at a lower table off to the side.

She made the best of the situation, chatting with her dinner companions, but welcomed the meal's finale—an elegant marzipan fashioned in the shape of a bear, the heraldic symbol of the House of Beroburg, in honor of their guest and his family. Now maybe they could get on with the musical entertainment, which—next to Willem—was her true passion in life.

His light touch on her shoulder sent a trail of tingles down her spine, and she rose to join him in front of the assembled guests, grateful for his rescue. They strummed a few chords, then began with some of the older songs, calling for the assembled crowd to join in on the chorus.

After a time, Willem whispered, "Are you ready to try the new piece, my lady?"

"As ready as I shall ever be," she assured him, willing away the queasy feeling in the pit of her stomach. What if they didn't find her melody pleasing?

He gave her a furtive wink and turned to address the hall. Margarethe was attending to the tuning of her lute, so she missed his opening remarks until she heard him mention her name. "My lady wrote the song—both words and music. As her instructor, I could hardly allow such audacity—" he paused to allow for a ripple of laughter— "so added an instrumental passage of my own. But for that single addition, this is the Lady Margarethe's own composition."

Willem's eyes twinkled as he glanced at her. She could hardly miss the fact that he was as handsome as ever—dressed as well as any of the lords in attendance, but in brighter colors. His parti-colored green and purple tunic

reflected her own gown tonight, as he had requested. And even her aunt had entered into the preparations, persuading her to leave off her girlish cap and substitute instead a veil and circlet. The effect, she'd had to admit, was quite different from her everyday look. "Enchanting," Willem had murmured just before they'd taken the stage.

He nodded his readiness now, and she led out on the lute. It was always a joy to perform with him, but tonight it was as if they had been created to sing together, so flawlessly did their voices blend.

They sang the simple verses by turns, beginning with Margarethe:

> *"Cheerful did the sun shine, sparkling on the brook,*
> *When my love came calling and on him I did look.*
> *In truth he was a fair one, wise and merry, too;*
> *And if he never leaves me, then I'll believe him true."*

The next lines suited Willem's elegant tenor:

> *"A lovely maid I saw there, tossing pebbles in the brook.*
> *Her song was sweet, her beauty rare, as on her I did look.*
> *Glad was I to go a'calling on the little country lass,*
> *For she is my dear wife now, 'til all my days shall pass."*

They harmonized on the chorus:

> *"We'll be together all our days—together, you and me.*
> *As ever on the brook flows down, constant to the sea.*
> *As it's renewed by snow and rain, our love's fed from above."*

Willem sang solo, *"I always will be true to you."*
And Margarethe answered, *"You'll always be my love."*

As the last notes faded, a shout went up in the vaulted hall. But instead of an encore, Willem summoned some other musicians to take their place and led Margarethe from the platform. "Well done, my lady. Still, it's best not to overtire your voice," he explained under his breath as he seated her.

She cocked her head. "I am not tired in the least, and we are in fine voice tonight." There. She was sounding like a petulant child, and he would be displeased.

"We shall let them call for us again. Meanwhile, you must talk with your guests." His smile softened the edge of admonition in his voice.

Margarethe wrinkled her nose and glanced about her in distaste. She was suspicious of the reason for Lord Otto's visit. It was more than a report

from the battlefront. Besides, Uncle Einhard was not much interested in Otto's war, as he called it. He much preferred to live in peace with their neighbors, and hardly ever squabbled over a few furlongs of land. There was quite enough to go around, it seemed to Margarethe.

Someone spoke, and she turned to see who had addressed her. It was Gregor, Lord Otto's third son, the least objectionable of the lot. He was rather attractive, but his nose and chin were both too big, which Margarethe reasoned kept him humbler than his brother Klaus, who could have been the model for the Roman statues in the castle chapel.

"Forgive me, Gregor. I did not catch what you were saying."

"I said that not only is Willem a fine musician, but he must be a superior teacher."

She favored him with a smile. "I perceive a compliment intended for me as well."

"Your perception is right on the mark," he replied, his left cheek dimpling. He had a cleft chin, too, and Margarethe wondered how he ever managed to shave around such lumpiness.

"I am grateful to God that my uncle had the wisdom to hire him. My music means much to me and keeps me company when I am lonely for my family."

From her left, Klaus spoke up. "Your uncle has always had your best interests at heart, Margarethe. You'd be wise to remember that in the days to come."

She suppressed a shudder. Klaus would have been appealing were it not for his pompous manner. But she tried to remember her training and concealed her irritation. "Thank you, Klaus." She turned again to Gregor. "When I was a child, you yourself were a good musician. Do you still make music?"

"I sing on occasion. . .but only for my own ears. I am not nearly so gifted as you, my lady."

"Do you play then?"

He held up his disfigured hands. "I have too long wielded the instruments of war, I fear."

Margarethe could not resist touching one jagged scar. "What a pity. Yet these hands and their skill with weapons of war have preserved your life."

Gregor's expression shifted subtly. "So you do care for this poor life of mine."

She was relieved when Klaus leaned over her to speak to his brother. "We are not being considerate of the entertainers," he said with a show of irritation. "Can't you keep still, Gregor, and listen to the song?"

Margarethe could not restrain a roll of her eyes for Gregor's benefit, and settled back in her chair to listen to the music, but not before Gregor covered her small hand with his much larger one.

While Willem pretended to take in the performance of two musicians—one playing a dulcimer, the other, a flute—he was really watching Margarethe sitting between the two sparring brothers. As for a prospective husband, Klaus would seem to be the more likely candidate. As Lord Otto's second son, he was in line to inherit, although it scarcely mattered. Lord Otto's wealth was a well-known fact, and there was plenty for all his sons, even Gottfried and young Albert.

Indeed, each son already held several estates and would likely have more if their father's victories continued. Only one major enemy remained before Otto would secure the valley with its roads linking Stuttgart with Zurich and Munich in the east with Strasbourg and the other great cities beyond. In fact, Lord Ewald's forces, weakened by years of war, might fall this very year.

If Margarethe were to be given her choice of the four unmarried brothers, whom would she choose? Even Albert was old enough to marry, and so she could take her pick. The subject was a sore point between them, and they had skirted the issue several times. But if Willem had to guess, he would say Margarethe might prefer Gregor. He was witty and kind and a fairly good singer.

Just then Margarethe caught Willem's eye, and he lifted his chin in acknowledgment. He hoped that she would find happiness in the home of her husband—whomever that fortunate man turned out to be. Willem himself had been attending Mass daily for the past few months, praying for Margarethe and her destiny.

Though she seldom attended Mass, he knew she prayed, for he had caught her at it in the chapel and in her study chamber. He knew, too, that she insisted on reading the scriptures for herself, asking Father Bernard to interpret difficult passages and asking all kinds of questions most people never thought to ask. But she had always been a curious child, and now that she was a woman, her bright mind still sought answers to the lofty themes of life.

Not long ago he had come upon Margarethe in prayer. When their lesson was concluded, he'd gently asked her about it, assuring her that he would understand if she chose not to share her private thoughts.

She surprised him by replying right away. "I was praying that I will be a good wife to. . .my future husband."

He nodded, a little sadly. "Then your prayers will be answered. As long as your relatives draw breath, you may be assured of having a husband."

She shook her head. "No. You don't understand. I pray for my future husband's safety and welfare, and that he will be blessed in every way. That he will love the Lord with all his heart, and I pray for. . .other things."

"Those are worthy prayers to be sure, my lady. I know that they will

be heard. Dare I ask what 'other things' you might have mentioned to the Almighty?"

Eyes downcast, she went on. "It is something very important about my husband. Father Bernard has taught me that the Scriptures instruct us to ask for what we want and to keep on asking—like knocking on a door until is opened, or seeking some lost thing until it is found." She grew pensive, and he waited. "Oh, Willem, I hope you don't think me a foolish child."

"Never, Margarethe," he said. "Tell me what it is you ask for."

"I have asked God to give me you for a husband. I believe if He can do anything—anything at all—then even this request is not beyond Him. . . ." With that, she broke down, sobbing pitifully, and he felt his heart wrench. What she was asking was completely impossible.

"I love you so, little Greta. And I will join you in that prayer, no matter how hopeless it seems," he promised.

As soon as he had uttered the words, he regretted them. But a promise given was a promise he intended to honor, no matter what. . . .

A sudden outburst from the dais brought Willem back to the present, in time to see Gregor capture Margarethe's hand. So. It was *this* son who would win her. That is, if God did not see fit to intervene. Willem might not be a warrior, only a simple musician. But he would storm the very gates of heaven with his petition for the love of his lady.

☙

Margarethe was most eager to see Willem this morning after their rousing success of the night before. Many people had told her how much they had enjoyed her song. Even Aunt Mechthild had seemed moved.

"You played and sang like an angel last night, my lady," Willem said when he joined her for their lesson. "Everyone is commending me as an exceptional instructor now."

Margarethe's joy was full. "They speak the truth."

"It is the student who makes the teacher proud," he said softly, lightly tracing her profile with one finger.

"We do sing and play well together, don't we?" She watched as he placed his lute on the table and turned back to her.

"That we do, my lady. Would that we could spend the rest of our lives discovering other things we do well together."

As naturally as breathing, Margarethe reached out as he drew steadily nearer, so close that she could see the little flecks of hazel in his eyes. "Kiss me, Willem. Please."

He swallowed and shook his head. "It would make matters worse, I fear." Despite his words, the next thing she knew, she was in his arms, hearing his whispered words, ragged with emotion. "I love you, my lady. I would die for you."

15

He had never held her this way before, and Margarethe scarcely moved, not wanting the moment to end. "I love you, too, Willem."

The moment was shattered by her uncle's stern voice from the doorway. "Margarethe. I will have a word with you."

They sprang apart, and Margarethe noticed the stricken look on Willem's face. She tried to still her own pounding heart and spoke as nearly normally as possible. "Yes, Uncle."

"I would speak with you also, Willem. Later. Wait for me in my office chamber."

"Please, my lord. Lady Margarethe is innocent. I was pleased with her performance last night and was over-familiar in my congratulations, that's all."

Lord Einhard put up his hand. "In my office, please, Willem."

"Yes, my lord." Willem bowed stiffly and moved past him, glancing back at Margarethe, who ached for him and could give him no sign since her uncle was regarding her steadily.

"So, Margarethe," her uncle began the instant Willem was out the door, "is what I overheard true?"

"Yes, Uncle," she said, then shook her head in confusion. "That is—he was congratulating me, but I am not innocent. I offered the embrace."

Uncle Einhard's glassy-eyed stare was unreadable. "I also came to congratulate you. Your performance last night was superb. You have become a fine musician under that young man's instruction."

"Thank you, Uncle," Margarethe responded, her eyes stinging. What would her uncle do now? She shivered involuntarily as he walked up to her and cupped her chin in one hand, slowly tilting her head to look deep into her eyes.

"Do you love him, *Liebchen*?"

Margarethe took a deep breath. "Yes, Uncle, I do. I didn't mean to love him, for I know he can never be a husband to me. But he did nothing to encourage me. In fact, he. . ."

Uncle Einhard silenced her with an uplifted hand. "Greta, you are of an age to marry. I want you to be happy, as do Mechthild and your parents. You will have a say in the matter when the time comes. It is unfortunate that Willem cannot be considered as a prospect, for he is a man of honor and a nobleman. But he holds no land, and I cannot risk your future. Please understand."

"I do understand, Uncle. I only wish that things could be different."

After her uncle left, Margarethe looked out the window, wondering what would come to pass. She knew Willem's story would match hers, for he would simply tell the truth as she had done. They would not reveal the depth of their feelings for one another, but otherwise, they had nothing to hide.

FOR A SONG

From the day they had met when she was but a girl of eleven, Willem had always treated her as a lady, had ever been considerate of her. When she stumbled over her chords, he did not laugh. And when she needed correction for some childish infraction, he was gentle. He had listened to her dreams and trusted her enough to share his dreams with her.

Margarethe wept softly as she thought of him now, facing her uncle alone in his chamber. What would Uncle Einhard do? He was a good man, a kind uncle to her, but he dealt with wrongdoers swiftly. And in the eyes of all those in authority—God and man alike—Willem was guilty.

Chapter 3

Waiting anxiously in the lord's solar, Willem prayed that God would grant him favor with his employer. There was no question that he was guilty—of love, at least. Thus, deserving of punishment.

His foreboding eased somewhat, however, when Lord Einhard entered the solar and gestured for him to be seated. "I have just had a most interesting conversation with my niece."

The bearded man's gaze was unwavering, and Willem felt compelled to answer, his voice coming out in a croak. "Yes, my lord?"

"I came to her study chamber to offer the two of you my heartiest congratulations. With your. . .uh, dedication to my niece, Margarethe has surpassed all her family's hopes and expectations."

Willem shifted uneasily in his chair. "I thank you, my lord. But it was God who gave my lady the gift of music. I only helped her bring it to light." Feeling his master's intense scrutiny once more, he lowered his gaze to the rush-strewn floor.

"Up until now, you have been an asset to this household, Willem," Lord Einhard continued. "But I fear that I have been selfish, keeping you on when you might have had a better opportunity elsewhere." Willem looked up, fully alert.

"I wanted to keep you on, partly because of Margarethe's affection for you, of course." Lord Einhard rose to warm his hands at the blazing fire in the hearth. "How *much* affection I have only just learned."

"Oh, my lord, if you knew how sorry—"

"Peace, Willem. Peace." The master turned his back to the warmth. In the morning light filtering through fashionably tinted windows and the flickering firelight, Lord Einhard looked fierce indeed—as daunting as the stag's head mounted on the stone wall above the mantel. Except for the compassion in his voice, Willem would have quite lost heart.

"I've called you in to tell you of an offer that has been tendered by Lord Otto of Beroburg Castle. He left before first light or he might be speaking for himself," Lord Einhard went on. "The position is an enviable one—that of chief musician. There would be no teaching duties—unless you desired them. However, Otto pays well, and he has a much larger household than I and entertains on a grander scale, so many more would benefit from your craft."

Willem already knew much about Beroburg. Situated on the trade route

between Stuttgart and Zurich, the castle commanded the most strategic location of any manor house in the area. From its parapets, one could actually see across the entire valley. The speculation was that Lord Otto had been successful in his assaults because of the ability of his scouts to spy out the activities of neighboring enemies, giving him the advantage.

In any event, the castle was in the thick of things, and Lord Otto's household was an active one, going about the business of war during the spring and summer seasons—and hunting, harvesting crops planted by the peasants, and generally making merry the remainder of the year. It would be an ambitious move for Willem. If it were not for his love for Margarethe. . .

Still, to be near her each day—with no hope of wedding—was sweet agony. Surely both of them would be better off without his daily presence as a reminder of what could never be.

"Would I be leaving your household in a poor position should I move on, my lord?"

Lord Einhard seemed visibly relieved. "Not at all. It is a very good offer—for you and for Otto. As for me—" he turned back again to the fire— "I thought to make use of Margarethe's newly developed talent and offer her your old position. I should think it would amuse her."

And distract her from thoughts of me, Willem couldn't help thinking with a trace of bitterness. Still, that his remaining here might rob his dear one of such an opportunity was a shattering thought. "Greta deserves every chance," he murmured, then regretted slipping into the affectionate name he often used with her.

With Lord Einhard's back turned at the moment, Willem could not read his expression, but when he swung around, there was nothing to betray the fact that he might be disturbed. "Good. I'll send a messenger to Otto at once, letting him know your plans. In the meantime, you are relieved of your duties as Margarethe's music instructor, although I hope you understand that, under the circumstances—" he cleared his throat—"I am not charging you with any wrongdoing."

The man was a saint! And while Willem must leave his Greta, there was no help for it. "I am more than grateful, my lord."

And he was grateful. But there remained the task of breaking the news to his beloved.

∞

From the window of her bedchamber, Margarethe watched the messenger thundering across the drawbridge and wondered what important message he carried—and to whom. She listened to the carefree song of a bird building a nest in the belfry and wished with all her heart that she could take wings and fly above her pain. Then, hearing the sound of footsteps in the hallway, she hurried to see who it was.

Flinging the door wide, she found Willem, shoulders sagging, passing by. "Willem!" she called.

He pivoted on the spot where he stood, and she read his heart in his eyes. "Tell me at once. What has happened?"

"I have been relieved of my duties at Adlerschloss and am to take up a new position at Beroburg."

The words fell like hammer blows. He seemed so remote, so distant. "Can't you tell me more? Have you been forbidden to talk with me?"

"It is not forbidden—" he let out a sigh—"merely unwise."

"Then come ride with me," she begged. "We could not get into any mischief on horseback."

A reluctant smile curved his lips, and she felt hope rising. "I suppose not. But I must notify your uncle, lest he think we're plotting to run away together."

"Now there's an idea—" She bit her lip, realizing the folly of it. "I'll get my riding wrap," she said quickly before he changed his mind.

She donned her favorite cloak, the purple one, lined in blue and trimmed with ermine, then ran down the stairs and out of the donjon. Willem was at the stable door ahead of her, saddling his horse, just as a groom led her mare up to be mounted.

They rode without speaking, past the castle walls and down the hill. Then they took the path off the road and into the forest. It was quiet here, lush with undergrowth, with only the sound of woodland creatures to disturb their thoughts. Here, too, the path widened between the massive conifers, allowing them to ride abreast.

The day was warmer than Margarethe had realized, a light breeze carrying the scent of evergreen and occasional whiffs of daffodil and narcissus growing at random in the moist earth. She scooped off her hood and turned to assess Willem's mood.

He was looking at her longingly, as if trying to memorize her features, and the awful truth overwhelmed her with its finality. Willem was going away!

Her heart swelled with an ache too great to be borne, and she began to cry, gulping in great breaths of air.

Willem nudged his horse nearer hers. "I feel it, too, little one. Is there some way I can ease your grief?"

She glanced up through her tears and seized at the first thought that occurred to her. "You could run away with me. We could be traveling minstrels."

But he was shaking his head. "We wouldn't get far, *Liebchen*. You're this castle's greatest treasure, and you'll be needed now more than ever. Besides, we must be strong—do what is right, not what our hearts dictate."

His hand, holding the reins, was a white-knuckled fist. "What I would really like to do right now is to take you in my arms, but I promised your uncle—"

"*I* made no such promise!"

"Then come here, my lady." He scooted back on his steed and gathered her into the saddle in front of him, nestling her close. "This is madness, you know. If someone were to oversee us—"

"But no one is about. The battlefield is far away, and the farmers are all at their farming. And it isn't the hunting season, so we're quite safe here—and alone." She turned to gaze up into his eyes. "Are you still praying—about our condition, I mean?"

"Yes, sweet lady. I gave you my word, didn't I?"

Margarethe's horse moved off in search of a grassy sot beneath the trees, and Willem allowed his gelding to follow for a few paces. Then he released the reins and pulled Margarethe back against him.

"I do not want you to go, you know," she whispered.

"No. But you see how dangerous it is for us to be together. Only this morning, I held you for the first time, and now here we are again—" He broke off on a ragged breath. "I don't know how I will live without you."

"Beroburg is only an hour away. Perhaps we could meet—"

"No, Greta. After today, we must not allow ourselves to be alone again. You will be another man's wife, and I will not shame you or wrong him by taking such liberties."

Margarethe felt a surge of despair. "But we are both praying, and maybe. . ."

"If our miracle happens, we will not be any the worse for staying apart, little one. But if God has other plans for us, then we will have nothing to repent of."

"Yes, Willem." She knew he spoke the truth. "I will not tempt you again. But when I visit Beroburg Castle in the future—and I shall—I hope you will speak to me there."

He chuckled—that deep, throaty sound she loved so much. "We will always be friends, sweet Margarethe, although after tomorrow, we will live in separate households."

"Tomorrow! It is too soon. I cannot let you go tomorrow." The tears that had been so near the surface spilled over once more, and Willem held her until she quieted and dried her eyes, then kissed them.

"Greta, *Liebchen*, do not stop praying. And ask God to give me an extra measure of strength and wisdom."

She nodded miserably and tucked one of his light brown curls under his hood, a liripipe she had made for him. Though her needlework was poor at best, she had worked each stitch with loving care.

"It is time, my lady. Call your horse. We should be getting back to the castle."

"One kiss?" There was a pleading note in her voice.

Willem hesitated only a moment, succumbing to her plea. "Perhaps one small, very proper good-bye kiss. Can we manage that?"

Her answer was swift—both arms thrown about his neck, her lips pressed to his in a gesture he thoroughly returned. Margarethe let her fingers linger on his face as she gazed at him, her wonder tinged with regret. "Now I know why you would never kiss me," she said. "It is true that no other lips will ever taste as sweet."

"Call your horse," he groaned in mock urgency. "We must get back."

Settled into her own saddle, Margarethe urged her horse to keep pace with Willem's, retracing their path through the forest as the shadows lengthened. By mutual and silent consent, they spoke only of pleasant things, sharing their memories of the day they had met.

"I don't recall what I was expecting when your aunt and uncle told me of the gifted child at Adlerschloss," Willem mused.

"And just what did they say?"

"That it was impossible for you to receive the musical training you deserved at home in the Schwarzwald, and so your parents fostered you to them in order for you to have the advantage of your aunt's talents."

"But she could not instruct me in the viel—"

"Yes—and so I was employed to fill that gap in your musical education." His eyes twinkled with the memory. "Now, of course, I understand why they called in another teacher. All your questions were exhausting them!"

Margarethe's laughter echoed across the forest floor, startling a squirrel, who darted into a tree. "I do not really ask so many questions, do I?"

A sudden sharp crack brought them to a halt along the trail. Willem inclined his head, listening. But there was no further sound and he continued.

"It must have been some forest animal. To get back to my story, I was not prepared for you. I had no notion what a gifted child looked like. And then you came in with mud-spattered clothing, your braids dragging the ground, and your hands behind your back. You curtsied politely when introduced, then told your aunt that you had found a new singer for the hall. 'He will fit right in,' you announced, then proceeded to plop a big, wet frog in her lap!"

"I really shouldn't have done that. Poor Aunt Mechthild. How she jumped!" Margarethe put her fingers to her lips to suppress a giggle. "But you never let me get away with such tricks, did you, Willem?"

"I learned to be wary when you hid your hands behind your back. Besides, your rascally grin usually gave you away." His expression grew sober. "If only you had grinned like that the first time you climbed into my lap, it

might have forestalled all manner of trouble."

"Pah! There is nothing wrong with a child sitting on her teacher's lap."

"True. But the child has become a woman," he reminded her.

They rode in silence for the remainder of the way. And when the castle came into view, they kept their mounts at a discreet distance.

⦾

Lord Einhard called on the jugglers instead of the musicians that evening at dinner, and Willem was grateful for the reprieve. With his departure so near at hand, singing with Margarethe again would have been sheer torture. The jugglers, too, were happy with the decision, since they normally worked in the kitchen and were eager to escape their chores.

Willem had fared well in this house, never having had any duty but that of singer and musical tutor, teaching Margarethe and a few others from time to time. He was highly esteemed and had been given his own chamber, like a member of the family. Therefore, his guilt was all the heavier this night, knowing that he had dishonored his lord and his lady by falling in love with their niece.

Worse still, he had done little to rebuff Margarethe's adoration. With her tender, young heart, he should have taken sterner measures to keep their relationship purely platonic. But in spite of all that, Lord Einhard had not dismissed him in disgrace and had even allowed him to accept another position. Surely the love of God was manifest here. Willem must thank the good Lord for His favor and repent of bringing trouble to this household.

⦾

Early in the morning, before dawn, Willem arose, packed his few personal belongings, and prepared to attend morning Mass in the chapel. Later he would load a borrowed pack horse, being careful of his instruments, and set out for Beroburg. But first, there was a pressing matter to attend to.

In the chapel, Willem prayed fervently, unmindful of anyone around him, so eager was he to set his heart right with God. When at last he looked about him, he was surprised to find Margarethe there. But she kept her hood over her face, as if she did not want to be recognized, and slipped out before any of the others.

After Mass, Father Bernard approached him and spoke warmly, offering a benediction: *"Dominus vultum suum ad vos et det vobis pacem,"* he said. "May the Lord show His face to you and give you peace."

Willem thanked the priest and added that blessing to the prayers he prayed for Margarethe.

She was breaking her fast in the great hall alone at a trestle table when he arrived. He slid in beside her and tore off a chunk of bread from the loaf in front of them.

"Did you speak with Father Bernard?" she asked.

23

"Briefly. He had a blessing for me."

"Good. God will go with you. But I wanted to help, too, so I brought you some cheese." There was a goatskin of wine and a brick of hard cheese, along with another loaf of the flaky bread. "Oh, do be careful! The road is dangerous this time of year. I've heard there are robbers and—"

"Shh." He covered her lips with his fingers. "Where is your faith, little one? I must hurry now before the family comes in. It wouldn't do for them to think I was making things difficult for you by delaying."

"Oh, Willem, there is so little time. And to think that, as a fosterling, I could have dined with you everyday for the past five years instead of at the lord's table. And now it is too late," she moaned. "Tonight you will sit at meat in Lord Otto's house."

He nodded. "We may well think of other things we could have done differently over the next few days—" and months *and* years, he added mentally. But let us remember the good things only. I pray you will be diligent with your music—remember the things I have taught you. Will you sing from your belly instead of your throat? And will you keep your youngest finger handy at all times when you are playing viel, instead of curling it up out of the way?"

"Yes, teacher." She laughed—a tinkling sound that echoed like the smallest handbell. "Some things I will never forget."

"Nor will I, sweet lady. Nor will I."

Chapter 4

Margarethe was grateful for Father Bernard's patience at morning studies. A fortunate thing, since she found herself calling upon it over and over again during her Latin and geometry lessons. When she immersed herself in history, asking many questions, the hour flew. But when it was over, she remembered that it was time for music and that she had no teacher.

"You will miss Willem, will you not, my child?" Father Bernard asked gently.

"You have read my heart, Father."

He chuckled. "It is your *face* I have read."

"I am used to having him around, and—"

"And you love him."

Margarethe cast the old priest a sharp glance. "Did he speak with you. . .about me?"

"There was no need. I knew. I cannot take his place, of course, but perhaps you and I could share some music from time to time."

She nodded, the idea holding much appeal. "I would like that." Father's singing voice was as rusty as an old coat of mail, but he handled wind instruments admirably.

He looked a little shy just now, a novel thing. "I'm free at the moment, as a matter of fact, having no more duties until after dinner."

Margarethe jumped up. "Which instrument do you prefer? I'll fetch it."

"A doucaine, please. I should think sackbut and lute would make an interesting duet."

Despite her longings for Willem, Margarethe was intrigued. "Then you must have a song in mind." She handed him his instrument and took up her lute.

" 'The Lady in Blue.' I will lead out, then. . .well, we'll see."

"I know that song. It's one of Aunt Mechthild's favorites." Margarethe tuned her lute, then nodded for Father to begin.

They were well into the chorus when she heard her aunt's rich mezzo-soprano behind her. Father Bernard switched to a harmony part immediately, evidence that he had seen his lady coming.

At the end of the song, Margarethe put down her lute and hugged her aunt. "I'm so glad you joined our ensemble. What shall we play now?"

"How about 'The Wood Clothed in Daffodils'?"

The bittersweet song was not so pleasing since it reminded Margarethe that time was marching relentlessly toward May Day. At the song's conclusion, and without consulting the others, she struck the beginning chords of '*Dominus Vobiscum.*' Lady Mechthild followed on her recorder.

Once the tune was underway, Margarethe slipped out of the chamber and into the music room, where she picked up a viel, checked the tuning, then reentered the room, playing in harmony with the other instruments.

The combination with this modal piece was haunting, and as the final notes trailed away, the three of them sat in silence, sensing the sacredness of the moment. Remembering that these were the last words she had uttered to Willem before he took his leave, Margarethe felt the sting of tears behind her eyes. "*Dominus vobiscum*—God go with you."

Inspired, she took up her viel again and began to play, her fingers flowing with the mood of the moment. The others listened, and when she repeated the melody, Lady Mechthild joined in.

Father Bernard laid aside his doucaine and reached for some parchment and a quill pen. "This one deserves marking down for the future," he observed. "We must play it again."

He left them then to prepare for the midday meal, and Margarethe laughed in delight. "What a pleasant morning, after all, Aunt. I had forgotten how well we make music together."

"Then we shall do it often. But now you are the teacher and I the student. I must learn how to make a viel sing as you do. The naughty instrument does not behave as well for me."

Margarethe smiled, recalling Willem's admonition. She had followed his advice, curling her smallest finger just so, and it had helped. Perhaps she *could* teach her aunt a thing or two. The notion buoyed her spirits considerably. But it did not remove the ache from her heart when she thought of her lost love.

❦

A thousand little memories plagued Margarethe during the long afternoon. Willem—dining with the other retainers at his trestle table at the noon hour. Willem—astride a stallion, looking as proud as any lord. Willem—tears sparkling in his blue eyes at their parting. . .

Feeling restless, she could not keep her mind on her dreaded needlework. She left the tapestry frame and went to the window overlooking the bailey. There was the little kitchen maid, throwing out a pail of water. The smithy was shoeing a horse. And from here, she could see peasants in the fields—pruning the grapevines. Everyone, it seemed, was busy, doing some useful work. Only she was left with nothing to do.

Leaving the room, she found Lady Mechthild teaching her youngest

child, Friedrich, in the solar. He was seven now and would soon be fostered to another household to further his education. He would begin as a page, like other boys his age, then go on to be trained as a knight, as befitted his station in life.

Her thoughts, apparently with a mind of their own, strayed again to Willem. But only for an instant as she willed her heart to obey. "Would Uncle Einhard be needing some help with the accounts?"

"Why not ask, my dear? He's in the next chamber." The woman turned again to answer some childish question about the story she was reading to her little son.

At the door of her uncle's office chamber, Margarethe waited until he glanced up from his papers. "Oh, so there you are," he said at last. "Is something wrong?"

"No, Uncle. Nothing. I was bored and thought I might be of some help to you. I have been practicing my letters with Father Bernard, and—"

Her uncle's grave expression halted her words. "Come here, Greta." She approached and took a seat cushioned in velvet. "I was just reading some of the proposals offered by your many suitors."

"Then I'm sorry I intruded. I'd rather not think of such things today." She rose and was about to leave when her uncle gestured for her to remain.

"I realize the timing is poor. But you are of age now, and we can no longer put off your betrothal, or your suitors shall all grow tired of waiting. One of them has long since given up and withdrawn his offer."

She was curious in spite of herself. "Which one?"

"Ludwig von Beroburg—the eldest son."

"Oh. He would have been a valuable ally for you. But he is Aunt's nephew, so you will still be joined."

"True. Still, these propositions have been coming since you were twelve. And now that you are a woman of substantial grace and beauty—" he regarded her once again—"not to mention your exceptional talents, it seems the list has only grown longer."

She had to smile. "And will you truly allow me to choose my husband, Uncle?"

"I said you would have a say in it. But I have narrowed your choices to these six." He indicated the stack of parchments on his table. "I would not want to overlook anyone who might be worthy to claim your hand."

"And have you a preference?"

It was clear that her uncle was loathe to answer. "I want you to be happy, child. At the same time, I must take into account what is best for our household. These are turbulent times. We have lost revenue in the fields due to the floods. Then this everlasting war of Otto's has involved us more than I would like." He rose to pace before the fire, hands behind his back. It was

as if she were not even in the room. "Still, it might be wise to strengthen our ties with the House of Otto. I have not supported him in battle as often as he might have wished, being reluctant to lose any of my own men for a cause so far removed from my borders."

He paced some more, and Margarethe waited, fascinated with his monologue, so revealing of the affairs of this family. "Of course, having our daughter Jolan there these past two years has helped, though she can form no lasting alliance since she is too closely related to marry any of Otto's sons."

At this, Margarethe spoke up, unable to contain her disgust. "Uncle Otto is the only person I know who is so fussy about cousins marrying. He's certainly not strict about other things forbidden by the Church!"

At this, Uncle Einhard let out a loud burst of laughter. "Aha! It seems I do recall being served meat there during Lent once—and finding it quite enjoyable, too." He straightened his face. "But Jolan is reconciled to having Albert as nothing more than a cousin, and besides that, we were speaking of your prospects, I believe. As you know, any of Otto's four sons would be an excellent match."

She supposed there was no hope for it, but perhaps she could put off the decision just a little longer. "Will Jolan marry soon? She is only two years younger than I."

Uncle Einhard returned to his chair and narrowed his gaze to look directly into her eyes. Margarethe knew that he suspected this delaying tactic, but he answered kindly. "It won't be long before she has her choice of suitors as well."

"Then I would like to allow her to consider Selig and Helmhold, along with the others. As for me, I shall choose one of Otto's sons, Uncle, for I know it would please you."

Uncle Einhard's gaze softened. "Good. Very good, Greta. I had hoped you would come to that decision on your own. Do you have a particular son in mind?"

She sighed, thinking again of Willem and wishing it could be *their* betrothal under discussion. "Yes," she conceded weakly. "Of those four, I would choose Gregor, I suppose."

Now that she had been so bold, she regretted it at once. "Still, I really don't know him very well. Perhaps I should speak with Jolan about him. Living in the same household, she would know. He could be foul-tempered or stingy or a boor, for that matter."

Uncle Einhard seemed amused, but he consented readily enough. "You're right to consider carefully. Besides, it is time Jolan came home for a visit. So I shall send for her. In the meantime, I'll tell Mechthild that you have agreed to marry one of her nephews—though I'll be sure not to mention which one. It shall be our secret."

He rose in dismissal and Margarethe followed suit, releasing a long sigh. Her uncle's attempt at humor had failed miserably. Instead of bringing a smile, Margarethe felt her cheeks growing moist with tears.

"Greta, dear child, I love you as my own daughter. I know how hard this must be for you. But all will be well, you'll see."

"I do hope you're right, Uncle. It will take me awhile to get used to—"

"I know, *Liebchen*. I know." He held out his arms, and she walked into them, sobbing openly. How many tears had she shed in these past few days? If this continued, she would not have to worry about marrying. No man would want a wife with red eyes and a voice as raspy and shrill as a shrew.

⌘

When Willem arrived at Beroburg, he was greeted warmly by Lord Otto's wife, Lady Edeltraud. "Otto will be sorry to have missed your arrival," she said. "But he was called to the battlefield. Would you like to get settled before we talk?"

Willem bowed over her hand. "I am entirely at your disposal, my lady. My journey was not overlong; therefore, I'm not tired. But I would like to rid myself of some of this mud." He swiped at his mud-spattered cloak.

"Refresh yourself then. We'll talk later." She summoned a page, a fresh-faced lad of about ten, who appeared instantly to show Willem to his quarters and help with his belongings. But the sack of musical instruments he carried himself.

He found his bedchamber slightly smaller than the one he had occupied at Adlerschloss. With the addition of an anteroom, furnished with a table and chair, the walls hung in rich tapestries, his accommodations were even more sumptuous. Indeed, this castle was quite large, having been added on to through the years, including garderobes, for which Willem was most grateful. Other options for taking care of personal needs were either inconvenient or downright crude.

Willem thanked the page and stowed his possessions in a coffer. Then after washing his face and hands in a bowl of water prepared for him, he joined Lady Edeltraud in the solar. She was eager to get on with the discussion of his duties, mentioning a handsome wage.

"And if that is not enough," she said, scanning his face anxiously, "Otto has authorized me to offer more—with an additional stipend for instructing our musicians and fosterlings, if you are so inclined."

He nodded thoughtfully. "You are generous, my lady. When can I meet with the other musicians?"

The lady sighed. Though she seemed physically robust—tall and broad-shouldered—the constant warfare of past years had surely taken a toll on her spirits. "I'm afraid there are only a few—some women and two men. All the others are with Otto in battle. It has not been going well this week."

"I will pray them Godspeed," Willem murmured, his stomach twisting at the thought that he might be similarly pressed into service one day.

Lady Edeltraud waved a hand. "You need not concern yourself. We've become accustomed to this way of life. Now, is there anything else we can do to make your stay with us more pleasant?"

"Well, there is the matter of a borrowed horse. I could return it on the Lord's Day if you cannot spare me on a working day."

The lady appeared to be thinking. "Not even those barbarians Otto fights will do battle on the Lord's Day, so the men will be home. Music would encourage them. I pray you might be willing to play for them then, or do you object to working on that day?"

Willem inclined his head and replied solemnly, "To serve you is to serve Him, my lady."

∞

On his way into the banquet hall, Willem was hailed by a young woman. To his delight, he saw that it was Jolan, striding briskly toward him.

"It really is you, Willem. Then have you finally given your consent to join this household?"

"I have. I might say that you're looking well, my lady." Like his Greta, the young girl had blossomed into a lovely young woman—though she was more like her father in appearance than her mother or her sweet cousin.

"How will Greta manage without her handsome teacher?"

"Ah. . ." To his utter embarrassment, nothing came to mind, and he felt a slow flush heat his cheeks.

"Never mind. Her loss is my gain, for we've been in need of a music instructor. My high notes—when I move from chest voice to head voice—are most unpredictable lately."

He suspected he knew the cause of the symptoms she was describing but restrained the grin that threatened to break across his face. At a certain stage in life, young lads had much the same problem. Her vocal problem was surely related to her age and would settle on its own. "It would be my pleasure to assist you."

"We have all been hoping that you would decide to come here. We've been too long without a voice teacher and someone to help us make merry in these dismal halls. But couldn't you have come sooner? The trip is not so very long except when it is raining or snowing."

"And, of course"—he went along with her jest—"it never rains or snows in Bavaria."

"Of course not!" Her rosy cheeks dimpled. "You'll do us all good, Willem." She glanced at the lord's table. "I had better go. Lady Edeltraud is scowling at me. Well met, Willem. Let me know when you will have time to help my poor voice."

"It is no small gift you have, my lady," Willem protested. "We shall meet again."

He watched her swift departure as he seated himself, then bowed for prayer before the meal. Jolan did look well, and she had matured considerably since she had been his student at Adlerschloss. Such a voice she had, and now that it had deepened a bit, he could work with it. Her sense of pitch was slightly lacking, but she had the resonant range of her mother, Lady Mechthild. He welcomed the challenge.

As the servitors brought in the food, Willem noticed that most of them were women. So it was true that Lord Otto had pressed nearly every available man into service. If this continued, it wouldn't be long before the lord of the castle would be calling on his neighbors at Adlerschloss for reinforcements. Thinking of the home he had just left—and Margarethe—brought a fresh pang of grief.

He was relieved when Lady Edeltraud called him forward to be introduced to the household. "Our new chief musician has agreed to favor us with a song," she said. "Come now, Willem. But please—give us anything but a battle song!"

Chapter 5

In the morning hours, Willem auditioned the musicians one by one, then assembled them as a group to rehearse for the evening's entertainment. In the process, he noted individual strengths and weaknesses, hoping to give encouragement where it was needed. There seemed to be a dearth of enthusiasm about the place—a general malaise hanging over the entire castle. He wasn't sure it was the war only that robbed these good folk of their life and vitality.

Shrugging off the effects of melancholy, lest it settle over him, he set off to find the chapel. At this hour, it would be deserted. All the better. He needed time to pray. For his new household. For the wisdom and discernment to know how to help them. And, of course, for Margarethe and her impossible dream.

Afterward, he strolled in the bailey, dropping by the stables to see to his horse and the pack animal he had borrowed from Lord Einhard. They had been fed and watered and were nibbling at the straw in the stall. He talked with the groom and the avener for a while, then went out again, noticing a commotion at the gate.

No one had expected the soldiers home that night, but it appeared that there had been a lull in the fighting, and Lord Otto, his sons, and many of his men arrived an hour before sunset.

Suddenly there were people everywhere. Knights in blood-stained armor. Squires stabling the horses, lathered from a hard ride. A flurry of maids and pages hurrying to lay out fresh linens for the baths, and extra cups and trenchers in the banquet hall. And Lady Edeltraud quietly supervising—instructing the steward to prepare several additional courses for the meal, then calling for the physician and other healers—including Lady Jolan—to help tend the wounded.

Ever practical, she arranged for a portion of the great hall to be curtained off as a bathing area and hospital. And soon there was a steady procession of servants bringing steaming cauldrons of water, strips of bandaging, and various medicinal herbs from the garden.

Willem wondered how he could help and remembered his prayer not an hour past. This would be his chance to offer encouragement. Music was as healing—to his mind, at least—as any herb, and he went in search of the other musicians to tell them of his plan and enlist their aid.

He was talking with some of them when he heard a manly voice call out, and he turned to find Gregor striding toward him. "Lord Gregor! How good to see that you escaped an enemy arrow or spear," he said as they clasped arms in greeting.

"I am well," Gregor announced. "Are you here for a visit, or has my father finally persuaded you to join this household?"

Willem grinned. "I'm here to stay—as long as I can be of service. And you and the other fighting men—what about you?"

"It depends on word from our scouts. We may be here for the night only, or we may rest another day. But it's good to be home and to have you here." He glanced around to make sure the other musicians had left, then added, "We can use some pleasant music in this drafty old hall. I've been longing to lend my voice to some harmonies but have had no inspiration until now."

Gregor looked so comically sad that Willem laughed. "You shall sing with us tonight. No doubt this group will want many songs."

A page appeared at Gregor's elbow. "Your bath is ready, my lord."

"Ah, and not a moment too soon. A hot bath is sorely needed about now. As for this evening's songs, Willem, I would suggest that long ballad you wrote about the victorious lord—"

"I've had my instructions from Lady Edeltraud. No battle songs were allowed at dinner today."

"So my mother has already made use of your talents." He nodded. "But we are here now, and the men need uplifting. We've suffered defeat lately on the field. Come, sit with me while I bathe, and I'll tell you about our latest skirmish."

Willem followed Gregor into the curtained-off partition, hoping the others would not find his presence offensive. Perhaps they would even be amused.

Inside, Willem dropped down onto a bench that ran alongside the wall while Gregor disrobed with the help of a page. Others stood about in various stages of dress—some being assisted out of their heavy mail and into one of four large wooden tubs filled with soapy water. One such tub stood waiting for Gregor.

He settled into the suds with a loud sigh and closed his eyes. "With this bath and a night's sleep, I may be fit for battle again come morning."

Willem launched into a rousing verse of a tune Gregor was likely to know. It wasn't long before the young lord was singing along, blending his voice in harmony.

When they were done, one of the other men—a knight judging from his age and scars—spoke up. "My lord, what I have heard about Willem is true. He can sing with anyone and make them sound good."

A hearty chorus of laughter rang out through the hall. This time,

when Willem struck up a tune, the others joined in lustily. A good quarter of an hour went by before a page entered to wash backs. When there was a lull in the music, he was quick to take advantage. "Pardon me, my lord, but Lady Edeltraud told me to ask all of you to bathe faster. The supper is cooling."

Gregor frowned. "You may tell my mother that I am not done with singing yet and that I will leave my bath when the songs are through!" he bellowed, obviously pitching his voice so his lady mother would hear.

"My lord, I love my life," said the little fellow, "and do not wish to cross my lady."

Gregor chuckled. "Wise lad—to know at such a young and tender age whose wrath to fear!"

⌒⌒

There was no music at Adlerschloss the night Willem left. Instead, Lord Einhard called for the games to be brought out after supper. Margarethe liked chess well enough and would have challenged Lady Mechthild, but she was occupied in some kind of child's play with young Friedrich.

When she realized that Lord Einhard had excused himself to attend to some business and that Father Bernard was also nowhere to be seen, she approached the youngest knight, who was sitting by himself at one of the trestle tables, his bandaged ankle propped on a stool.

He appeared alarmed when he saw her with her game board and her leather bag of chessmen and glanced about the hall nervously, as if seeking escape.

"Greetings, Sir Johan," she began. "Will you be my opponent tonight?"

"Uh. . .with pleasure, my lady. But I hope you don't mind a short game."

She gave him a curious look. "And just what do you mean by that?"

"I am quite good at chess."

She laid the board on the table between them and got out her playing pieces. "Then mind your moves. It wouldn't be wise to let down your guard just because I am a lady."

⌒⌒

Willem had difficulty falling asleep. It had been Lord Otto himself who had briefed him on the progress of the war, inviting him to the solar while he gave the news to Lady Edeltraud, Jolan, and the rest of the family at home. It was clear that Otto was concerned that he might have failed to consider his enemy's superior strength—now that he had obtained replacements and supplies from some unknown source. To regroup, therefore, Otto had broken off the battle at the first opportunity and had fallen back. In the meantime, he would wait for the reports of his scouts, who had set up a relay system to forward messages to their general.

With Albert's castle in jeopardy, Otto had dispatched his youngest son

there with what he hoped would be an adequate armed guard and a unit of archers. It was not likely that the nearby villagers would be threatened, but they should take no chances.

"I have no idea where Ewald has gotten his extra support," Otto fumed. "He can hardly afford mercenaries, so I fear that one of our neighbors may have reconsidered his alliance with me. If that's the case, we may be facing war on two fronts."

His audience was stone silent as he paced in front of the fire. At length, he looked up, searching the faces until his gaze fell on Willem, and his countenance brightened. "Ah, there's a good man. It is you, Willem, who have fortified us today with your songs and your merrymaking. I was questioning the wisdom of falling back until I realized that the men were receiving far more than a few hours' rest and a hot meal. They've received hope—from your music. Already you are proving to be an asset to this house." He squinted at Willem. "What is it, my good man? You appear disturbed. Is Edeltraud paying you well enough?"

"It's not that, my lord. I was just wondering if you would call for troops from among your allies."

Otto sighed and resumed his pacing. "This is really my battle. But I could use some help. Still, it's a complicated situation. I would hate to risk my friends' goodwill. . ." He seemed to be mulling over the idea but offered no further enlightenment.

"Forgive my inquisitiveness, my lord," Willem murmured, fearing he had overstepped.

"Nonsense. As a new member of this household, you have every right to know what is going on under this roof and abroad."

Sleep was elusive now as Willem tried to retire for the night. His thoughts roiled as he considered just what Lord Otto might do. He knew the cause—protecting his family and their possessions—was just, and Willem had no qualms about lending his support. But Lord Einhard should be advised.

Still sleepless, Willem arose, lit a candle, and wrote a letter to his former employer. While Willem owed his new master his loyalty, he could not put aside his years as chief musician of Adlerschloss. And there was more. He would not desert the one he loved more than he loved himself—Margarethe. If Lord Otto's army lost the war, her life might be at risk as well.

⚭

Albert roamed the battlements of the castle, scanning the countryside for signs of activity. Even at twenty, he was strategist enough to know that movement of troops at night would spell trouble. Indeed, every male in his father's household knew, by the time he was a lad of eight, that an ominous silence could well signal the eve of battle.

At midnight, a scout rode in with the news that a large battalion of foot soldiers was moving in their direction from the southwest. Albert called for his squire and a messenger, the first link in the relay system. "Tell Lord Otto that he is to come at once. We may not have much time before we are under siege."

He whirled to summon a page. "You, boy! Rouse the knights and the other fighting men and tell them it is full armor. But before you do, bring me the captain of the guard. I need a word with him."

"Yes, my lord." The lad bowed and flew to do his bidding.

Sir Jakob was not long in coming. "You called for me, my lord?"

Albert nodded. "Choose the most convincing of your men and send them into the village. Have them wake the people and bid them come within the castle walls at once. They will find sanctuary here."

Such was not the case only two years past, when his father had first invaded this small pocket of civilization, Albert knew. Fearing the lord of the manor more than the approaching enemy, the villagers had refused to take asylum in the castle. Instead, they had faced Lord Otto and his men, confident that their lives could be no worse off with this invader.

In truth, the "barbarian" invader had proven to be a benevolent ruler. Otto had built them a church, lowered their taxes, and otherwise looked out for them in the face of growing political unrest. Not only that, but hadn't his father appointed Albert himself to manage castle affairs, including protecting the people from their enemies—whoever those enemies might happen to be?

He could only pray that they would listen to the knights he had dispatched to warn them. He could only pray. . . .

☙

Leaving her bed sometime in the night, Margarethe fell on her knees, reasoning that if she were to be sleepless, she might just as well put the time to good use. As it was, there were plenty of targets for her prayers.

She began with the one dearest to her heart. "Willem—" The very mention of his name sent a shaft of pain deep into her heart. "If I should not love him, Father, then change my mind and fill my thoughts with more useful things. I know Lord Otto has other plans for me, but I cannot imagine finding a better husband. Not in all of Bavaria!"

She thought of her loneliness and prayed that her uncle would send quickly for Jolan. It would do her good to have another young woman about—someone she could trust with her dreams of Willem. Still, she must guard her tongue lest she speak too much of him and betray her heart.

She prayed silently for a few minutes more until she realized that her prayers had all been selfish ones, directed toward her own sad state. She must remedy that at once, and so she addressed the matter of others—her

aunt and uncle, the cousins, Father Bernard—

Margarethe was unaware that she had been nodding until she awoke from a startling dream. She had seen Albert, riding horseback through a village, crying out in despair! Strewn about like so much litter were dead bodies, and smoke drifted about from sacking fires.

For a moment she was embarrassed to realize that she had fallen asleep at her prayers, then wondered if it was God who had sent the dream. Then, fully alert, she gave herself to a frenzied barrage of prayerlike arrows aimed into the darkness, not knowing where they would land. Only God knew. She prayed her aim was true.

∞

Willem was surprised to see Lord Einhard's messenger, who arrived while the household was still at table breaking their fast. The message must be extremely important and reminded him that he had an urgent message to send.

"Stay, Sir Messenger," said Lady Jolan when the young man handed her the scroll, "while I read this to see if a return reply is expected."

Recognizing the lad, Willem smiled as he walked up. "Greetings. Any luck with that serving maid yet?" he whispered behind his hand.

"Uh. . .yes," said the boy, glancing at the lady, who was absorbed in her letter. "In fact, we are going to take a walk today," he whispered back.

Relieved that he would have swift transit for his message, Willem smiled. "Then you are going back right away! You can take a letter for Lord Einhard."

"Indeed, I would go with you now," said the lady, showing her dimple, "had I not been promised a voice lesson first." She looked especially beguiling when she pursed her lips in that way, Willem thought, wondering how such a thought had come to him with Margarethe constantly on his mind.

The messenger, it appeared, was in no hurry to be gone—despite his plans for an outing with the scullery maid. "I must let the horse rest. I'm afraid I rode him too hard on the way here."

"Then let him rest and ride the horse I borrowed. He needs to be returned to Lord Einhard anyway."

Willem walked out with the messenger and stopped off at the stables to wish the lad Godspeed and send him on his way. He was appalled to see the condition of the horse the messenger had ridden in.

"How would you like to run so far with a great beast on your back?"

The lad had the grace to blush. "I wouldn't like it at all. And the groom has already abused me on this same point."

"He's a good man then." Willem nodded. "Now be off with you. And treat this animal better. Ride and walk alternately on your return trip."

Willem watched the messenger mount up and begin his journey home

to Adlerschloss. Immediately the vision of the familiar halls beckoned. How he wished he could be making that trip right now—back to Margarethe.

∞

Shortly after midnight, Albert was dismayed at the turnout. Only a handful of villagers had answered his summons and shown up here at the castle. But he greeted them all courteously. "Why didn't the others come?" he asked one old man, who had shuffled over to stand by the fire.

"Because they were all warm in their beds and felt no need. They have forgotten the former invaders before you. Begging your pardon, your lordship, but there are few of them who remember the rapings and burnings and such like that went on."

Willem was truly concerned now. "Good sir, would you ride back into the village with my knights and speak to your people? I fear for their lives."

"I will go if you require it, my lord."

"I do not require it. I merely ask it."

The old man nodded. "Then I will go."

Albert arranged for a good horse and a sturdy cloak for the man and sent him out with instructions to the knights who accompanied him. "Take care now. And bring him back with you—along with all the others you can persuade. I think I see the glint of armor in the morning sun."

An hour later, when the knights returned, there was still only a trickle of peasants coming in from the countryside. And when the last of his soldiers, including the old man, were safely within the walls, Albert reluctantly secured the gates and posted archers on the walls.

Chapter 6

L ord Einhard took Willem's letter into the solar to read as soon as
it arrived.

He found Lady Mechthild there, working on her tapestry—an
intricate design of flowers and leaves bordering a forest scene. "What is it?"
she asked, looking up from her loom.

"Willem writes to tell me of the situation at Beroburg. I did not know
the war had taken such a turn. He says Otto will not ask his allies for troops
but may hire mercenaries instead."

Mechthild appeared puzzled. "He hates that practice. Why would he
do such a thing?"

He handed over the letter so she could read it for herself. "It sounds
quite serious," she observed, clearly alarmed.

"I am stricken with guilt that he would not call on me for help." He
rose to pace restlessly, then turned to regard his wife. "Would Otto take
offense if I sent troops without consulting him?"

She cocked her head and gently posed a question. "Would you do it out
of a guilty conscience or because my brother truly needs your help?"

He shook his head. "It is this letter, Mechthild. Willem has always had
keen discernment. If he senses that Otto's army is depressed, then I believe
it. A few extra men might lend encouragement. Besides, hiring mercenaries
could take weeks. Ewald might hit Otto hard before a new contingent of
forces could be ready to fight."

Einhard stood and gazed out the window at the soldiers drilling in the
field below. "I will put it to the men."

෴

The attack—a flurry of arrows launched over the castle walls—came just
before dawn while Mass was being said. Tower guards also reported enemy
activity in the nearby village. It was a minor siege, broken off after scarcely
an hour, thanks to Albert's well-executed defense. There was only one
casualty—an archer on the wall, who took a crossbow bolt in the neck.

Unfortunately, the unprotected villagers had not fared as well, he feared.
To assess the damage, Albert mounted the turret and looked out over the
valley. It appeared that the enemy had withdrawn, but the source of the heavy
smoke was surely other than random cooking fires, built by the peasants as
they went about the business of preparing their morning meal.

"We suspect there might be soldiers still in the village, my lord," the lookout said.

At that, Albert felt a wave of disgust, confident he knew what the marauders were up to. "Any sign that the main body of the army is simply feinting?"

"No, my lord. From what I could see, the main force has withdrawn."

"Then keep a sharp eye until relieved and report any further activity." He waved the young man away and descended the stairs to the bailey to learn the latest from his scouts who had ridden in.

The enemy troops seemed to have pulled back, at least for the moment, but Otto's men, who had been alerted as to the problem at Engelburg and should have set out by now to reinforce the castle guard, had not yet been spotted. It was not a good omen.

Albert summoned his men, and they gathered in the early morning sunlight, plumed helmets gleaming, shields reflecting the morning sun. It was a small but formidable-looking battalion, and their mounts shifted restlessly beneath them as they awaited orders from their commander.

"We must ride into the village at once. Bring back—alive—any soldiers you find loitering behind. I must learn today where Ewald has drawn his extra troops."

Albert then called for his squire to bring his warhorse. "My lord, surely you would not risk your own life on such a mission," the squire objected.

Albert donned his helmet and swung into the saddle. "These are my people, and it is my duty to protect them. You there, Sir Jakob, half the foot soldiers will remain here with you to guard the castle. The remainder will follow me. Forward!"

With that, he moved out in front and, taking the lead, clattered across the drawbridge, down the rutted road, and toward the village at full gallop.

To his horror, the first sight to greet him was the bodies of two small children, sprawled lifelessly along the road. "See to a proper burial for these little ones," he ordered a couple of his knights. "In the churchyard yonder."

Then, noticing the destruction of a portion of the church he had ordered built, he barked out a few brisk orders, dispatching some of his knights to enter and search each building and hut. "The villagers must be persuaded to return with us to the castle where they will be safe," he said. "But go gently. So great will be their terror that even we will be suspect."

Riding down the path in the central part of the village, he saw the smoking remains of several thatched-roof cottages, the dairy, and the blacksmith's hut. But not a solitary soul was in view. They must be huddled inside, poor souls. Or worse still—dead.

Suddenly he was aware of a fluttering movement through the open doorway of a merchant building. "Ho, there! Are you friend or foe?" There

was not a sound. Perhaps it was one of the enemy soldiers, caught in the act of looting. On the other hand, it could be a villager.

"If you are one of us, we mean you no harm. We've come to give you safe escort back to the castle."

In a moment, a sallow-faced, middle-aged woman emerged, holding on to the doorframe, her features contorted with pain and horror.

"Good woman, get you to the castle, where you may find sanctuary."

"I cannot leave my husband," she said, despair ravaging her voice.

"He is welcome as well. Is he inside?"

"He is dead. All of the merchants are dead, save me."

"Then praise be to God who has spared you," he said, not knowing what more to say to ease her grief.

"I hid in the cellar. They did not find me, for the door is underneath the bed. I could hear all the screaming. . .and did not come out to help. I stayed there and let my husband and neighbors die—" Her voice trailed off in a keening wail.

"There is nothing you could have done, madam. These barbarians are heartless wretches."

Albert's squire caught up with him and waited for his lord to turn to him before speaking. "I stopped the rascal and turned him over to the prison squad."

"And here is one of our people who will be glad to hear it. This good woman needs escort to the castle. Make sure she has her belongings with her." He calculated the damage done to her establishment with a practiced eye. "It will be some weeks before she can return—and only when the danger is well past."

"And where will you go next, my lord?" the squire asked.

"To the mill to see what might be left of it." Without the mill to grind their barley, rye, and wheat, the villagers could well go hungry come winter.

Albert moved off, but it was only a matter of minutes before the squire caught up with him again. "My lord, there are so many dead."

Albert glanced sharply at the man, whose usual ruddy complexion had paled to the color of parchment. "Are those who survived now consenting to go behind the castle walls?"

"They are reluctant to leave their loved ones behind. But I think they would be willing to follow us, my lord."

Albert let out a long sigh. "There will be time to bury the dead. But we must make haste to assure that there will be no further loss of life this day."

They rode in silence until the mill was within sight. Before he had come abreast of the oak tree in the bend of the road, Albert could hear the blood-curdling screams of a woman in distress and urged his horse forward, his squire following.

The cries came from within the mill itself, and Albert and his man dismounted. "Tether the horses, then wait here."

With that, he drew his sword and hurried into the mill. What he found there sickened him. A blood-smeared wall. A young woman who lay pinned to the ground by a dirty, disheveled soldier. Another soldier, his face a mask of mockery, holding his unsheathed sword to the neck of the miller, forcing him to witness the rape of the girl—perhaps the poor man's daughter.

Enraged, Albert had to restrain the impulse to remove both the soldiers' heads on the spot. But he satisfied himself with hauling the rapist to his feet and dispatching him with a swift upward thrust to the chest beneath his mail bishop's mantle.

Instantly, hearing the other man's booted feet running toward him, he whirled to face his attacker. Albert was grateful for the protection of full armor, though it made him ungainly, for this one was obviously a seasoned fighting man, all scars and wariness.

Albert's rage fueled the fight in him, and he struck the first blow, which was expertly parried by his opponent. In fact, to his dismay, Albert could not land a single thrust at first, so deftly did his enemy counter every move.

"Is the fine knight getting tired now?" the soldier taunted. "Drop your sword and I will give you a little rest."

Intrigued by the man's accent—one he could not identify—Albert attempted to keep up the conversation. To do so might be crucial to discovering the identity of the invaders. Still, this duel could take much too long, and the girl needed attention and transportation. That, he resolved to supervise himself lest she suffer further embarrassment and shame.

"You have a fine voice, ruffian. Likely you are a singer," Albert baited him, hoping he would give himself away before dying.

"I am the delight of every girl back home," the man boasted, momentarily dropping his guard. "These women here in Bavaria are nothing but simpering fools."

Albert pressed his advantage and backed the soldier to the wall, then finished him quickly. Glancing about the room, he called out to the miller, crouched between his daughter and the body of the fallen soldier. "Miller, are there any more of these cursed soldiers in the place?"

"No one, my lord. Only these two. But they have caused harm enough," he croaked out in a raspy voice.

Albert approached gingerly, not wishing to alarm them. The girl was conscious but unmoving. Her clothes were torn, and an angry bruise was forming on her face and one bare shoulder. She lay in stoic silence—an ominous sign indeed.

"Is there wine or ale in the house?" he asked.

"I don't know," the miller whispered, tugging at his daughter's torn

tunic in a futile attempt to cover her.

Seeing the small dwelling next to the mill, Albert entered, found a gourd, and filled it with water from a pail. He carried it to the miller. "Good miller, give this to the girl."

The miller obeyed, and she sipped. "My only living child," he explained. "My wife died of a fever last winter, thanks be to God, for what has happened here this day would have sent her to her grave."

"Perhaps I can be of some help. May I speak with your daughter?"

The miller nodded and blinked, his red-rimmed eyes tragic in his white face.

"Miss?" Doe-brown eyes—a study in grief—flickered to his for a moment and then away. "She does not seem to want to talk now. But we'd best find the source of this bleeding. Did she strike her head?"

The miller examined his daughter's face and neck, running stubby yet gentle fingers over her head. "Seems the bleeding's near stopped," he said. "Perhaps it happened when the knave forced her."

Albert took a steadying breath. "Would that you had both been at the castle."

"Hilda begged me to go," the miller howled in remorse, "but I refused. Business has been brisk, and I had wheat to grind. 'Tis my fault this shame has come upon her."

"Peace, Miller. This is the fault of those two there, none other," he said, nodding toward the lifeless bodies on the floor.

The girl glanced over at one soldier and began to retch. Her father cradled her head and wept.

Albert left the pitiful scene to speak with his squire, who was waiting under a tree outside. "What news here?"

"Two of the men have reported few survivors," he said. "The strike was thorough, if brief." He surveyed his leader with a quizzical look. "What happened in there?"

"Two ruffians injured a girl. They will not do it again. One of them spoke with an accent of some kind. I will question the merchant woman. Perhaps she heard it, too, and can tell us what she makes of it."

"Did you not keep them alive for questioning?"

Albert shrugged. "It could not be helped. I had to work quickly, or more lives would have been lost. The girl will need transport to the castle. Stand guard, and do not allow anyone to cross this threshold."

When Albert returned to the miller and his daughter, he found them somewhat calmer. "I will arrange for your daughter to be taken to the castle for safekeeping. Will you go with us?" he asked the miller.

But it was the daughter who answered. "No!" she moaned. "Please don't carry me away from my home!"

Albert eyed her skeptically. "Why not? There is a healer, a gentlewoman who will tend your wounds."

The young woman sighed and met his gaze. "People will know what has happened to me and will talk. I would not disgrace my father."

"Nonsense. You have disgraced no one. You are hurt and need attention."

"Could I go somewhere else?" The dark eyes were brilliant with tears.

"Please, sir knight," the miller begged. "My daughter has suffered enough humiliation."

Albert pondered his dilemma. He could not leave his post to take this young woman to some remote region. "I could have a man take you to my parents' home."

She began to weep and whispered something to her father.

"She trusts no one but you, sir," he said in a plaintive voice.

There was no need for further speculation. "Then I will escort you personally," Albert said decisively. "We'll be off as soon as my squire has located some blankets."

Outside, there was a hasty conference with the squire. "I will be making a quick trip to Beroburg, it seems. I need you to ride ahead of me to let them know what has happened here today and to alert the physician. I am certain that our message went astray last night, else Father would have sent help." Spotting one of his knights, Albert beckoned to him, and he came straightaway.

"Yes, my lord?"

"I will be away for a few hours. I'm leaving you in command of this operation. Evacuate the rest of the village and bring them to the castle. I'll go for help."

◎◈

When a minor incident in the chapel called Father Bernard from her lesson, Margarethe went looking for her aunt in the solar. Lady Mechthild was gazing out the window overlooking the bailey where Lord Einhard was addressing his men in the field. "What is Uncle doing?" she asked.

Lady Mechthild put her arm around Margarethe's slender shoulders. "He is asking them if they would be willing to join Otto's forces in their fight."

"Oh," Margarethe breathed. "Then maybe my dream was true."

Puzzled, Mechthild drew back to regard her niece. "What dream?"

"I could not sleep, so I was praying. As I asked God to direct my prayers, I fell asleep. I dreamed that Albert was riding through a village weeping in despair. The village was in ruins, and there were bodies everywhere."

"What then?"

"I woke to a strong desire to pray for Lord Otto's men, but especially for Albert."

Lady Mechthild looked stricken and reached inside her long sleeve to withdraw a piece of paper. "Read this. It's from Willem."

Margarethe scanned the letter. "There is great danger, Aunt. Both Willem and I sensed it when we were in prayer. Uncle needs to send help right away."

"Then we must tell him at once."

But when they looked, they found the men dispersing. Without waiting to consult her aunt, Margarethe flung back the shutter and cried, "Uncle Einhard! Wait! Don't send the men away!"

Rushing down the stairs, followed by Lady Mechthild, she ran out to greet him, pulled him aside, and told him of her dream.

Lord Einhard stared hard in concentration, then strode back to his troops, calling them to attention. "The situation has changed. We must prepare to defend Beroburg. We leave at once."

∽

Willem was working on some music for the entertainment of some special guests when a page dashed into the hall in search of Lord Otto. "Troops approaching, my lord!"

"From what direction?"

"From the east, sir."

For the first time, Otto smiled. "Einhard." Looking immensely relieved, he rose and quickly left the hall.

"Thank you, Father," Willem breathed, striking a chord to harmonize with the prayer he sent heavenward.

Chapter 7

Willem ran to the door to hear the news when it was rumored that Lord Albert's squire had ridden in alone—the first sign that something was very wrong. When Willem learned that the village had been attacked and the message system had failed, he was appalled. Even more so when, in lowered tones, the squire told Lord Otto of a savage crime committed against a village girl.

Lord Otto called Jolan over at once. "I hope you don't mind delaying your visit home for a while. I will need your healing skills for an unfortunate young woman."

"Of course, Uncle," she murmured. "I'll help in any way I can."

He gave her a grim smile, then inclined his head toward the squire. "See that a page carries your message to the physician, then get some dinner. You have ridden hard and long."

"I beg your pardon, my lord, but I need to get back to Lord Albert."

"We will see Albert soon enough. Right now we must summon my knights for a war council."

❧

Lord Einhard's entire household was in a state of chaos at the news that their soldiers would be joining Otto's war. Lady Mechthild, in particular. She had not expected her husband to accompany his troops, and Margarethe could tell that her aunt had been weeping, along with countless other women—from chambermaids to knights' ladies.

So it was that Margarethe made a bold suggestion. "I know it is not the usual time of day for songs in the hall, Aunt, but perhaps it would help to ease the tension."

Mechthild nodded thoughtfully. "A good idea. We could have some music before the dinner hour. Let's sing some of the psalms to fortify our hearts."

Margarethe called over two of the other musicians, who helped gather a few instruments. They started with the psalms as her aunt had suggested, and went on to some other uplifting tunes. Indeed, some said later, it was as if a blanket of peace had descended over that portion of the hall where the stringed instruments and voices blended in celestial music.

❧

"Come with me, Willem, and sing us off," Lord Otto said as he strode to his waiting horse.

This was no invitation; rather, it was a direct command. With his horse saddled and ready, Willem mounted, accepting his lute as if it were a saber from the hand of a servant who stood by.

At Lord Otto's signal, he advanced to the head of the troops just outside the gate, listened to a brief rallying speech, then led out in the fiercest battle song he knew, followed by an invocation of God's blessing on their efforts that day.

As the troops paraded by, banners streaming in the balmy breeze and lances poised, Willem watched with a kind of mingled pride and dread. So many men. But how many would return at battle's end?

The last man rode by, and Willem turned to ride back to the castle when Lord Otto halted him with an upraised arm. "Stay. That must be Albert coming. We'll hear what he has to say."

Near the outskirts of the village, a cloud of dust signaled an approaching horseman. As the rider drew nearer, Willem could see that he was carrying something that appeared to be the figure of a woman, slumped forward in the saddle in front of him.

"Father, well met. Greetings, Willem," Albert hailed them.

At close range, Willem could see that the maiden's face, bearing the pallor of battle shock, was badly bruised and that she was trembling. She did not meet their gaze but glanced quickly away.

"Father, this woman was attacked by one of the enemy soldiers. I have brought her here to recover. She is Hilda, daughter to the miller."

"Greetings, Hilda. Would that we had met under more pleasant circumstances. But you will be avenged—that I can promise you."

"My lord Albert has already avenged me," she said softly, "and it is enough."

Lord Otto then turned his attention to his son. "Did you discover why the relay system failed?"

"The second messenger was murdered moments after receiving the message. I found his body and that of his horse not a furlong from the relay point."

"Then we should have had a backup messenger. Einhard and his troops have just ridden out with ours."

Willem noticed that Hilda shifted a little in her seat.

Albert glanced at her and nudged the horse forward. "That is good news. How did he know to come?"

Lord Otto and Willem fell in beside him, and they rode three abreast. "Willem wrote of our troops' sad lack of morale."

"So you are visiting then, Willem?"

"Ah. . .no. Your father has prevailed—"

"Willem has consented to join our household," Lord Otto said with

surprising pride. "He had written Einhard to ask for troops for the next battle when young Margarethe revealed a dream she had last night."

As Lord Otto was speaking, Willem watched Hilda's eyes grow large and fearful.

"A dream? How so?"

"Apparently she fell asleep while she was praying." Otto recounted the details as he recalled them.

Albert nodded in understanding. "Margarethe has always seen more than others. Would that she could join our household as well."

"God grant that it may be so," his father agreed.

Willem felt a flush heat his cheeks, then caught Hilda stealing a glance at him.

"Father, one of the foot soldiers spoke with a strange accent. There is a merchant woman among my people at the castle. Perhaps she heard it and can help us."

"And the foot soldier?"

There was a long pause. "I could not let him live to violate another maiden." He cast Hilda a quick look, and she squeezed her eyes shut. "There must be others in the prison who could be interrogated. Meanwhile, we have work to do right here."

Lord Otto nodded. "It is a good thing Jolan has not left for her journey home to visit her parents and Margarethe. Her healing skills will be of help to our miller's daughter."

Albert looked thoughtful. "Yes, and Margarethe would also be a good companion for Hilda. They are about the same age, and Margarethe's gifts would be helpful to her."

"Let us send for her then."

Once more Willem had to restrain his emotions, lest his face betray his heart. They rode in silence to the very door of the donjon, where Lord Otto waved off a bevy of curious servants.

Willem suspected that Lord Albert, in his heavy armor, would have difficulty in dismounting with the maiden still clasped in his arms. But when Lord Otto instructed his son to hand Hilda down to him, she leaned hard against the young lord and clung to his surcoat.

Lord Otto appeared completely bewildered.

"The maiden has learned to trust me alone, Father," Albert explained. "But we do have a problem, Maid Hilda," he said, leaning down to speak gently. "You will have to allow someone else to carry you until I can rid myself of this breastplate."

"Forgive me, my lord," she whispered back. "Can Lord Willem help?"

At the nod, Willem hastened to dismount, handed his lute to a servant, and put up his arms to lift Hilda down from the horse's back.

"Use care, Willem," Albert cautioned. "She is injured and cannot stand."

Willem gathered her into his arms and waited while Albert dismounted. But before he knew what was happening, a flash of blue whirled past. It was Jolan, Margarethe's young friend. She took both of Albert's hands and stood on tiptoe to kiss his cheek.

"Albert," she cried, "I am so sorry about your village and your people."

Albert appeared not at all flustered but immediately took her into his confidence. "Greetings, Jolan. This is Hilda, the miller's daughter. She will need rest and quiet and the ministrations of a physician. But in the meantime, I thought you might befriend her," he said under his breath.

Jolan regarded the trembling girl with great sympathy. "Bring her to my chamber. It is more private than the infirmary." She looked at Hilda, lying in Willem's arms. "You will be quite safe with us, and well in no time."

And with that, Jolan led the way to her chamber, where she ensconced the maid in her own bed and covered her tenderly.

❧

As the servitors brought in trays laden with steaming venison soup for the noon meal, Margarethe arranged for an hour of rehearsal in the banquet hall after dinner. Even Lady Mechthild agreed to be one of the players. If nothing else, Margarethe thought, the diversion would provide her aunt a welcome respite from thoughts of the war.

She sat beside Lady Mechthild at the table and talked a little with young Friedrich who was permitted to join them today.

"Cousin, do you remember how to catch frogs?" he asked, leaning up on his elbows to speak to her around his mother.

Margarethe laughed at the child, his impish face all ears and earnestness. "I suspect I'm a little out of practice."

"Well, you should catch up on your music at least after this afternoon's rehearsal," her aunt observed.

Margarethe dipped her head in a little bow. "I count it my small contribution to the cause, Aunt."

"Cousin, I would be honored to help you practice catching frogs," the boy persisted.

She stifled a smile. "How thoughtful of you, Friedrich. But we should wait until the weather is warmer and we can hear them singing in the rushes. Then we'll know for sure where to look for them."

Friedrich pursed his lips in a pout. "They never sing until almost May Day. And that's such a long time from now."

You're wrong, young Friedrich, Margarethe thought to herself. *May Day will come all too soon.*

❧

Troubled by the events of the past day, Jolan rose early the next morning for

Mass. It was not her usual custom, but extraordinary circumstances required extraordinary measures. In assisting the physician, she had learned the nature of all of Hilda's injuries. Of course, she was no child and had heard of such things. But to sit and talk with someone who had suffered such an atrocity was new to her.

If Hilda recovered quickly, she knew that Albert would be greatly encouraged. And so she prayed—out of pity for the maid, out of love for her favorite male cousin. Still, it was Margarethe who was her true favorite.

How she wished they could be together now. Margarethe and her parents had invited her for a visit, and she would have left this very day, except for this dreadful turn of events. Now Hilda needed her, and there was no help for it but to stay. She could not be so selfish as to leave on a holiday or even to beg Margarethe to come here instead. She must do her duty. Albert had requested it himself.

"Help me, Father God," she whispered into the near-empty chapel. "I have no wisdom in such things. Tell me what to do. Or send someone else to help Hilda. She cries all the time, and I don't know how to comfort her."

Jolan noticed that Willem, too, was attending Mass and wondered if he came often or only when he was in trouble as she did. No, that couldn't be. Willem was older and wiser and could handle anything.

Leaving the chapel, Jolan allowed Willem to catch up with her, using his familiar springy step. "Good morning, my lady. How is your patient?"

"She is quiet this morning, thanks be to God. But she cried most of the night. I'm at my wits' end as to how to help her."

"And so you have come to the chapel to pray. A very good start indeed. I trust God will answer all your prayers, my lady."

"Thank you, Willem," she answered, her cheeks warm. "I hope God answers all your prayers as well."

He walked at her side in silent speculation, then spoke up. "If I recall correctly, you are to have a voice lesson today. When would you be available?"

Jolan shook her head. "I don't know when Hilda might sleep, and I don't want to leave her. Since the...incident...she seems afraid of men—" Suddenly realizing what she had said, she clapped her hand over her mouth.

"No matter, Jolan. I know what happened to her. She trusts me, it seems. Perhaps we could have your lesson in your chamber, where Hilda could listen."

The idea was pleasing, and Jolan hurried back to tell Hilda of the plan.

The maiden's eyes grew round. "I would be most happy to hear you sing, my lady, if your voice is as fine as your cousin's."

"Oh, it's not nearly as fine as Margarethe's. She has true talent."

"Margarethe? I know no Margarethe. I was speaking of Lord Albert."

"Oh." Jolan laughed. "I suppose his voice is fair. When did you hear him sing?"

"Yesterday, on the ride from the village. He sang lullabies and other soothing melodies."

Jolan nodded and smoothed her skirts. "I remember hearing him sing to me when I was small. He treated me like a little princess in those days. He always had time for me."

"And that is why you love him," Hilda stated matter-of-factly.

Jolan felt her eyes widen. "I love him because. . .well, because he is Albert. He's a good and gallant man."

"Will you marry him then?" Hilda asked quietly.

"Oh, no. Our family does not believe in cousins marrying. But he will make a fine husband—Margarethe's, I hope."

"I thought she was a cousin, too." Hilda was clearly puzzled.

Jolan smiled. "It's quite complicated, but I'll try to explain. My father, Lord Einhard, is Margarethe's mother's brother. But Albert's father, Lord Otto, is my mother's brother. So, you see, Margarethe and I are cousins, but she and Albert are not."

Hilda blinked and put her hand to her head. "That will take some pondering."

"While you are pondering, I had best go to table before they decide I am not coming at all." Jolan rose and patted Hilda's hand. "And when I return, I'll bring Willem with me, and we will make music. A merry heart is just the medicine you need."

⚭

Margarethe was summoned to Lady Mechthild's chamber shortly before dinner. "Sit down, Greta," her aunt invited, holding a letter in her hands. "This is from Lady Edeltraud, suggesting you come at once. There is something of an emergency at Beroburg."

"Oh. I thought Jolan was coming here to visit," Margarethe said, holding her breath. What if something had happened to Willem?

"The plans have changed. Albert brought in a young maiden who had been violated by one of the enemy soldiers. She is in need of healing in body and in spirit. Jolan is caring for her, but Albert and Otto both felt you might be of some help."

Margarethe frowned. "I don't like leaving you alone, Aunt, with only Friedrich and your maids," she said, but it was Willem she was thinking of. How could she bear to be near him again, knowing they could never wed?

"Don't be concerned about me, my dear." She waved one smooth hand. "I will be fine. I know you have been missing Jolan's company. I wonder, though, if it would be painful—seeing Willem again."

How like Aunt Mechthild. Reading her like a book. Margarethe sighed. "It would be difficult. But we have agreed never to be alone, so that will help."

"Jolan knows nothing of your feelings for Willem, I hope."

Margarethe shook her head.

"Then I trust you can keep your feelings to yourself." Lady Mechthild gave a wry smile. "Even if she is my daughter, I will have to say that Jolan is not known for her discretion, and Edeltraud has enough on her mind without dealing with matters of the heart."

"Have no fear, Aunt. Jolan is also easy to distract."

"You're right, my dear." Lady Mechthild gave a little laugh, rose, and tapped the parchment against the palm of her hand. "Then I will write Edeltraud while you gather your things. Sir Johan will escort you. His ankle will not permit him to engage in battle, but he can ride with you. Is that suitable?"

Margarethe rolled her eyes. "As long as he will promise not to taunt me with tales of his recent victories in chess!"

☙

Jolan's singing lesson went well, but Willem found himself frequently glancing in Hilda's direction, fearful that she might be tiring of hearing the scales sung in a less than perfect pitch. Her eyes were closed much of the time, and he could not tell if she was asleep or listening.

"One last song together, Lady Jolan," Willem said, "and then it will be dinnertime."

Hearing a gasp, Willem turned toward the bed, where Maid Hilda was sitting upright.

"What is it, Hilda?" Jolan asked, rushing over to comfort her.

"Forgive me. But it can't be time for dinner. You've only just begun to sing!"

Jolan laughed, and Willem chuckled gently. "I think that our guest likes music very much," he said.

"Oh, it would be my life," she said, clasping her hands together. "But I have no training."

"Then, when you're feeling better, you shall have some," Willem promised.

At that moment they heard a noise in the bailey, and Jolan went to the window to look out. "It's the messenger back from Mutti. I hope it is the news I've been waiting for," she said.

They sang one last song, a cheerful song of spring that Willem had chosen especially for Hilda's benefit. During the last verse and chorus, he noticed a page standing by the door.

The lad waited for the song to end, then sprang forward. "Lady Jolan,

Lady Edeltraud would have you know that your cousin is coming this afternoon, as she requested."

Jolan jumped to her feet, laughing in delight. "Margarethe! The answer to my prayers!"

Willem stood, scarcely able to breathe. *And to mine,* he thought.

Chapter 8

Willem spoke little during dinner, to the disgust of his dining partner, who had chosen her place opposite him hoping to be the recipient of his renowned wit.

But the only person on his mind was Margarethe. He had not expected to see her again just two days after leaving Adlerschloss. He had thought there would be time to adjust to her absence. She was coming, of course, to help with Hilda, whose care was a little daunting for one so young as Jolan. Still, he wondered what the great God—He who arranges all things—must be thinking to allow them to meet again so soon.

Sweet Margarethe. He knew her every feature, her every thought and feeling. She had hidden nothing from him in nearly two years, when they had first spoken openly of their love.

Once Margarethe's sense of humor had matured beyond childish pranks, she had developed a delightful ability to mimic various castle visitors with an artful expression or hand gesture discreetly rendered behind her veil. It was often all Willem could do to keep a straight face when she imitated some speaker who droned on past all endurance.

Sometimes her mischief was turned on him. At such times, her teasing kept him both amused and embarrassed by turns. One hot day they had gone for a ride on horseback through the countryside, stopping by a creek to rest. Hoping to cool themselves, they had waded into the water. "I don't suppose you would consent to going for a swim with me?" she had asked, her eyes demurely downcast.

But when he had bent over to see if she might be truly serious, she had splashed him, giggling like the young girl he had known for so long.

He chuckled in remembrance, drawing the curiosity of the woman seated across from him. "Were you daydreaming, sir?" she asked with a coy expression.

"Do forgive me. I was merely thinking of going for a swim."

She dropped her mouth, baffled by his answer, and immediately left off any further questions for the remainder of the meal.

❧

Margarethe wondered what it would be like to see Willem again. He had been in her heart constantly since their parting, and she looked forward to the moment. But it would be quite different, she knew. For one thing, he

54

was no longer her music teacher. For another, she must treat him as she did any other gentleman, neither seeking him out nor paying him any special attention should they chance to meet. While they would be able to carry on a conversation from time to time, she must take care not to be alone with him, lest her emotions run away with her. What agony—this forbidden love!

It was amazing that only the day before yesterday they had said good-bye for the last time. Or so they had thought. And now they would again be face to face—though not heart to heart or lip to lip. Never that. Never again.

She wrenched her thoughts from what could never be to the task at hand. She would need to pack only a few clothes for herself. But on the chance that the miller's daughter would need something to wear, having left her home so hurriedly, Margarethe added a few garments that had grown too short for her. Since there were instruments aplenty at Lord Otto's, she would take only her lute.

Jolan would need some help in the use of herbs, so Margarethe also packed her precious copy of *Causae et Curae,* by Abbess Hildegard of Bingen. The book contained all sorts of useful information and had been given to her by Father Bernard who had painstakingly transcribed the copy himself from a copy his sister had obtained at the very abbey in which Abbess Hildegard lived and worked.

Finally, Margarethe put in a few dried herbs from the castle infirmary. What with treating battle wounds and injuries, no doubt such supplies would be scarce at Beroburg.

On the road with Sir Johan and his squire, Margarethe saw that the daffodils were blooming at the edges of the woods. The sweet smell wafted to them on the breeze, the cheerful yellow heads bobbing in time to the music of the skylark. Though the birds of early spring were fewer in number than they would be in the merry month of May, their song seemed all the sweeter.

So lovely was the day and so fragrant the flowers that before they reached Lord Otto's castle, Margarethe asked her escorts to stop so that she might pick daffodils for Jolan and Lady Edeltraud. Pleading his sore ankle, Sir Johan remained on his horse. But his squire willingly dismounted to help gather armfuls of the flowers.

Upon their arrival at the castle, Jolan was waiting to greet her, quickly followed by Lady Edeltraud and a swarm of maids and pages, who bustled about to carry in the trunks and bundles.

"So the late snow did not kill them, after all," observed Lady Edeltraud, burying her nose in the buttery yellow blossoms. "Come in, child. Have you dined? And you, sir," she said to Johan and his squire, "you are both welcome at our table."

"Thank you, my lady, but we have eaten," he said pointedly, directing his words to the young man, whose countenance fell.

Margarethe smiled up at him. "I thank you for bringing me here, Sir Johan. I hope your ankle heals quickly and that you will soon be able to go on to more interesting duties."

Still mounted on his horse, he bowed. "I shall miss our chess games. You are a worthy opponent, my lady."

"Oh, I intend to improve still more. I shall be practicing here with some truly great players. So the next time we meet, you'd best be on your guard."

He bowed again, reined his horse around, and rode away, his laughter trailing over his shoulder.

In all the commotion, Margarethe had not yet laid eyes on Willem. She spotted him as she and Jolan, her arms laden with flowers for Hilda, were starting through the back of the great hall on the way to her chamber. He came straight over, offering to carry Margarethe's lute.

"So you've come to visit then?" he asked, his eyes all merriment and love.

She shrugged, trying for an indifferent attitude and failing miserably. "Jolan needed me to help with that poor village girl, and so I came."

"That's good. Jolan and I have found that the patient loves music, and she is quite wearing us out with her requests. Now you may take a turn."

"Willem, don't be ridiculous," Jolan chided. "She is hardly wearing us out. Margarethe, don't listen to him." Looking about, she gave a great sigh. "I need a large container for these flowers. Now where are all those lazy pages anyway?"

"Ah, I think they are carrying Lady Margarethe's things to her chamber, my lady," Willem reminded her.

Margarethe knew his thoughts, knew that he was repressing a big grin.

"Well, I will just have to find one myself," Jolan said, dumping the daffodils into Margarethe's arms and flouncing off.

"I know the way, my lady. I will take you there," Willem said, his hand light on her back. He glanced around the hall, then lowered his voice. "It may not be wise to count on Jolan for escort. She is a flighty one."

Margarethe laughed lightly. "She has ever been so. But I cannot see around these flowers. Do not let me trip on anything on my way up the stairs."

"Then let me take them." He slung the lute on its strap around to his back and held out his arms for the flowers, his hand grazing hers in the transfer.

"Oh, Willem," she breathed. "Will there be any time for us? Any time to make music as we once did?"

His gaze was tender. "I'm sure of it." Margarethe noticed that his tone was still measured and respectfully distant—as they had agreed—though it grieved her to hear it. "The people in this household love music. I will be playing every Lord's Day and many other times as well. Perhaps there will even be an occasional day off when I can pursue my own pleasure."

Margarethe smiled over at him. "And what would you do with a day off, sir?"

"I would write music and make new arrangements and catch up. . ."

"Watch out!" Margarethe warned. "We are coming to the first step now." She laughed as Willem groped blindly with his foot. "Do you perform all your silliness for Lord Otto's house as you did at home?"

"Of course. I even sang a duet with Gregor—your future husband—while he was in the bathtub."

Margarethe did not dare respond to such a remark and rushed a few steps ahead, then turned to confront him. "Willem," she said softly but sternly, "there are things you should not tease me about."

He gazed at her sadly. "You are right. Please forgive me, my lady."

"Of course I forgive you," she said, striving for a lighter tone. "And if you are agreeable, I will even join your musical group and help you out."

"Now that would be a boon indeed—a welcome change from some around here who aspire to make music but do not possess your gifting."

Reaching the top of the stairs, Willem led Margarethe to a chamber door and paused outside. "Maid Hilda? It is Willem and Margarethe. May we come in?"

"Enter," came a small voice, whispery-soft.

They entered the room, Willem partially obscured behind the mass of flowers in his arms, while Margarethe advanced toward the bed. She felt a rush of pity for the young woman lying there with that great bruise on her face, doubtless more hidden beneath the bed coverings, and untold bruises in her spirit.

"I am Margarethe," she introduced herself. "If I know Jolan, you have heard all about me."

"Greetings, my lady. I hope you had a pleasant journey."

"It was a fine day for a ride. And just look what we found along the way. Jolan has gone for a container."

"Lady Jolan has told me that you are very talented. . .in music. She and Willem have been so kind to let me listen to them practice."

Willem cleared his throat. "The three of us together are even better. And just wait until you hear Margarethe sing with Jolan. Even the angels stoop to listen."

Margarethe was laughing when Jolan burst into the room with a crockery jar for the flowers, took them from Willem, and plopped them unceremoniously into the water, sloshing a bit of it onto the floor.

Jolan stood back a little to admire the effect while Willem found a towel and mopped up the spill. "There, Hilda. Margarethe has brought the outdoors in." Turning to Willem, she said, "Would you please step out for a minute? We ladies must talk."

He gave a little bow. "I'll be right outside if you should need me."

"Yes, yes. I'll call you. Now go." She gave him a little push and turned to Hilda as soon as he had closed the door. "Now, Hilda, you have been in bed for some time. Do you need anything—perhaps to use the privy or take a bath?"

"Oh, please. I would be so grateful. But the bath can wait as long as we can have music."

Margarethe and Jolan helped her out of bed to tend to the necessities. "You shall have music," Jolan promised. "Then before supper, we will see about some other things to make you more comfortable."

When Hilda was settled back in bed, they called Willem in. This time he brought in his lute and a leather bag of wind instruments. "I thought Maid Hilda might enjoy a small concert."

No comment was necessary. Her joy was reflected in her radiant face as she clasped her hands together in anticipation.

"Is there anything special you would like to hear?" Margarethe asked.

"Does anyone play the viel? It makes such a lovely sound."

"I will fetch a couple of viels from the music chamber," Willem said. "Jolan can observe this time," he added with a rueful grin.

"I have inherited my mother's lack of congeniality with the viel, I'm afraid. She is like Margarethe—she can play any instrument. Any instrument but the viel, that is."

"Jolan, we have not sung together in months," Margarethe reminded her. "We should warm up while we wait for Willem. You start."

Jolan began one of their old favorites—a round with three verses. On the second, Margarethe spotted Willem waiting at the door. When Jolan began a new phrase, he took up the melody, then joined in the third verse to finish the exercise.

There was laughter at the song's conclusion except for Maid Hilda, who breathed, "Wunderbar!"

Willem handed Margarethe a viel, and they tuned up. "What shall we play?"

"I was playing *Dominus Vobiscum* with Aunt Mechthild and Father Bernard the day before yesterday when a new song came to me in the same mode. Could we play the old song? Then I will play the new one, and you can join me the second time through."

The first melody—slow and stately—soared to its majestic conclusion, the two viels in close harmony. Afterward, Willem dropped out and allowed Margarethe to play the new tune. As planned, he joined her, blending in a simple harmony. The song ended on a sustained note that rose past the vaulted ceiling and into the heavens, it seemed.

"Oh, Margarethe," Jolan said, "I've never heard anything so lovely."

Willem, too, was moved. "Have you written a lyric?"

"Not yet," she replied and noticed that tears were rolling down Hilda's cheeks. She hurried to comfort her. "Oh, I'm so sorry that the music made you sad."

"Oh, my lady, it's just that it was so beautiful—and now I am wondering how people like you, who can create such beauty, could care for me?"

"It is no mystery. You are one of God's precious ones, and we love you. It's as simple as that."

Jolan bustled over with a handkerchief. "Uncle Otto told me of a new love song you and Willem have been singing, Margarethe. I want to hear it. Would you like that, Hilda?"

"Yes, please," she said. Jolan sat beside her on the bed, one hand resting lightly on Hilda's arm, the other making a commanding gesture in the air. "Then let the music begin."

Margarethe picked up her lute and found it already tuned. How like Willem to be so thoughtful, she thought, feeling another pang in her heart.

He picked up his own lute and laid a soprano recorder where he could reach it and nodded to her. They sang that song, played the instrumental passage without a flaw, and seeing Hilda's obvious delight, sang the chorus an extra time, ending with a repeat of the last four lines.

> " 'Til all our days shall pass,
>   We'll be together, you and me.
> As ever on the brook flows down
>   Constant to the sea.
> As it's renewed by snow and rain,
>   Our love's fed from above."

"I always will be true to you," Willem sang in his rich tenor, and Margarethe answered in her sweet alto: *"You'll always be my love."*

Only when the sun sank low in the western sky did they stop to care for Hilda's needs. But even with the other women in the room, Margarethe's heart was bonded with Willem's once more—as if they had never been apart.

Chapter 9

With the troops coming home the next day—the Lord's Day—Jolan had to plead for enough hot water for Hilda to bathe. While servants brought in great kettles of water, heated over the fire, Margarethe made an infusion of soothing herbs to sprinkle in the bath. Hilda would be able to soak her aching muscles instead of sponging off as was the custom. But to everyone's surprise, the men arrived early, making a great commotion in the vaulted halls.

Jolan was relieved to hear the shouting and joshing among the men. "When the battle goes poorly, they come home sullen and silent. This noise is a good sign," she explained.

"I hope all continues to go well for them, though I must admit I do not understand this war at all."

Jolan was quick to supply a brief overview of the turbulent history of their border. "Back when all this started, Uncle Otto and a few others noticed that we had too many robberies on the roads. Uncle sent out some of his men disguised as merchants to see what was going on. From their report, he suspected that these were not ordinary thieves. Indeed, it turns out they were Lord Ewald's men all along."

"But I heard that Lord Ewald and his allies were stopping people on the road and demanding huge tolls."

"True"—Jolan looked off as if deciding whether to continue—"along with other crimes. And in exchange for the tolls, the travelers were offered protection from the robbers."

"What gall!"

"Exactly. Of course, Uncle Otto and the other honest people asked Lord Ewald to stop this abominable practice. When he refused, Uncle and his allies broke off trade relations. Unfortunately, this only fueled Ewald's resolve to steal even more."

"Why is it that so many goods pass through this area?" Hilda put in for the first time.

Ah, a hopeful sign, Margarethe thought. That the maiden should take an interest in something besides her own sad plight was a small indicator of her recovery.

"The east-west road that intersects the valley is a major trade route," Jolan explained. "It connects with several other well-traveled roads. Or they

would be—if not for the threat of robbers—and this awful war."

She rose to straighten Hilda's bed coverings. "And the north-south route that links Bavaria with the other German lands runs straight through the disputed valley."

Margarethe was now curious about this war she had long disdained to be informed about. "Jolan, what other crimes did Lord Ewald commit besides the robberies and collecting tolls he wasn't entitled to?"

"He is cruel to Jews. He taxes them more heavily than others. And one night in Rogensruhe, he burned their homes and shops, and many lost their lives."

Margarethe was horrified. "How could he do such a thing?"

Jolan shrugged. "I can't fathom it myself. But I do know it triggered the war, for Ewald himself had a large house in Rogensruhe, filled with lovely things, and—"

Margarethe snorted. "Most of them stolen, no doubt."

"Someone went to Ewald's house in Rogensruhe and burned it, just as he had done to the Jews," Jolan continued. "Assuming the deed was ordered by Uncle Otto, Ewald retaliated by declaring war."

"And was it true—that your uncle ordered the burning, I mean?" Hilda asked in a soft voice.

"I don't know, but someone I trust says Uncle was not displeased when it happened."

Then Jolan told Margarethe of the recent attack on Albert's village. "Hilda could tell us more—if she's willing," she said, glancing toward the pale girl propped against the pillows. "Sometimes it helps to share the things that trouble us most."

Hesitantly at first, but with growing confidence, Hilda related the whole sordid story, reducing them all to tears before she was through.

"I'm glad you felt you could share your pain with us," Margarethe said. "And we are both here if you care to say more."

"Thank you, my lady," Hilda murmured. "You and Lord Albert are so kind to take a stranger into your family." She eyed Margarethe with a puzzled expression. "But then you are not a true cousin to him, if I understand correctly."

Jolan grinned and bobbed up from the stool where she was sitting to poke at the fire. "We are all hoping she will be related soon."

"I will, in truth," Margarethe said with a little sigh. "I am to marry one of Lord Otto's sons."

Hilda's eyes grew wide. "Which one?"

"All four have proposed, but my uncle and father have assured me that I may have my choice when the time comes." Thinking to change the subject, which was always burdensome, Margarethe hurried on. "But shouldn't you

get out and dry off? The water is nearly cold by now."

Jolan and Margarethe gently eased Hilda from the tub, wrapped her ribs, helped her into a fresh smock, and tucked her into bed again. All this time Hilda was studying Margarethe with a measured look.

Noticing, Margarethe asked, "Do you have an opinion as to which of Lord Otto's sons I should choose?"

"Oh, no, my lady. I have met only Lord Albert, though I must say he is the finest man I have ever known, save for my father. He rescued me and prayed for me and sang songs to help me forget my ordeal. And all of this without ever mentioning that he was a wealthy and powerful lord. In fact, it was not until we were within sight of Beroburg that it came up at all."

Jolan sat on the bed by Hilda and gestured for Margarethe to do the same. To Margarethe's discomfort, the maiden was still gazing steadily at her. "Albert is a fine man, but I will not tell you which I favor," Margarethe said. She glanced sharply at Jolan. "And you must promise not to tell, either. I would prefer Hilda's unbiased opinion."

"Once you are able to come down to the hall for meals, you will be able to meet all of them," Jolan told her. "In the meantime, perhaps we should ask Margarethe what she is looking for in a husband."

The two women waited expectantly while Margarethe gathered her thoughts. "Well, he must be kind—"

"They are all kind!"

"I would like someone who has a good sense of humor," Margarethe went on, overlooking Jolan's interruption.

"Then that lets Klaus out." Jolan again. "He's as sober as a monk."

"Not to mention pompous and self-important," Margarethe added. She grew serious again. "I need someone who honors God, someone who can sing with me and make music whenever the mood strikes."

"Albert," Hilda began, then blushed at the slip of her tongue. "That is, *I* know that *Lord* Albert is a praying man and he likes to sing. He has a most pleasant voice."

"Yes, he does," Jolan agreed. "But Gregor also likes to sing. Now Gottfried, on the other hand, has no sense of pitch, and Klaus can sing but finds it pointless." Jolan made a face that set the others to giggling. "Klaus will need a wife with an excellent sense of humor, for he has none whatsoever."

"It sounds like a choice between Lord Gregor and Lord Albert then," Hilda wisely decided. "And since I have not met Lord Gregor, I suppose I can be of no further help."

Margarethe hesitated, wondering if she should mention her final criterion. "There is one thing more. My husband must be even-tempered. I do not care to be shouted at or abused. Nor could I bear to have my servants or my children mistreated." At this, she watched Hilda's face for evidence

that she might have erred in suggesting this ugly reminder of the poor girl's recent experience.

Not surprisingly, a worried look crossed the maiden's face. "That may eliminate Lord Albert, my lady. He was quite angry—justifiably so, of course—but he did kill two men in defending my honor."

There was silence while they pondered the matter. Then Jolan ventured an opinion. "I do think it's the only thing he could have done. Else the brutes would have been free to terrorize other maidens. And I have never seen Albert angry—only kind and gentle."

Touched by their concern for her decision, Margarethe wanted to know more. "Jolan, how do you find Gregor's disposition?"

"Oh, I have seen him irritated by small annoyances, but mostly he treats all of life as a great joke. Still, if it were up to me, I would rather have Albert any day."

Margarethe grinned over at her cousin. "I already knew what your opinion would be. You've always adored Albert, followed him around like a puppy." She turned to include Hilda in the conversation. "My cousin was always trying to impress him—plying him with flowers or frogs—"

"Frogs! You should talk about frogs! Hilda, Margarethe was the best frog-catcher around. She would hide them behind her back, then plop them in someone's lap without warning!"

From the smile on Hilda's face, it was clear that she was enjoying the account. Then a sudden frown creased her brow. "Lady Jolan, how old were you when you were following Lord Albert about?"

"Oh, I must have been three or so, and Albert was nine. He's six years older than I."

"Then if you are fourteen, that would make him twenty now—"

Before Jolan could respond, there was a knock at the door and she rushed to answer it. It was a page summoning them for supper.

Margarethe noticed the look of alarm on Hilda's face. "Is something wrong?"

"Nothing, really," she said, picking at the bedclothes. "I'm being silly, I suppose. I'm sure I will be just fine here alone."

"If you feel lonely, we could stay with you during the meal. But after supper, Jolan and I will both be working."

"Working?" Hilda seemed genuinely confused.

"Yes. The men will want music until late at night. I'm afraid we will both be needed in the hall to help Willem," Margarethe said, carefully watching for Hilda's reaction. No doubt the poor thing was frightened of the boisterous soldiers she heard romping about the castle. She certainly had reason to be fearful after the shameful act that had been forced upon her.

Jolan was quick to sense Hilda's alarm as well. "I'll call a guard. Shall I

tell him that only Lord Albert or Willem is to be admitted?"

"Oh, would you, Lady Jolan? I would be ever so grateful." She looked so wan and defenseless lying there. "I do hope you don't think me foolish."

"Of course not. But we shall hope that by tomorrow evening, you will be joining us in the banquet hall. After all, without your counsel, Margarethe cannot make up her mind who is to be the lucky man to claim her hand in marriage."

☙

Willem was relieved to see Lady Jolan and Margarethe taking their places at table. Not yet knowing the full potential of the other castle musicians, he intended to work the two young ladies mercilessly. They would love it!

Right now, observing the warm greetings bestowed on Margarethe by her suitors and the way she responded to each of them with equal warmth, he felt a pang of regret. Why couldn't he be one of those favored few contending for her hand? Still, no one else made music the way the two of them did, and soon she would be singing with him again—even if there was a large audience to hear them.

After supper, Willem called on Margarethe for the first song. They had played for perhaps half an hour when Willem noticed a page running down the stairs and back up again. Following that, another page brought a chair and placed it near the back of the hall.

A lady, supported by the first page, slowly descended the stairs. Even from this distance, he could see that it was Maid Hilda. And when she was seated, he whispered to Margarethe and Jolan, and they struck up a lively tune that the maiden had enjoyed.

While the other musicians were playing and Willem was taking a break, Gregor called him over. "How about that drinking song? We could try a duet if you're agreeable? And Father doesn't mind a little dancing, either, now that the Lenten season is behind us. Perhaps a little Saracen dance music, with the chimes and drums and those wailing shawms. I see some toes already tapping."

Willem bowed. "As you wish. But I'll need Lady Margarethe on the shawms," he teased.

Gregor looked so comically mournful that Willem relented. "Perhaps she won't be needed on all the numbers," he said, at which Lord Gregor's countenance brightened at once.

Willem couldn't help liking Gregor in spite of the fact that this would probably be the man who would take Margarethe from him forever. And he had to wonder what his attitude would have been if he'd known that only a few days ago, Willem had been kissing his intended!

At the end of the song, Willem announced Lord Gregor's request. Tables and benches were pushed against the walls, and the hall cleared for

dancing. As the music played—Saracen-style—the lords and ladies formed a circle and began the ring dance.

Before the first dance had ended, Willem leaned over and spoke into Margarethe's ear. "The next tune will be a couples dance, so I won't need you to play."

"If I don't play, I'll have to dance!" she whispered back fiercely.

"I believe that's the idea."

"How much did Gregor pay you?" she demanded, sounding snappish and not at all like the Greta he knew.

Willem laughed. Better that than speaking his heart. The idea of another man holding her in his arms was too much to bear. So. . .best to get the whole thing over.

He signaled for order as the dance ended, and Margarethe put down her shawm. Instantly, Gregor was at her side, looking smug, and Willem overheard their conversation as he asked Margarethe to dance.

"I'm a very poor dancer, I'm afraid, Gregor," she began. "The music I make requires fingers and lips—not feet. Therefore, I've never learned what to do with them."

"I'll take my chances, my lady," he said with a grin. "Besides, it would give me great pleasure to be your instructor." He gave Willem a sidelong look. "It occurs to me that your tutors have much readier access to you than anyone else."

She appeared to ignore the implication and rushed on. "And for every dance I dance with you, I will have to dance one with each of your brothers as well."

"Then you shall be busy indeed, for I plan to dance with you at least seven times this night. Come, lovely lady."

She allowed him to lead her out onto the floor and even managed a smile as the music began. True to her prediction, she danced the night away—first with each of the brothers in turn, then with Lord Otto and Uncle Einhard, returning to Gregor again and again. It was too much to be endured, Willem thought.

At last, leaving the music to a trio of players who had proved themselves adequate musicians, Willem found the nerve to approach Margarethe. Willingly, she drifted into his light embrace with a whisper of long skirts. He easily spanned her small waist with his hands while she placed her hands on his shoulders. Even in this stiff and formal manner, he was near enough to see the pulse beating in her throat, to smell the sweet gardenia fragrance of her skin. The torchlight cast interesting shadows across the planes of her face as they danced, and she kept her gaze fastened on his until the song ended—much too soon.

Regretting the moment, he bowed low and kissed her hand, then

whispered, "Rest for a while, then we'll sing our song for Maid Hilda."

But when he glanced toward the back of the hall, he could see that Hilda's chair was vacant.

☙

Later, Margarethe and Jolan stole into the chamber where Hilda was staying to see how she was faring. They were surprised to find Albert sitting beside her and singing softly, accompanying himself on a lute.

"Albert, I didn't know you were here. The poor thing will never recover if you keep her up all night," Jolan scolded.

"She asked for music when I carried her back upstairs from the hall. But she is sleeping now, I think."

"Is there any news from the village?" Margarethe whispered.

"Yes. Good news. More of the people were safe than we thought, for they hid in the woods when they heard the troops coming. We had feared many more casualties—or perhaps even capture."

"Hilda will be so glad to hear that when she wakes up," Margarethe said.

Jolan gave an exaggerated yawn, and taking the cue, Albert rose and placed the lute gently on the table.

"I will let you ladies get your rest now. Let me know if there is something else I can do to be of service."

"We will, Albert," Jolan assured him. "Good night."

"Yes, good night, Albert," Margarethe echoed. "And thank you."

Albert tipped his head. "For what?"

"For caring for Hilda so tenderly, and for absenting yourself from the dancing. It saved me several dances, for which my feet are grateful." She winced.

Albert grinned. "Hilda says that you will choose a husband soon. If you make your choice known, that would save you many dances."

"No doubt it would."

"Klaus was just saying tonight how he'd love to have you as his bride," Albert teased.

Margarethe narrowed her eyes. "Good night, Albert."

He smiled, leaned over, and kissed her cheek, then Jolan's, and with a wave of his hand, he was gone.

"Klaus, indeed," Margarethe muttered.

Chapter 10

After Mass, Willem greeted Margarethe and motioned for her to sit across from him at table while waiting to break their fast. "How is Maid Hilda this morning?" he asked.

"Sound asleep. I stopped by her chamber to check on her, and Jolan says she cried out but once in the night. She seems to be improving each day."

"Excellent." He raised an eyebrow. "And your feet?"

She gave him a mock scowl. "Just fine, now that they have rested."

Laughing, Willem turned to greet Lord Einhard who was on his way over to join them. "Good morning, my lord."

"Good morning, Willem, Margarethe." He seated himself beside his niece.

At that moment the servitors brought in the meal—great golden loaves of bread and mugs of cider. After the blessing, they broke off chunks of the bread and began to eat, each apparently waiting for the other to speak first.

"Willem, not long ago I asked you to write some music for May Day—for a certain occasion," Lord Einhard began.

Willem listened quietly, wondering what Margarethe might be thinking.

"We have not spoken of it since, but the assignment is yours, if you are still willing."

"I am willing, my lord," Willem said reluctantly. "But it would help with the composition of the piece if I were to know what choice your niece has made."

Lord Einhard glanced at her. "Margarethe knows that she is at liberty to discuss the matter with you as soon as she has made her decision. She also knows," he said, frowning a little sternly, "that time is running out and she must decide soon. Naturally, she will talk with the man himself before she discusses her plans with any of us."

Willem nodded respectfully. "Of course, though I suspect she was dancing with him just last night."

Margarethe shrugged as if disgusted with the whole business. "Naturally—since I had to dance with each of the brothers, which is tedious indeed to keep track of so many. I may make my choice known soon just to be free of the accounting!"

Einhard chuckled, and Willem forced a smile. "About the commission

for the music—I will double the amount I originally told you, Willem, since you are no longer in my employ."

"Thank you, my lord. I will do my best," he said, a lump forming in his throat.

Lord Einhard leaned over the table. "I know how difficult this is for you, and I appreciate it all the more," he said holding Willem's gaze. "I wish things could be different."

Willem sensed the man's sincerity and wondered at it. Did he not consider Gregor a worthy man for his niece? Or did he favor Willem for some reason? Surely Margarethe could come to love Gregor as other women had come to love their husbands in arranged marriages. It was he—Willem—who would have no wife, no love, ever. His memories of Margarethe would have to last him a lifetime.

He could find no reply for Lord Einhard and ducked his head to consider the spicy liquid in his mug. Just then, he felt a small hand under the table, reaching for his. She gave it a brief squeeze before releasing it. He dared a quick glance in her direction and saw the tears starring her eyes. How could he bear it?

They ate in silence before Margarethe spoke up. "How long will you help with the war, Uncle?"

"I will stay with my troops for another week at least. Then, if all goes well, I will leave them with Otto and go home next Lord's Day. I'm sure Mechthild is anxious."

"As any wife would be, Uncle."

Willem heard the slight catch in Margarethe's voice and knew she was dreaming of how it would be if it were she, sending Willem off to war.

"Is your patient doing well?"

"Much better, Uncle—now that we have found that she loves music as much as we do."

"Have you asked what instrument she plays? It is likely that she has talent. Her mother was quite musical, as I recall."

"Hilda has not spoken of her mother, but Albert told me she died last year of a fever. Did you know her, Uncle Einhard?"

He nodded. "She was a noblewoman, a younger daughter for whom no husband was found. She pleaded with her father to let her marry the miller, and he was persuaded to do so. It was a love match, as I understand it, and they were very happy together." Lord Einhard grew pensive, then excused himself from the table and left the hall.

Willem watched him go, then looked at Margarethe, who was gazing sadly at him. "Why do you suppose he told us that story?"

She shook her head. "I don't think he meant to tell it. I doubt that he even realized how it would affect us until afterward."

Willem sighed deeply. "I am a nobleman, but I would be better off if I were only a commoner. . .one with a mill."

"Perhaps you can find one at a good price and buy it," she teased, then bit her lip as he gazed at her, his longing written all over his face. "I'm sorry, Willem. So sorry," she whispered. This habit of jesting when in pain—he couldn't remember if he had acquired it from her, or she from him.

"I would make a poor miller," he said, going along for her sake. "Perhaps I could buy a pig farm instead. I could spend my days making music and hire a pig herder to do the work. Would you be available for the job?"

Her mouth dropped open, but her eyes were sparkling—more like the old Greta. "Me? Highly unlikely."

Gregor, who was approaching from behind Margarethe and had overheard her last remark, dropped down beside her. "And just what is highly unlikely, Margarethe?"

"Willem here fancies himself a pig farmer, with me as his hired hand. Can you imagine it?"

Gregor joined in their game. "Willem, you've always had a rare gift for searching out a person's talents. Still, I would never have thought of Margarethe as a pig herder until you suggested it. But now I can see it quite clearly."

"Well, I have no pigs as yet, and I have bathed. So why does no one sit beside me?" He threw up his hands. "Even Lord Einhard has left us."

"Speaking of Lord Einhard, he told me something interesting yesterday," Gregor said, turning to Margarethe. "He said that you have decided not to marry one of his other allies, but one of the four brothers of Beroburg. Is that true?"

"It is true. I desire a good mother-in-law, and the others could not promise me anyone so kind as Lady Edeltraud. So I will do what I must."

Gregor's face lit up. "Excellent! You will make me a fine sister-in-law."

Willem watched the disbelief spreading across Margarethe's face. "Sister-in-law?"

Gregor gave Willem a conspiratorial wink. "Klaus will be so pleased. He has wanted to marry you and tame you since you put that frog in his shoe."

"That poor frog," she shuddered, in an attempt at lightheartedness. "But it is not Klaus I will wed. He needs a wife with a very good sense of humor—and much more patience than I."

"He does, indeed," Gregor agreed, nodding vigorously.

Seeing the direction of this conversation, Willem decided to withdraw. "I have work to do," he said, rising. "And it is best that I get to it. If you or your patient should like some music this afternoon, Lady Margarethe, send for me. I'll be in my study."

"Thank you, Willem," she said. The love and longing in her eyes pierced him through, but there was nothing he could do about it.

☙

Hilda was disappointed when she discovered that she had slept through morning Mass. At home, she never missed a service on the Lord's Day. Still, she did feel rested, and for that she was grateful. Jolan, too, had overslept in the adjoining room and emerged sometime around midmorning, yawning and rubbing her eyes.

"Good morning, Jolan," she said, realizing her error almost at once. "Oh, forgive me. I meant to say, *Lady* Jolan."

"No matter, Hilda. I would be happy if we forgot about using titles altogether. It is only an accident of birth, after all, that you were born in a village and I was born in a castle. Now shall I help you to the privy?"

"Oh, I've already taken care of that. I'm feeling ever so much stronger today."

"It is the rest and the healing herbs, I think. Wait here," Jolan instructed her, "and I'll see about breakfast."

But she went only as far as the door. "See what someone has left for us? Whoever it could be is taking very good care of you."

"Yes. . .He is," Hilda agreed, thinking how gracious God was to send her such loving new friends.

They broke their fast together, eating in silence. Then Jolan helped her dress, and Hilda braided Jolan's hair in return.

"Is there anything you would like to do today, Hilda?"

"I need to write to my father. He will have the news from Lord Albert, but he would much prefer to hear from me. That is, if there is paper I can use."

"I'm sure there's some in the music room, though Willem always uses parchment for writing music, because it is easier to erase."

"The music room?"

"Yes. Instruments and music and such are kept there. It is an inner room, fairly safe from the damp. Would you like to see it?"

"I would love to see it—and all the instruments, too."

They left the chamber and walked toward the music room, surprising Willem there as they pushed the heavy door open. He was sitting on a stool at a cluttered table, plucking a lute. He turned at their entrance, and Hilda could see that he had been crying—a very strange sight indeed, for she had been taught that men, once they are grown, never cry.

Without thinking, she went to him and put her arms around him. He put the lute down and returned her embrace ever so gently.

As they drew apart, Hilda saw that Jolan was looking on in amazement. "Willem, what is it? What's the matter?"

"It's all right, Jolan. A small matter."

Jolan stared at him curiously for a bit, then turned to Hilda. "There is paper here for your letter. Do you want to bring some back to our chamber?"

"Or you may use this table if you wish," Willem said, clearing a place for her at the table.

Jolan seized upon the notion. "A fine idea, Willem. You can stay here, Hilda, and write while I make some infusions in the infirmary."

"Very well," Hilda agreed, taking the chair Willem held for her.

When Jolan had left the room, Hilda spoke what was on her mind. "Now it is my turn to listen. If you should want to talk, Willem, I am here," she offered.

Willem sat very still, saying nothing, gazing at the blank parchment before him.

"If you will not, or cannot, tell me what is troubling you, then I will simply pray that the Father of us all, who knows all things, will give you whatever it is you are praying for."

She was a little surprised to see the tears welling again in his eyes—so much so that they began to trickle down his cheeks like a spring rain. She covered his hand with hers and set about to beseech the Heavenly Father to comfort Willem, that good man.

"Thank you, Maid Hilda. You are most kind," he whispered. "I must say, though, that I seldom weep this way—and certainly not before an audience."

She smiled. "And don't I understand tears? I've shed enough of them in the past few days. I've heard that God stores every one of them because He knows our pain."

Without another word, she began to write, only half-hearing the melody he was picking out while she worked. Almost unconsciously, she began to hum along. And when Willem joined in, taking the lead, she switched to an alto harmony, their voices blending flawlessly.

When she looked up from her writing, the look on his face startled her. "Oh, I've taken liberties, I know! Would you forgive me?"

"Oh, it isn't that. Not at all. It's just that I was surprised to hear your harmonizing. If that tune were a song, would you prefer that it be a chorus or a verse?"

"Verse," she said with great conviction. "The melody line of the verse needs to be simple so that the words will be prominent. The words of the chorus will be remembered for their many repetitions." She paused. "But who am I to tell you such things. You're the musician."

"No more than you, it seems, Maid Hilda." He appeared strangely moved. "What else do you know of music?"

"I can sing a little—when my ribs are not cracked—and I can play rebec, shawm, and recorder, the instruments I had as a girl."

"Your mother taught you," he stated, surprising her.

"How did you know?"

"Lord Einhard spoke of her at breakfast." He looked very sad again, probably because he feared bringing up such a painful subject.

"Lord Einhard knew her long ago, before she married my father."

"I see." Willem nodded but did not pursue the matter further. "Do you have any ideas about the chorus?"

"Have you a recorder here? I am under physician's orders not to sing." Willem passed her a soprano recorder.

"Thank you. Now what words have you given the chorus?"

"I haven't written the chorus yet. My head and my heart are working at cross purposes today."

Hilda paused to pray silently, then played the tune of the verse again before launching into something else entirely—a melody that carried the essence of the verse but was bold and triumphant and proud.

Willem stared at her, transfixed. "Can you play that again?"

She nodded and obeyed, noticing that Willem was paying close attention. He picked out the tune on his lute, looking to her for approval, then transcribed the music while Hilda finished her letter.

"Hilda, this may not be the music I should be writing today, but it is a worthy tune. If it earns me a commission, part of it is yours," he said, looking perfectly serious.

"Oh, no, Willem. I couldn't take anything. Mine was only a small idea. You had already done the important work. Besides, I have no need of money." There was no way she could ever save up enough to replace her lost dowry anyway—money lost to the physicians her father had secured for her mother, against all hope.

At that moment there came a tapping on the door frame, though the door was standing ajar. Looking up, she saw that it was Albert. "Greetings," he called out to her. "I was told I might find you here."

"Greetings, my lord," she said, pleased to see him again.

"Hilda has been most helpful with a composition I was working on," Willem told him.

"The lady loves music. I'm looking forward to hearing her sing when her rib has healed."

Gazing at the two men looming over her, Hilda felt her throat begin to close and a suffocating feeling overtook her. While she wanted to flee, her knees buckled beneath her when she tried to stand, and she put her hand to her head to ease the dizziness. Her heart, pounding wildly, felt as if it would leap from her chest.

Albert pulled up a chair and sat down near Hilda, saying nothing.

"What's wrong?" Willem wanted to know.

Albert shook his head, frowned, and whispered, "Play something soft and soothing."

Willem obliged, and Albert held out his hand to her. As the music flowed through the room, her pulse gradually ceased its rapid fluttering, and her breathing slowed. Closing her eyes, she held tightly to Albert's hand.

"What happened, Hilda?" Willem asked gently when the lovely piece came to an end and she had regained her composure. "What frightened you so?"

"I really can't say. I suppose it's just that I suddenly became aware that I was alone in the company of two men. It makes no sense, for I count you both friends." She sat very still, pondering the problem and clinging to Albert's hand.

"I understand," Albert said. "I've had such fears when facing battle—or worse yet, recalling the horrors of past battles. It's as if some darkness overtook my spirit for a time."

"That's it exactly! Do you often have these sensations at night as well?"

"They're worse at night than at any other time. But they won't last forever." She could tell he was trying to comfort her. "As the experience dims, so will the night terrors."

She thought Albert looked very tired, as if he were remembering something even now.

"I, too, have had nightmares, frightening dreams that I cannot remember when I awake," Willem added.

"You have company, I see," said Jolan from the doorway.

Albert smiled. "Come join us. Hilda needs some hugs."

Jolan laughed as she entered the room and put her arms around Hilda. "I have not had enough hugs since I left home myself," she said. "They're good medicine—like music," she said, catching Willem's eye.

"Oh, Hilda," said Albert, "before I forget why I came here, I must tell you that I will be leaving after dinner today. I want to go home to see how my people are faring before I return to the battlefield tomorrow. I can take a letter to your father if you wish."

"I have only to seal it." How thoughtful Albert was, she thought, always anticipating her needs before she asked.

"And since it is two hours until dinnertime and my armor is cleaned and polished, I have nothing further to do. I was hoping to find a chess partner."

"Music is better than chess," Hilda suggested, looking at Willem and Jolan in turn.

Willem frowned. "I have a composition to write."

"It's the Lord's Day, Willem. Write it tomorrow," Jolan said with a saucy toss of her head.

"Very well. Let us have music then."

Jolan was pleased. "I'll go fetch Margarethe."

Hilda thought she saw another wave of pain cross Willem's face at these words. Had Margarethe been the cause of his tears earlier? She decided to pray the more earnestly for both of her new friends.

❧

Where the time flew Hilda could not say. But after Margarethe joined them and they took their instruments to the hall to play, the moments took flight with the wings of a dove. It was all so delightful—choosing and carrying the melody without stopping between songs, until all the music blended in one harmonious whole. At a nod of the head, someone new picked up the lead and started another tune. With the beautiful sounds enhanced by the high and vaulted ceilings, the hall began to fill with eager listeners.

By dinnertime, Hilda was quite tired but happy. Still, seeing her begin to sag, Albert appeared concerned, and she wasn't surprised to hear him say, "You three continue without us. I'll take Hilda upstairs."

She did not protest when Albert picked her up at the bottom of the stairs. "Thank you, my lord. I will be strong again soon, I hope, and will no longer be a burden to you."

"You are no burden at all, Hilda."

Was this how it was with these people? Always tender and compassionate toward others? Or was there some special bond that linked her with this man—the man who had rescued her on the most terrible day of her life?

Chapter 11

After dinner Margarethe rode with Gregor as she had promised. She wore her favorite riding habit to help ease her nervousness and concentrated on enjoying the sun on her face and the spring breeze scented with the perfume of hyacinths and lily of the valley.

The shadow of a cloud slid across the fields as they cantered down the hill; it moved slowly but could not be halted. Margarethe was reminded of May Day's inevitable approach and that she was doing something today to smooth its way.

She and Gregor spoke of many things. Family traditions. Favorite pastimes. The war. Now, better informed, Margarethe found herself in complete sympathy with Lord Otto. "I thought his war was only about land. I never realized how much more was involved. I'm ashamed that I have never prayed for victory for you."

"It isn't too late to begin," he teased her.

"And so I have, good sir."

"Good. I hope you also pray for my safety."

Margarethe thought about that. "Are you ever in real danger?" she asked. "As a captain in full armor, I would think you are much safer than one of the foot soldiers or archers."

"True," he conceded. "But war is still a bloody business, and anything can happen. I covet your prayers, my lady."

Margarethe glanced over at him. He looked so strong, as if nothing could ever harm him. "I will pray," she promised. His smile was quick and contagious, and she found herself smiling back.

They followed the main road for a furlong, then Gregor suggested that they take the forest path. It was cooler here, and Margarethe was glad for her warm cloak. They stopped in a glade ringed with daffodils.

She looked around, delighted. "How lovely," she breathed.

"I thought you would like it." His eyes were for her alone, she noticed, not for the flowers nor the lush forest foliage. She had always been comfortable with Gregor. If she felt awkward now, it was only because of the serious subject they must explore together.

"Gregor, you know you can speak the truth with me, don't you?"

"I would hope so. It's not as if we haven't known each other since we were children."

"This morning you said I would make you a good sister-in-law. . . ." She stopped, her courage wafting away as on a sudden breeze.

"You would, indeed," he said, nudging his horse next to hers.

She sighed. "Gregor, must you put me through this humiliation?"

"I think you are doing very well. Do go on." He appeared to be enjoying this little game.

She shook her head. "I must know the truth about the proposal you sent my uncle two years ago."

"Three."

"Very well then, three years ago. I know it would not be honorable for you to withdraw it if you changed your mind—"

"Not to mention expensive," he interrupted. "When Ludwig withdrew his proposal, he had to give gifts to both your father and your uncle."

"Neither of them shared those gifts with me," she pouted, and Gregor laughed at her comical expression. "Three years is a very long time, and I want to know if you still wish to marry me—if you ever did. Perhaps it was your father who made you send the proposal."

Gregor nodded. "I must admit it was originally my father's idea. But that was back when I was a lad and before you were all grown up. Now it's very much *my* idea." He took the reins from her hand and began leading them deeper into the forest.

"Father began talking about one of us marrying you when he first met you as a child of seven. Through the years, other young ladies were considered, of course, but you were the only one I ever wanted to be my wife."

She smiled at him through a veil of tears and took a deep breath. "Well, since you would probably make a poor brother-in-law, and I do have to marry one of you, I was wondering if you still wanted—"

In the shadows, she could not read Gregor's face as he dismounted and strode over to her. But she could see that he was quite intent as he lifted his arms for her. She slid off her horse and he held her, searching her eyes.

"We are always jesting, you and I, Margarethe. But I truly believe we can bring much happiness to each other. Will you marry me?"

She stood gazing up at him, breathless. The moment she had dreaded was upon her. There was nothing else she could do. "Yes, Gregor, I will," she whispered.

He pulled her into his arms and held her tight. She tried desperately to hold back the tears, but to no avail. Poor Gregor. He was kind and gallant and deserved so much more than she could offer him. But there was room in her heart for only one. Willem. Always Willem. . .

Gregor pulled away to study her face. "What's this? Tears? And this our betrothal day? I *much* prefer your laughter."

He held her closer, and she leaned into him, steadying herself, surprised

to find that she was enjoying his warmth. She felt a stab of guilt. What kind of person was she, and how could she go through with this farce?

He kissed her forehead and stood back to let her look at him while he spoke of serious matters. "I won't rush you into marriage, Margarethe. But I would like your kisses in greeting and farewell. Do you think you could manage that?"

Striving for a casual tone, she cocked her head. "So your brothers will remember whose I am?"

"Something like that. But I am quite proud that you have chosen me, Margarethe. I admire you greatly."

"I admire you, too, Gregor. I always have."

He smiled mischievously, and Margarethe was instantly on her guard. "It occurs to me that if we will be kissing publicly, perhaps we should practice privately, don't you agree?"

She looked up for a moment, pretending to consider. "Very well," she said and stood on tiptoe to brush her lips against his.

He laughed, caught her to him, and kissed her soundly. It was pleasant enough—something like kissing Jolan or Uncle Einhard or Aunt Mechthild. Nothing like the all-too-brief kisses she had shared with Willem that had only left her wanting more.

Gregor seemed disappointed and a little anxious. "I can see that we will have to practice often until we get it right."

She smiled as he gave her a leg up to remount, hardly necessary since her horse was small and her legs were long. On the way back, they spoke of Gregor's holdings and his castle. They talked of possible wedding dates, what to wear, whom to invite. They spoke of many things, but they did not speak of love.

The cloud shadows moved faster and faster across the fields until, pelted by large raindrops, Margarethe and Gregor were forced to gallop for home.

☙❧

In the hall, Willem worked on the lyrics for the music he and Hilda had composed. Feeling the need to be near people rather than closeted away in the music room, he had come here where there was always a bustle of activity—pages scurrying about on some errand, kitchen maids preparing the tables for a meal, and an occasional visitor passing through on an inspection of the castle.

His musical partners of the morning had scattered. Lord Albert had left after dinner, Hilda was abed, Jolan was nowhere to be seen, and Margarethe was out riding somewhere with Gregor.

Truly, his writing was not going well. The music was more suitable for battle than a betrothal—a betrothal, he felt sure, that was being arranged this very afternoon. Just one step nearer to the time when his love would be

lost to him forever. He had to think of something cheerful, or there would be no songs of any kind this day.

Hilda had surprised him with the wild exuberance of the chorus she had been inspired to write. Perhaps it had been born of her recent ordeal—something far worse than anything he had experienced. He studied the blank piece of parchment and thought about her rescue, her faith. The concept would make a worthy song, though the attack itself could never be set to music. It was far too terrible. Still, there might be some way to use its message.

He was absorbed in the process when Margarethe and Gregor entered the hall. At the sound of their voices, he looked up from his writing and met her eye briefly before she glanced away. Then she and Gregor walked toward his parents' solar.

Willem picked up his writing materials and went back to the music room. Solitude was better than staying here to witness what would surely come next.

In the music room, Willem prayed for Margarethe—the prayer he had covenanted with her to pray, though each day it seemed the answer was more remote than the day before. "It's me, Lord. Willem. Father, You know my heart. You know that I desire Margarethe as my wife more than anything on earth. And You know which of us would be the better husband for her. Please help me. Teach me how to pray for her. Help me to desire Your will more than mine.

"I could also use some help with my music—the music you gave me and Hilda. As for the maid, Lord, I ask that she would grow strong in body, mind, and spirit. Hear her prayers and reunite her with her father. Lord, since she may have trouble finding a husband after being dishonored, I ask You to send her a good and loving man who will not hold it against her." He continued, praying for all those he cared about, even Gregor—the man who stood between him and the love of his life.

෴

At supper, there was wine at every table, a most exceptional occurrence since the retainers usually had only ale or cider to drink. Some of the soldiers took the opportunity to drink too much and became inebriated before the final course was served. Willem was tempted, but stayed with one cup.

Against his will, his gaze kept straying to the head table, where Margarethe and Gregor were chatting and laughing together. They seemed quite happy and content. Even Lord Einhard and Lord Otto were in an unusually jovial mood, considering the fact that they would be heading back to the battlefield on the morrow. Only Klaus looked somber and morose.

As soon as the last course was cleared, someone in the crowd called for music, and Willem gathered the ensemble for the first set and began. People

were in a festive mood tonight, which only served to heighten his despair. Attempting to rid himself of his melancholy, he chose lively tunes and called on Jolan to help him.

When Margarethe beckoned, he strolled over, strumming his lute as he went. "Yes, my lady?"

"You can count on me for my share of the music, Willem," she said. "I would be happy to play or sing."

"As would I," Gregor put in. "I know the baritone parts to all the old songs."

Willem was struck with a sudden inspiration. "I will call on you soon. Your lady also."

He noticed Margarethe's grimace at hearing the term. Gregor, on the other hand, beamed with pride.

As it turned out, when the time came for some new songs, it was the four of them singing in a quartet that drew the heartiest applause. Following that performance, Willem wisely changed the mix, using Jolan on small drums and Margarethe on lute. She and Gregor sang an old comic duet that featured an argument between a husband and wife. The sketch was always hilarious even when done poorly. But tonight, with the talent and personality of the actors, it was a great success.

After a short instrumental interlude, someone called for Margarethe's love song. There was no way around it. To decline would be to invite rumor and speculation. And so Willem called Margarethe over and whispered, "Can we do this?"

"Have you stopped believing that God answers prayer?" she retorted.

His doubts fell away as he read the determination in her eyes. "Lead on, my lady." They sang as well or better than ever, and he was cheered by the reception the song received.

When the time seemed right for some silliness, Willem made a great show of selecting a special group of singers—Lord Gregor, Lord Einhard, Lord Klaus, Lord Gottfried—Gottfried rolled his eyes, knowing that it had to be a joke—Lord Ludwig, and Lord Otto. "And I, of course, shall be a part of this carefully chosen chorus." There was a ripple of approval and a few cheers.

With great deliberation, Willem went to each man and whispered the name of a song in his ear. At his cue, each one began to sing a different song. The crowd realized what had happened a second before the men did, and roared with laughter. Willem knew it was a trick that would work only once, but it had been worth it to see the reaction all around. As the laughter began to subside, Willem closed with a worshipful number that ended the evening on a high and holy note.

It was quite late, and many had already drifted off to bed when Willem

found Hilda sitting in the back of the hall. "Have you enjoyed the evening, Maid Hilda?"

"Yes, Willem, thank you. You are not only a master musician, but excellent with people."

He was impressed again with her cultured speech, recalling that this was not some simple village maid, but a woman of noble birth through her mother. In addition, he was pleased with her compliment. "I do enjoy making merry, and I try not to offend while doing it. Are you getting tired?"

She nodded. "I think I shall retire now, but I can walk on my own."

"That won't be necessary when I'm around." He scooped her up, carried her up the stairs, and set her down in Jolan's chamber.

"Thank you, good sir." She stood, gazing up at him expectantly.

"You are most welcome, my lady," he said. He studied her for a moment longer, then said, "Earlier today you said you would pray that my prayers would be answered."

"Yes, Willem."

"I hope you intend to keep your pledge."

"Of course I will, for I know you must have something important on your mind."

"Very important. The scriptures tell us to pray in faith, but some days my faith is weak and I have need of a strong friend."

She smiled. "I prayed today for you."

"And just in time, too," Willem said. "Of a truth, my lot has been bleak of late, but your words give me courage, even though the situation still looks impossible."

"God is good with impossible things. Remember the man born blind? No one had ever healed someone who was blind from birth, but Jesus did."

"I will remember. Good night, Maid Hilda, and thank you for your counsel."

He left the room, and as he descended the stairs, he murmured to himself, "I have much to be thankful for, indeed. I was not born blind. My only problem is that I was born *second*—to a man with little land."

⁂

Remembering all that had happened, Margarethe had difficulty falling asleep. Even her dreams were fragments of the day's events. Gregor's proposal, his kiss. Lord Otto and Lady Edeltraud's joy when they heard the news—a joy that would be for naught if, by some miracle, her continual prayer were answered.

Nor could she forget the look on Willem's face when they came into the hall. His pain was so visible, so raw. It was all she could do not to tell Gregor it was all a mistake and run to Willem on the spot. No matter the consequences, no matter what she had promised her uncle.

She recalled the clever staging Willem had contrived with the evening's music, especially the bit with the singing lords. How was it that he was able to make people laugh even when his own heart was breaking? Margarethe cried herself to sleep.

She woke, frightened, from a dream she could not remember. Her face was wet with tears. Afraid to sleep lest the dream return, she lay still for some time. Then she rose and dressed herself in a woolen tunic and surcoat. It was too dark to tell what colors she had chosen. And her hair was likely a mess, so she put on a cap and tucked her braids underneath.

She left her chamber quietly and walked toward the chapel. She would surely be the only one there at this hour, so long before dawn. But when she arrived, she was surprised to find the chapel packed with fighting men. She would have withdrawn except for a man near the door who saw her and made room for her. As Mass had just begun, she stayed.

Margarethe looked around the chapel until she spotted Gregor, then gave her attention to the ritual and prayed along with the priest.

Afterward she waited by the door for Gregor. He came looking for her, and seeing her, he put out both hands in greeting. "I am touched that you came. I didn't realize that you knew about this early Mass for the fighting men."

"Oh, I didn't know, but I couldn't sleep and needed to pray."

"Well, I'm glad you're here. We will be leaving after we break fast. Would you keep me company until then?"

She smiled and nodded, and they made their way to the banquet hall, where the servants were already placing baskets of bread and mugs of ale on the tables. Gregor led her to the head table, where they sat down with the other captains. Looking out over the vast hall, she saw all those young and vulnerable faces, so very different from the men who had laughed and sung and shouted the night before.

"Just before going off to battle, they are quiet," Gregor began. "They're wondering who will come home again and who will be buried on the field of battle."

She looked at him as if she'd never seen him before. How different their worlds. And how necessary the life he led to the security and comfort of hers. She took in Gregor's clothing—quilted breeches and aketon with a chain mail hauberk and the surcoat embroidered with the family crest—and felt apprehensive. "You do wear plate armor, don't you?"

"Yes, but not until we reach the battlefield. As you may imagine, it's quite awkward and uncomfortable."

"I am beginning to understand that this war is real and not just a fanciful tale for storytellers and minstrels," she said, feeling an unaccustomed pang of fear.

Gregor covered her hand with his. Again, she noticed the scars marring the bronzed skin. Fearing for him, she clung to his hand all the way to the gathering place on the grounds outside the hall.

At this hour of the morning, it was still cold, and she shivered in the pre-dawn chill. Gregor put his arm around her and drew her close while a squire brought out his warhorse, prancing and neighing, the stallion's breath pluming in the frosty air. The great beast stamped his feet as if eager to be off.

When it was time to mount up, Gregor hugged Margarethe close. "God be with you," he whispered.

"And with you, Gregor. I shall be praying for you, for all of you. Do not allow yourself to be injured, or you will have to answer to me."

He gazed down at her for a moment longer, then bent to kiss her. She returned his kiss willingly. She had promised, after all.

Gregor swung into his saddle and, with one last little salute, rode to the front of his battalion. Lord Otto and Uncle Einhard were already mounted, waving their swords to signal the call to move out.

She watched with a sinking heart as the men trotted their horses through the gate. They would be gathering more troops from allies along the way.

With no trace of dawn tinting the sky, Margarethe felt smothered by the oppressive darkness. She would never love Gregor with her whole heart—as she did Willem—but she could not bear to see him marching into certain peril.

Chapter 12

Willem was surprised to find Margarethe in the hall when he came from Mass. When she explained that she had stumbled onto the soldiers' worship service by accident, he nodded. "It is the custom here, I've learned."

"Willem, we should not be seen together in front of Lord Otto's people. I do want to talk with you, though. Would you have time to visit with me later today?"

How could he resist her? "It seems I'm giving voice lessons to nearly everyone in the castle these days, but I will always have time for you, Greta."

The familiar nickname came without thinking, and he noted her pleased smile. "I am not overly busy with my patient, so if you need help with some of your lessons, I'm available."

"An excellent idea, my lady. I may take advantage of your kind offer."

She left him with a nod and made her way to the head table to join Lady Edeltraud. Willem could not take his eyes off her. He wondered at her choice of clothing today. He had never seen anyone wear a green surcoat over a blue tunic. The effect was startling.

His thoughts were diverted by a group of his students who joined him at the table, broke bread with him, and made conversation. He assigned lesson times for each of them and then asked if anyone would like to receive instruction from Margarethe. Two of the women were enthusiastic about the idea.

The afternoon passed pleasantly enough. Willem worked on Hilda's story, changing it so that she was rescued just before the assault and making it vague enough that there could be no disgrace to her. He used no names, of course, but the people close to her would recognize the story.

The music lessons went well, and Willem introduced the two women to Margarethe, who put them through a series of exercises. After the women had left, Willem and Margarethe sat together in the chamber—much like her study chamber at home. They were alone, but only until the next student arrived, which should be any time now.

Apparently Margarethe was feeling more and more uncertain about her betrothal, and voiced as much to Willem. He listened to her fears and misgivings, trying to ignore his own pain. "Truly you are in a worse position than I, for I need not pretend to love anyone else."

Margarethe's eyes filled with tears. "I am pretending nothing, Willem. How can you say that?"

"I have seen you with Gregor. Either you really do care for him, or I have taught you more of acting than I meant to."

"Of course I care for him," she said a bit defensively. "Gregor is a decent man, and I will treat him decently."

"Does that include kissing?"

"I believe it is expected of betrothed couples."

He could see the pain in her eyes but pressed on. "So I see. And do you enjoy kissing him?"

To his surprise, Margarethe grinned. "Indeed, I do. Kissing Gregor is much like kissing my aunt!"

Willem laughed with her for a moment, then grew serious again. "Forgive me, *Liebchen*, for suggesting that you would be dishonest with Gregor. But I wonder what you would say if he asked you about me."

He could see that she was studying on the matter before replying. "I will not lie to him, but neither will I tell him anything he does not ask."

She hung her head and looked so sad and small that Willem wanted to take her in his arms and comfort her. He satisfied himself with holding her hand instead. "I know you for an honorable woman, Greta. This must be very hard for you."

She did not answer but sat very still. After a time she said softly, "Willem, should not people who are betrothed speak of love? I have said nothing of love to Gregor, and he has said nothing of love to me."

☙

On Friday Hilda persuaded Jolan and Margarethe to wash her hair. It was a delicate operation since they had to remove the bandage beneath her cap and take pains not to disturb the injured area on the back of her head.

While Hilda's long, golden blond hair was drying, Margarethe asked the others to pray with her for the men on the field of battle. "The three of us can accomplish so much more than one," she said. "Remember Christ's words? Father Bernard has told me that our Lord said, 'If two of you shall agree on earth as touching any thing that they shall ask, it shall be done for them of my Father which is in heaven'?"

The others readily agreed, each one having someone dear to her who was facing danger. Each in turn prayed for all that was on her heart. When it was Margarethe's turn, she gave thanks for these women who were sharing their lives so willingly.

But something Hilda had said stirred her curiosity. The maiden had asked God to bless Willem and to answer his prayer. What prayer? Could it be that he had confided in Hilda? Surely he would not betray their love!

On Saturday night the men came home, loud and boisterous once more. Margarethe dutifully sought out Gregor and kissed him. "You might do well to have a bath, my lord," she suggested, pinching her nostrils shut with one hand.

"I can see that you will be one of those wives who is always giving orders," he teased.

"And I can see that you will be one of those husbands who needs much instruction," she countered, smiling. "There is plenty of hot water, and singing as well. Your mother tells me that's a combination you can't resist."

"My mother is right, as always." With a jaunty wave, he headed off for the bathing area. "When you see me next, you won't recognize me," he called over his shoulder.

Margarethe listened to the rowdy singing coming from behind the curtains in the portion of the hall assigned to the bathers. Willem's voice was unmistakable, and soon she could hear Gregor joining in. Then Willem dropped out, and a moment later she could hear him say, "You're wounded!"

Gregor's answer was muted, but she caught the mention of her name, followed by a round of laughter and a voice Margarethe did not recognize. "Ewald's captains he does not fear, but Lady Margarethe is another matter."

She was relieved. It must not be a serious injury. She went to the page who was guarding the entrance to the bathing area and announced, more loudly than necessary, "Please ask Lord Gregor to meet me in the infirmary when he is finished."

"Yes, my lady," said the page, and the laughter behind the curtains resumed.

Margarethe found the infirmary quite busy when she arrived. The place was filled with soldiers—none of them seriously injured—with Jolan and some other women mixing herbs and making poultices.

"While you're waiting, you could roll that linen material into bandages," her cousin suggested.

Margarethe finished one roll and set about straining some fresh infusions. Then, feeling someone watching her from the doorway, she looked up. "So there you are, Gregor. Are you badly hurt?"

He shrugged. "It's only a scratch. I had your prayers protecting me, didn't I?"

She nodded but gathered up an armful of ointments and bandages anyway. "Come. There's no room here to treat you. We'll have to find another chamber."

She led the way to the solar. "Where is your wound?" she asked when they were behind closed doors.

He removed his tunic and showed her a nasty-looking scrape, surrounded by a purpling bruise on his side. Bringing a candle closer, she inspected the injury.

"Judging from these marks, I'd say this was made by chain mail." She looked Gregor in the eye. "How did you get this?"

"From a lance belonging to one of Ewald's captains."

"Were you wearing your breastplate?"

He ducked his head sheepishly. "Not at the time. You see, that plate was made for me three or four years ago, and I've outgrown it. So I left it off just this once."

Margarethe found herself trembling. "A lance goes through chain mail like a flame through paper. Had that captain a better aim—"

"His aim was true, but his horse slipped," Gregor explained. "The fellow was most disappointed. As for me—well, I was lucky."

Margarethe drew in a sudden breath. "When did this happen?"

"Yesterday, about midmorning."

She felt the sting of sudden tears. "It was not luck, Gregor. It was the hand of God. Some angel tripped that horse. Jolan and Hilda and I were praying for you at that very moment." She began to cry, and Gregor gathered her into his arms.

"Then keep on praying, my lady," he whispered as he held her. "Your prayers are more powerful than the enemy's weapons."

Eventually she moved out of his arms and got to work, using soothing ointments and wrapping his ribs with strips of linen. "No broken bones, at least," she said. "We can thank God for that."

"And I must thank the other ladies who prayed for me. Jolan, did you say, and Hilda? Is she the maiden Albert brought in from the village?"

"Yes. She seems like one of the family already." Margarethe tied off the bandage and gave Gregor a final pat.

"God is so good. In my prayers I have been thanking Him for you," he said shyly.

She was stricken with guilt. "Oh, Gregor, I don't deserve your praise," she said, thinking of her deception.

"Whose idea was it to pray yesterday?" he interrupted.

"Mine," she whispered.

He gazed at her steadily. "God used you to save my life. Even if something happens and we never wed"—she felt an icy premonition—"I will be grateful that you were in my life long enough to save it."

☙

It was good to be at morning Mass on this Lord's Day, Hilda thought with satisfaction. She thanked God for her continuing recovery. She rejoiced that the life of Margarethe's betrothed had been spared. It proved to her that

God had been listening when they prayed, which gave her hope that her own personal petitions would be answered as well.

Lord Albert, who had also attended Mass, met her on the way out. "Are you planning to break fast in the hall today?"

She nodded, feeling her cheeks heat beneath his curious gaze.

"Then let's go over together."

They walked in companionable silence to the hall, and Albert seated her, then surprised her by sitting across from her at the trestle table. "I go home after dinner today, Maid Hilda. Will you have another letter for your father?"

"I've started one to tell him of our answered prayer on behalf of Lord Gregor."

"Gregor told me about that last night. He also said that he had an appointment with the armorer today, Lord's Day or no, to have his breast-plate altered. On Margarethe's orders."

Hilda laughed. "Margarethe will see to that. And you were right to believe that she would choose Gregor over the rest of you."

Albert speared a chunk of bread with his knife. "We're all relieved that she has finally made her choice. She and Gregor are suited to one another, and it frees the rest of us to look for other life companions."

Hilda's puzzlement must have been plain to see, for Albert went on to explain. "Each of us proposed to Margarethe, and none of us could seek other wives until she decided. Ludwig got out of it by gifting Lord Einhard and Margarethe's father handsomely."

"Did she know you were waiting to hear from her?"

He shrugged. "Most men would disregard any proposal that is not answered within six months. But we were truly hoping she would consent to join our family. So, other than Ludwig, we chose to do the honorable thing."

They spoke of lighter matters as they ate, then Albert escorted Hilda to the music room, where he left her to finish her letter to her father.

Later on, Hilda climbed the stairs—somewhat slowly and painfully— and went to Jolan's chamber, where she played a rebec until Albert came. She stood to greet him.

"Your father will be glad to hear from you. He misses you but wanted me to assure you that you have his blessing to remain here until you have completely recovered."

She was comforted. "I do feel at home here at Beroburg. Everyone has been so kind to me."

He stood gazing down at her for a long moment. "Would you pray for me? I feel the need before I take my leave."

Gladly she stepped up to him, took both his hands in hers, and prayed,

asking for his safety first of all, then for wisdom and victory and for his future happiness. When she was finished, Albert added his own prayer for her, including a request for her future husband—that God would prepare him for her.

He concluded his prayer, then smiled down at her. "I do hope you don't mind my imploring the Almighty for your future husband. But for all I know, you might be planning to join the sisters at the monastery."

"That isn't my calling," she assured him.

Suddenly, however, the awful incident of a few days past rushed over her like a tidal wave, threatening to engulf her, and she felt Albert's arms catching her before she slipped, unconscious, to the rush-strewn floor.

೦೫

In Margarethe's chamber at Adlerschloss, Lady Mechthild waited by the window commanding the best view of the road. She was hoping Einhard would be home today. And when she saw a lone rider in their colors approaching, she left the chamber and went to her own to check her appearance in the mirror. She was wearing her husband's favorite ensemble—a scarlet surcoat over a slate tunic. Her braids were coiled over her ears, and it was warm enough to do without a head covering. Still, just in case, she got out her scarlet cloak and carried it with her.

In the hall outside her door, she found Sir Johan polishing his armor yet again and greeted him. "I think Lord Einhard is on the way. I spied him from the window."

"That's good news indeed, my lady. I shall look forward to hearing about the battle and joining the rest of the troops soon."

"You must be anxious to do just that. Is your ankle well?"

"As well as can be—thanks to the skill of your healer, my lady."

Mechthild smiled. This young knight had as yet seen no battle as a knight, only as a squire. And like all the gallant young men, he was eager to be a part of a cause greater than himself.

She started out of the hall, donning her cloak as she went, then walked briskly to the stable, knowing it would be Einhard's first stop. She was not disappointed.

He had already dismounted by the time she arrived and greeted her with a hug.

"Oh, Einhard, I'm so glad to have you back safe and sound," she said, offering a silent prayer of thanks. "What news do you bring?"

Summoning a page to take his things to the donjon, he walked with one arm around his wife. "For one thing, our niece has chosen her husband at last."

"Gregor?"

He nodded. "Just as we predicted."

"Does Margarethe seem happy with her decision?"

"Well—" he faltered. "She is trying. She rose very early this morning to attend the fighting men's Mass, then came out to the field to see him off. She seems to care about his welfare."

"Oh, that's a good sign. I do hope she can get over Willem quickly and make a good life with Gregor."

She noticed that Einhard was thoughtful for a long moment, and she wondered about his silence.

"I'm still sorry about that. Margarethe and Willem should be wed. They're so right for each other."

She looked over at him with a coy smile. "Einhard, ours was an arranged marriage, and we have been very happy together, haven't we?"

He squeezed her hand. "But neither of us was in love with anyone else. Margarethe and Willem truly love each other, the way you and I love each other. Perhaps she will learn to love Gregor, but I fear she'll never be as happy as she would have been with Willem."

She could not answer, or she would weep. And it wouldn't do for her people to see their lady's tears and wonder what had caused them.

☙

Inspired to write another verse for the battle song, Willem went to the music room immediately after dinner. It did not take him long to get his thoughts down on parchment and then to shape them into verse. "Thank You, Lord, for helping me. I know it serves some purpose of Yours."

He read the verse over again and was satisfied. It told of a captain saved from certain death by an angel sent in answer to the prayers of the women at home. Willem reflected on a truth he was just grasping. A battle can be won or lost by the actions of people who are nowhere near the battlefield.

And now he had an idea for the chorus. Still, he must speak with some of the soldiers who had seen battle and could give firsthand reports.

With two verses and the melody of the chorus written, and driven by the need to complete his project, Willem carried paper and pen with him and went back to the hall to see who might be about.

There he found Gottfried talking with two knights and asked if he might join them.

"Of course, and welcome." Gottfried moved over on a bench to make room for him. Seeing the supplies in Willem's hand, he asked, "What have you there?"

"I've been working on a song, and I want to include some heroic tales from this war. I was hoping you might tell of some exploit that should be remembered so that I might put it in the song for all to hear."

"A worthy project, indeed, Willem. Have you met Sir Osgood and Sir Johan?"

Willem nodded. "Sir Osgood I've seen about the castle, and Sir Johan I recall from Lord Einhard's house. Have you just joined us?"

"Yes," said the younger knight. "The healer finally said my ankle was well enough for me to fight, and I've been most eager to perform some heroic deeds of my own." The other men laughed and clapped him on the back.

"Much of war is mud and blood, I fear," admitted Gottfried. "Heroic deeds are sung about because they are so rare."

Far into the night, the two knights talked, recounting their adventures on the field of battle and others they had heard told around the fire. Willem scribed furiously. And when everyone else had left the hall and the two knights had retired at last, Willem was still writing.

Chapter 13

On his next foray into the village, Albert stopped by the mill and spoke at length with Karl, an interesting man, all the more so for being Hilda's father.

"My lord, will you marry?" the miller asked over a mug of mulled cider.

"It is expected of me. And so I shall."

"Have you chosen your wife?" Karl scratched his chin, dusty from the grain he had been grinding.

Albert shrugged and shifted uncomfortably on his hard stool. "My father has put several choices before each of us. I'm not particularly valuable for making alliances, since I am but the youngest son. But perhaps I can help solidify some alliance we've already made."

There was a long silence while both men gazed into the fire, pondering their own thoughts. Then the miller let out a sigh. "It is sad that nobles must marry for politics and not for love."

Albert set his mug down and wiped his mouth. "Oh, I have some say in the matter. In fact, since Lady Margarethe made her choice known, I have been praying more than ever that the Lord would show me the wife He would choose for me."

"And I'm persuaded that He will. Take your brother's escape from the lance. 'Twas an amazing thing," said the miller, his eyes wide with the memory of the tale. "And I know that my Adelie—God rest her soul—was an answer to my prayers for a good wife. For not a finer woman ever lived—unless it would be our Hilda." His face, beneath its coating of flour, flushed scarlet. " 'Tis a hard thing to forgive the man who stole her virtue—"

A log blazed higher, sending a spark spiraling out onto the wooden floor. Albert rose to grind it out beneath his heel, then turned to regard the miller with compassion. "Be at peace. I happen to know that your daughter has already forgiven him and is making a good recovery from her ordeal. The physical scars have almost healed, and with the help of the Almighty, she will be able to put the whole sordid business out of her mind and heart. In fact"—he gazed off into space, remembering their prayer before they parted—"I am truly impressed with the goodness of her spirit."

Karl smiled, his chest swelling with obvious pride. "It is because of her mother. My wife was of the nobility, you know—and a godly woman. She taught the girl well."

"Yes." Albert turned again to peer into the fire, watching the flames dance as if they were responding to some unseen wind. "Yes," he said again, thinking, reflecting. "She is quite a remarkable young woman—your Hilda."

☙

Willem was utterly distracted. Whatever he was about—whether coaching a vocal student or strumming his lute in the privacy of his own chamber—the song would not let him go. It plucked at his heartstrings with a relentless will of its own. Even when he tried to pray for Margarethe, the words came, unbidden, to his mind: "Write the song. Write the song." Not the betrothal music he'd been commissioned to write, but another. A song of such force that it took his breath away.

☙

By midweek, when Margarethe and Jolan examined Hilda, instructing her to breathe deeply, they were convinced that her rib had healed sufficiently to permit her to sing.

She was ecstatic. "How can I thank you? I have had the best healers in Bavaria!"

"And now we'll see just what kind of voice you have," Margarethe said. "We've been needing a third person for a trio."

Hilda laughed with delight. "So that was your motive then. You thought to mend me so as to put me to work! But I must warn you—I didn't inherit my mother's warm, rich alto voice."

They were soon humming together, finding Hilda's range and proclaiming her to be a low soprano. Before long, they were harmonizing on a song Jolan and Margarethe had sung for Hilda many times during her convalescence.

At the end of the second time through, they were startled by the sound of clapping coming from the open doorway and turned to find Willem standing there. He was looking most handsome this morning, Margarethe thought with a catch in her heart—dressed in the blue that so enhanced the blue of his eyes.

"*Wunderbar!*" Those eyes were twinkling now. "Well, Maid Hilda," he said, "I'm happy to see that you've progressed in your recovery—and that we have a fine new attraction for our after-dinner entertainment."

Margarethe sensed his delight, knowing that discovering new talent was a great adventure for him.

"Perhaps—if you would excuse us, Lady Jolan"—Willem gave his most courtly bow—"Margarethe and I might have some time with Maid Hilda to explore her gift a bit more."

Jolan waved her hand. "Oh, I have work to do." She lifted a volume—*Causae et Curae*—from the table. "I must copy some passages for the infirmary, so I should be busy all afternoon. But if you need me later for any reason—"

"Such as the three of you helping with some music for the end of the week?" Willem asked.

Margarethe cast a doubtful glance in Hilda's direction. It might be too soon for the injured maiden to be facing a roomful of people. But her fears were quickly allayed.

"I've sung at village fairs and in our church with my mother," Hilda explained with a reassuring smile. "I should welcome an opportunity to repay all of you—and my host and hostess—for their kindness to me."

Willem lifted her hand and kissed it. "Dear lady, I hope you plan to stay for a very long time. You are sorely needed here."

Knowing the gesture meant nothing, Margarethe felt only a small pang, soon replaced by the exhilaration of watching Willem at work.

In the music room, the afternoon sped by as he put Hilda through a series of vocal exercises, making notes and pointing out areas of strength and weakness. While she sang, Margarethe wandered about the room, finding some parchments on the table that looked interesting. There were verses about heroic deeds, written in a style unlike anything she had seen. Another contained some music, scrawled hastily—a verse and a chorus. She had picked up the parchment to study it more carefully when Willem caught her in the act.

"And what do you think, Greta?" he said softly, having left Hilda to stand in front of a mirror to practice some scales.

Margarethe smiled sheepishly. "I think you are writing something of great importance—such wonderful tales—though I can't imagine what the occasion would be."

"Nor can I." He shrugged. "I only know that when I pray a certain prayer, these words pop into my head: 'Write the song.' And I know that it is this song."

"Will you hum the tune? I couldn't make it out over the background music in the room."

By this time Hilda had joined them at the writing table. "What song is this you speak of?"

"You'll recognize the chorus," Willem said, moving the page so she could read over his shoulder. "You gave it to me when I had nothing but the verse."

She seemed surprised. "You would want to use that chorus?"

"If you'll agree. But I shall give you credit."

"Indeed, you will not. I gave it freely. Besides, it is not mine anyway, for it came after prayer—when you mentioned to me that you needed an idea."

Margarethe, who had been listening intently, was struck with wonder. "Then *God* is writing this song."

Willem nodded in agreement. "It seems so." He moved to pick up his

lute. "I'll sing what has come to us so far."

He sang the verse about Gregor's miraculous delivery from death on the battlefield, then hummed the melody to the chorus.

Margarethe clasped her hands together when he had finished. "It's magnificent, Willem! Truly inspiring. We'll pray that the words to the chorus will be revealed to you."

"God will send them when He is ready." Willem set the lute on the table and dropped onto a stool with a long sigh. "It is the music your Uncle Einhard commissioned that concerns me now. I'm not sure why it won't come." She saw that he could not meet her gaze.

Margarethe felt her own heart sinking at the thought. "But it will be needed in less than a month. Surely you have at least started it."

"That's just the trouble. I had started it when this music came and consumed my mind entirely. I'm not sure what to do."

"Forgive me," Hilda put in. "But may I ask what music you're speaking of?"

"Lady Margarethe's uncle has asked me to compose a song for the announcement of her betrothal on May Day," Willem answered with an uncharacteristic note of bitterness in his voice.

"Oh. Is that what you meant when you told me you had to compose a score but that your mind and heart were at cross purposes?" Hilda asked gently.

Margarethe held her breath, waiting for Willem's reply. "I do not want to see her wed. She would move to Gregor's castle, and I will miss her. . . music."

It was enough. Hilda need not hear the whole truth. But when Margarethe saw the tears gathering in Willem's eyes as he put the music away, she read what his lips had not uttered—and must never utter again.

❦

On the evening before the Lord's Day, the newly formed trio performed in not one, but four songs. Willem was hugely pleased with the response of the hall and with the expertise of the performers. Truly he was blessed to have such singers in the castle—and such friends.

Willem watched Hilda closely throughout the evening. She seemed to be recovering well from her injuries. She tired before her companions, but otherwise seemed much better. Still, at times it seemed that her body was present while her spirit was elsewhere. Willem prayed for her, knowing that more healing must come before she was fully restored.

"It is your turn to sing again, Sir Willem," called someone in the crowd. And with that ridiculous application of a knight's title, he laughed, then obliged them with a song.

At the evening's end, Willem looked for Gregor in the hallway outside

his chamber—the first time he had been able to catch the man without Margarethe at his side all day. "I would have a word with you before you retire."

Gregor frowned. "Shall we return to the hall?"

"No, my lord. I'd prefer we talk undisturbed. This is a private matter," he said, feeling a growing apprehension.

"In my chamber then." Gregor jerked his head toward the door.

Willem walked in with him and surveyed the room as Gregor uncovered two cluttered stools where they could perch. Surely Margarethe had never seen this room, Willem thought, or she would already be lecturing him about housekeeping.

"What is on your mind, my friend?" Gregor asked.

"It is this war. I find myself very much in sympathy with the cause, and I want to help." Willem watched Gregor's eyebrows rise and made himself sit still while the knight contemplated.

"You help us already, Willem. You can't imagine how refreshing it is to come home to music and laughter and dancing. The atmosphere of this place has improved sevenfold since you came."

"Thank you, my lord. I trained to be a knight, but since there was no war, I have never seen battle."

"Are you saying you wish to fight with us?"

"I am."

Gregor dropped his gaze and studied the toe of his boot, propped against the table leg. "How long since you were in training?"

"Six years."

"Much has changed in weaponry and strategy in the last six years. You don't own armor or a warhorse, and being afoot is too dangerous for any nobleman." He narrowed his gaze. "How is your archery?"

"I am. . .*was* deadly accurate," Willem replied. Was there no way he could prove himself?

Gregor appraised him with a sweeping glance. "You're strong; there is no doubt of that. Perhaps you could still string a bow."

"I would be proud to do so," he replied, his spirits falling. He *needed* to go to the field as a knight. It was knights who did the great deeds. It was knights who were sometimes rewarded for their acts of courage.

Gregor's expression was grave. "Willem, I am pleased that you want to help. And I am honored that you came to me to offer your services. But I cannot allow you to fight in any capacity in my battalion. You're too valuable to risk. Men like me are expendable, but a man who can bring an entire castle joy simply by opening his mouth cannot be replaced."

"Would it not be my own life I'd be risking?" he pled. "Have I no choice?"

"My father needs you to hold the household together. The depression has lifted since you came to us. And your life is not your own. You're a believer, bought by the blood of Jesus Christ. As your Supreme Commander, it is He who gives the orders."

Convicted, Willem fell silent. "I had not even thought to pray about this," he confessed. "I must do what He calls me to do."

"There is another reason I cannot let you fight in my battalion," Gregor continued, speaking with soft intensity. "If something happened to you, Margarethe's sorrow would overwhelm her. She loves you so." Willem froze in his seat, not believing his ears. "It's true. You're her closest friend, and I could not bear to see her hurt."

After another lengthy silence, Willem sighed. "Then I will do what I can without fighting. Some are called to fight, and some are called to sing."

"I would gladly trade you callings, my friend."

Gregor rose to see Willem out and cuffed him lightly on the shoulder as he bade him farewell.

That night Willem could not sleep at all. His prayers were filled with thoughts of Margarethe. "Write the song," came the familiar response.

"How can I write of what I do not know, Lord?" Willem groaned. As he waited for the answer, an idea dawned—like the rising of the sun.

∽

Margarethe was up before first light and attended the fighting men's Mass as she had once before. Gregor seemed to be expecting her and had saved her a seat. He was becoming so affectionate and considerate that her guilt increased each time she saw him.

During the stillness of communion, she prayed, "Father, please help me find a way out. I don't want to hurt Gregor, but I feel I belong to Willem. Only You can bring order to this chaos, and I humbly ask You to do it."

After Mass, she walked beside Gregor, turning only when she heard Willem's voice calling out. "My lord, I could not sleep for an idea that will not leave me alone."

"Willem," Gregor said sternly, "I gave you my answer."

"It is not what we talked about—yet it is," Willem began. "Shall I tell you in front of your lady, or will you turn aside for a moment?" He was short of breath, and his eyes were dancing with excitement.

Margarethe stared until Willem noticed her, but he quickly looked away. What could he be thinking of? She questioned his sanity, so strange was his manner as well as his attire, for he wore traveling clothes.

"Margarethe, I will join you when I can," Gregor said, dismissing her.

Once again Willem caught her eye and glanced toward the ceiling. From that gesture—their private signal—she knew he was imploring her to pray. But for what?

Help Willem, Lord. Give Him your wisdom. Let him know what path he is to take. He seems so desperate of late. Comfort him. Let him know that I love him still. I do not know what he is scheming with Gregor, but if the idea is from You, then please bring it to pass.

She continued to pray as she went to break her fast. At the table, she sat and waited for the men to come in, nodding to some who drifted in from other parts of the castle.

When Willem and Gregor entered the hall, she could see their heightened enthusiasm, which only increased her apprehension. What was even more curious was that they headed directly for the main table and passed her by on their way to speak to Lord Otto. She could not overhear the exchange that was made, but from the back-slapping that followed, she could only assume they were well pleased with something.

"Stay, Willem, and sit with us," Gregor invited when he had left his father and returned to Margarethe.

To her surprise, Willem remained, dropping into the seat to her left while Gregor took the right.

"What is happening?" she asked, glancing from one to the other.

"Meet our new camp minstrel, my lady," Gregor said with a broad smile.

At first she could not make out what he was telling her. But when understanding came, she smiled. "It is well, Willem. You will find the missing words for the chorus there." She fought the thickness forming in her throat.

"Then you do not mind?" He stopped suddenly and tipped his head to one side, an eyebrow raised.

"What? Mind leading the evening music and teaching all your voice lessons?" she said with mock indignation, trying her best to hold back the tears. "My lord," she said, turning to Gregor, "I know this bandit is paid for teaching. Will you let him treat me so?"

Gregor laughed. "Indeed. Teaching will keep you out of mischief while I'm away." He dropped his voice. "We need him, Margarethe. Morale is low in the field, and he can encourage us with his music. Do as you please with the students. But you will be serving us well if you can keep the people happy at home."

She nodded miserably and applied herself to her bread and cheese. When it was time for the men to go, they rose. A feeling of near panic threatened to cut off Margarethe's breathing.

"It is a wet morning, my lady," Gregor said. "I'll bid you farewell here."

She stood on tiptoe to kiss his cheek, and he drew her to him to whisper in her ear. "Willem could use a hug as well. He was concerned about leaving you with all his work."

She faced Gregor as he released her, then turned to embrace Willem. "God be with you—and keep you from harm."

Chapter 14

For the next few days, Margarethe was completely occupied with teaching and coordinating the nightly music. All of the students were pleased that they would not have to be without instruction while Willem was away. But as for all other matters pertaining to the music of the house, she was careful to consult with those who had shared the chief musician's post before his arrival. They seemed pleased to have been consulted—equally pleased to be free of the responsibility.

Margarethe had never known a house so fond of music. On previous visits, she had assumed that the rich musical variety offered after supper was in honor of the guests. Not so. Here at Beroburg, musicians were used regularly, with jugglers and acrobats simply offering a diversion while the singers rested between sets.

So preoccupied was Margarethe, in fact, that it was Thursday before she noticed Hilda's silent withdrawal from the routine activities. Concerned, Margarethe began to look for her.

Not finding her anywhere about, she went to Hilda's new chamber adjoining her own. Finding the door ajar, she stepped in. Hilda was standing at the window, gripping the cold stone sill with a white hand.

"Hilda? Greetings. I've been missing you in the hall—"

When the maid turned, Margarethe could see that her eyes were red and swollen. "What is it? What's wrong?"

Hilda shook her head. "I hope it is nothing. But I've been calculating the dates. . . ." She sighed deeply, then dropped her gaze, unable to meet Margarethe's eye. "My monthly blood is late."

Margarethe caught her breath at the implication but fought for composure—for Hilda's sake. Rushing over, she took her friend's hand. "Women are sometimes late for no reason."

"I have *never* been late."

"But I have heard that when a woman has had a serious injury, it is not unusual for her whole body to react to the pain. . . ."

"No, Margarethe," Hilda continued sadly. "I was not severely injured in body. But now I'm so very frightened—" she sobbed and fell into Margarethe's arms, where they wept together.

◎⅛

With orders to remain at base camp with the cooks and other servants during

the daytime hours, Willem used the hours to finish his song. Sitting cross-legged in the tent he shared with Sir Johan and his squire, he peered out into the misty rain, praying and thinking.

The words for the chorus came to him the first day out. But when they began to formulate themselves in his mind, he waited, resisting the urge to record them at once. Drawing aside, he prayed, needing to be sure that they were divinely inspired. At the same time, he was consumed with a sense of urgency to complete the song.

On the third day in the field, the battle took a bad turn. The men came in discouraged, and fights broke out among some of the foot soldiers. The rain that had been falling when they left Beroburg was now relentless, pounding against the tops of the tents, the dampness seeping into everything. The bedrolls were soggy, water was standing in puddles inside, and there was not a thread of dry clothing among them. Supper was late because the bread was ruined, and the cooks had to send runners to Lord Albert's castle for more.

In the midst of all this, Willem walked among the men, attempting to spread a little cheer. But for the most part, they turned a deaf ear.

If ever there was a time for a rousing song, this was it. Still, Willem wanted to be sure and knelt in a corner of his tent to pray. The longer he prayed, the more he was certain that this was the night to introduce the new music.

After their meager supper, the men grew restless, and at Lord Gregor's direction, Willem stepped to the front. "A song!" someone cried. "Give us a song!"

"And high time, I'd say," called another.

Thus encouraged, Willem gathered his lute, stood in the entry of the main tent, and struck the first chord. One by one, he led them in some of the old familiar songs that had been favorites at the castle. He could feel the tension draining away.

Finally, when he had their full attention, he spoke. "I have a new song this night. I cannot take full credit for writing it, for most of it came to me only after much prayer. This song is about you, and it is a gift to you from the Lord God."

Willem strummed the opening chords, whispering a prayer as he did, "Here it is, Lord. Use it as You will." He sang the first verse to utter silence. During the chorus—that wild and proud sound, accompanying words of love and courage—there was a stirring among the men. The second verse was received much like the first, with rapt concentration. By the fourth chorus, the men had risen to their feet and were clapping in time to the music. Hearing a voice join his, he turned to find Lord Albert harmonizing.

Even so, at the song's conclusion, Willem was not completely prepared

for the response. The men cheered heartily and threw their hats into the air. There was a general stampede as some clapped comrades on the back or shouted their approval. He himself was mobbed by the lords, and his lute was whisked away somewhere.

"*Wunderbar*, Willem! Exactly what we needed!"

"How did you gather all those stories? It must have taken months."

"Well done, Willem. Is there a baritone harmony you can teach me for the chorus?" That, from Lord Gregor.

Soon their conversation was interrupted by a widespread chant: "*Wieder*, Willem, *wieder. Wieder*, Willem, *wieder*!" they shouted. "Again, Willem, sing it again!"

Gregor escorted Willem back to the tent entry, and the squire who had taken his lute into the tent to keep it dry returned it to him. A cheer went up as he positioned his lute.

"It's a very long song," he called above the din of rain and raves. "Are you sure you want the whole thing?"

"The whole thing! Don't leave out a note!" came the enthusiastic reply.

They were of one accord, except for one ruddy-faced fellow, who yelled, "How about adding more about women?"

A roar of laughter went up—a good sign, indeed. Surely this was the song he was meant to write, for it was hitting the mark—much like an arrow, aimed true, striking the heart of its target.

So Willem sang the entire song again. This time, he was joined on the chorus until an entire male choir was ringing through the night:

> "*To trade and travel freely,*
> >   *No tyrant taking aught;*
> *Our families safe, our farms secure—*
> >   *This is what we've sought.*

> "*Maidens, wives, and mothers*
> >   *Doing battle on their knees—*
> *Praying as they work all day;*
> >   *God has heard their pleas.*

> "*Partners with us in the conflict—*
> >   *Mighty without sword;*
> *We fight for freedom, heart to heart,*
> >   *Contending for the Lord.*

> "*Inspired by their example,*
> >   *We have a sacred trust.*

And so we have the courage
To do all that we must."

Though there were calls for more, Willem backed off, yielding the floor to Lord Otto, who led in a prayer for victory—something that had never happened in their history, to anyone's recollection. But on the way back to their tents for the night, it was the melody of Willem's new song they were humming.

⌒⌒

On Friday a messenger arrived from the battlefield with news of a great change among the troops.

Lady Edeltraud summoned Margarethe and Jolan to the solar. "Perhaps the two of you can help me make sense of this. Remember how rainy it was the first four days of the week?"

"Yes, Aunt," Jolan replied.

"All the men were wet and miserable and deeply despondent. Then Willem sang a new song, and suddenly the black mood lifted." Lady Edeltraud rose, pacing the room. "Now I know the messenger to be a sober young fellow, but he vows this is the best song he has ever heard. Everyone is singing it as they go about their business, and praying as well.

"Even Otto has been leading the men in prayer." Edeltraud's eyes were huge. "On Thursday our men gained ground—a significant amount, I understand, and today the enemy retreated entirely." She peered into the two faces. "Tell me, if you know—how could a song bring such a change?"

There was a slight pause while Margarethe searched for the right words. "It is not the song, Lady Edeltraud, but the God who gave the song that made the difference. We, too, need to pray."

"Yes, yes, I can see that. I pray this victory will continue in spite of Ewald's reserves. Oh, and that is something else I learned from the messenger." Margarethe waited expectantly. "The extra soldiers came from Austria, as we suspected. Ewald gave a daughter in marriage to an Austrian lord in exchange for troops for this season."

"What does his daughter think of that?" Margarethe wondered aloud.

Lady Edeltraud sighed. "I do not know. I know only that I could never trade a child of mine to win a battle."

⌒⌒

Friday evening Willem and Gregor talked by the blazing fire outside their tents. "Never have we had a musician stir us as you have, Willem. My father wants to reward you at the end of the campaign. Think now. What reward would you have?"

Willem shrugged. "What does every man want?"

Gregor surprised him by laughing. "The one thing my father has more of than any man in Bavaria-land."

Willem nodded, gazing into the fire. "And if I had that which every man wants, my life would still be empty, for it would come too late."

"Too late? How could land come too late?" Gregor asked.

Willem turned a sober look on him before he glanced away. "Forgive me, Lord Gregor. I talk too much."

A heavy silence descended between them before Gregor cleared his throat. "Willem, let us sing a song, just us two. Do you know 'The Lady in Blue'?"

Oh, yes. And in green, and brown, and scarlet. She was lovely in purple as well. "I do."

They sang softly so as not to disturb anyone, their voices blending.

As the fire died down, Gregor clapped Willem on the shoulder and went off to his bedroll. But Willem sat, watching the dying embers, and allowed his tears to fall.

ᔆᔆ

After getting ready for supper at the end of the week, Margarethe stopped in to see Hilda. "How are you?"

"The same." Tears welled in the blue eyes. "Except that I grow more fearful each day."

"God will be with you—and Jolan and I will stand by to help. I'm sorry my new duties have called me away so much and I could not be with you more."

"It is well. Jolan has been with me, and singing helps." Hilda looked so hopeless that Margarethe felt a rush of grief for her friend. At least the men would be home tomorrow night. Hilda seemed happiest when Albert and Willem were near.

"Perhaps tomorrow we will be able to hear the new song that has so stirred the fighting men," Margarethe suggested, hoping to distract Hilda's gloomy thoughts.

But it was not to be. "I'm so ashamed to see them. Especially Lord Albert. How will I tell him about. . .my problem?"

"You have nothing to be ashamed of. But do you need to say anything? You are not even certain yet."

"Perhaps not. But he will have only to look at my face to know there is something amiss."

It was true. Hilda's usually rosy cheeks were pale, and her eyes were puffy from weeping. "Still, he has made himself your protector. He may know a way to help you."

Hilda shook her head. "Some things cannot be helped. I am praying that I am not with child, that it is something else instead. But if I am—"

Margarethe sat with her, holding her hand, and thought about the situation. What a tragedy. The poor thing had already suffered cruel abuse. Now she might be called upon to bear pity and humiliation as well. Not to mention the suspicions of the village folk. She had hidden herself away at the castle and had not returned to her home since the attack. An unmarried woman with a child would have a sad life, even the daughter of the miller, a man of some means.

The very best thing would be for Hilda to marry immediately so that the child would be assumed to be her husband's. Else she might be shunned for life. At the very least, tongues would wag.

Still, Hilda was not betrothed and had no prospects of marriage. Nor did she have a dowry, what with her mother's long illness taking all their money. And even if Margarethe's uncle was willing to provide a suitable dowry, she was almost sure the proud Hilda would never accept it.

Margarethe stirred, pressing her friend's hand before she rose. "I must go. Will you come down to supper?"

Hilda sighed and followed her out the door. "My appetite is poor. But I will come. Perhaps the change will do me good."

∽∾

Margarethe's was the first face Willem spied when he arrived at the castle with the troops, more joyful than usual after a report from a scout had revealed that the enemy had fled the fighting field.

"I've heard about your new song and am anxious to hear it," she said, her smile warming him—heart and soul.

"Then you shall—most likely this very night," he said, feeling his love for her shining through his weariness. "How went this week for you?"

"Your students and the music kept me very busy. I'll tell you all about it when you have the leisure to listen."

"I will seek you out when I do—after a good hot bath." He stood, admiring her for a moment. "It was a good week, a necessary week, but I missed you," he said softly, hoping that Lord Gregor wouldn't come along to spoil this moment.

But it was Lord Albert who passed by with a little wave and a salute. "Willem," she whispered urgently after Albert had moved on, "pray for Hilda. She needs us so."

∽∾

Just as Willem left for the bathing area, Gregor came in. Margarethe greeted him with a kiss as he had requested, grateful that both men were home safe once again. How very strange it felt to love one man with all her heart, the other with only half.

She heard the news from the front, rejoiced with Gregor, then saw Albert rush down the stairs, take his mother aside, and go with her to speak

with his father. Lord Otto frowned, then the three of them walked out of the hall together. *Father,* Margarethe prayed silently, *if this has something to do with Hilda, please work Your way in it all.*

Jolan caught her eye across the room and gestured for her. Margarethe obeyed, seeing that her cousin was surrounded by fighting men, fresh from their bath, claiming to need massages even though they had not been wounded.

The men, who had been clamoring for her services, dropped back at Albert's approach. "Cousins," he said, "I need your prayers, though I cannot explain why just now."

"Is it something to do with our friend?" Margarethe asked.

He nodded.

"You can count on us, Cousin," Jolan assured him. "We have nothing pressing to do here anyway." Her glance swept the group of men who were clustered nearby, waiting for the conversation to end.

"Then I can proceed with courage."

"And where are you going, Albert?" asked Margarethe.

"To the home of Karl, the miller," he called over his shoulder as he strode away and disappeared through the door.

The miller! she thought. *Hilda's father!*

☙

Willem was accustomed to good treatment in this household, but now he was treated with the respect accorded a great hero. At supper he was given a place of honor at the lord's table, and afterward, a cry went up for "the song."

He looked about and caught Margarethe's eye, then rose and accepted the lute one of the other musicians handed him. Without introduction, he began the song, his heart swelling as a group of the soldiers joined him on the chorus, filling the hall with the glorious sound.

At the end of the song, a great cheer went up, and Willem felt the joy he saw radiating from Margarethe's face. It was well. She was pleased—more than pleased.

Lady Edeltraud rose from her seat and came to see Willem. "I did not understand all the fuss about a mere song. But now that I've heard it for myself, I can see how one song could inspire men's hearts and put an end to war."

Willem bowed low over her hand. "Thank you, my lady. But I believe God is the composer of that song."

"I believe it, too. And I pray He continues to use it."

If he received any more acclaim, Willem thought to himself, he would have to pray against that deadly sin—pride!

☙

Hilda stayed in the hall long enough to hear the stunning song everyone

was talking about. Her eyes filled with tears at the sheer beauty of it. She recognized her story, of course, and was happy for Lord Albert, who had been made a hero forever through his part in the song.

But now she was wondering how he was faring with her father—and what their business might be. Feeling the need to visit the garderobe, she did not remain for the rest of the music but climbed the stairs for the small chamber down the hall.

She was inside only a short time and emerged, flushed with happiness and relief. Her feet fairly flew down the steps on her way to share the good news with her friends.

Then she went back upstairs to give thanks to God and to await Lord Albert's return. For whatever he was arranging for her would now be for naught.

Chapter 15

Margarethe was doing a ring dance with a group of ladies when someone tapped her on the shoulder. She turned to find Hilda, wreathed in smiles, with Albert and his parents. They all looked so happy that she withdrew from the dance to learn what had happened. Hilda offered a hug instead of an explanation while Albert left to fetch Jolan.

At the back of the hall, he launched into an announcement. "We've splendid news! It appears we have discovered a solution to Hilda's dilemma."

Margarethe and Jolan exchanged bewildered glances.

"You're both aware of the. . .uh. . .the difficulty Maid Hilda has been experiencing." At their nods, Albert continued. "Well, my first thought was that she must marry immediately."

Jolan shook her head. "We thought of that as well. But it's impractical, of course, since she is not even betrothed. Besides—" Where was all this leading? Hadn't Hilda confided that the grievous assault had not left her with child?

Albert grinned. "Yes, now—thanks be to God—there is no need to rush into a marriage for the purpose of saving her honor." Well, so now Albert knew as well, Margarethe thought.

"In spite of all that, however, the lady has consented to marry a man of whom she has grown quite fond."

Margarethe watched, astonished, as Albert leaned over to plant a kiss on Hilda's cheek.

"So there is to be another wedding in this house," Lord Otto said, with Lady Edeltraud on his arm, smiling proudly.

Margarethe could only gape as Jolan let out a little squeal and threw out her arms to both Albert and Hilda. Then Margarethe collected herself. "I am so happy for you both," she told her friend. Yet even as she kissed Albert's cheek, she thought of Willem. Such happiness would never be theirs.

⤫

Willem looked on as the little tableau at the back of the hall unfolded. Still, he had not an inkling of what was going on until the radiant couple approached. "Willem, Hilda and I are to wed."

Willem covered his surprise by drawing them both into an embrace. "My heartiest congratulations, Lord Albert, Maid Hilda." Then he inclined his head toward the maiden. "I must say you've a job ahead of you, taming

this one." Hilda made a face but clung to Albert's arm.

Had Margarethe known all along? Is this what she'd had in mind when she'd asked him to pray for Hilda? How strange—that a lord could marry a miller's daughter, when a nobleman could not marry a lady simply because he had no land.

⚭

In spite of a sleepless night, Willem rose early on the Lord's Day and attended Mass. Toward morning his thinking had cleared, and he realized that a miracle could still occur for himself and Margarethe. She was betrothed to another, but that was not the same as being wed, and the betrothal had not yet been made official—with May Day still a fortnight away.

If Margarethe broke it off after that, it would be an insult to Gregor. Insulting the knight was not something Willem cared to do. He had not intended to like the fellow, but now that they were friends, he felt an unexpected loyalty.

Hilda joined him at table. "Forgive me, Willem, but you seem sad today. How can this be when God has given you such a wonderful song to encourage the men? Why, you're a hero!"

He shook his head mournfully. "I am no hero. I'm a failure."

"A failure?" Her eyes grew round. "You are so gifted and talented, and everyone loves you." He made no answer but sat watching the servitors bring in the meal. "Does it have something to do with this prayer you have been praying?" she asked.

He gave her his full attention and nodded. "The prayer that has *not* been answered."

She tapped the table with a fingernail, pondering. "You have never shared with me the nature of your prayer, but did God not instruct you to write a song when you prayed?"

"Yes. And I obeyed."

"Then surely the answer to this prayer is on the way. Can you not see? It is something like going to a bazaar to purchase something from a merchant. At his booth, you choose some cloth. The merchant tells you how many coins, and you lay them on the counter. After all that, would you then walk away without the cloth?"

"Of course not."

She gave a little smile. "There you have it. You should be thanking the merchant and picking up your purchase. Do you not think that our Lord is much like that merchant, and you—the buyer?" She eyed him expectantly, and Willem blinked in amazement.

"That is a weighty matter," he said, clearing his throat. "I will have to give it some thought."

At that moment Jolan and Margarethe joined them. "Are you planning

to purchase some cloth, Willem?" Jolan asked.

He felt the beginning of a blush. "Not likely." Then he changed the subject. Looking about, he saw none of Lord Otto's family. "Where are all the lords?"

"They are meeting in the solar," Margarethe replied.

She was lovely today in light blue and purple, a combination she favored.

"For what purpose?"

She shrugged. "Gregor was secretive. Did Albert mention anything to you?" she asked Hilda.

"Nothing."

"I need to talk with you today, Willem," Margarethe began, "about your students and the music for this week. Jolan, you should come, too, for you've had your share of students."

Willem bowed. "I shall be ready whenever you need me, my lady—in the music room."

He quickly finished eating and excused himself. In the music chamber, he took up his lute. There he strummed as he considered what Hilda had said. The maiden made good sense. The answer might well be on the way.

Thanking God for that which had not yet come, Willem hummed a tune he heard in his mind, then plucked the strings, feeling his way through the song. Before it slipped away, he reached for parchment to seize the moment. The Lord continued to surprise him at every turn. Maybe Maid Hilda was right, after all. . . .

☙

"A messenger, my lady, with a letter from the Schwarzwald," announced a page, interrupting the music lesson Margarethe was giving.

Offering no explanation, she excused herself and dashed down the stairs. She had seen her parents only twice in the nine years she had been a member of her uncle's household, and news from home was dear. In fact, because of the danger on the roads, they had all been advised against traveling, and so it had been several years since she had seen them.

With trembling fingers, she took the letter the messenger handed her, unsealed it, and read:

> *Our dear Greta,*
>
> *Too much time has passed since last we were together. And now we learn that our little one—only a babe yesterday, it seems—is to wed.*
>
> *With the improved roads and the battle far to the south, we are told that travel to Beroburg is safe, and we long to help you celebrate your betrothal at the feast on May Day.*
>
> *Until we meet again,*
> *Papa and Mutti*

Margarethe wiped a tear with the back of her hand. Would that her parents were coming for a visit only—and not to celebrate the beginning of her lifelong imprisonment—a marriage she dreaded with all of her heart.

∽

It was late on Lord's Day Eve when the fighting men returned, more boisterous than ever. Margarethe ran down the stairs with Jolan and looked for someone who could tell them what was happening.

"Willem!" she called, spotting him among the men. "What is the news?"

"It was a complete rout. Ewald's men turned tail, and Lord Otto gave chase. The front has been pushed all the way to his castle," he said, grinning. "I rode along when I heard. It was glorious! I may have to add another verse to the song."

Jolan grimaced in a comical expression. "I hope I never have to learn that long song."

"Oh, Willem, is it almost over?" Margarethe asked.

"Very likely. The scouts from the south reported that many of Ewald's hired Austrian troops did not stop at the castle but kept going toward home."

Someone sent out a cry for a healer, and Jolan responded, leaving Margarethe and Willem alone. "My parents will be here soon," she said, suddenly feeling awkward.

His gaze pinned her to the spot, and she felt as if she could not draw her next breath. "I know you will be glad to see them."

"Yes, but. . .oh, Willem, why did it have to end this way?"

Glancing about to be sure they were not being observed, he leaned close to her ear and whispered, "Remember, our God can do anything. Never give up hope."

Gregor came in just then and enveloped her in a hug. "Sweet Greta, how goes the battle at home?"

"We are still praying, Gregor." She looked around for Willem, half expecting him to be gone. But he stood there, grinning.

"Did Willem tell you why we are so late tonight?"

"Yes, and it is good news indeed. Do you think the war may be over before midsummer?"

"Sooner than that, I'd wager." Gregor lowered his voice, "I cannot tell you here. Shall we find a more private place?"

She nodded. "The music room?"

"Very well. You go first," he instructed. Margarethe was curious about the wink Willem sent her way, but she preceded Gregor through the rowdy mob and toward the stairs.

Gregor followed, closing the door behind them and sinking wearily onto a stool at the table. "Ah, it is good to be home again."

FOR A SONG

For a moment she wondered if he would expect the kiss she had
neglected to give him upon first greeting him. But he seemed content to sit
and rest. And their kisses were unremarkable anyway, so she held her peace.

But what was this that could not be discussed in front of the others?
She was curious.

"The war, Margarethe, my dear, may be over this coming week."

"But how? It would seem to be time for a siege now, and those are most
tiresome and drawn out."

"True. But we will parley. Messengers have been sent to all of our allies.
If they all appear, it will be a most impressive sight, and Ewald will be hard
put to resist. Your uncle arrives tomorrow, and my father will have him do
the talking, as he is the best diplomat among us."

"You will go on this. . .excursion?"

"Yes. I am counted as one of the allies, as are my brothers."

"Oh, Gregor. I hope your plan is successful. I fear for you, for all of you.
When you came close to taking that lance—" She shuddered, feeling the
pain as if it were her own.

"It was not one of my best moments," he admitted, rubbing his side
and wincing a little. "But I was spared—thanks largely to your prayers, my
lady." He took her hand and smiled into her eyes. "You are the angel God
has given to bring me safely through this war."

Margarethe forced a smile. How could that be—when her own heart
did not bear witness to his?

He rose reluctantly. "We must get back to the hall. The men will be
assembling shortly for further instructions about our venture later this week.
But keep my secret, my lady. We need the element of surprise."

"Will you be armed?" she asked in a small voice.

"We will dress to make an impression, I can assure you. And we will
take along a secret weapon." He grinned at her look of puzzlement.

"I will cover you with my prayers as always, but won't you please wear
the mail hauberk underneath—just in case?"

At this, he tugged her into his arms and held her tightly. "For you, my
lady, I would give my life."

Margarethe closed her eyes and yielded to his embrace. Perhaps—just
perhaps—she could learn to love this man, after all.

☙

At Mass on the Lord's Day, Margarethe was surprised to see Gregor, Willem,
and Klaus dressed—not in mail—but in traveling clothes. She waited outside
the chapel for them, hoping to find out what they were up to.

"An affair of state," was all Willem would confide when she asked.
Klaus looked watchful and as stern as ever, but Gregor reserved his most
tender smile for her. "Once more we'll need your prayers, my lady."

110

"And you shall have them." She eyed him suspiciously. "Are you wearing the mail under your tunic as you promised?"

At that moment, Gregor looked no older than little Friedrich, and he ducked his head in embarrassment. "I fear I forgot."

"The lady is wise," Willem put in. "We should pray as if everything depends upon God, and be as prudent as if everything depends upon ourselves."

"Hmmph!" Klaus snorted. "We're wasting time if we have to add the hauberk. But come, Willem. I have an extra that would fit you."

Seeing their haste to be off, Margarethe gave each of them a fond farewell. But Gregor held her a moment longer than the others, then gestured for her to follow him to his chamber.

She hesitated only a moment. After all, they were betrothed, and—if the mission failed—this might be the last time she would ever see him.

Inside, she could not resist a quick look around. The man surely needed a valet, even in these temporary quarters in his father's house. With no one to keep order here and lay out his garments, no wonder he had forgotten to put on all the necessary armor.

"Well, Greta, have you decided what we will be doing this day?" he asked, beginning to remove his outer clothing.

She averted her eyes, looking instead at the cluttered room and mentally rearranging the furnishings. "Since you chose not to arm yourself, I suspect you are not going into battle today but may be planning a rendezvous with some of your allies to persuade them to come parley with Ewald tomorrow. Am I right?"

He grinned. "Your reasoning is most admirable, my lady. Ewald will not be convinced to surrender if certain allies do not appear. Therefore, we need our very best diplomat."

"Well, then, that explains Klaus's part. Despite his morose attitude lately, he is known to be the best diplomat among you brothers. But what of Willem? He is not a soldier."

Gregor would not answer directly. "Trust me, my lady. He is needed. Now you must leave so I can prepare myself as you directed." He gave a little bow and pushed her toward the door. "But I have one last request. We will break our fast along the road. So don't come to see us off. We've said our farewells, and time is short."

She nodded, brushed her lips against his cheek, and left the room. But when the three men mounted up to ride out of the courtyard, she was watching from her chamber window. Carefully strapped to the back of Willem's horse was a package the size of a lute.

She left her room to go to the chapel to pray and did not emerge until dinnertime.

Chapter 16

When Margarethe went to the hall for dinner, she found that her aunt and uncle had arrived, along with young Friedrich. She laughed as she flew into her aunt's outstretched arms. "Oh, Aunt Mechthild, it feels like years since I've seen you! I've missed you so."

"Ah, Greta, you're looking well," said her uncle, giving her an assessing glance.

"Greta, when are you going to show me around this great big castle? It's the biggest castle I've ever seen!" Friedrich piped up. "I want to see everything! The secret hiding places and the dungeons and all the best ponds to catch frogs!"

There was a round of hearty laughter as they were escorted to the head table, where Jolan was already seated, waiting for them.

"From what Otto tells me, Son," began Lord Einhard, sliding into the seat a page held for him, "Margarethe has been much too busy to explore her surroundings."

"True, Friedrich," she admitted. "When I first came here, I helped your sister, Jolan, care for a lady who had been sadly injured. And since Willem has been away with the troops, I've been helping with the music students."

"Did the sick lady get better?" The freckled face grew sober. "Or did she die?"

"She is quite well, I'm happy to report. Oh, and I took care of a wounded captain, who also recovered."

Friedrick was all ears. "What happened to him?"

"One of the enemy soldiers charged him with a lance. Unfortunately, our captain had neglected to wear his breastplate that day."

"Then he should be dead," said Friedrich, philosophically.

Margarethe nodded. "And he likely would have been killed, too. But as it happened, the enemy soldier's horse slipped in the mud, and his lance only grazed the captain's side."

"Were you there?" Friedrich asked, obviously intent on learning every detail of the incident.

"Oh, no." Margarethe laughed at the earnest little face. "At least not in the flesh." She leaned closer to look him directly in the eye. "But your sister, the injured lady, and I were there in another way. We were praying at that very moment."

"And which of your fighting men was so lucky as to have your prayers?" asked Lady Mechthild.

"Gregor," Margarethe replied, lifting a mug of warmed cider to her lips.

"Oh, so it was your betrothed. How interesting. You must love him very much if you are so faithful to pray for him."

"Oh, Mutti," Jolan said, "they're always together. Gregor is in our Lord's Day musical group as well, along with Hilda and Albert and Willem."

"Fine musicians all," Lady Mechthild commented. "Do you play here in the hall as you did at Adlerschloss?"

"Of course," Jolan spoke up. "In fact, Margarethe and I will sing for you this very evening, if you like—though we've had no time to prepare for your coming," she said with a trace of reprimand in her voice.

Mechthild nodded, pleased. "So we surprised you then, my dears?"

"Yes, and what a nice surprise," Margarethe said. "My own parents will be here soon for the betrothal feast, though they will leave my younger sister at home this trip. She prefers to wait for the wedding."

Friedrich made his voice heard from the other side of the table. "When will I meet your father—the great man I am named after?"

"Very soon, child," Mechthild answered for Margarethe. "But you must keep quiet now. We have important matters to discuss."

Lord Einhard leaned over the table. "And where is Lord Gregor today, Margarethe? I was looking forward to seeing him."

"He is on some mission with Klaus. They will return very late tonight," he said.

"And I do not see Willem about, either," he remarked.

"They are together—on the same mission."

Lady Mechthild's eyebrows rose. "Gregor. . .and Willem? They get along well?"

"Oh, yes," Margarethe said, wickedly enjoying the growing alarm on her aunt's face. "They are probably best friends. Would you not agree, Jolan?"

"I would say so. They even bathe together," she said, bursting into laughter.

"Hmm. . .it must be some very important mission indeed," Einhard observed," to send them out on the Lord's Day."

☙

Margarethe waited for the men's return, praying that nothing had gone amiss. When she heard the sound of horses' hooves clattering through the gate, she dressed hurriedly, left her chamber, and met them in the hallway.

"You are up late, my lady," Gregor said softly with a warning look she could make out even by torchlight. Klaus seemed miffed; Willem, triumphant.

"I waited up to see how you fared on your mysterious mission," she

replied. "Were you successful?"

"Completely," Gregor replied. "Perhaps we will be able to tell you about it soon—but not tonight."

She couldn't hide her disappointment. "Uncle Einhard has been looking forward to seeing you and was disappointed when he found you gone," she said, hoping Gregor would relent and share the news now.

"He will not be disappointed when he learns the whole story. But, Margarethe, it is late and we are spent. Thank you for your prayers."

She nodded, still wishing someone would tell her more. Why must men keep secrets? "Good night then, Gregor. Good night, Klaus, Willem. God bless you all."

Gregor pressed her hand to his lips, then left for his quarters. Klaus, too, bowed and passed by. Only Willem was left. "Do not ever stop praying, my lady," he said, taking her hand. "God was with us tonight, and I know your prayers had something to do with it."

"Then I will never stop."

Willem smiled and lifted the hand he was holding to kiss her fingers. "Good night, *Liebchen*," he whispered, brushed her cheek with the back of his hand, and went on.

Feeling more and more confused, Margarethe returned to her chamber, undressed, and got into bed. Willem had seemed so confident for the past few days—almost as if he were in a world of his own. He had even told her some fanciful tale about a cloth merchant—something Hilda had taught him. Then he had proceeded to baffle her even more by telling her he was thanking God for answering his prayers—even though there was no visible sign of the answer. Perhaps, after she and Gregor were wed, Willem would become a priest like Father Bernard. It did seem his thoughts were loftier these days, more focused on heavenly things.

Sleepless, she lay awake, pondering. Willem was praising God for something He had not brought to pass as yet. Was that the secret of prayer?

Here on the eve of her betrothal to Gregor, Willem might well have come to terms with the truth and changed his prayer to one of acceptance. But if he had not—if he was still praying for some miracle for them—she prayed fervently the good Lord would answer. For if He did not and she married Gregor, Willem's faith might be shattered.

In four days, the betrothal would be accomplished. Only four days. God could still work a miracle. But she, too, ought to pray like Willem. She would try. She recited her list of family and friends—concentrating on their needs instead of hers. She prayed for wisdom and discernment, for an end to all war. For peace in her own troubled heart.

As dawn streaked the sky, trailing fingers of pink and purple, Margarethe at last gave up and prayed Willem's prayer. "Father, you know

the prayer I have been praying since I met this man as a little girl. I thank You for hearing me. I thank you for hearing Willem's prayers. You have been so faithful to answer other prayers, and I know You are answering this one as well. Perhaps not as we would hope—but Your ways are best and right. I praise You for being a good and loving God, One who knows what we need—even if we do not always get what we want."

She continued thanking and praising God until she fell asleep, completely content as she had not been in many months.

◌⊗◌

On Tuesday morning, at the shout of the lookout in the turret, Margarethe ran to her window to find a large mounted party approaching from the west. Hurriedly tucking her errant hair under her cap, she ran down the stairs.

"Greta, you must let me dress your hair," Aunt Mechthild said, half scolding. "There is yet time before Friedrich and Ida are within the castle walls. Your mother must not see you in a little girl's cap."

Margarethe could not resist a teasing retort. "It keeps my head warm, Aunt."

"Back up the stairs with you now. I'm sure you brought something we can use."

Margarethe allowed her aunt to rebraid her long blond hair and select a becoming veil. Today she had chosen her second best gown—a dove gray tunic with a murrey surcoat. Margarethe liked murrey; it reminded her of berries.

Putting the finishing touches on the new hairstyle, her aunt anchored the veil with a gold circlet studded with garnets. "There now, you look more like a young lady who is soon to wed—and not a naughty child tormenting her poor old aunt." Lady Mechthild chuckled fondly.

Skimming the stairs to greet her parents in the hallway below, Margarethe embraced them, then stood back so that they could get a good look at her—and she at them. It had been so long. Her parents seemed somehow much smaller than she remembered them. Papa's hair was touched with silver at the temples, and Mutti—well, when she spoke, her voice held the same lovely rich timbre Margarethe recalled as a child when her mother had sung lullabies at bedtime.

"You are grown, my little Greta," she said, holding Margarethe at arm's length. "Taller than your Mutti. And to think, you are soon to be a bride."

The thought was less than reassuring.

◌⊗◌

"Mutti, let us make music together as we used to do," Margarethe suggested just before supper. "Aunt Mechthild is anxious for us to entertain, and we might provide a diversion from thoughts of this never-ending war."

115

"Ever thoughtful," Lady Ida said, patting her daughter's hand.

"Hmm. Yes," her father muttered fondly. "Ever thoughtful—unless she's playing a joke on someone." His smile removed any sting his words might have caused. "Am I invited to make music with you ladies?"

"Of course you are, Papa. Come and help me carry some things." He accompanied her up the stairs and to the music room, where Margarethe chose an assortment of wind instruments and put them in a bag, then took up her lute and a viel and bow.

He frowned. "Will you promise me not to let Mechthild play that thing?" he asked as he eyed the viel with misgiving.

Margarethe laughed. "So her fame on the viel reaches even to the Schwarzwald."

"Her infamy, more like," he said as he took up the bag and the lute. "Has anyone heard from Otto?"

"I have heard nothing yet. The parley was to last only one day, though." Despite her prayers, this comment triggered a spark of terror. What if negotiations failed? And now she had not one man to worry about, but two.

They descended the stairs together in silence.

"This delay is unnerving," her father continued. "We should be hearing something. Still, I cannot picture Otto in peacetime. It seems unnatural somehow. After all, this conflict has gone on for the past twenty years. I suppose war is a way of life for him."

Margarethe couldn't help thinking that perhaps Lord Otto had changed his mind and decided there should be no truce at all. Or maybe they were all being held hostage. . . . For a dreadful moment, her faith faltered, and a thousand horrors came to mind.

○ざ

On Wednesday Margarethe rose early for Mass. There were more people than usual on their knees this morning, likely praying for peace, as she was, and for the men who had gone to make the peace. She tried to pray without fretting, but there had been no word at all, and her natural instincts rose up to crowd her mind.

Lady Edeltraud had considered sending a messenger to find out what was happening, but she dared not do anything that Ewald might construe as a hostile act. And so they had waited.

During the Mass Margarethe decided to use her new method of prayer—the one Willem had taught her. Doing her best to put her fears aside, she praised God, thanking Him for all that He had already done for them—Gregor's escape from certain death; Hilda's healing, both physical and mental; her growing friendship with Gregor; her love for Willem and the miracle they desired—if, in truth, such a miracle was best for all concerned.

As she prayed, a small kernel of joy began deep within and bubbled to

the surface until she felt that she would burst. "Bless Willem, Father. And Gregor and Klaus and Uncle Einhard—especially Uncle, for he is to be doing the talking today. Bring them home safely. . .and bring peace."

☙

With the preparations for the betrothal feast and the anticipated homecoming of the fighting men in full swing, the castle was abuzz with activity. Once again, Hilda had to be moved to accommodate the many guests who would be arriving soon, it was hoped.

"We keep moving you about, Hilda," Jolan said while helping the maiden relocate from the private chamber she had occupied for only a short time back into Jolan's chamber. "I do hope you don't feel neglected or unwanted."

Hilda laughed her gentle laugh. "Not at all. I know you care for me. You've proven it in a thousand ways."

Margarethe winced. "I feel guilty, for I have had my own chamber all along."

Jolan gave an exaggerated sigh. "Don't remind me. However, since you are the guest of honor here, I suppose we must concede. Even the lords are doubling up to make room."

"I wonder what poor soul will have to share Gregor's chamber," Margarethe mused.

Hilda covered her mouth with her hand, her eyes wide, and Margarethe realized too late how her remark must have sounded.

Jolan straightened and gave her a searching look. "In just a few months, *you* will be that poor soul. And what would be so bad about sharing with Gregor anyway?"

"Nothing, if he had his valet with him here. He sorely needs one. He leaves his clothes strewn about everywhere," Margarethe explained.

"Oh," Jolan said slyly. "I thought perhaps he snored."

"Now what," Margarethe demanded, "would I know about that?"

"Then how do you know how he keeps his chamber?"

"Please don't quarrel," Hilda begged, with a look of alarm on her face. "It serves no purpose."

"Ha! If you think we are quarreling now, you should have seen us when we were younger."

"I remember wishing I had a sister—or a very close cousin," Hilda said thoughtfully. "Perhaps it would not have been so wonderful, after all."

That brought an end to the chiding as Margarethe and Jolan erupted in gales of laughter.

"I have a younger sister whom I barely know," Margarethe said, suddenly serious. "I am looking forward to seeing her. . .at the wedding." But she was not looking forward to the wedding.

117

In the afternoon, Margarethe and her aunt and mother had called their own truce over the garments she would wear for the betrothal feast—a purple tunic with bands on the sleeves, embroidered by her mother, and a light blue diapered cloth surcoat her aunt had had made. Since she herself favored the colors, everyone would be satisfied.

With that decision behind, Margarethe was eager to get on with a more pleasant activity—a family musical concert. They were playing their second number—a driving dance tune called an estampie—when a general stirring in the hall outside reached her ears, and she laid aside her viel and bow.

Gregor was the first man through the door. He strode over, lifted her off her feet, and swung her in a circle. "Ewald has surrendered, my lady! Unconditionally!"

"Oh, Gregor, my heart is so full—" she cried—"of gratitude for God's goodness in sparing you and the others."

"It might have gone either way, had it not been for your prayers." Noticing the little group gathered around, he turned to greet them. "Forgive me. These must be your parents, Margarethe. You resemble your mother—a legendary beauty indeed. Lady Ida." He bowed over her hand.

Her mother dimpled, her eyes twinkling. "And you're much more dashing and distinguished than when you were a boy."

Margarethe could not help thinking that perhaps Gregor should be the family diplomat—not Klaus, who was always so dour.

At that moment Lord Friedrich stepped up to extend his hand, sizing Gregor up in a single look, she observed. Her father would not be able to find anything to fault in Gregor, she thought. Nothing except his housekeeping, at least.

"So this is the young lord who will marry my daughter," her father said, still skeptical, or so it appeared.

Gregor smiled and would have replied, except Lady Mechthild spoke up just then. "I must find Einhard," she said, rising from her chair. "Oh, there he is now."

When Lord Einhard strode over to greet them, it was Gregor who spoke first. "Here is the hero of the parley. Never have I seen such courage and persistence."

Lord Einhard clapped Gregor on the shoulder as he passed him to embrace his wife, and then his sister, Lady Ida, and Lord Friedrich. "I must confess I never worked any harder on the battlefield. But—"

Glancing toward the door, Margarethe saw Willem enter just as her uncle finished his statement—"There is the real hero."

All of the lords attending the parley and their allies sent messengers to their

homes with the good news, called for their families to join them at the castle, then stayed for supper, with music and dancing far into the night. Margarethe had never before observed such a sight. She herself, caught up in the excitement, was a part of many of the musical presentations. And she noticed that her cousin Jolan—when she was not playing an instrument—danced every dance, most notably with two of their young allies, Lord Selig and Lord Helmhold.

Throughout the evening, Margarethe sang often, blending her voice with others in a variety of performances. Once she sang a solo. And when someone called for the love song she had written, she felt a bittersweet pang as she sang in harmony with Willem, feeling his gaze resting on her tenderly. There was a request for the war song, but Willem refused, and Margarethe wondered why.

He shrugged. "It is Lord Otto's idea. I am to play it tomorrow."

She smiled weakly at him. "Instead of the betrothal music you were to write?"

"In addition to that," he said, smiling broadly.

Before she could press him further, Gregor claimed her for a dance, and she whirled away, looking back over her shoulder at Willem. He was a puzzlement to her. How could he appear so cheerful on the very eve of her betrothal to another?

It was quite late when she finally retired, but she could not fall asleep right away. Strangely though, in thinking of the morrow, she felt neither fearful nor sad. Instead, she spent some time in prayer, thanking and praising God before a gentle blanket of peace descended over her, and she slept.

☙

After Mass, Margarethe could not find Jolan anywhere. She looked all over the castle, then returned to Jolan's chamber. "Hilda, have you seen my cousin?"

"I think she went somewhere with Willem. Do you need her?"

"Well, I need someone. This hair is too much for me alone. I am to wear it loose for the feast, so I need to wash it right away, else it will not dry. Aunt Mechthild is nowhere to be seen." She waggled her fingers in the air. "Besides that, my father is in some meeting with Uncle Einhard and Lord Otto and Gregor. I don't know what is going on. I would have thought they'd have had everything settled by now."

Hilda seemed to be ignoring her perplexity. "Is the water ready?" she asked in her calm way.

At her words, Margarethe was brought back to her current quandary. "Oh, I asked for it last night to be sure they would bring it this morning."

"Then let me help," Hilda offered. "You have such lovely hair that it would be a pleasure."

When her hair was thoroughly clean, Margarethe sat with her back to the window, her head in the direct sunlight. "Perhaps we should take the longest part of your hair and toss it out the window to dry the quicker," Hilda suggested with a smile.

"And if a bird chances upon it, we will have to start over. No. I think not, Hilda."

"You seem quite happy, Margarethe. You must have grown to love Lord Gregor very much."

A long look passed between them. "Let's just say I am at peace. God's in his heaven, and all is well." How she *knew* such a thing mystified her, but she was confident that it was true.

"I will be praying for you today. It is too bad that the peace treaty had to come at the same time as your betrothal announcement. It will not get as much attention as it deserves—as *you* deserve."

"I don't mind." Margarethe had never felt so certain of anything in her life. "It is peace that is the most important thing."

◌◌

Gregor was Margarethe's dinner partner, a novelty only in that she had not seen him all morning. During the last course, he took her hand. "I want you to know that I truly admire you, my lady."

She narrowed her gaze in speculation. "Well, thank you, my lord. But I would find it rather odd if you found your future wife *objectionable*."

As soon as the tables were cleared, the herald quieted the hall for Lord Otto. Margarethe had never seen the man looking so jovial. Gone was the fierce, almost menacing countenance. He was actually smiling, which gave him a different appearance altogether.

"As you know, after a long and valiant struggle, we are at peace." He waited for the cheers to subside before outlining the terms of the peace agreement. "If all abide by these terms, we should enjoy many years of tranquility and prosperity within our borders."

Margarethe drummed her fingers on the table until Gregor covered her hand with his own. After-dinner speeches were so boring. Would her future father-in-law just conclude the business so they could get back to their music making?

"Now for the business at hand. There is one man in particular I wish to honor here this day. A man who never took up arms, but one whose skills and encouragement have led us to this moment."

To Margarethe's surprise, Lord Otto turned to look at Willem, sitting at the end of the table. "Willem, will you honor this hall with the battle song that brought us victory?"

Willem nodded, made his way to the front, and sang the stirring words that told of courageous deeds done in the name of love and loyalty, with

the help of Almighty God.

At the conclusion of the verses, the men joined in the chorus, their strong masculine voices filling the place with rich sound. Once more the herald was called to quiet the hall before Lord Otto could speak. "After due deliberation," he began, "my sons and I have decided to reward this hero."

A great shout went up as the fighting men confirmed the decision with their cheers, and Margarethe glanced at Gregor, whose eyes were moist.

"The only reward our chief musician would accept was a small plot of land," Lord Otto went on. "But in view of his unique contribution to our cause, we have decided that in addition to the land, he should be given a fitting dwelling as well." Once again the hall erupted in shouts and cheers. When the applause had died down, he finished, "And so I give you Lord Willem of Waldbergen Castle!"

Margarethe sat, stunned, as the fighting men of Lord Otto's household stood to their feet and launched into another chorus of the battle song. Gregor, she observed, remained seated, too, leaning forward to make a comment. "He is a true nobleman—as gallant and brave as any knight."

Tears filled her eyes. She was happy for Willem, but his land had come too late. Her betrothal to Gregor was to be announced this very day. She could not dishonor Gregor when he had been nothing but kind to her.

"Our announcement pales by comparison," she said, bravely trying to meet his eye.

He shook his head. "We need make no announcement, dear Greta."

She frowned, trying to understand. "But my parents have come all the way from the Schwarzwald for the occasion."

"They came for the announcement of your betrothal, my lady."

Was he mad? "That is what I just said, Gregor."

"No, you said something about *our* announcement." When she continued to stare, uncomprehendingly, he said, "I care for you deeply, but are we not more like brother and sister? You deserve a man who truly loves you—and here he comes now." He nodded toward Willem, who was walking toward them with that endearing bouncing gait. "And so I release you from our betrothal."

She turned to Willem as he bent to speak with her. "Your uncle and Gregor did battle for me, and your father and Lord Otto are agreed. All I need now is your consent, my lady. Do I have it? Will you marry me?"

Through a veil of tears, she saw the dear face she had adored since she was but a girl of eleven. "I will, my lord." She stepped into his arms, and he kissed her tenderly, to the great delight of the hall.

Gregor, standing to the side, beamed his approval. "You both have my blessings," he said. Then, stepping back, he announced, "Now I have work to do, if you will excuse me."

Margarethe sat down again, with Willem at her side clasping her hand tightly. He sang softly in her ear:

> " 'Til all our days shall pass,
>   We'll be together, you and me,
> As ever on the brook flows down
>   Constant to the sea.
> As it's renewed by snow and rain
>   Our love's fed from above
> I always will be true to you—"

"Oh, Willem," she cried, "and you'll always be my love! Our prayer and our song have both come true, haven't they?"

She turned to see Gregor, Albert, Jolan, and Aunt Mechthild taking their places at the front of the dais, where they performed a merry piece Margarethe had never heard.

"Our betrothal music," Willem explained. "The inspiration came soon enough when I knew that *I* would be your betrothed."

"So that is why you've been so happy of late." She gazed at him with wonder and admiration. "When did you write this music?"

"A fortnight ago."

"So you have known all this time about your land?" she asked.

"Oh, no. I learned about that only this morning."

"I still don't understand. How did you know a fortnight ago that you would be my betrothed?"

"That is when I began to thank God for what He was doing for us. He gave me such joy. Then these past few days I have seen the same joy shining in your eyes, and it gave me even more hope."

They sat smiling at each other as the song ended and the hall erupted in loud applause. "I will have to listen to that song sometime—when I can truly hear every word," Margarethe murmured.

Lord Otto stood to his feet to make the betrothal announcement—quite different from the original one planned. Margarethe's heart was full as she and Willem rose to acknowledge the good wishes of the audience—dear family and friends all.

"So this was your prayer," Hilda said when at last she could make her way to the happy couple.

"Yes," they said in unison. "And God bless you for praying, Hilda."

"I thank you, too, for the story about the merchant," Willem said, nestling Margarethe closer to his side.

And then Gregor was back to hug each of them in turn. "I know of no two people who deserve greater happiness," he said graciously. "You're

a fortunate man, my friend."

Safe in Willem's embrace, Margarethe put her hand on Gregor's arm and, cocking her head, said in a mischievous tone, "I have a little sister at home, my lord. And she's nothing at all like me!"

Gregor's grin lit up the vast hall. "So your father tells me," he said. "So your father tells me."

Flip over for another great novel!

FRIEDA'S SONG